FORGED

M.B. THURMAN

Forged
Copyright © 2025 by M.B. Thurman
All rights reserved.

First published in the United States by Contrarian Publishing

www.contrarianpublishing.com

Summary: Hadley Weston and Fitz MacGregor travel back in time to Forfar, Scotland 1662 in order to prevent a family heirloom from falling into the wrong hands. But as they survive the rampant witch hunts and connect with Fitz's ancestors, they must decide if they will allow time to take its natural course or if they will chart a new way forward.

www.thesummonedseries.com

Library of Congress Control Number: 2025910687
ISBN: 978-1-965422-05-2
ISBN (ebook): 978-1-965422-06-9
First Edition

Cover illustration and design by Jon Stubbington

Book design by Jamie Ryu

F✹RGED

BOOK THREE IN THE SUMMONED SERIES

M.B. THURMAN

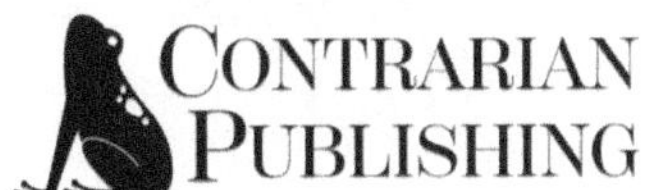

Brooklyn, NY | Est. 2024

FORFAR
THE FAIR FOLK

FORFAR LOCH
HIGH STREET

BRUCE HOMESTEAD

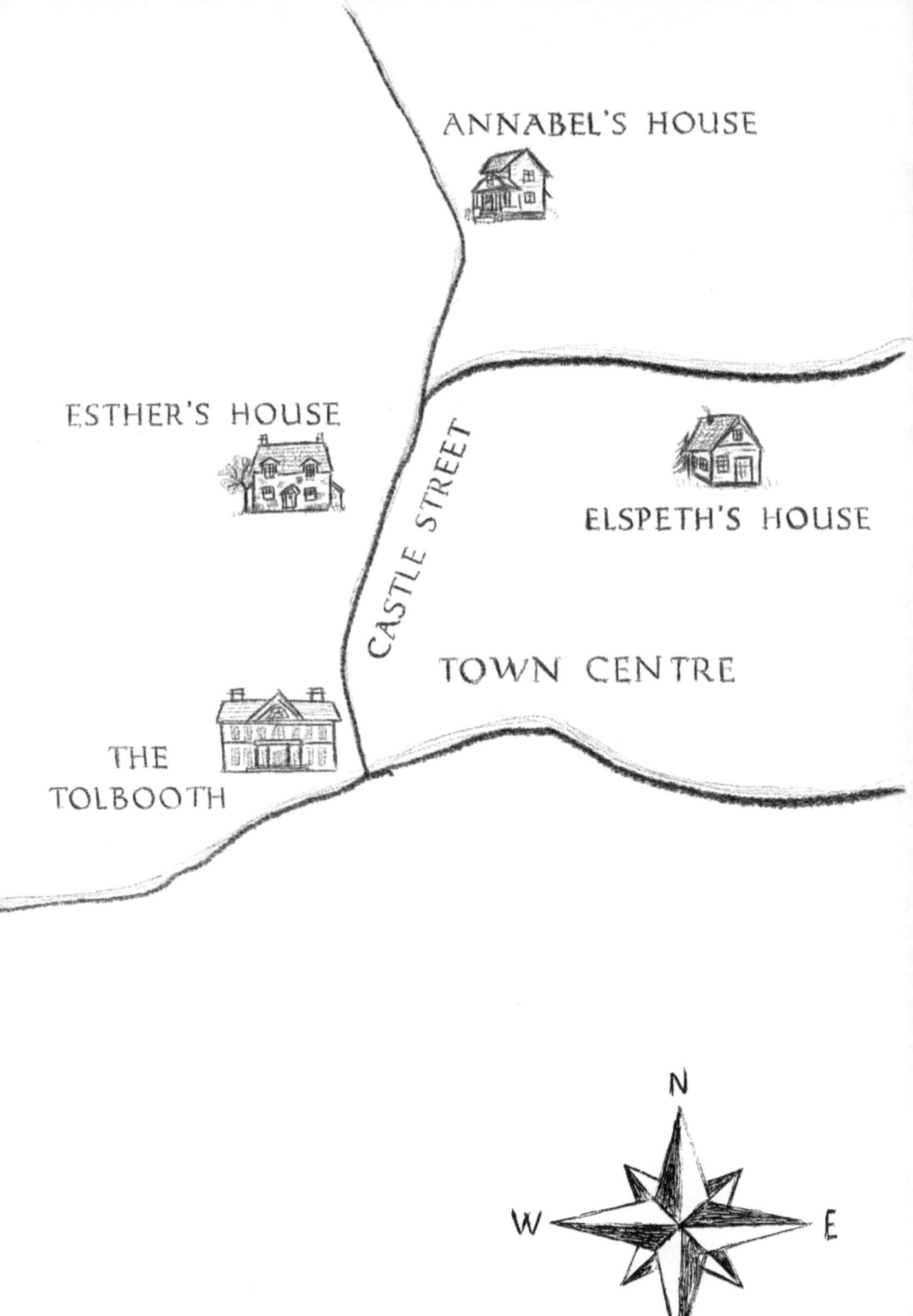

ANNABEL'S HOUSE
ESTHER'S HOUSE
ELSPETH'S HOUSE
CASTLE STREET
TOWN CENTRE
THE TOLBOOTH
N
W
E
S

*Though this story is fictional,
it was born from events that were not.*

*This book is dedicated to the real women who lost their lives in
the witch trials of Forfar, Scotland.*

You are not forgotten.

"They didn't burn witches. They burned women."

— Unknown

AUTHOR'S NOTE

When the original idea for *Summoned* came to me, I began researching the history of witchcraft in Scotland and first came across the North Berwick Trials, which were fueled by King James I of England. I was appalled to discover that while I had been taught that he united the kingdoms of Scotland and England and had the Bible translated, there was a darker history I had never known. As I traced the larger notes of his foul legacy, I found *Daemonology*, a vile book he wrote to "educate" his kingdom on the subject matter of torturing women believed to be witches. As I studied the prejudice he infused across his kingdom, I followed the trail to other trials throughout Great Britain and stumbled across the Forfar Witch Trials, which ranged from 1661–1663.

I can't pinpoint what made the Forfar trials stand out more than the rest to me. Perhaps it was the simple fact that I had never heard of them, and I sought to understand why some witch trials were internationally known—household names even—while others seemed to simply be forgotten. As I learned what had happened, I mourned for those women… and I wanted the world to remember the names of those who were persecuted with such senseless fear and hatred.

The character of Esther came to me quickly after, and I knew instantly that Hadley's story was meant to cross Esther's—that these two witches were bound to one another in some way across time and space.

This is how *Forged* was born.

Though these pages contain a fictional story, I hope to shed light on the real events of the past, to consider how life must have felt to the women of this time. This has been many years in the making: countless hours of research, many tearful writing sessions, a connection that was forged across centuries. Though these women lived hundreds of years ago, their stories feel so close to me. I have done my very best to honor our ancestors in my work, and now I can only hope I have done these women justice.

Before you dive into the story on these pages, I invite you to take a moment of silence to remember those persecuted:

(As listed in *Confessions of the Forfar Witches* and/or in town records)

Joanet Howit

John Tailzeour

Isobell Shyrie

Elspet Alexander

Joanet Stout

Ketheren Portour

Agnes Sparke

Isobell Smith

Helen Cothill

Marjorie Ritchie

Elspet Bruice

Margaret Guthrie

Elizabeth Guthrie

Girzell Simpson

Marjorie Bruce

Helen Guthrie

This list is woefully short and incomplete, but records of all persecuted during these trials have proven to be elusive.

The Forfar Witch Trials ranged from 1661–1663, though for the purposes of this story, I have moved all events to the year 1662. For anyone seeking an accurate timeline of events, I recommend the following resources:

Visit Angus: Angus Archives
Angus Alive
The National Archives: Angus Archives

CONTENT CONSIDERATIONS

# PART ONE

PROLOGUE

November 2, 1662
Esther

I leaned through the open window, taking one long breath of air, and found that it had soured like wine long turned to vinegar, ripe with fear and despair. The dreary day meant to earn its place in November, saturated with gray clouds, strong winds, and the echoes of falling rain. The birds were far quieter than usual, and only the occasional chirp broke the somber air. Even the crows were silent—ne'er a caw was heard all morning, and the woodland creatures clung to the forests, forsaking even the breakfast I had left in the garden. Something was amiss, of that I was certain, but my visions had eluded me for days. I pulled the window closed, shivering from the cold, damp air, and returned to the fireside.

Intuitive as ever, Millie had seemed to sense my troubles before they even appeared, and she had placed a bit of mugwort tea on the fireside table just after breakfast. Millie had returned to us only a few weeks prior after falling ill in September. My aunt, Annabel, had sent help to us in Millie's absence. Though my husband, Hamish, and I were grateful for the assistance, I had been elated when Millie returned. The tea's warmth trickled through me as I took a sip, providing a bit of relief, though my nerves bolted through me like lightning crackling across the sky. They wouldnae be easily quelled today.

I closed my eyes and searched the elements—the air filling my lungs, the fire warming my skin, the earth and water soothing my throat—and I asked Fate once more: what news eluded me? What was amiss in Forfar?

Nae vision surfaced.

Again, I breathed deeply, and upon its release, I attempted the vision once more. A scene nipped at the edge of my mind, but I couldnae pull it forward. My heart thumped strangely; the vision wouldnae bring braw news. I couldnae stall my efforts now. I looked to the fire, pulled at the air, and asked my mind's eye to remove the protections that blocked my vision.

Sparks jumped furiously from the swirling fire, and in the flames, a scene took shape. A woman was dragged from her home by three men. She thrashed about violently, kicking and clawing as she attempted to free herself. The men tightened their grip, forcing a blood-curdling scream from her lips. The woman's desperation was pungent, but even so, defiance rested in her dark eyes. I focused with all my might, and her features cleared.

My teacup clattered to the ground, its earthy warmth soaking through the green fibers of the rug.

Millie threw the door open, rushing to my side.

"What is the matter? Are ye well?"

I shook my head. "'Tis Agnes," I choked out, barely able to form the words.

"What of her?" Millie prompted.

"The witch hunters will take her from her home. I must warn her," I said, turning my gaze to Millie. The fear on her face was surely echoed by my own, but we had nae time to give way to our fears… no if we were to warn Agnes in time.

"Have ye forgotten our orders?" Millie asked.

We were meant to keep ourselves from intervening in human affairs.

"The Forfar Council be damned," I said.

Millie arched an eyebrow.

"Aye, and the coven too."

Millie exhaled deeply, but she nodded in turn. "What will ye say to her?" she asked. "She'll ken the truth if ye warn her of things to come."

"Ye dinnae think she already kens?" I asked. "She's kenned me all our lives. We spent little time apart as bairns. 'Tis far too late for caution with Agnes."

Millie bit at her lip, her face torn, but she nodded once. We gathered our cloaks and rushed from the safety of our home toward the village center.

Though the rain persisted and the cold cut through my bones like a frozen blade, town was as active as a spring's hive of bees. Even with the bustling energy of the villagers, the ominous air clung to me as Millie and I wove around the meandering townsfolk, a sign that my vision hadnae been quick to reveal itself on this occasion. We had neared the edge of the market when the jeers of villagers reached my ears. A woman's shriek pierced my soul, and my eyes met Millie's.

We were too late.

Agnes stepped into our line of sight, dragged by three men whose stoic faces mocked us with their cruelty. In contrast, the shouts of the villagers only grew louder.

"Witch!"

"Burn the witch!"

"The devil's mistress—make her pay for her sins!"

My heart sank with my spirits, even as it beat wildly in my chest, as though opposing forces were at work in my body. I wanted to run as far away from the burgh as my feet could carry me, and I longed to rush at the guards and free Agnes. But my vision swam, deciding my course for me. I clung to Millie's arm for support.

A man broke from the growing crowd bearing a knife, his arm poised to bring his own justice against Agnes. Before I could cry out, one of her captors pushed his weight against him. They fell to the ground, wrestling in the muck, and my nerves grew loud at the thought of the man fighting his way free. How could he be so cruel? Agnes was innocent of all charges—she was certainly nae witch— though the villagers would ne'er be convinced otherwise. Tears welled in my eyes as I considered her likely fate.

The crowd began parting, allowing Father Evans, the new minister of our burgh, to pass through. He had arrived only at the close of August, but already, he had sewn seeds of discord that would be impossible for us to weed out. For years, many of our kingdom's monarchs had planted suspicion of witchcraft through our country, and I had long witnessed our local townspeople's belief in their lore. But this minister's arrival had sparked the old sentiments afresh, which now fanned into blazing flames.

The minister was followed closely by Malcolm Campbell, the head of the Forfar Witches' Council. Little surprise, I thought. If the minister was causing trouble, Malcolm was certain to be found at his side. Though Malcolm worked with Father Evans as a means to protect us, I couldnae stomach the thought of our safety coming at the cost of innocent human women.

Father Evans's dark eyes were set under a strong brow, and his features were cloaked in their usual persuasive position. He threw back his shoulders, making the most of his tall figure, and when his deep voice sounded, the crowd quieted, fearful they'd miss even a crumb of the minister's instruction.

"Violence is not the answer!" His London accent was still strange. "Judgment is yet to be determined. Do not bring harm against this woman."

The crowd erupted in murmurs—some in agreement, others in doubt.

"There's only one thing Agnes is guilty of," Millie muttered to me, "and that is being a woman in this godforsaken burgh of bloodthirsty men."

I couldnae disagree. The minister and the magistrate were hell-bent on ridding the burgh of *witches*, and the townspeople were either too frightened to fight back, too enamored with the teachings of Father Evans, or simply content to allow it so long as it kept trouble from their own doorsteps. Several coven members thought it wrong we didnae intervene or influence the humans to think better of their course, but the council gave nae heed to our concerns.

"Assist us in taking this man to the tolbooth," the minister commanded. Father Evans would certainly have him held in the tolbooth's jail, though unlike Agnes, this man would again walk free.

A few of the village men made their way closer, but nae one yet entered their tussle.

"If this… woman is guilty, justice will be served in due time," the minister reassured.

This woman. Aye, Agnes was meant for the gallows, to be sure.

With this reassurance, the crowd reluctantly obeyed his wishes, and the attacker was secured and quickly removed toward the tolbooth. Another villager took the missing guard's place, and Agnes was once again in motion. The crowd observed the proceedings more peacefully than before, seeking the minister's favor.

"Justice will be served, my children!" Father Evans called, nodding to those he passed. "Walk not in darkness during this time but trust in the Lord and his instruction!"

"What does he know of the Lord?" I muttered.

The minister continued at a slow pace, calling the villagers by name and giving further instruction. As Agnes grew close, she looked pointedly at me before turning away. The act didnae escape the minister's notice, and his glare burned through me as he passed by, his eyes searching into the very depths of mine as though he kenned my every secret.

The men dragged Agnes around the corner of the tolbooth. Agnes and I had been dear friends as girls, two wild bairns running through the nearby forest and vexing our mothers. Agnes's parents were more determined than mine to raise a proper lady, and when our girlhood gave way to young womanhood, her mother had forbidden her to pass time in my company. Though we had drifted apart, I maintained a fondness for Agnes that hadnae faded. Perhaps the same was true for Agnes, but I couldnae lie and say that I wasnae worried that they would pull confessions from her that would compromise me.

Perhaps I should remove those early memories of myself from her mind. The closer in proximity to her, the better for completing such a task, and I kenned a guard who exchanged favors for a bit of coin, so I—

I squeezed my eyes shut, horrified. I was frightened, to be sure, but that was nae reason to betray my childhood companion. She had kenned my ways when we were younger, and she had ne'er betrayed our confidence. My stomach churned at what we'd each been reduced to by these trials. I'd nearly allowed men's prejudice to fracture the bonds of sisterhood.

I turned to Millie, steadying myself. "We should return hame."

"Aye," Millie agreed, taking my arm. "Let's get ye warm by the fireside."

CHAPTER ONE

Present Day
Hadley

The gravel crunched under the weight of our car traveling down the familiar, winding road. My mate, Fitz, and I hadn't spent time together at Lake Crescent since we'd said our tearful goodbyes near its tumultuous waters before our forced separation over two years ago. So much had changed since then. Fitz had helped me find myself as a witch, and I had helped him begin to solve a family mystery rooted in Scotland's seventeenth-century witch trials… a journey that had set us on a mission to stop Lorenzo Belmonte from fracturing the peace between our folk and humans.

Though I'd faced earth-shattering moments at the lake, I had always found a curious comfort at its shores. But this time, I feared even the sparkling lake I had once called home couldn't ease the burden that I carried, the grief that had taken hold of my chest. Our distress over the loss of Fitz's father, Ian, was stifling, as was the weight of everything else that had happened in Opimae—the battles, the betrayal, the chamber removing us from our mission. And there was still everything that was yet to come with our mission into the past. Opimae hadn't been kind to us, and I imagined seventeenth-century Scotland would also hold little tenderness.

The proprietors of the Cedar Creek Inn, Ben and Sarah, who were like second parents to me, had been kind enough to lend us their car for the drive. Though I had anticipated the light of Earth's sun to be jarring after months under the strange Opimaean suns, I wasn't prepared for just how difficult it would be to act… *normal*. I also hadn't anticipated Ben being part of the welcome party at the portal. Knowing about us put Ben and Sarah at risk with our witch-kind government. Just another decision the councils had made for Fitz and me, just another reason for us to be angry with them.

Fitz's sister, Izzy, and mother, Ann, had traveled out to the Mac-Gregor lakeside cabin the day prior. Soon enough, we'd be standing on my mother's doorstep, and the delicate balance we kept with my human loved ones would continue. For now, I was grateful for the car ride alone with Fitz, no matter how brief it was. The strain between us was impossible to ignore, but at least worried eyes weren't studying my every move, as though I might crumble at any moment.

Green blurred in my periphery with flashes of blue peeking through the forest as we wound through the countless evergreen trees along the back side of the lake. Though our circumstances weren't peaceful, when I closed my eyes, the tranquility of the lake washed over the edges of my anxiety. Something was mysterious about these waters, but despite that, a calming energy radiated from its depths.

An old wooden dock flashed through a brief opening in the trees, sweeping my mind back to happy memories with my best friends,

Jordan and Tanner, and the many days we spent lazily on these very lakeshores. Now, they both remained in Opimae, carrying forward the mission that Fitz and I had been removed from. I pushed thoughts of them aside before my guilt and concern could pull me under.

"Not that I'm not grateful for some quiet, but we have to talk," I finally said.

Fitz's eyes remained glued to the road, though his energy stirred restlessly.

"Fitz," I said softly.

His gaze shifted briefly to mine, a smile gracing his lips that did not quite reach his eyes, before returning his focus to the road.

"I'm sorry, my love," he said, his voice low and gruff.

"You're distracted," I said.

"I know, Hadley. My mind… it's a bloody mess," Fitz began.

"We could talk about it."

"Are you ready to see your mum?" he asked, changing the subject.

My brows furrowed. I supposed I wanted to talk about how I was feeling about as much as he did.

"We do have decisions to make about our mission," I said.

Fitz sighed. "That has me entirely stuck. I'm not sure if we'll ever agree."

I couldn't deny that. Chloe and Solomon had traveled back from Opimae with us as Cardinal Court representatives, and though I was glad they had been selected, they sure hadn't helped us reach an accord any faster when we'd tried to talk over a plan.

There were so many threads to sort. There was Fate. Then there was Fitz's family, the townspeople, Esther's foretold death… it was a lot to wade through. And while the councils had their thoughts, they didn't have the right to call the shots this time.

The choppy waves of the lake still sparkled beyond the tree line, the water as alive as my own thoughts.

"I know what you're going to tell me," I said, "but I don't really care what the councils have to say about this."

He cut his eyes in my direction.

"Be as tart as you'd like about it, but it's the truth. The councils won't be in the past with us—they can't be. So, we'll be navigating this with our best judgment."

"Aye—best judgment. Sometimes you confuse that with your own will," he said.

"Nice, Fitz."

He gave no response.

"No, I'm serious," I continued. "Our councils won't be there. The Opimaean councils don't even know we're doing this. I mean, realistically, we need to ask ourselves what Fate wants and what the consequences are for going against her will if that's what it takes to make this right."

"I hope our interests are aligned with hers," Fitz said. He could hope all he wanted, but we both knew that wasn't likely. "But if they're not, she might prevent us from reaching Forfar in the first place. Or she might take something dear from us. Then, there's the chance that we might do something that alters the natural course of history in a way that results in… death."

I swallowed hard.

"And despite whatever we decide on, we only have one chance at this," Fitz said.

"You mean if we mess up in the past, we can't come back to the present and try to time-walk to the same place again?"

"Aye, the same travelers can't replace history twice. Fate won't allow it," he said. "She won't reveal the threads to me twice. We have one chance."

"So, we figure out a solid plan, and we don't screw this up," I said.

"That will be difficult since we don't know exactly when or where we'll land," Fitz said. "We don't want to have more time than we need—that leaves more room for errors."

"You have doubts about how closely you'll meet our mark?" I asked.

"Aye. Time-walking isn't an exact science, and we're traveling hundreds of years. I believe I will bring us close, but we'll be lucky to land within a week of when we wish to arrive."

"So, we might be gone for longer than we anticipated," I said.

"Aye, and every day spent in the past is a day traded from our present."

I hadn't considered it that deeply before, and the very thought worried me after our return from Opimae. We should have crossed the portal into February on Earth, and yet October was nearly gone. The last thing I wanted was to lose more time. "We can't just return from the past to our starting point?"

"No," Fitz said. "Our lives don't extend simply because we're skipping through time. Fate requires a trade for every day she allows us to be elsewhere. That time will be lost to us."

I nodded. "So, we trade the days we'd have in our present for our passage into the past. It's basically paying a toll."

"That's one way to look at it," Fitz said.

"So, you try to land us as closely as possible," I said. "Then we seek refuge with Esther or…?"

"Or we camp, I'd reckon. I am uncertain of the reception we'll receive from my ancestors. Solomon said they'd send us with a bit of money, but if we stay in a lodging house, we'll raise suspicion."

I sighed. Scotland in November wasn't exactly prime camping season. "I'll just pray that Esther takes pity on us, then."

Fitz nodded. It was all I could expect in response.

"So, Esther's ring… any new thoughts on how we find it?" I asked.

"We cannae risk exposing our plans too quickly," Fitz said, his accent thickening. He was still angry then. We had quarreled when we had discussed everything with Chloe and Solomon.

"I'm not suggesting we do anything that'll blow our cover."

Fitz's eyes cut to me.

"I think we use the spell to find the ring," I said. "We can't do anything without at least knowing where it is. Once we figure that out and gauge the relatives, we can work from there."

"It might already rest on Esther's finger."

"But if it doesn't, then we need to find it quickly."

Fitz rubbed his temple with his free hand, his other still holding a death grip on the steering wheel.

"What?" I asked.

"This is my family," Fitz said. "Of course, the plan is to find the ring, but I dinnae wish to dishonor them to accomplish our goal unless it's absolutely necessary."

"I haven't suggested dishonoring them!"

"Aye, but if you lose yer temper… I already see that impatience creeping into yer eyes, and I hear it in yer tone, Hadley."

I huffed. He could give me a little more credit than that.

The car jostled as we hit a particularly nasty pothole, and I gripped the door handle. I winced as pain shot through my shoulder and cursed the state of the road. If this was the beginning of the winter season, I hated to think what the road would look like by spring. Fitz sighed and decreased his speed.

"Are you all right?"

I ground my jaw but nodded. This injury from Opimae just didn't want to heal.

We remained silent, but after a beat Fitz stole a glance at me.

"Deny your impatience if you wish, but that doesn't make it any less true."

I sat back in my seat, arms crossed, breathing slowly as I brought my heart rate back to an even thump.

"I'm concerned about countless factors," he continued, "but I worry for your safety most of all."

He was always worrying about my safety.

"We can be discreet until we figure out how receptive Esther and Hamish might be," I said, refocusing the conversation. "But Annabel…."

"You think she'll be difficult to convince," Fitz said. "That, we agree on."

"I suppose we can't say for sure, but if she was willing to break the rules to protect Esther…."

"Aye, she'll be less reasonable than Esther herself. Hamish will be difficult too, I'd reckon."

"I don't think we can reasonably decide on our strategy with them until we actually meet them and see who we're truly dealing with."

"We cannae step in the middle of their lives, cause issues, and not face consequences from it. I dinnae wish to alter their course in such a way," Fitz said.

A crow swooped across the road, its wings spread wide in flight, and landed in front of us. Fitz slammed on the brakes. His hand shot out in front of me, and I gripped the door handle as the car's tires skidded to a halt. The bird did not falter—it faced us as it tilted its head curiously. It stood in a patch of sunlight that filtered through the trees, and its black feathers gleamed as brightly as the glowing waters of the lake. It cawed, refusing to move, and Fitz and I exchanged a wary glance.

"Death," I said.

"That's only one possible omen of a crow," Fitz countered.

"I've always just heard that it means death."

"Most of your life was spent with humans."

Finally, the crow took flight, though Fitz and I sat in silence for a few seconds before he stepped on the gas pedal again.

"Fine. What else does it mean?" I asked.

"The crow is a symbol of intelligence. It might tell of transformation or destiny."

"I can see where that might be fitting," I admitted.

"Witches who are gifted in communing with spirits have often claimed crows serve as an intermediary between the living and the dead."

Goosebumps rippled across my skin, as if to signal the truth of Fitz's words.

"What do you think our visitor signaled today?"

"I don't know," Fitz said. "We'll speak to Iz about it."

I nodded. Talk of Fitz's sister inevitably reminded me of Esther. I knew from my spirit-travels how much they looked alike. Perhaps they might share more than just physical similarities.

"I wonder if we'll be able to speak honestly with Esther," I said.

"After studying her story for so long, something tells me she just might be reasonable."

"I hope she is," I said, mulling over my next words. "But if she isn't... all I'm trying to suggest with the ring is that we have a backup plan—something we set in motion if we need to go around her to get to it."

"And all I'm suggesting is that we don't do anything reckless that we'll then be forced to sort."

Silence.

"You recall where she and Hamish live?" he finally asked, breaking the quiet tension.

"Yes." I had followed Annabel to Esther's home through my spirit-travels when we were first searching for the ring. Forfar was small enough during that time period. "I can find it again."

"We need to sort whether we lead in with my connection to her or not," Fitz said.

Chloe had posed the question yesterday, and we owed her and Solomon an answer by tonight.

"I dinnae think I'll lead in with that—that I'm her descendant."

"You could," I countered.

"She might think we're both off our heads."

"She's a seer. She knows about time-walking."

"Aye, but that's a loaded initial statement."

I hated the edge in his voice. The distance in his eyes. How much he was struggling under the surface.

"So, what? We tell her our names and that we'd like to call on her?"

Fitz's energy wavered. As much as he spoke of my impatience, *he* was the one displaying that particular trait today… an increasing pattern since we'd lost Ian.

"Aye, then we'll tell her we've traveled from afar to visit her."

"If she asks where we've traveled from, then we say what? The future?" I asked.

We sat in silence for a few seconds.

"You'll have a read on her fairly quickly," I said. "Maybe we feel her energy and decide."

"Iz told me yesterday she believes there's a strong chance that Esther has seen us coming. This debate might all be for naught."

I considered the thought. "I doubt she's watching our futures. I mean, I don't know how she would know about us. Unless…."

"Unless?" Fitz prompted.

"Unless she's seen us because she's watching her future, and we've turned up in her visions."

Fitz nodded thoughtfully. "If she's seen us coming, then I reckon we'll know rather quickly if she and Hamish plan to offer us refuge."

"I know a lodging house might be risky, but there's still an argument for staying elsewhere—we'd change Esther's fate less if we weren't staying in the house with her," I said.

"But by staying in their home, our mission will move forward quicker."

"I suppose you're right. We'd get to know them faster. And we'd get eyes on the ring easier, I'd bet."

Fitz agreed, but his energy was distant. My anxiety nipped at my mind and sent my nerves tingling. I never wanted to be out of sync with Fitz, but especially not now, not when we were about to time travel over three-hundred fifty years into the past.

Finally, my mother's cabin appeared, and we dropped down the hillside to greet the wooden, two-story structure. Sunlight broke through the trees, glimmering against the forest-green tin roof. I smiled, recalling how proud my dad had been the day he'd finished it. My heart still tightened at the thought of him… everything would feel better if he were still here. It was easy to imagine him alive and well from a distance, but the memories of this lake house haunted me. His absence could be felt at every turn.

Fitz put the car in park as my grandmother waved from the front porch. A big smile rose to her face, and I waved back, mustering my courage.

Fitz squeezed my hand, but something was off. He had been different since his father's death—understandably—but nothing felt sturdy anymore. I was grieving for more than our loss of Ian.

"I know you aren't ready for this," Fitz said. "But your mother loves you, and Gram will support you through it. You've faced Lorenzo Belmonte. You can handle this conversation with your mum."

"Yeah, well, Lorenzo Belmonte has never met Rachel Weston."

Citing business he needed to handle at his mom's cabin, Fitz left me to talk with Gram after a quick greeting. We stood in the living room near the large windows facing the lake. The autumn sun warmed my skin, which was a comfort considering my anxiety was shooting chills all the way to my core.

"Take a seat," Gram said. "I had just taken the kettle off the stove when you were pulling in—perfect timing."

Of course she had.

Gram's "knowing" had always been a subject of discourse in our family. Even when we were apart when I was a child, she had known just when to call or precisely what was on my mind. And she seemed to have a sixth sense when it came to things like the weather or the soil of our earth. Even Jordan had wondered at Gram's uncanny abilities, never quite satisfied with any explanation she dreamt up during our discussions about her.

"Where's Mom?" I asked as I sat down and Gram traipsed into the kitchen.

"She should be home soon," Gram called through the doorway. "She's on that performing arts committee, and they had a meeting this morning that she couldn't get out of."

Gram emerged with a couple cups of tea, and joined me on Dad's favorite sofa.

"I'm selling the place in Mississippi," Gram said.

I turned to her, a slight intake of air betraying my surprise.

She simply nodded.

"But you love your house."

"I do. It's where I made a life with your grandfather. It's where I raised your father. It holds a lot of happy memories for me. I'll miss it, but if I'm being honest, that house is full of ghosts now. Those memories will always be with me, priss. Your mom needs me, and I reckon I need her too. Maybe this house has its fair share of ghosts, but we have enough life ahead of us to fill it with happier memories."

My insides were churning, and my heart felt like it might burst from the guilt it harbored. My mother needed me, and I couldn't be here for her. But Gram could, and I knew that counted for something.

"When your mother married your father, she became my child too. I couldn't desert her."

Momma had seen Gram as a mother as long as I could recall. I'd never known my mom's parents. Her mother had died in a car accident before I was born, and her father had died when I was an infant. Truthfully, I didn't know much about her side of my family.

I squeezed Gram's hand. "Thank you," I whispered.

"It's made me feel useful again," Gram said.

"Gram," I whispered.

"A part of me died with Matt," Gram said simply. "A mother shouldn't have to bury her children."

I nodded. A part of me had died with Daddy too.

Quiet fell.

"I imagine my move is pretty shocking, but so was hearing my granddaughter was taking off on some wild adventure we couldn't know anything about."

"Gram, I'm so sorry." I had wanted more than anything to share everything with her. She wasn't only my grandmother—she was one of my best friends. But I couldn't tell her that I had been involved in a secret crusade against an evil witch raising an army on a foreign planet.

"Oh, pshh," she muttered, waving her free hand. "Don't go apologizing for doing what you had to do. I'm just saying is all."

"I wish things were different." My voice shook. Gram would never be able to understand the full weight of my statement. I wanted so badly to turn back the clock and do better by my family.

"Course you do. No one ever asks for the kind of burden you carry. But it was given to you for a reason, and one of these days you'll understand why."

"I'm glad, in a way," I began, twirling the tea-stained string in my hand. "I'm glad no one else has to carry this."

"You're more fit for this role than you'll ever give yourself credit for. I know you that well. I'll wager you're as gifted as anyone ever could be."

I shook my head softly.

"Hadley," Gram paused, smiling as she tapped her nails against her teacup. "There are some things you should know about."

"What do you mean?"

"My mother was gifted." She cleared her throat. "Gifted like you."

"What are you saying exactly?" I asked, bracing myself.

"She had an uncanny intuition, but it was more than that. There seemed to be some kind of influence that guided her in everything she did, from big decisions to her everyday life. I always knew that about her, but then one day I saw her walk over to the stove. The fire had gone out, and the black-eyed peas hadn't boiled." Gram smiled, closing her eyes to the memory. "She didn't know I was nearby, and she dropped her guard. She closed her eyes, and the peas instantly boiled."

I gasped.

"When she realized I'd seen the whole thing, she made me promise never to tell anyone. And I kept that promise to her—that is, until now."

"Did you ever see her do anything else strange?"

"Many times. She was less guarded when I was older. What was the point in hiding it from me anymore?"

"Did you ever really talk about it again?"

"My grandmother was even more gifted than my mother—and a little reckless. After we lost her, I had to know the truth. My mother didn't want to tell me all of it, but over the years, she finally came out with a truth that I already knew."

"Which was?"

"My grandmother was a witch. My mother was half witch. I'm only 'bout a quarter at best. I've never had any real power, but I have my ways. What I can't figure out is how you have all this magic in your blood after all this time."

I placed my teacup on the table and pulled my shaking hands into my lap. I was entirely overwhelmed with a swirling mix of emotions. I had longed to know more of my magical ancestry, and Gram had held some of the answers all along.

"Why haven't you talked to me about this before?" I asked.

It was Gram's turn to set her teacup down, and she fiddled absentmindedly with her wedding band as she found her response.

"Don't be angry."

I nodded.

"I was forbidden—by your parents."

"But... they didn't know."

"Well, not exactly. You see, when you started showing signs of power, your dad came to me. He's always known my ways, but it was still tough for him to hear the truth. Your parents knew you were different—gifted—but to believe you were a witch? Well, that was an entirely different matter."

"So, they never came to believe you?"

"Your dad did, though we owe that to Fitz. Once Fitz told him how dangerous it was for humans to know about magic, your dad didn't want to tell your mom. She didn't believe what I had told her anyway, and he said it was fine to let it lie. He just wanted you both to be safe."

"So, he told her Fitz and I were the same kind of 'different' but didn't lead her to believe it was magic necessarily," I said, recalling an earlier conversation with Fitz.

"Exactly."

"But he still didn't want me to know about myself?"

"Matt believed what Fitz told him, and he wanted to keep you safe. And anyway, your mother was against us talking about your abilities in any capacity. She said I wasn't to put fanciful ideas in your head. If I had ever shared any of this with you and your parents found out... well, there wouldn't have been any more summers in Mississippi to say the least."

"Gram, I am so sorry. I can't imagine what a difficult position that was."

"Don't you go worrying about me. None of that means a hill of beans now."

I couldn't agree but held my tongue. My insides were coiled tightly, and my mind was churning. I could have understood myself so many years sooner, but Gram had been silenced—and by my own mother. The one person who should have been most in my corner had betrayed me. A wave of nausea slithered through my stomach.

"I kept my eye on you over the years. I see so much of my grandmother in you. Your energies are so similar." She smiled sadly. "And when Fitz showed up, I knew things would turn out all right."

"You knew?"

"The moment he and Izzy turned up on our doorstep," she said, grinning. "Those two had magical energy spiraling all over the place."

She chuckled, and I couldn't help but laugh myself. Fitz and Izzy were powerful, and I couldn't deny that their magical footprints were sizable.

I sipped slowly at my teacup as Gram told me more about my great-great-grandmother—about how powerful she was. And I told Gram our theory that magic resided in my mother's lineage as well. We wondered at Fate and how my parents had rekindled lost magic from two bloodlines when they'd brought me into the world. Gram wanted to know of my mission, and though I could share very little, she was encouraging.

"I'd like to believe that I've made my ancestors proud, but I feel like all I've done is make a mess of things," I admitted.

Tears spilled hotly down my cheeks. Ian's death, Keoni's death and betrayal, Fitz's and my dismissal from the mission, our upcoming journey… it all bubbled over.

For a second, the tick of the clock was all that disturbed the peaceful air of the sunlit afternoon. Gram took my hand in hers.

"I don't know what you've experienced, but from what I gather… well, I reckon it's pretty bad." Her eyes traced over the scars on my arms before lingering on a large, slow-healing bruise, and I felt exposed.

"Ian's dead, Gram." Of course, she already knew that, but I needed to say it out loud.

"I know, sweetheart. I'm terribly sorry about that."

I wanted to confess how I felt, but I nodded instead, holding back the words I wanted so badly to say aloud. I wanted to tell her how I shouldn't have pushed for us to go to Lorenzo's fortress that day… how Ian would still be alive if I hadn't.

"Your mother is pretty shaken up about it. We both are."

Of course they were. He'd died on the very mission I was continuing on.

"It's dangerous work," I said, my words barely a whisper.

"I don't know how we'd go on without you," she said. "After losing Matt… I know something about how that would feel."

I looked at her through teary eyes, and hers weren't any less clouded.

"You have to promise me that you'll be careful."

I nodded, and she looked down at her tea.

I was suddenly aware that my leg was shaking violently, and the surface of my tea rippled as I rattled agitatedly underneath it. I took a deep breath and steadied myself.

"If anyone can do what they set out to do, it's you, Hadley. If anyone can overcome whatever this is, it's you."

"It's not that easy."

Gram nodded. "When you break it all down, things are usually less complicated than we paint them out to be."

"There are so many threads with this. So many stories, so many lives. Everything—" I stopped, looking into Gram's storm cloud eyes.

Something in them beckoned me to continue. "Everything is interconnected. It's all jumbled, and I don't know who I can trust."

"Can you trust Fitz?" Gram asked.

"Of course," I said without pause.

"Then, that's something. The two of you can untangle the mess. You've always had a way with each other."

I couldn't argue that. We might have been in a delicate place after everything that had happened to us in Opimae, but he was still mine, and I was still his. We would sort it out, I told myself for what must have been the hundredth time.

"Talk each other through it. Start at the beginning. Maybe the threads *are* all jumbled up. So, tease 'em out. Go all the way back and sort out this mess. Where did it all start? What's the root cause of it all?"

Lucio, I thought. Lorenzo's father.

"There's a spark in your eyes that I thought I might not see this time," Gram said approvingly. "Wherever your mind just went... start there. Work your way forward. You can't go back and change the past, but you can sort things out in the present."

Gram was wrong about that... I *could* go back in time, and that was exactly where it had all begun—in 1662 with Lucio. And a ring that was forged centuries ago that was never meant to be his. I searched Gram's energy, and I thought that somehow, she knew more than she let on.

Gram squeezed my hand gently.

"I always knew you were born with a big purpose, priss. From the beginning, you were a child with real gumption."

I smiled, taking my grandmother's hand, and for the first time, the faint echo of magic in her blood responded to the surge of my own.

My grandmother—part human, part witch, and fully divine—had carried a torch through her veins that one day ignited within my own.

We were still in conversation when my mother returned home, and though my stomach flipped at the squealing hinges of the side door, an internal smile flitted through me. That door was always needing more oil, and the familiarity offered a bit of comfort that pushed back against my nerves, enveloping me like a warm blanket. Her keys clinked as she set them in the ceramic dish that had been shaped and painted as a black cat—just like my favorite childhood pet. I smiled in spite of my nerves, in spite of the fact that she was the one who had kept me from learning the truth about myself as a child.

When she rounded the corner, our eyes met, and my anger faded as emotion flooded into her face.

"Momma," I whispered.

She crossed the room and wrapped me in a tight embrace. The room was quiet except for the sniffles that came from the two of us, and Gram's footsteps as she padded back to the kitchen. I was sure she meant to retrieve some tincture of hers to soothe our nerves. When my mom released me, she sat and took a tissue from the wicker holder on the coffee table and passed it over to me. I accepted her offer as I took a seat across from her.

Gram returned with a cup of tea that smelled of lavender and chamomile. Something to soothe us indeed. I blew at the steam swirling from the cup before feeling my mother's gaze on me. A familiar warmth channeled through me, tugging at my witch's eye. It was weak, but it was there—the subtle hum of magic. Not enough to make a witch, but enough to have passed the legacy to me.

My mom looked at me—really looked at me—for the first time, and though she kept her expression carefully even, her hazel eyes were uncomfortably observant as they studied me. I took a deep breath at the sight; there was something in them that bordered on fear. And there was something else… something different about her, though I couldn't quite account for it. It wasn't a new hairstyle or new clothes. It wasn't even in her speech or the way she carried herself, but it was there, silently plaguing me.

I was grateful to have my grandmother there with us. Gram prodded us along in conversation, everything from how she was enjoying her time in Washington to the garden's first crop to Momma's charity work. But unspoken words peppered the air around me, and I could barely function under their weight. Finally, and rather abruptly, I threw the conversation into disarray.

"You haven't once asked me about myself."

Something flashed through my mother's eyes, an anger I recognized, but they fell flat again.

"I don't know what I can ask."

"I—" I broke off, unsure what to say. I clasped my hands together and looked down at my lap calculating my next move.

"You what?" my mom asked. "I've asked countless questions, but there are never any answers."

"I do answer your questions."

"Yes, with half information. You answer cryptically that you can't answer my questions."

I nodded, unable to argue with her.

"I know nothing. Where you've been, what you've been doing, who all you've been with… nothing. My child left on a dangerous mission months ago, and I know nothing."

Her voice shook slightly, though I couldn't decide if it was due to anger or nerves. But her next statement made it clear.

"Ian didn't come home, Hadley. And I'm sure he told Ann and Izzy the same things you told me. I'm sure he said not to worry, that he'd be okay, that he'd come home. But he didn't, did he? And he never will."

Tears spilled down my cheeks, but I couldn't seem to speak. My mother's eyes flickered with sympathy, but I knew better than to believe she'd let me off the hook that quickly.

"Do you know what it's like to be in this position?" She shook her head violently, her blonde strands swinging with the motion. "Of course not. You told me this is for my protection, but I have never once asked you for that. What I *have* asked you for is honesty. I'd rather be in danger than destroying myself with all this worry."

"What if knowing the truth made you worry more?"

"I don't think that's possible. I mean, Hadley, I already know you're on a dangerous government mission, and I know that Ian was killed on that mission. I know you're somewhere you can't talk to me. The worst is already running circles in my mind."

I nodded softly. The thought of coming clean sent a wave of nausea rolling through my stomach again, bringing with it perspiration across my skin. My nerves felt like live wires.

"Hadley, are you all right?" Gram asked.

My mom ran her hand across my back. She'd moved from her seat and was crouched on the floor near me.

"I'm okay."

"Anxiety?" she guessed.

I nodded.

"Take some deep breaths and talk when you're ready. Gram and I will wait."

My thoughts churned. This was dangerous… could I really tell her what I was? My dad had known, and Gram knew, too. And besides… witch DNA resided within my mother's veins. That had to be true, or I wouldn't be sitting in front of her rolling with magic.

I opened my eyes and truly took in the sight of her. And there it was—I was finally able to name what I saw. It was the culmination of her grief over my father compounded by her concern for my safety. She was hollowed out, frail, and the realization blew through me like a gust of wind that was hellbent on my punishment.

I wavered momentarily before my decision was made.

"Momma, you might want to sit back down."

I met Gram's eyes warily, and her face was resolute. She nodded once, and I began.

The back door groaned its announcement of Fitz's arrival. His warmth grew stronger with each step that brought him closer to me. It was one of the most comforting parts of our magical connection. He stopped upon entering the room, and his eyes darted inquisitively across the three of us.

"What's happened?" he asked.

Momma rose from the couch and embraced him. He froze before wrapping his arms around her, though his voice sounded through my mind.

"Hadley, what is going on?"

I flashed a nervous smile. *"Just a minute."*

When Momma released him, she sighed, dropped her hands resolutely to her side, and crossed the room once more to reclaim her former seat on the couch.

"She knows," I said aloud. "They both do."

"They know," he repeated almost absentmindedly. "They *know*," he said again. "Everything?"

"Nothing classified, but they know what we are."

Fitz's energy bubbled through me. I'd surprised him, though he recovered quickly, and his light laughter filled the room. He took a seat on the arm of my chair and slid his hand onto my shoulder.

"You know…" he said before shaking his head. "Actually, never mind."

"No. What is it?" I asked.

"You already know the consequences well. You've made your decision. It's done."

I nodded. "It wasn't an easy one, I assure you."

"I know, Hads." Fitz turned to my mom. "How do you feel, Rachel?"

Her eyes drifted to the window as she pondered her answer. After a few seconds, she turned back to us.

"In a way I'm relieved, I suppose. I watched Hadley struggle to fit in all through her childhood, and even into adulthood." She fidgeted with a loose thread on the beige linen couch. The couch was practically a relic, but because it had been Dad's favorite, it might as well have been nailed to the floor. "I also feel guilty because…" she trailed off, looking to Gram.

"Gram knew," I said.

Gram nodded. "Course I knew."

"I didn't believe Gram, and Hadley suffered for that."

"To be fair, I know how it must have sounded," Gram said.

My mom looked earnestly at Gram. "I'm sorry."

Gram waved her hand dismissively. She had never been one to hold a grudge. She then nodded to me, holding my mother's gaze.

My mom turned to me, her face scrunched. "You suffered because I didn't believe. I am sorry for that, Hadley."

"It's okay. I've found my place. Feeling bad about the past won't change it."

Momma nodded. She wouldn't let it go that easily, but as I considered the dangerous mission ahead of me, I was happy to not dwell on it. I didn't want to spend precious time being angry if I could help it.

"More than anything, I'm scared," Momma said.

"Does it help to know more of the truth, or is it worse?" I asked.

"More information is always better. I wish you could tell me everything, but I better understand why you can't, at least." She looked to Fitz. "Ian's loss *does* bring fear to my doorstep in a new way."

"Of course," Fitz said, his voice barely above a whisper.

"I've worried every day since y'all left. Every phone call stops my heart because I wonder if someone is going to tell me that my child will never come home again. I'll worry every day until you come home for good… I can't help it."

My guilt grew heavier with her words.

"Hadley is one of the strongest beings I've ever known," Fitz said. "And not only in her will, but with her magic… she's a marvel."

"Course she is," Gram said, smiling.

"She works strong and impressive magic. Perhaps it helps a wee bit to know that," Fitz said. "And not that she needs it, but I'm by her side every step of the way. I'll always protect her. You have my word."

I reached for Fitz's hand and met his gaze. We smiled softly before I turned to my mother. Tension still clung to the air, but gradually, it eased with our unburdening.

"Thank you, Fitz," Momma whispered, tears falling down her cheek.

The air rippled, shifting with the comfort of familiar energy. I turned to Fitz, who smiled.

"What's going on?" Momma asked.

"There are other witches nearby," I said. "We know because we feel the shift in the air."

Her eyes widened.

"That'll be Mum and Izzy. They were keen to see you—I hope that's all right."

"Oh, we'd be thrilled to see them," Gram said.

"Please," Momma said, smiling through her tears. "Let's make use of that old fireplace on the deck. It's been far too long since we all gathered out there."

CHAPTER TWO

My heart ached as we drove around Edinburgh from the airport. It was cruel to see our city at a distance without the opportunity to stop at our flat for even an evening. But with our time limitations, Fitz and I had been forced to choose between the lake and our home, and seeing my mother had been a priority for me. Emotionally, I was worn thin, still cloaked in the remnants of our Opimaean losses and reeling from our conversations at the lake. At least Izzy was with us for this leg of our trip. Fitz and I both found comfort in that.

The early morning drive to Forfar was brief, the occupants of the car quiet. I studied the jewelry hanging from a chain around my neck, the moonstone ring that was an exact replica of Esther's magical one. This small, unassuming object had changed the course of all our lives. The slim golden band was hammered lightly and held a smooth, pearl-colored moonstone in a round bezel. The stone caught passing headlights, casting an ethereal glow across the glassy surface, reminding me of its namesake. I'd always loved this ring. Not only had it amplified my connection to Fitz because he'd channeled his magical energy into it, but it had brought me closer to Esther as well. The crystal's properties had been beneficial in soothing my anxiety, and I suspected I would have a distinct need for that where we were headed.

Chloe and Solomon had been tasked with finalizing the last details with us and giving instruction from the rest of the Cardinal Court, and as the car neared the streets of Forfar, they began discussing our final business before crossing over.

"Have you learned anything new about the loss of time between Opimae and Earth?" I asked.

I didn't miss the concerned look exchanged between Chloe and Solomon before she answered, "We still don't know much of substance, but we've confirmed this isn't normal."

We had thought perhaps time moved slower in Opimae, which would account for us missing eight months of our time on Earth. Since so much information had gone missing between our worlds, we'd assumed this detail had been simply lost. But apparently not.

"Something to do with the portal, then?" Fitz asked.

"We believe Lorenzo might have discovered our plans to cross back to Earth and attempted to stop us," Solomon answered. "In doing so, he might have further disrupted the portal, which led to this loss of time."

I recalled the trouble we had originally traveling to Opimae and how Keoni believed Lorenzo was affecting portal crossings.

I met Chloe's troubled eyes in the rear-view mirror, and I was reminded that it wasn't only Fitz and me who'd lost time. I gave a tight smile in return.

"We'll continue to look for answers while you're gone," she said.

"And speaking of which," Solomon began. "We really must reach an agreement on one last piece of this mission. What will you do if the family refuses to hand over the ring peacefully?"

Fitz's energy stirred.

"Fitz?" I prompted.

His eyes dropped to his hands, which were coiled tightly in his lap.

"Is this truly my decision?" he asked.

Chloe and Solomon exchanged a troubled glance.

"We won't be there to consult with you," Chloe said. "So, yes… it'll be your decision."

"But we are entrusting you to make the right one," Solomon said.

Fitz hesitated a few seconds before finding his response. "Hadley and I will await Esther's death, and we'll take the ring before Lucio does."

Hearing the words aloud was jarring, and I imagined it was equally difficult for Fitz.

"What if he gets to it first?" I asked.

"That's always your argument," he said. "But we won't let that happen."

"He might beat us to it. I mean, we can't control any of the factors around Esther's execution."

"We willnae know any of that until we're there," Fitz said firmly.

I met his gaze before raising my hands in surrender. Of course, we'd know more once we made it to the past, but I didn't see the harm in running through this scenario now.

"If you can reach an agreement for them to hand it over when it was meant to be collected by the family, that does sound like the best case," Chloe said. "But be mindful of Lucio. Once he arrives in the past and realizes you're there for the same reason, who knows what he might do?"

"Aye, that alone might alter the course of history," Izzy said.

"So, we need to be very careful. Try to outsmart him," I said.

"We'll do our best, but if we must, I believe Hadley and I are strong enough to overpower him."

I hoped Fitz was right.

When we arrived at the car park, I met Izzy's gaze. She smiled softly, though her eyes were filled with sadness. My nerves tingled down my arms, and I opened the car door before I lost my courage. I had faced a foreign planet and a great evil already, I reminded myself. I could handle some overzealous witch hunters. Solomon popped the trunk, and we grabbed the backpacks that held what we hoped to be seventeenth-century-appropriate layers for us to don just before our time jump. The first morning light was just glimmering on the horizon, and the wind blew cold across the rippling waters of the loch. It nipped against my face, seemingly reminding us of what lay ahead, and I zipped my jacket to my chin. The weather in the past wouldn't be any kinder to us once we landed in November of 1662.

Chloe looped her arm through mine as we began our walk down a paved path. We meandered in silence along the trees, and to our right, a bright green field stretched up a gentle hill to meet the autumn sky, which shone with reds and oranges—a sunrise worthy of the season. Horses dotted the field, some trotting around while others grazed lazily. Soon enough, the trees enveloped us on either side of the narrow path, granting a sense of seclusion to our journey. The path grew dim, and the world was quiet, likely owing to the early hour.

The wind picked up slightly as we reached our destination, and I took my final few steps to the Forfar Witches' Memorial. A rectangular stone rose from the ground, its edges rounded. The text simply read:

THE

FORFAR

WITCHES

JUST

PEOPLE

Twenty-two circles had been carved between the two blocks of text: the number of women murdered during the witch trials. I dropped to my knees in front of the stone and ran my fingers across the ridges, like a sailor drawn to a siren's song. Izzy knelt beside me and pulled flowers from her bag. Their bright purple blooms and prickly leaves gave them away in an instant.

"Scotch Thistle?" I asked.

"Aye," she said softly as she laid them to rest at the base of the memorial. "They might be the national flower of Scotland, but they're more than that. These flowers are hearty, able to grow in even the harshest of environments."

I nodded, understanding.

"Where you're going… it will be harsh, difficult. But I know you will persevere," she said. "You'll fight bravely alongside our sisters, and I know you will come home."

Tears sprang to my eyes, and again, I simply nodded, unable to voice what I was feeling.

Izzy turned and touched her fingertips to the stone, closed her eyes, and whispered softly in Scots Gaelic. She then drew herself up and turned to the lake, singing boldly in her nation's tongue—a lament, it seemed. Fitz pulled me into his arms, and we stood frozen, captivated by Izzy's melancholic voice until she released us from the trance.

Chloe and Solomon walked to either side of us and faced each side of the path, closing their eyes briefly. When they turned back around, they nodded. No one was nearby. It was time to change our clothing and slip through time. Fitz called to the elements to shield us as I pulled our new garb from the backpacks. Fitz helped me through my layers: a chemise, a petticoat, a pair of stays, my outer garment and overcoat. We changed as expediently as the clothing of the time period allowed and then dropped the shield.

Izzy took in the sight of us and giggled.

"I know," I said. "I feel completely ridiculous."

My black velvet dress held embroidery of colorful floral details, and thick, golden bands detailed around the neck and down the center of the dress. The overcoat was no better—the puffy sleeves were extraordinarily large, and the gold detailing was just as loud as what lay underneath.

"Is the petticoat meant to be that... full?" Izzy asked.

Chloe shrugged. "Apparently. We didn't have much time, but we learned the style of the seventeenth century isn't heavily documented. We were told this was generally the style of the time."

I didn't know much about seventeenth-century fashion, but the extravagance didn't feel quite right for the Scottish countryside. But there was no turning back now.

Fitz's garments were equally opulent. He wore a red tunic with a black velvet overcoat whose gold detailing was clearly meant to complement mine. His matching black velvet cap held a red feather. After truly taking it in, I couldn't help but laugh.

"Aye right. Throw your punches while you still can," he said.

"I'm glad this could be our parting gift to you," I said to the group, holding out my arms in full display.

Izzy pulled her attention back to the memorial, and it only took a beat to understand why. A small black cat with large green eyes sat to the left of the stone.

"Well, hello, you wee cutie!" Izzy said.

The cat studied us, but it gave no inclination of any emotion.

"I wonder if it's friendly." I took a step forward.

The cat stood, flicking its tail while making a great show of stretching its limbs. It walked around the stone and seemingly... disappeared. We rushed over to look, but the cat was simply gone.

"Well, that's odd," Chloe said.

"An omen, perhaps," Izzy said.

"We encountered a crow at the lake, too," Fitz said. "I meant to speak with you about it, Iz."

"Two appearances by animals who walk between the living and the dead," Izzy said. "That does seem strange."

"They're both said to be messengers of Fate," Chloe said.

"I wouldnae be feart," Izzy said. "I don't believe them to be bad omens. But watch for other messengers. Be vigilant."

With that, we began our goodbyes. Chloe was the last to embrace me as Fitz hugged Izzy, sadness radiating between the two of them. He then grasped my hand tightly with a brave smile, our discord forgotten in this moment. I glanced over my shoulder, and Izzy nodded, her brows knitting together as she fought back tears. I twirled to face Fitz, wrapping my arms around him like I'd done a thousand times before.

"I love you," Fitz said softly. "On purpose."

An echo of our promises made on Opimaean soil… and it meant as much to me in this moment as it had then. This was his promise. Together, we'd find our way through it all.

"I choose you," I said.

Fitz smiled. "Hold on tight, love."

"Don't lose me," I whispered.

Fitz laughed in response, but the noise was dark and distorted like some horror from a haunted house. The air rippled as he connected to the threads of time, which echoed through my body as the in-between beckoned us forward. As my vision slipped from this reality, the sky changed overhead. It darkened with storm clouds as strong gusts of wind whipped across the loch. We braced ourselves at the onslaught, and it enveloped us in a wind tunnel, much like the one I'd witnessed Chloe work against one of our Parsian stalkers, Allette, in Opimae.

I tore my gaze from the scene to face Fitz. His eyes were wide, but it was wonder rather than fear I found in them. The elements had never behaved this way when we had time-walked, and gauging by his reaction, Fitz hadn't experienced this either. I channeled my focus and thought of the past, setting my intention as I had done many times before.

"There will be no stopping it now," he called over the chaos. "Fate has decided, and time is pulling me under."

The darkness enveloped us, and I lost all comprehension of time—had we been in the in-between for hours? Minutes? I didn't know, and truly, we never would. When a glimmer stretched across the horizon, I knew the end of our journey was near.

Patches of green and gray came swirling into view, much like the colors of the beach when I'd first time-walked with Fitz. How long ago that seemed. Our feet found solid ground, and a chill pierced the air. After a few seconds, my eyes acclimated. There was no one in sight—and not the slightest indication of humanity.

Though the loch was certainly beautiful in our time, this was something else entirely, and I had to wonder if we'd remained true to our course. Evergreens towered from the overgrowth of dormant grass and shrubs, while thick, verdant moss cloaked much of the smaller trees. Wind whistled through the upper limbs, and the bare branches of the smaller trees groaned from the weight. I couldn't catch sight of the loch, but the trees were so dense, it was little wonder. However, nothing suggested we hadn't made our mark, and I thought that might be win enough for the moment.

A slow smile spread across Fitz's features. He removed his cap and ran his hand through his chestnut hair.

"Well, we aren't in the town square. A braw sign. What do you reckon?"

"Thank god for that," I mused.

I craned my neck, searching through the trees, but found nothing of significance. A gentle breeze broke through the thick foliage before nipping at my skin, sharpening my senses. Though cold, the air was fresh and vibrant—clean in a way that I had rarely tasted.

"Only us," I whispered.

Fitz pulled me close, kissing my forehead. "Aye. That's enough for me."

Fitz and I grew still, searching the elements for clues. Water echoed through my senses.

The loch.

"To the water?" Fitz asked.

"To the water," I confirmed.

He placed his cap back on his head, prompting a snicker from me.

"What now?" he asked, feigning annoyance.

"Hold still."

I adjusted his cap and nodded once. "There," I said. "A bit more presentable."

He smirked, and we headed toward the loch. "If we've hit our mark, town *should* be that way."

"And what do you feel?" I asked as we trudged through the tall grass and meandered around the tree trunks.

Fitz paused, closing his eyes. "We've hit our mark."

"Of course we did." I smiled proudly. And apparently my smile was contagious.

"I can't believe it."

"I can," I said simply.

I planted a kiss at the nape of his neck. The tension and grief of the last few weeks eased as we wondered at the beginning of our new adventure.

I glanced around, considering the feel of a strange energy that grew firm on my skin. The warmth would have been pleasant if not for the unsettling fatigue that lingered behind it. I wanted nothing more than to curl up at the nearest trunk and fall fast asleep.

"The energy shift?" Fitz asked.

"The air changed, but there's something else…."

"Aye, and it grows stronger near that densely wooded area just there."

The energy tingled across the right side of my face.

A soft, golden glow caught my eye. It zipped quickly into the forest and disappeared.

"That light…" I said. "It looked like a lightning bug."

Fitz's brow furrowed. "I've never seen a firefly in Scotland," he said. "A glowworm, aye. But nothing like this."

I turned back to the forest, studying its depths. "Have you felt anything quite like that before?"

Fitz cocked his head. "I don't think so. There was something familiar in the feel of it, but I can't place it."

"Wonder what it could be," I said, almost to myself, as we resumed our path.

"It could be a great many things. Countless beings are rumored to wander the Scottish forests, lochs, and moors."

"Like?" I asked.

"You've probably heard of our mythical beings like the kelpies or the selkies, and faeries, of course. We have other folklore as well," Fitz said as he pushed a branch aside for me. "Beings like the redcaps, the Bean Nighe, or the fuaths."

"What on earth are *those*?" I asked.

Fitz chuckled. "Malevolent spirits. Some are said to be water spirits, and you know, we *are* close to the loch."

I grabbed his arm. "Do *not* start that with me, Fitz MacGregor."

His smile widened. "Whatever that was back there, it was strange, but it wasn't a bad spirit. We're fine, Hadley."

How many of Scotland's mythical beings were real? There had been a time in my life when I didn't believe in magical or mythical beings, but that time had passed long ago. After all, I'd found out one day that I was a witch. Perhaps all of the myths were true, and the real danger lay in disbelief.

In the distance, waves broke along the shoreline. I smiled. "Next, we'll confirm our heading and just… casually knock on Esther's door?"

"Aye, I suppose that is still the plan. Assuming we're not greeted by angry villagers with pitchforks."

I winced.

Fitz stopped and took my hand in his. I turned to face him. "What's the matter?"

I swallowed, my throat suddenly dry. "Honestly? We're *here*, Fitz. We're in a time where women are hated… men are suspicious of us. I can't use my magic—not openly. I'm…." I sighed. "I'm *nervous*."

Fitz nodded, his eyes gently flickering across mine. "Should anyone try to harm you, they won't live long enough to see it done."

"Fitz," I whispered.

He rested his forehead against mine. "Fate and Forfar be damned," he said. "No harm will come to you, I swear it."

I kissed him then, and his breath came short by the time his lips left mine.

"All right, then?" he asked.

I nodded.

A sparkling loch stretched before us, and though the banks were surrounded by considerably more trees, there was no doubt in my mind—this was Forfar Loch. The elements were untamed, uninhibited by modern life. I closed my eyes, drinking in the radiant energy of the natural world, recharging in the elements after our taxing journey through time.

A large gust of wind blew violently across the loch, and every bit of my exposed skin ached, protesting against the chill.

"Let's get going," I said. "Even with all these layers, I'm cold."

Fitz chuckled. "It's Scotland, love."

The piercing wind blew again, folding over the grass. We trudged along the loch briskly, though moving in my new wardrobe was challenging. But even so, I was happy to be active, steadily growing warmer with the exercise. We wound around the loch faster than I expected and had just reached a small clearing when the nearby brush rustled. My eyes met Fitz's, and he signaled for me to halt.

The tingling sensation of new energy danced through us—there was another witch close by. A shiver ran through my body, and this time it wasn't from the cold.

Leaves crunched underfoot; the witch was closing in. Fitz positioned himself in front of me, but I stepped to my left, allowing myself a better view. I clutched at the moonstone ring hanging underneath my chemise with one hand and took Fitz's hand in the other.

A beautiful woman stepped around a nearby tree, her green eyes lighting in recognition. Long, auburn hair was braided down her back, and her ethereal presence sent magic dusting the air all around her. She was just as I remembered from my spirit-travels. I had once met Izzy MacGregor in much the same way.

The woman's smile was apprehensive, but I didn't have to wonder long if she knew who we were.

"Fitz. Hadley. I am Esther… I've long been expecting ye."

CHAPTER THREE

"Esther…" I said, choking up. An urge to embrace her swelled in my chest, though I thought that might not be welcomed. "We're so pleased to finally meet you."

My blood hummed with both Fitz's energy and my own, and the rush was almost dizzying.

Esther's smile widened. She studied us, shaking her head softly, seemingly in wonder.

Fitz's eyes were wide, clearly surprised by this woman's similarities to his sister. I wondered if he was surprised by her age—she couldn't have been any older than the two of us. I eyed him meaningfully.

Esther looked down. "I am blest with foresight—perhaps ye are aware," she said, her accent and dialect deeply Scots Gaelic.

"Aye, we're aware," Fitz said, his voice a bit gruff.

Esther raised her eyes to her many times great-grandson. "I told myself I wouldnae trouble ye today. I dinnae wish to make ye uneasy…."

"You aren't," I said.

She nodded. "I have been visited by visions of ye for many months. I'm… weel, I'm quite overcome seeing ye here."

"We understand the sentiment," Fitz said, his voice softening. "Your story has been so close to our hearts… I feel as though I already know you."

Fitz had spent countless hours with his father researching Esther's story, and I imagined Ian's loss was only amplifying the emotion he felt in meeting Esther.

Esther nodded, as if not trusting her voice. And it was then that I succumbed to instinct and embraced her. Our energies teemed wildly between us as she squeezed me tightly. Her magic was warm and inviting, much like the rest of the MacGregor family, and it instantly put me at ease.

When Esther pulled back, she held onto my elbows for a few seconds longer before releasing me to take stock of us once more. Her gloved hands rose to cradle the sides of her face.

"Och, the sight of ye both!"

I smiled, feeling much the same. I had often noticed Izzy's similarities to her own mother, Ann, but seeing Esther again, I thought perhaps I had been wrong in that comparison. It was uncanny how much Esther and Izzy favored.

"I must apologize. I dinnae mean to stare. 'Tis more than the visions." She paused briefly, and we waited silently until she was ready to go on. "Fitz… ye're proof that my bairns live on after my death."

Fitz's energy sang warmly through me. He closed the gap between them quickly, holding his many times great-grandmother as she processed something unimaginable. She'd foreseen her fate—we knew—but to see the implications of it firsthand was another thing entirely.

When Esther pulled away, she was quick to apologize.

"Whatever for?" I asked.

"Ye willnae find me often overcome with feeling," she said, seemingly embarrassed.

"I understand," I said, nodding. "Though this seems like an appropriate time for it."

"Aye. I think we're all a bit overwhelmed," Fitz added.

"Weel, let's get ye out of the cold, shall we? Hadley is about to freeze through."

I laughed, nodding gratefully, and we set off on our journey toward the village.

After a few moments, Esther cleared her throat. "Ye've journeyed to a dangerous time, ye ken."

"Aye," Fitz answered. "The witch hunts have begun?"

"Five arrests this last fortnight. Ye ken Helen's tale?"

"She and her daughter were arrested, and she's made most of the claims against the persons arrested?"

"Aye, she's implicated many villagers. Nineteen arrests thus far. Twelve deaths. None of the recent arrests have been convicted yet, but in time…."

Dread slipped through my veins. Even though I'd expected danger, nothing could have prepared me for the moment this all became real.

"*We've arrived a bit early,*" Fitz said to my mind.

"*You've brought us to the right place and time,*" I said, knowing he'd be hard on himself. "We'll do our best to lay low for now."

"The humans are restless, frightened," Esther continued. "They need only take notice of the slightest oddity to make their claims to the new minister. Father Evans bathes in their accusations, and the villagers desire to remain in his good standing—for fear of being next in the noose."

"So they'll compromise their neighbors to ensure the accusations stray from their own doorstep," Fitz said.

"Aye, and it hasnae done much in the way of neighborly felicity."

"And Helen is a human?" Fitz asked.

"Aye," Esther said. "Though ye'll ne'er convince the villagers otherwise."

"Do you expect we'll be targets?" Fitz asked.

"Och aye."

"If you don't mind me asking… are the villagers suspicious of you already?" I asked.

"Aye."

"But they haven't made any formal claims yet?"

Fitz looked at me, his eyes filled with apprehension.

"I know. I'm sorry," I said. "I just wanted to know—"

Esther waved her hand, cutting me off. "Ye wish to ken just where ye are in time," she said. "I understand. Accusations have been made against many villagers. The minister is working through them—for now, I am safe."

"We'd like to make ourselves as inconspicuous as possible," Fitz said.

Esther paused for a moment, surveying us with a critical eye. "A new wardrobe is our first task."

"We were hoping the councils got this right," I said, pulling at my clothing.

Esther's mouth twisted.

I laughed. "But clearly they didn't."

"This is a bit…." She paused. "Weel, a bit ornate."

"They're too much." Studying Esther's clothing, it was clear. Our garments were ostentatious compared to her simple pieces: a dark brown overcoat, beige stays, simple olive skirts.

"Ye'll stand out, that's for certain."

I groaned.

"Dinnae fash. 'Tis easily remedied," Esther said. "But our work willnae end there."

"We've worked on our story," I said.

"Let us hear it."

"We've come from the Americas. My father moved our family to Stratford seeking religious freedom amongst the unrest here in his homeland. I was only a young girl when we moved, and I remember little of this country."

"It accounts for yer strange speech and manners." Esther nodded. "We have a bit of work ahead, but it'll do."

Esther was right about my speech. Both the accent and dialect of this time and place would take time for me to truly understand.

"My account is similar," Fitz said, "though I was older when my family left. I met Hadley, and we both wished to come home to Scotland."

"Ye sound closer to our speech, so ye'll find yer way a bit quicker than Hadley. Ye're also a man, which benefits ye—they arnae quite as keen on dragging men to the gallows. Ye'll do fine."

A dangerous time for women, indeed. My magic rippled from my witch's eye, a warning of sorts.

"We'll do our best to keep safe," Esther said.

"Is that even possible as women?"

Esther took a beat. "Nae," she finally said. "They will be suspicious of ye simply because of what ye are. If it eases yer mind, their vitriol extends to most women in the burgh. Ye'll hardly be unique in drawing their attention."

"We'll do what we can to conform quickly and not draw more attention to you—or me."

Esther nodded once. "I gather all ye have with ye is the clothes on yer backs?"

"Aye."

"Nae bother. We purchased extra fabrics at the market over the last six months in preparation. We only wanted yer story to draw up yer clothing properly."

"That's generous of you. Is there some way we might repay you?" I asked. "We have little in the way of money right now, but I'm sure we can figure something out."

"Dinnae fash. Ye'll earn yer keep soon enough." Esther grinned, and we laughed lightly. "Come now. Let's get ye hame."

"We didn't want to assume that we'd be welcome in your home…" Fitz said softly.

"Ye're family, are ye no? Of course, ye're welcome." Esther spoke with confidence, but her energy wavered.

We continued our conversation while we navigated through the trees, laying the lightest foundation between the three of us. Once we cleared the thicket of trees, Esther paused, allowing Fitz and me to take in the sight before us.

"Even with the danger… Dad would have loved this," Fitz whispered.

I gripped his hand tightly, smiling at the thought, and we pushed onward until the structures came more clearly into focus, their chimneys smoking in the distance—the chimneys of Forfar in the year 1662.

CHAPTER FOUR

The burgh of Forfar was small in comparison to what modern society considered a large town, but I knew that for the time, Forfar hummed with activity. As we neared the edge of town, villagers moved about the streets. But even with the bustle of the afternoon, the energy that nudged at my witch's eye was uncomfortable. It was too strong, and the undercurrent worked a prickle down my spine that left me unnerved and anxious.

"Do you feel that?" I asked to Fitz's mind.

"The strange energy? Aye."

Esther stopped just short of the narrow, muddy road that led deeper into town.

"I ken ye must find the burgh's energy worrisome, and it should be so. The villagers are vexed—filled with fear and suspicion. Carry yerselves with dignity and honor. Show them strength."

Without awaiting our response, she moved on.

Fitz extended his arm, and I looped mine through his, allowing him to accompany me along the street as we quickened our pace to keep time with Esther. I bent my thumb to fidget with my engagement ring and found only a smooth surface. The diamonds would have drawn far too much attention, so we'd replaced the ring with a simple gold band instead. The only familiar objects that remained with me were the moonstone ring and two pieces of jewelry I'd acquired in Opimae—the amulet from Queen Marina and the black tourmaline from Jess—all of which were placed on a long gold chain and tucked under my chemise to keep them out of sight. But they lent a bit of comfort still, and I was grateful for any boost in protection.

The first villager to notice us was a blacksmith working in an old stone building with the wooden doors thrown open. The warmth of his fire was appreciated, but with it came his attention. He paused his work and narrowed his eyes, studying us thoroughly as we passed by. Esther's attention remained fixed on the path in front of her.

"Not an ally, then," Fitz said under his breath.

I gathered myself, pulling my shoulders back and raising my chin. My pulse thumped in my throat, but I refused to show even the slightest sign of fear. It wasn't until we rounded the corner that the clack of metal striking metal sounded again. But the blacksmith was only the first of many. As we meandered deeper into the burgh, the stares grew frequent.

Storefronts were scattered in buildings at the center of town, and a market appeared to be in full swing in the center courtyard. In the shadows of a two-story stone building, stalls were nearly stacked on top of one another. Vendors chattered with other villagers, peddling fabrics, baked goods, paper, and more from crude wooden structures and covered carts. But even the fresh scent of breads and pies couldn't overpower the filth and waste that permeated the air. We were lucky to visit while it was cold—I could only imagine the summer months—but this was the reality of the time. I longed to take in the sight—to truly process where I was—but danger was palpable, preventing me from truly reveling in the fact that I was in another time.

"This market is approved by the crown," Fitz said, his eyes turned upward.

Despite the overwhelming sights and sounds, I had to smile. This must have been fascinating to my favorite historian.

"How do you know?" I asked.

Fitz pointed to a round stone structure. Standing roughly ten feet tall and of equal width, it resembled a monument of sorts. The market stalls encircled it.

"That's a mercat cross," he said, as though that explained everything. "It grants the townspeople the right to hold a regular market. Since it's just in front of the tolbooth, this is where they'll try and execute women convicted of witchcraft."

A shiver ran down my spine.

As we moved past a stall selling fabric, a middle-aged woman approached, carrying herself with a stately air. She stood out, her blonde hair pulled into two twists that met atop her head, and her wool dress stitched with a heather pattern. Her hands were delicate and her nails clean as she swept a woolen swatch over me. When I met her blue eyes, which sat above a button nose, I found a hint of condescension in them.

"Perhaps a new dress for the lady," she said, her tone suggestive as she scrutinized my dress.

"Thank you, but no," I replied.

Her eyes widened at my speech, and though I should have been concerned at my first interaction already setting me apart, I was a bit smug at her surprise.

I turned my eyes to Fitz, and we hastened our steps. When we were out of earshot, I turned to Esther.

"Is my dress just too formal, or is it out of fashion as well?" I asked, concern flooding through me.

Esther paused, and confusion flashed across her features. I rethought my word usage.

"Is it too elaborate? The woman back there," I explained.

Esther waved her hand. "Ah, Fiona," she said, resuming her walk. "Ne'er ye mind her."

I glanced around, realizing most of the women were wearing skirts that were less full than mine, and my overcoat was certainly more intricate than the ones the other women in the market wore. Where theirs were simple and practical, mine was loud and overdone.

"I *am* out of fashion," I said, my voice betraying my horror.

"We shall remedy that, as I've said," Esther said. "But dinnae let Fiona make ye ill at ease. She's discovered a connection betwixt making women feel less than fashionable and selling fabric."

Her sales tactic had worked on me. But I *wasn't* blending with the locals, and it was all I could think of.

"Well, that's unkind," I managed to say.

"Her husband was injured last year and cannae work the fields any longer. She does as she sees fit to care for him and their bairns."

As we continued along the stalls, the crowd grew louder, and the energy ripped through me like a current. We now stood by the mercat cross, and I surmised the building in front of us must be the tolbooth. The rectangular two-story structure was made of stone and held two large wooden doors at the front. The building housed the government happenings in town, along with the town's accused—including Helen Guthrie, her daughter, and the other poor souls accused of witchcraft. The few small windows it held had been boarded up. I looked to Fitz and Esther, my head tilted.

"The villagers fear the power of the witches inside," Esther said sarcastically. "If the witches cannae see them, it decreases the effectiveness of their curses on the villagers."

"Fascinating," I said, matching her tone. "I didn't know witches' powers were stunted by wooden boards."

I didn't want to linger too long, didn't want to draw attention to myself, so it was with difficulty that I pulled my eyes away. Women sat tortured just on the other side of those stone walls as village life carried on.

A group of villagers stormed through the market, stopping just short of the tolbooth's front doors.

"Bring forth the witch!" a man yelled. "Show us Helen!"

"Aye, bring her forth!" another exclaimed.

"Hang the witch!" the group shouted repeatedly.

Fitz tightened his arm, pulling me closer to him, and he laid his opposite hand on top of mine. Esther nodded to us, and we walked on.

Many faces in the crowd turned to us, watching our progress with interest. Several whispered and a few even pointed toward Esther—and then at Fitz and me. Though I allowed my eyes to sweep over the many faces, I didn't want to appear unnerved. Esther's energy stirred apprehensively, but her face was set in stone as she weaved through the crowd. I followed her example, swallowing hard and pushing forward. Once we reached the other side of the courtyard, I looked back, taking in the scene. In a tumultuous sea of shouting and raised fists, one person caught my attention. A frail woman with honey-blonde hair wove through the crowd. Her gait was slow and uneven, and the look of determination on her features suggested the task wasn't easy for her.

As the crowd grew more volatile, so did my unease. I worried someone would harm her, even by accident, or that someone might take notice of her. I'd read countless times that walking with a limp, having an eye that squinted, really anything that the villagers might consider a physical abnormality was enough to serve as proof that the person was a witch—especially if that person was a woman. I realized I was holding my breath and released it as the woman drew near.

Esther reached out and took the woman by the hand. As her gaze settled on Esther, fear flickered through her blue eyes, and she hesitated only briefly before placing her delicate hand in Esther's and gripping it tightly.

"Are ye well, Katherine?" she asked.

Katherine's heart-shaped face was framed by hair that had fallen from her braid, and though her features held the markings of grief, she was still young. Though witches typically showed our age slowly, I guessed she couldn't be more than forty.

"Aye, well enough. Get on with ye—dinnae slow yerself for me." Her husky voice didn't invite discussion, but as Esther's energy tightened, the hint of a smile quickly crossed Katherine's lips.

"We willnae leave ye behind," Esther said, turning to Fitz and me with a pointed look.

"Of course not," Fitz said.

Katherine's eyes widened at Fitz's response. "Glory be," she whispered before turning to Esther. "Is this…?"

"Aye, Fitz and Hadley."

Katherine's eyes filled with wonder.

"You know who we are," I said.

When Katherine's eyes met mine, a spark of energy jolted through me. It was fleeting, but it was impossible to ignore.

Esther turned to us. "Please allow me to introduce my dear friend, Katherine Sampson."

"We are so pleased to make your acquaintance," Fitz said as he bowed his head.

"Aye, 'tis a pleasure. Now, let us move swiftly before these barbarians take us all to the tolbooth."

A shoe sailed above my head, and I ducked. It connected with a man's head. He spun around quickly and locked eyes with another—though I couldn't say he was the culprit. It was enough. The first man pushed through our small group, nearly knocking Katherine and Esther over as he rushed at the other man. Fitz and I stabilized the other half of our party, locked eyes, nodded, and pulled Esther and Katherine away as a scuffle broke out.

"Lead the way, Esther," I said.

Fitz supported Katherine, and I walked at her other side to act as a barrier to the crowd. Fitz eyed me nervously, but I nodded—I was fine. Esther moved just ahead of us, scouting for the best route to get us away. As we rounded a corner, Esther nearly slammed into a towering man with large green eyes and a scruffy red beard. He jumped back and spit in Esther's direction.

"Witch," he muttered.

The man raised his hands in the sign of the cross before walking toward the market. A woman trailed him, her eyes troubled, and a solemn look rested on her features. She slowed her pace and turned to Esther and Katherine.

"Put an end to this madness," she whispered urgently. "I ken ye can do so."

"What is it that ye're asking of us?" Esther challenged.

"I ken what ye are—the both of ye," the woman said.

"Mary!" the red-bearded man called, looking around. "Where have ye gone, woman!"

Mary looked hard at Esther once more. "Put an end to this madness!" she repeated before running toward the man.

He grabbed her by the arm much harder than necessary and dragged her along. I couldn't make out his words, but from his posture to his anger-ridden face, it was clear she was being berated.

My blood boiled, and Fitz flinched, his gaze set over his shoulder and his eyes narrowed. I placed my hand on his forearm and shook my head. Our instinct was to fight—of course it was—but we weren't Opimaean warriors in this time. We needed to blend in.

I glanced in Katherine's direction. She was clutching at Fitz's elbow, holding tightly for support. His features softened, and he sighed. We'd have all been tossed in the tolbooth alongside Helen if he reacted, and that was assuming we'd survive the attack of the angry mob. We'd have to be incredibly strategic if we wanted to return home without making everything worse.

Relief flooded through me when Fitz finally stepped forward, and we pushed toward Esther's home. My mind had been mission-focused as we navigated the crowds, but upon reaching Esther's front door, I realized I was frightened in a way that had never touched my heart before.

A young girl took our overcoats, and I realized I'd observed her during my spirit-travels while learning about the ring.

"Thank ye," Esther said before inviting us into the sitting room adjacent to the entryway. We helped Katherine settle into the chair nearest the fire and took our seats. It was then that I allowed my eyes to wander. The room was crafted of wood and stone and was of decent size, trending toward natural woods and forest tones, and I found it comforting. Large, cushioned chairs and a sizable sofa were positioned near a roaring fireside. Everything was just as I recalled from my spirit-travels: the chaise near the window, the large stone hearth that lay at the center of the room, the shutters that allowed light but restricted prying eyes.

"Shall we bring refreshments?" a woman with dark hair and delicate features inquired.

"Aye, that'll do well, Isla. Thank ye."

Isla bowed and exited the room.

Esther removed her gloves, and I noted she did not wear the moonstone ring.

"*No ring*," I said silently to Fitz.

Fitz's eyes darted to her hand before turning to the window.

We'd surely have many things to consider in our first days in Forfar, but the most important task on our list was to begin locating the ring.

My attention was pulled away as a tall man walked through the doorway. He was brawny and well-dressed in a wool ensemble of visible quality. His eyes were the deepest shade of blue, the color of summer storm clouds or salt water in the depths of the ocean. He advanced toward us, his skepticism hanging noticeably on the air as he ran his hand through the blond strands that had escaped the tie at the nape of his neck.

"Hamish MacGregor," he said plainly. He sighed deeply. "So, it begins."

CHAPTER FIVE

Hamish took a seat on the sofa near Esther. She reached for his hand, and Hamish's gaze turned tender as he looked at his wife. Like Esther, I imagined he was in his thirties, and his demeanor was right out of a folktale. I could easily envision him charging into battle, ready to slay the English for his Scottish cause. Or sailing the ocean in his search for new land—his Viking blood showing itself as prominently as it did. He had great, square shoulders, and Esther's small frame was dwarfed next to his strong build. His voice was deep and gruff as he spoke to her in Gaelic, I presumed, and Esther's brows knitted.

But before she could respond, Fitz spoke to Hamish. "*Tha mi toilichte coinneachadh riut.*"

"Ye speak in our tongue... though strangely." Hamish studied Fitz. He had Ian's eyes—or rather, Ian had inherited his. I wondered if Fitz was also stunned by the similarity. "Yer look isnae so strange that ye'll draw notice… once we outfit ye properly."

"He requires nothing that cannae be remedied easily," Katherine said, waving her hand dismissively.

"Aye," Hamish said. "Ye need work, but ye'll do."

Esther's eyes met Fitz's, a plea resting in them. She wouldn't interfere just yet, but her energy buzzed anxiously around the room.

What was she holding back? What did she wish to say?

I was studying Esther so intently that I didn't realize I was the focus of Hamish's attention until his witch's gaze prickled my skin. His eyes pierced mine when I finally shifted my attention.

"And ye? Do ye ken Gaelic?"

"I'm afraid not," I said.

"Hmph."

"I told ye I didnae think she would have much time to learn before her travels here. Fitz and Hadley have been on a dangerous journey."

"Do ye ken of the danger of this time?"

"I inherited Annabel's journal and her grimoire," Fitz said simply.

Hamish's eyes widened ever so slightly. "Then ye ken ye willnae find any less danger here."

"We'll sort it," Esther said.

As Esther and Hamish looked to each other, I wondered at what was passing silently between them.

"Esther believes that all will be well in the end, nae matter what comes. I am *no* of that opinion. I'll speak plainly. Ye are welcome here because Esther wishes it so. I dinnae much care for this arrangement. Ye'll draw more notice to this hame at a time we cannae afford it." His eyes burned holes through me, and I didn't miss the quick glance he shot in Katherine's direction.

"That's not our intention in coming here," I said.

"That doesnae matter!" Hamish's voice rose. "Ye can intend whatever ye like, but that doesnae make it so. Ye come all this way to what? Ensure Esther is taken captive and get yerselves murdered along the way? Aye, ye'll do a fine job of that."

Fitz laid a hand across mine and squeezed gently.

"We will help them, Esther and I," Katherine said. "All will be well."

The tips of Hamish's ears were tinged with red, and his neck grew splotchy. He clearly wasn't pleased with any of us, and he didn't care to mask his feelings for the sake of being polite.

"Dinnae start, Katherine," Hamish snapped. "Ye have as much reason to fear their presence as anyone."

Katherine's head rolled to the side, her expression dull as though she was bored of Hamish's anger.

"Hamish," Esther said softly.

Hamish tore his eyes from me, and they cooled as they met Esther's. The connection between them was palpable. Esther wasn't the cliché embodiment of delicate softness that lulled her angry lover into tenderness. Rather, Hamish's love and respect for his wife seemed to curb his anger into something manageable. I considered the knowledge that must haunt them both. I understood why Hamish saw our presence as a threat to Esther. Her fate surely tortured him. As much as I wanted to plead our case and reassure him of our intentions, I decided against it. I would wait for Hamish's initial anger to pass before talking with him… and perhaps our business would be concluded quickly, and Fitz and I could be on our way.

We were interrupted by Esther's staff bringing in refreshments. I inhaled deeply, taking in the earthy scent.

"*Mugwort*," Fitz said. "*Meant to calm us.*"

It couldn't hurt.

The two women bowed ever so slightly and then left us to our arguments.

"Why have ye come?" Hamish asked, returning his focus to us.

Fitz went to respond, but Esther cut him off.

"Hamish! Ye gave me yer word."

"I dinnae see the harm in asking," Hamish countered. "We cannae trust so easily in such dangerous times."

"The harm in asking is that it is rude, and it makes them feel unwelcome." Hamish began his protests, but Esther would have none of it. "We beg yer pardon. It seems Hamish has forgotten his manners."

"We dinnae mean to trouble you, and we dinnae intend to trespass on your kindness for long," Fitz said. "Perhaps we can speak more of this later? The journey has been quite taxing on us both."

He was buying time, and luckily, we were in complete agreement. Hamish was in no humor to entertain conversation about Annabel's ring.

"I reckon I willnae ken the purpose of yer visit for some time if Esther has her way of it—but my patience has its limits. And when it has run dry, I'll toss ye out with yesternight's scraps, aye?" He nodded once. "I willnae allow ye to make things worse for my wife."

"Of course. We understand that's your greatest concern," I said softly.

"Esther tells me ye both have a bit of fight in ye."

"Aye, when it's needed," Fitz said.

Katherine grinned, and Hamish nodded curtly.

"As do I. Ye'll need it when ye cross paths with these witch hunting bastards."

"And there are witches on the witch hunting committee?" Fitz prompted. "Have they not offered to assist you in any way?"

"They claim to help manage the damage the humans are set on, but I cannae see it."

"Many believe they are protecting themselves so the accusations will fall on others," Katherine said.

"From what we know… I agree with them," I said.

Hamish's energy stirred. I'd surprised him.

"Ye dinnae think they'll help us?" Esther asked.

Fitz and I looked to each other.

His lips pulled into a tight line. "No."

"I paid a visit to Malcolm Campbell, the leader of the Forfar Council," Hamish said, "just after Esther's vision first surfaced. He gave me his word that he would offer any assistance in his power. A liar and a gowk."

I didn't recognize the word, but context clues suggested it wasn't a compliment.

"Dinnae ye suppose that's a bit unfair, Hamish?" Esther asked.

"Is it?" Hamish scoffed. "He demanded that I leave matters in his hands and that if I took action to protect Esther that wasnae ordained by the council that the consequences would be severe."

"The coven doesn't intervene in these trials solely because of Malcolm?" I asked, thinking of the woman from town who had bid Esther to help end the trials.

"A year past, a woman stood against Malcolm," Katherine said, eyeing Esther meaningfully.

"Malcolm's involvement was ne'er confirmed," Esther countered.

"What happened to her?" I asked.

Esther hesitated, but Katherine's glance prompted her to continue. "She turned up in the eastern woods covered in bruises and muttering incoherently."

"She was perfectly coherent about one thing."

"Katherine," Hamish warned.

She glared at Hamish as Esther studied our reactions.

"'Tis all nonsense," Esther said quickly, though a small wavering line formed above her head.

"*The air is heavy*," Fitz said.

We had both been gifted with the ability to detect lies, and each of our magical instincts signaled that Esther didn't believe what she said.

"Many believe he silenced the woman," Katherine continued. "They believe he enacted an elaborate scheme against her."

"What happened?" I asked.

"Malcolm doesnae have the sense God gave a fly," Hamish said. "Perhaps he harmed that woman, but an elaborate scheme? Aye, 'tis nonsense all right."

A thread hovered above Hamish.

"Nonsense, aye?" Katherine replied tartly. She then turned to Fitz and me. "Whatever the case, the poor soul was taken to her hame where she was cleaned and treated, but she refused to eat and would only lay upon her bed unresponsive. After going on in this way for a fortnight, she passed."

My chest tightened. Hamish eyed Esther meaningfully.

"*They're definitely hiding something*," I said to Fitz.

"The truth of the matter is this: most of the coven believes he harmed that woman. And none have stood against Malcolm since," Esther said.

"Aye, but every season has its close. He willnae prevent me from changing Esther's course. God help the man who stands betwixt my wife and her safety."

I understood Hamish's sentiment perfectly, and quite frankly, I liked him all the better for it.

"Ye cannae alter my fate," Esther said softly.

"But ye can," Hamish said. "I can help ye."

Hamish stood, stepping heavily toward the fire. The wooden planks creaked under his weight, and he exhaled. When he turned to Esther, his face was marked with anger.

"I ken, Hamish," she said, responding to something unspoken. "But what would ye have me do? There is nae land far enough away that we might take the bairns and find refuge."

Hamish clenched his jaw.

"We'd always be running, *mo ghaol*," Esther continued.

My stomach twisted. It had been little less than a year since Fitz and I'd had a similar conversation. Back when I hadn't yet matched to my powers, when our councils had sought us out for breaking their rules. I had been prepared to run for all eternity if that's what it took for us to remain together, and looking into Hamish's eyes, I saw that same determination. Esther might not want that life for her children, but Hamish would fight to the bitter end if she'd only say the word. A flurry of energy pushed through my system, and the onrush of emotion surprised me. I held back tears, but my body quivered under the pressure.

Fitz rubbed his thumb gently against my hand. I wondered where his own thoughts lay. Even with the events of the day, Fitz's eyes were filled with a sadness that our adventure could not reach. A grief that I could not touch.

"Ye understand as few could."

"Aye," Fitz said, barely above a whisper.

"Have ye faced this in yer time?" Hamish asked.

"Not witch hunters," I said. "But Fitz and I faced the councils of our time. We had plans… we were willing to run forever if that's what it took." I hoped my honesty might prompt something in Esther and Hamish.

Hamish turned to Esther, the sentiment in his eyes seemingly saying, "*See*, we can do this."

"We'll speak of this later," Esther said softly.

"Do your children know anything is amiss?" I asked.

"Only our eldest, Callum," Hamish said. "They're under the charge of family in a place they are unlikely to be found. It isnae an easy time to be a MacGregor, but 'tis harder still to be a witch in Forfar."

I nodded, a supportive smile springing to my face. "You're doing what you can for them. I see that."

Hamish took a seat again on the sofa and slid an arm supportively around Esther. She turned toward him, sinking into his protective bulk. I considered them. Though they weren't of noble status, Hamish was clearly doing well for himself in trade, and Esther was neither widowed nor destitute. None of the usual factors seemed to apply to Esther. She had no physical ailments nor was she a midwife or a healer… or at least, she didn't practice healing openly. So, how was she compromised?

Katherine slid forward in her chair.

"Ye arnae going so soon?" Esther asked.

"Aye, I am in need of rest."

"Are ye well, Katherine?" Hamish asked.

"There's nothing much the matter with me," she said, waving her hand. "Nae more than usual."

Katherine turned to us and smiled.

"Can we help you home?" I asked. I didn't want to insert ourselves where we didn't belong, but I worried for her safety after the volatility of the crowd and her difficulty walking earlier.

I considered Katherine. She reminded me of someone, though I couldn't place who, and I felt a bit protective of her, inexplicable as it was.

"Nae, I dinnae live far, and after this brief rest, I am well enough to see myself up the road."

My face must've given away my concern.

"My legs arnae so strong as they once were. The physician says I am weakening with time and that one day I will simply wither away. I dinnae much care for slipping away quietly into the night, and I dinnae much believe him."

"Why is that, if I may ask?"

"He believes me to be a witch, so he'll hardly examine me. Nearly knocked over a vase in his haste to exit my cottage the last time I sent for him." She shook her head but chuckled softly. "He has little sense, but he does amuse me."

I couldn't help but smile.

"My body has weakened, but I ken my limits well, aye? I'll be fine today." With a bit of assistance, Katherine rose from her chair and tested her legs. She nodded. "Aye, they'll do fine."

CHAPTER SIX

Esther led us to a room on the opposite side of the house from her and Hamish's quarters, which were separated by her children's empty rooms, the sitting room, and the large foyer. On the other side of us were the dining room and the kitchen.

Our space was more private than I had anticipated. Even with my limited knowledge of seventeenth-century comforts, our room seemed lavish. Hamish must have been doing quite well in trade for he and Esther to have such a comfortable home. A large, four-poster bed sat against the middle of the back wall draped in thick, navy-toned curtains and topped with several blankets. Simple wooden nightstands of the same dark wood flanked the bed, and a writing desk was positioned near a window. The view wouldn't be revealed until morning, and thick wooden shutters and heavy drapes warded off the chill of the night. Along the nearest wall was a large fireplace, crackling and sizzling with its evening charge. Millie, Esther's lady's maid, had stoked the fire just before we'd retired to our room, and she was due back within the hour to ensure it would last as far into the night as possible.

I scanned the bathtub tucked into a corner by the fire, along with the kettles hanging nearby. I had always preferred a shower over a bath, and truthfully, I had dreaded the lack of plumbing more than anything else—even more than the absence of electricity. Between the roaring fire and our candles, the room wasn't terribly dim, but the thought of drawing a bath tonight… I sighed and turned to Fitz.

"Esther mentioned she's going into town tomorrow. I thought about asking to accompany her, but Hamish…."

"Aye, a punishable offense, I am sure. I could accompany you," he said as he shrugged out of his tunic. "Although, it does put us directly in the path of the villagers."

"You did say you wanted to avoid that."

"That might have been wishful thinking."

"How so?" I prompted.

"If there's a path forward that allows us to keep a low profile, it's lost to me."

"We're probably the talk of the town already. Strangers walking through town with Esther? That's a story for sure."

"All the more reason for me to accompany you."

"However… if we stay here while she goes out, it might be a good chance to look for the ring."

Fitz paused his undressing. "I think we should spend a bit of time with Esther and Hamish first."

"Because Hamish is going to be so forthcoming with details on the ring?" I asked.

"I didn't say that. But might I remind ye that this is my *family*, so you'll have to excuse me if I dinnae mean to rush right into betraying them."

I winced at his words. He'd delivered them with an air of condescension I hadn't heard from him before.

"I didn't mean it like that. I just...."

"I didnae either," he said, his lips pulling into a hard line.

"There's a lot on your mind."

"Aye, and this mission has me a bit mixed up, but that is no excuse to be rude."

I gave a soft, forgiving smile.

"What I should have said is that I worry we'll rush into this mission without taking the proper time to stop and assess." Fitz resumed his previous task. "And that would have grave consequences."

"As much as I think we need to start doing some reconnaissance on the ring, I see your point about getting to know Esther better. And it wouldn't hurt to see more of the town and get our bearings."

"Agreed."

"And if we can't escape the villagers, we might as well learn about the town while we bond with Esther."

"A fine decision. I'll be joining you." His tone didn't invite discussion, and luckily for us both, I wasn't in the mood to argue. "Let's get to know them a bit first and see where it leads, aye? Perhaps we'll learn something useful—maybe they'll even become allies by the end of it."

"Sure."

I sank onto the bed and watched Fitz as he advanced about the room. He moved a candle nearer to the wardrobe to the left of the doorway. Millie had scavenged for a few garments that Esther and Hamish no longer wore and had a quick fitting with us. She said she wanted us to have something a bit less *gallus* to wear until the household staff finished our new clothing. She had been quick with her alterations.

Fitz looked discerningly at the trousers before nodding once and moving on, studying everything he found in the room. A historian, through and through. The fireside was warm, and I was tired after the full day we'd had. But I couldn't quite fall into relaxation—not with everything going on, not with what was happening with Fitz. I wanted him to talk to me, to let me in. His grief hung heavy across our connection. I couldn't do it anymore. We had to talk—about Ian, about our loss. I decided to take a new approach.

"So," I began, running my hands along a MacGregor tartan blanket. "How are you doing with all this? I can't imagine what you're feeling after meeting your distant relatives, especially after the rollercoaster this past month has been."

Fitz took a seat on the bed before he raised his eyes to mine. His face was a bit pale, and I froze.

"Hadley, not now. I'm begging you."

"I'm just worried—that's all."

"Aye, I understand. But I dinnae want to talk about this just now."

I bit my lip as I thought through my response. I opened my mouth to speak, but Fitz was faster.

"Beyond all of this," he said as his eyes swept our surroundings. "I'm exhausted from the journey here. The distance took a toll on me."

Fitz had walked us through time, met his many times great-grandmother and grandfather, tasted the vitriol of the villagers, and was now sitting drained before me. Of course he was.

"I'm sorry. It was insensitive of me to not think about that. You've had the more difficult work of the two of us today, and even I'm exhausted." I rested my hand on his cheek and gently turned his head to face me. "I won't pry any more… tonight."

Fitz's breathy laugh was a welcome sound. I'd have done almost anything to hear it again and again. His warmth pulsed through my veins, and the look in his eyes shifted from hollow to smoldering in a second. My breath caught in the back of my throat, pulling a wicked smirk to his lips.

"One of these days I think you'll learn to mind your tongue, Ms. Weston."

I bit my lip at the shiver that rippled through my body at the gruffness in his voice.

"And who's going to teach me that lesson, Professor?"

He might have been too tired to unpack his grief, but his want resounded through both of our bodies. Coupled with my desire, I knew we'd get less sleep tonight than we should. Fitz rose from the bed and stepped to face me before placing his hands on the mattress on either side of me. At eye level, he pierced my gaze, and my hands rose instinctively to cup his face. My senses roared to life at his scent. I had always likened it to a whisky that held notes of oat, fruit, and spice. My eyes traced from his chiseled jawline to his piercing green eyes before dropping to the lips that felt like home. It would never be lost on me how beautiful he was.

"Always challenging me, aren't you?" he continued, though I knew he was acutely aware of my body's response to him.

"I don't think you actually want it any other way," I said.

He pulled my hands away from his face and kissed the inside of each of my wrists. Butterflies danced in my stomach, my eyes closing with his touch. He dipped his head further to kiss the tender skin behind my ear.

"Aye, you're right. Frustrating as you can be at times, I'd never want you any different than you are."

I laughed lightly.

"Turn for me," he commanded.

I followed his direction.

"Very good, my love," he whispered in my ear, sending tingles all through my body.

He ran his hands along my arms, gently rubbing the tired muscles, and my head tilted back. Fitz's grasp moved carefully to my shoulders and then my neck, melting tension off me in waves. His fingers slipped around my neck and tilted my head further back, meeting me in a slow, deep kiss. I leaned into him, and his lips traveled to my neck. I was teetering on the edge of losing myself to him when a rap at the door halted our progress.

I spun around, and Fitz took my hands in his as he called to our visitor, beckoning them in.

Millie gingerly stepped through the doorway. Her cheeks were lightly flushed, though from her evening labor or her shy nature, I wasn't sure.

"I beg yer pardon for the intrusion, but I wasnae sure if ye wanted assistance with drawing yer bath?"

I smiled. "Thank you, but no. We'll manage."

"Aye, verra well, then. Yon water is fresh," she said, pointing to two large containers tucked into a corner near the fireplace. "I shall address the fire and be on my way."

"Thank you, Millie," Fitz said.

She smiled timidly, nodded, and set to work.

"I'll wake ye in the morn," she said a few minutes later. "We start the fires and wake the family an hour before dawn. Master MacGregor prefers to breakfast with the earliest morn light to set off to his trade by full dawn. Shall we arrange the same for ye?"

"That'll do quite well," Fitz said, really leaning into the accent and dialect of the time. "Thank ye for asking."

Millie curtsied, wished us a comfortable sleep and exited the room.

Fitz quickly had his hands around my waist, pulling me closer.

"She's a sweet lass, but I couldnae breathe the whole time she was in here." He kissed me rather breathlessly, as though to illustrate his point. I sighed contentedly, and it hastened him forward. He grabbed at my hips, pulling me away from the bed. With my skirts, my legs couldn't grasp his waist as they were accustomed to, but I looped my right leg around his, and we made our way toward the fire. He worked deeply against my lips one last time as my feet met the stone floor, and he pulled away.

"Time to sort this bath, I reckon," he said, his voice husky.

"If you move the water, I'll heat it. And after we're done bathing, I guess...."

Fitz's eyes shifted to the window. "Aye, you have yourself a deal."

He extended his hands toward the buckets, and water rose in a steady stream as he sent it toward the bathtub. My hands grew warm and tingly before they burst to life with red and yellow flames that licked the air. I channeled my energy as dangerously hot as it would allow and connected to the molecules of water, allowing my heat to mix with it until it steamed.

"Ready," I said to Fitz, who was watching the whole affair with a heated gleam in his eyes and a satisfied smile across his lips. He sauntered across the room, and my pulse quickened.

"Allow me to assist you, milady," he said softly.

Fitz began the work of deconstructing my seventeenth-century layers, and through a mixture of kissing and hands moving against skin, I was soon in only my chemise. I ran my lips along his neck before pulling back and making short work of his clothes. Then he untied the top of my chemise and pulled it back over my shoulders. As it fell to the ground, Fitz's eyes swept my body.

He shook his head lightly. "You are so bonnie. Sometimes, I hardly believe you are real."

"Come here," I whispered.

He stepped closer and pressed his lips hard to mine. Where his touch had been tender before, an urgency now echoed between us. We stepped closer to the bath, and he pulled away to lower himself into the water. As I followed him, his hands guided my hips to turn my body around, and I sank into the magically charged water and onto his lap. Goosebumps rippled across my skin at the feel of his skin on mine, and the warmth of the water intensified the sensation.

Fitz ran his fingertips along my arms, shoulder, and back before pressing firmly into the muscles of my lower back. I released a satisfied sigh, encouraging him as he pressed and thumbed his way along my spine. His fingers moved up and down the center of my back before massaging all around my shoulders and my neck, and as he worked lower, I beckoned him forward through the movements of my hips. His hands worked along my thighs, and he moved forward, pressing against me. I leaned to the side, tilting my head back, and he met me again in a deep kiss, working slowly, though urgently against my lips.

Fitz lifted me, his muscles flexing with the effort, and he lowered me slowly into place—just where he wanted me. I gasped at the feel of him, and sparks floated gently on the air all around us.

And there, in the year 1662—amongst the fear, doubt, and uncertainty—we met each other in perfect rhythm, finding the respite we both so desperately sought.

CHAPTER SEVEN

I woke to the sound of screaming.

I bolted upright and thrashed around in utter panic.

"Hadley, it's all right," Fitz coaxed. "You're all right. I've got you."

Tears streamed down my face, and I gulped at the air, needing more than my lungs could hold. Fitz held me securely, and I rested my head against his chest, listening to the thumping of his heartbeat. It was a bit irregular, and when I finally mustered the energy, I found my voice.

"I scared you," I said simply.

"Aye, waking up to your panic was unsettling. What's happened?" he asked.

"I had a nightmare… but it was so real."

"Battle?" he guessed.

I nodded.

"Your terror woke me before your screaming even started."

"I'm sorry," I whispered, rubbing my hand across his.

"Don't you apologize."

"It was Isamu." I felt a humorless smile mask my features. Isamu had been part of the team that had tried to take Jordan and me hostage in Opimae. And he'd harmed Fitz after.

"What did he do?"

"We were fighting. He had the ring, and he was winning."

I couldn't escape the ring. It haunted me even in dreams.

"Things were all jumbled up. The pregnant woman from Adamo was there too. And there was blood. So much blood…."

Fitz's hold on me tightened. His warmth and pressure felt safe, and both my breathing and my pulse slowed into something more manageable. I reached for the ring hanging from my neck, its smooth moonstone surface bringing another wave of calm.

"Do you want a dram? I'll bet I can fetch a wee bit from the kitchen."

"No, I don't want you to go anywhere." I gripped his hand tightly.

"All right," he said softly. After a moment, he continued. "We should find a way for you to get some exercise while we're here."

We had learned meditation and exercise reduced my anxiety. Losing my routine would be easy to do in this new time, but Fitz was right. I needed to find a way to expel all that extra energy.

"Great timing for this, isn't it?"

"There's no braw time for PTSD, my love," Fitz said.

PTSD. Of course.

I wasn't sure if putting a name to what I was experiencing made me feel better or worse. There certainly wouldn't be any resources for me in the seventeenth century, but I knew that at some point, I would have to deal with this new trauma.

Fitz helped me settle back under the covers and wrapped himself around me protectively. The room fell quiet, but a thought surfaced that I couldn't suppress.

"What will happen in Opimae while we're here? We didn't get ahead of Lorenzo before they sent us packing, and the fact that they kicked us off the mission after we lost—" I broke off.

"We lost Dad," he finished.

"Yeah," I said, barely more than a whisper. "I just… feel like a failure."

"Well, that isn't true." Even with his words, I couldn't help but wonder if Fitz blamed me for Ian's death. Had he considered it in the same light I had?

"We'll never be whole again," I said, barely audible.

Fitz pulled me deeper into his warm embrace. As distressed as I was, sleep called to me. I stifled a yawn just as I registered the cozy energy enveloping me.

"Are you working a spell on me?" I asked him.

"Back to sleep with you," Fitz whispered before laying his head on mine.

I meant to protest, but the spell was taking effect, and I was far too tired to form a coherent argument. I was quickly lulled into the hazy edge of consciousness, only vaguely aware of Fitz speaking so softly I couldn't register his words… before I realized they were in Gaelic. A lullaby. The cadence of his voice was soothing, and I smiled before slipping into a deep, dreamless sleep.

The following morning arrived too early. Dawn was miraculously late during November here, but the effects of time-walking ravaged my body. When Millie swung open the drapes of our bed, the commotion startled me awake, the events of the previous day having fallen almost to myth overnight. Her round face was touched by the rosiest hue on her cheeks, and her dark hair was swept into a simple white cap atop her head. She smoothed down the matching white apron that sat over her gray, woolen dress and straightened her posture.

"I didnae intend to startle ye," she said by way of greeting.

I nodded groggily.

"Nae bother," Fitz said.

"Do ye require assistance with yer garments, Mistress MacGregor?" Millie asked, her hand sweeping toward something I couldn't see.

It took me a couple of seconds to realize she meant me. She thought Fitz and I were wed.

"Oh, I don't go by that last name," I said, unsure if it was okay to share that we weren't married.

Millie's brow furrowed.

"I dinnae understand. 'Go by?'"

"My surname is 'Weston.'"

Millie's eyes widened, but she quickly cleared her throat and nodded.

"What's the matter?" I asked.

"I dinnae wish to overstep. 'Tis only… weel, 'tis quite strange. I was told ye are meant to blend with the villagers, and they will certainly—" she trailed off.

"It'll raise suspicion," Fitz said.

"Aye. They will think ye unmarried—*impure*."

And that would place us in danger.

"Then I shall go by MacGregor," I said. "Thank you for letting me know."

Millie's gaze lingered on me, and though I had attempted to carefully navigate the situation, her energy was dicey. As her magic zipped around me, I found more than simple curiosity in it. Had I offended Millie? I hadn't thought the witches of the day would be troubled by the lack of a human ceremony, but perhaps I had miscalculated.

I leaned forward to catch a glimpse of my dress in the firelight, returning to Millie's initial question in the hopes of dispelling the tension in the air. The fabric was dyed so deeply blue, it bordered on purple. I sighed at the thought of burdening myself with the constrictive garment, though I was happy I would, at least, be warm.

I was unsure how to answer Millie's question. It was surely improper for me to inform her that Fitz would assist me, wasn't it? I didn't want to further offend her, but the thought of others readying me for the day wasn't a proposition I wanted to accept. I might have been thrown into the seventeenth century, but I would protect my own boundaries as best I could.

"Perhaps I'll send for you if I'm in need of assistance?"

"Verra well," she said. "If there's nothing else, I'll return to readying my mistress for the day."

We released Millie to her usual duties and set to work preparing ourselves for our first full day in Forfar. Fitz's assistance was comical, and my own instruction wasn't any more helpful than his intuitiveness—or lack thereof—in assisting me.

"You had very little trouble with my laces last night," I said.

Fitz laughed lightly. "Easier to remove than to piece back together, I'm afraid."

But soon enough, he had sorted it out, and I turned toward the mirror. I hardly recognized the woman who stared back. The royal blue over-bust stays accentuated an hourglass figure, and the front narrowed into a deep V at the end of my torso. My daywear chemise was of finer quality than the one I'd been given for evening wear, and it emerged from the stays to cover my shoulders and the full length of my arms, gathering snugly around my wrists. The matching skirts were full and lent their assistance in creating a small, shapely upper body. I twisted my hair back and pinned it into a bun at the crown of my head to complete the look.

Fitz pulled another garment from the dresser for me: a beige waistcoat embroidered with swirling patterns of blue. He held out the garment and helped me slide my arms into the sleeves. I then tied three linen ribbons across the front of the coat, which held it in place.

No puffy sleeves, no intricate floral embroidery, and no gold detailing… even with the deep color of the fabric, it was certainly less ornate than the outfits the council had sent us in. I caught Fitz's gaze in the mirror. He gave a tight smile. Worry lingered in his emerald eyes… or was it grief? I hardly knew anymore, and I stifled my urge to ask. The evening had worked its magic on us, but in the morning light of Forfar, the edge threatened to creep back in.

I turned to Fitz, surveying his dress.

He held up his hand. "Dinnae say anything."

I attempted to hold back a smirk but failed. "Nice," I said, nodding.

He sighed as he reached for his vest. It was olive green with beige detailing, which matched the olive trousers he wore. He buttoned it into place over his shift, which was tucked into the woolen trousers. It was longer than the waistcoats Fitz wore in our time, sitting well below the waist. The style made him appear older somehow.

"It could be worse," I said. "Do you remember all those paintings we saw at the castle and in the museums? Lots of frilly pieces and puffy trousers from the past. At least this is the clothing of respectable Scottish tradesmen."

"It's far better than what the council outfitted me in, so I won't complain," he said as he smoothed down the vest and reached for his coat. "This is hardly the worst part of seventeenth-century living." His eyes turned to the chamber pot that sat in the corner, and I giggled.

With our layers secured, we padded down the hallway in search of breakfast.

The dining room was lovely. There were more windows in the room than I'd seen anywhere else in the house, and the subtle light of dawn revealed a view of the vast park behind the MacGregor home. Just yesterday—over three-hundred fifty years in the future—the same park had contained a walking trail, a small boating club, and a clear grassy area for soccer. Now, it held a muddy walking path with untamed shrubbery and countless gardens spread across the wild expanse.

Fitz helped me to my seat, eternally the gentleman, before proceeding to his own. Hamish watched us curiously, but Esther's face lifted into a smile.

"I wasnae certain if ye would breakfast with us this morning," Esther said.

"Oh aye," Fitz said. "We thought it best to begin acclimating."

Hamish remained focused on his porridge, but Esther nodded.

Our breakfast was hot porridge and honey, sausage, and warm bread. It must have been luxurious for the time, and I wondered if this was a normal meal for the MacGregors or if Esther had planned a more extravagant first breakfast for us.

Millie set a teapot down before me.

"Is this…." I trailed off.

"Aye," Esther answered.

"Is tea commonly traded yet?"

"Nae," Hamish answered gruffly. "It was quite the feat to bring that to our wee village."

"Our queen is fond of tea," Esther said. "She has established its popularity across much of England. It isnae so easily found in

Scotland just yet, but its popularity will increase." Esther's enthusiasm was contagious, and it was fun to see her enjoy some of the knowledge that came from her gift of foresight.

"What happens after breakfast?" I asked as I poured a healthy serving of black tea into my delicate teacup.

"Hamish conducts his business about town," Esther answered quickly. "I will go to the market with Millie and look over the latest imports."

"Fitz and I would love to come with you if we won't be too much of a distraction."

Hamish opened his mouth—to argue, I was sure—but Esther was faster. "I would find the company most welcome."

"Only with an abundance of caution," Hamish said. "Ye dinnae blend with the villagers."

"I will do everything in my power to keep us safe," I said.

Hamish nodded curtly, but it was an acknowledgment, not outright hostility, so I took that as a win.

After breakfast, Fitz helped me into my woolen cloak. Considering the frost sparkling across pretty much everything beyond the windowpanes, I was confident I'd be grateful for the extra warmth. The downside was that the cloak was almost as cumbersome as my gown, and I was nearing overstimulated territory. Coupled with my nerves over our intended outing, my breath grew shorter.

"What's troubling ye?" Fitz asked.

I pointed to my clothing. "This is just a lot—wearing these stays especially. I'm feeling a little overwhelmed."

"There's more," he said.

I took a beat. Would speaking my fear make matters better or worse?

"I'll walk down those streets with my head held high, but Fitz… It's already tough for me to be here knowing how many men will hate me for simply being a woman. The air is polluted with hatred. It's difficult to breathe."

He nodded encouragingly.

"This is only the beginning," I said. "We've barely scratched the surface. There's so much more to come, and the fact that I won't be able to use my magic to protect myself?"

Fitz placed his hand along my cheek. "I know you feel out of step. This time, these humans, the trouble we've faced… but Hadley, I will protect your life with my own. Remember, I am your shield, *mo chidhe*."

I placed my hand on his while he kissed my forehead.

"Now, let's do a bit of meditation before we meet Esther. Aye?"

"Okay," I said simply.

Fitz and I lingered in the quiet, and after a few minutes, I had calmed enough to put on a brave smile. Skepticism lingered in his narrowed eyes—he knew me well—but he didn't argue.

"How are we feeling about the garments?" he asked.

"I survived Opimaean battle armor. I *will* conquer seventeenth-century women's fashion."

I straightened my cloak, and then we headed for the foyer to meet Esther.

By the time we'd left the house and meandered into the main intersection of town, the burgh of Forfar had roared to life. Villagers were negotiating with vendors, and the shops were either dotted with patrons or with shopkeepers sweeping their entrances and wiping down their windows. Though it was early in the day, it wasn't too early for some to watch us warily, their eyes drilling holes into our skin. And though many vendors called out to passersby, no such greetings were extended to us. Even Fiona seemed content to allow our passage without so much as a condescending look at my gown. Someone must have told her we were witches bound for hell. Word traveled fast.

We stopped along a few stalls, and though no one refused to serve us, their distance was noticeable. Esther seemed to pay it no mind as the vendors avoided close contact or darted their eyes around to see if their neighbors were watching. I was tempted to read the minds of the villagers, but I'd grown too proficient in my mind reading power to let it run wild. Back in my training with Maka, I had promised I wouldn't read others' minds unless I was in danger or directed to do so by the councils. The villagers' thoughts wouldn't benefit my nerves anyway, so I wouldn't pry unless it became necessary. I had a feeling that, soon enough, it would be.

We followed Esther into an apothecary. The walls were lined with wooden shelves holding remedies, plants, and dried herbs, and we were greeted with a pleasing, earthy scent. I smiled, thinking of Izzy. She'd love to spend time in a place like this.

We trailed Esther as she meandered to the counter. A young couple stood on the other side, their heads bent over the countertop while the man poured herbs through a funnel and into a small burlap bag. The woman looked up at our approach, her ocean blue eyes widening at the sight of Esther. She had a slim, angular face and an abundance of hair like golden cornsilk. She recovered quickly from her discomposure. She moved around the counter and met Esther, extending her hands in greeting.

"Did all go well?" she asked.

Esther turned and looked to us.

The woman smiled before placing her hands over her mouth. "This is them? Truly?"

"Aye," Esther said. "Fitz, Hadley, I'm pleased to introduce ye to Elspeth and her husband, Thomas."

My skin danced with the soft, familiar nudge of a friendly witch's glance.

"We're pleased to make yer acquaintance," Elspeth said.

"Aye, that we are," Thomas said, shaking Fitz's hand.

"Glad to meet you," Fitz said.

Thomas and Elspeth exchanged a pointed glance.

"Our speech?" I asked.

Thomas chuckled, and Elspeth gave a tight smile.

"We dinnae mean to make ye uncomfortable," Thomas said. "But aye, 'tis a bit strange."

Thomas's gaze sent an odd prickling sensation across my skin. Where his wife's attention felt calm and sincere, Thomas's was quite the opposite. Though a broad grin graced his lips and his tone of voice was warm, his energy was odd, unsettling.

"It's quite all right," Fitz said. "We expected we'd need to study your speech to help us blend in better."

"We trust yer travels werenae difficult," Thomas said.

"We cannae complain," Fitz said. "No difficulties, and Esther was awaiting our arrival."

"Ye were justified in yer calculations, then," Elspeth said to Esther.

"Aye, upon the hour and midway down the loch."

Elspeth smiled as she shook her head softly.

"A marvel ye truly are, Esther."

Esther waved her hands. "Ne'er ye mind that. I've come for more Rhodiola rosea."

Elspeth nodded and moved back behind the counter. She pulled a large glass jar from a shelf behind her. "Still no sleeping well," she said, scooping dried strips of the plant.

"I *am* following yer instructions," Esther said.

Elspeth tied the bag and handed it over to Esther. "I willnae scold ye. I mean to help ye as best I can."

Esther glanced down momentarily before nodding. "Aye, I ken the Tailyours mean well."

Tailyour… where had I heard that name before? I was just about to ask Fitz when the horrifying answer surfaced. There was a man by the name of Tailyour who had been accused of witchcraft during the trials, I realized.

Thomas slipped an arm around Elspeth. Though it was subtle, she flinched, and a look flashed in her eyes that didn't quite make sense. He was her husband, so what would make a wife dislike her husband's touch? I shuddered at the thought.

"I am glad ye and Hamish came to dine with us last week," Thomas said.

Esther's smile was uneasy, but Thomas continued, seeming to pay Esther's wavering energy no mind.

"The coven means to keep us apart," he said. "That isnae natural for us. 'Tis time we take our stand."

Esther's eyes traveled in our direction, and she cleared her throat before answering.

"*She seems uneasy that Elspeth and Thomas are speaking openly,*" I said to Fitz.

"*Aye, but it's more than that. Something odd is at play here.*"

I returned my full focus to their conversation.

"I long for the coven to reconvene. I have wished it so for many weeks," Esther said quietly.

Elspeth looked uncertain, and it didn't escape Esther's notice.

"What's the matter, Elspeth?" Esther asked.

"She's had a nervous condition as of late," Thomas answered. "She seems afraid of even her own shadow."

"There is much to fear these days," Elspeth said.

Though her statement was true, her energy was conflicted, and something in her power told me that Elspeth did not frighten easily.

A bell jingled above the doorway, alerting the shop owners of a new customer. Human energy filtered through the space, quieting the conversation and signaling that we should take our leave.

The quiet comfort of the apothecary faded as we navigated the streets of Forfar. Commotion had increased near the front of the tolbooth, making our path more treacherous than before. The crowd strained against one another to catch a glimpse of a woman whose hands were bound in rope. She stood defiantly at the mercat cross, her head held high as her mahogany strands whipped in the cold breeze while her captors held tightly to her and the crowd hurled insults.

"We'll send ye back to the devil from whence ye came!" a woman with dark orange hair shouted. Her fist was raised high in her fit of passion.

"Aye! Send her back to hellfire from which she was forged!" a tall man exclaimed.

I turned to Esther and instinctively reached for Fitz's hand. He answered my silent request as Esther turned to me, her face like stone.

"Is that Helen?" I asked.

"Aye," Esther said. "The villagers have cried for a glimpse of her since the night of her capture."

"This is the first time they've agreed?"

Esther nodded.

"So, we really can't predict their behavior."

"Nae," Esther said.

A man with dark eyes and hair to match stepped to the right of Helen.

"Do not fear, my children!" he said, his voice raised above the crowd. "The power inside this witch is no match for the will of God!"

"What does he know about witches?" I muttered. Clearly, not much, or he would know Helen was no witch. Not an ounce of magical energy coursed through her.

The man's accent was strange—English, I thought, though I couldn't place it exactly.

"Is that the minister?" Fitz asked.

"Aye. 'Tis Father Evans. The man to his right—that is Malcolm Campbell—our Forfar Council leader."

My head snapped in their direction, studying them carefully. Father Evans was thin and lithe with sharp features, but Malcolm was tall and domineering. He had fiery red hair and pale skin, and his build was large—similar to Hamish's. The minister might be one to fear because of the villagers he so clearly commanded, but Malcolm was not only a physical presence; he was a magical one too. Even from a distance, with a bit of focus, the force of his power teemed all around me. It made me uneasy. I understood why some might speculate about him—his power had a dangerous feel to it.

I looked to Fitz, who was tense and observant, ready to strike at a moment's notice. I was equal parts relieved and fearful. Perhaps we could put up a fight if the crowd turned on us, or even escape… but at what cost to Esther?

My eyes met Helen's and something deep within my soul stirred. Perhaps it was the connection to another woman… a woman damned for no reason other than that a man wanted her dead. Helen would implicate Esther—I knew it. But she would ultimately pay for that with her life. Standing in that square with an angry mob chanting for her death, I couldn't find it in me to hate her. I noticed a small bracelet tied around her wrist. It was made of yellow fabric, as simple as it was curious. I wasn't sure if it was necessary quite yet, but my mind wandered into Helen's, and I didn't stop it. Her thoughts were vivid, and fear gripped my chest.

Helen's thoughts were erratic, but as the town's minister came into view, my blood boiled. Her memories burst to life as she watched Father Evans speak to the crowd, the scene prompting memories of him. Helen's prison was a tiny cell comprised of cold stone and stale air. The minister visited her often, begging her to relinquish her relationship with the devil and shouting that she was a harlot in equal measure. He persuaded her to speak ill of her neighbors and even her own friends by entering the neighboring cell, which held her daughter.

"Force is not my way," the minister said, kneeling by Helen's daughter and taking her chin into his grip. He looked toward Helen's cell. "But I will not risk the souls of this burgh by falling prey to your wicked ways. I will not temp the devil with my mercy."

"Naw!" Helen screamed. "Leave her! She is innocent, Father."

"Any child of yours is not blameless," he said, gritting his teeth. He stood and made his way back to Helen's cell. Red colored his cheeks and flushed his neck. He was more than angry… he seemed almost flustered.

"Father, please," Helen said, moving closer.

Father Evans raised his hand as though to prevent her from coming any closer. "Be still, witch! You shall not temp me."

Helen thought of her daughter, Janet, and though her anxiety over her daughter's fate was her primary concern, memories bubbled to the surface of their happier times together: Helen rocking Janet to sleep as a baby, Janet giving Helen a yellow bracelet made of scrap yarn, the two of them feeding their chickens behind their home and singing together in the kitchen as they prepared their meals. It was apparent they didn't have much, but the two had made the most of it. Their bond was palpable through her memories.

I shook my head and freed myself of Helen's thoughts, a wave of guilt crashing over me for entering her mind. Countless scenes had raced through my consciousness, but I didn't have time to process them. We needed to distance ourselves from the minister, from the crowd.

"Burn them all!" a woman shouted beside me.

I met Esther's gaze, and she nodded to the opposite side of the crowd. I meandered around the villagers, holding tightly to Fitz's hand as though letting go would mean losing him forever. As we neared the far side of the crowd, a woman turned toward Esther.

"Another witch roaming free!" she yelled. "Ye'll get what's coming to ye soon enough, ye MacGregor filth!"

Esther kept her head high and her eyes forward.

"Och, and Millie Gilroy. Ye bring shame upon yer family, falling in with this lot!"

Millie followed Esther's example.

The crowd's focus was shifting uncomfortably in our direction, and every single fiber of my being screamed at me to fight. My thoughts raced through battle plans and exit strategies, adrenaline coursing through my system. Their hatred channeled through me, resulting first in fear—and then in anger. I reminded myself of every reason I couldn't lose control, grinding my teeth with the effort. This was neither the time nor place.

"Hadley," Fitz said lowly.

"I know. I'm trying to calm down," I said a bit too harshly.

Fitz eased his arm from mine and placed it around me, pulling me close.

We pushed forward quickly, freeing ourselves of the crowd, and we walked briskly toward the nearest street. As we rounded the first corner, a tall figure hurried down the lane.

Hamish.

"Esther!" he called. He wrapped an arm protectively around her. "What is the matter?"

"They've brought Helen outside the tolbooth," Fitz answered.

Hamish sighed, and his eyes dropped to Esther. "Yer fear gripped me."

Esther responded too softly for me to hear.

Hamish urged us home, and as we followed him down the streets of Forfar, I bit back my worry. Would we neutralize the threat of the ring before the villagers came for us?

CHAPTER EIGHT

When we returned from our outing, we entered the foyer to the heavy click of boots across hardwood floors. It was Annabel, pacing restlessly. At the sight of Esther, Annabel's hazel eyes flooded with relief, and her skirts billowed as she moved hastily in her direction. She paused at the sight of us, her energy coiled tightly like a snake ready to strike. Fitz's gaze was fixed on Annabel, his expression carefully guarded. Had it not been for his nerves mingling with my own, I'd have wondered what he was truly feeling. Esther's eyes darted between us before holding out her hands. Her aunt grasped them eagerly.

"Dinnae fash, Aunt. All is well," Esther said calmly.

"Ye were at the market?" she questioned, her eyes sweeping across Esther as though she'd suddenly find something amiss. "And with *ootlins*?" She nearly spat out the last word.

"Aye, I was at the market, and nae, I wasnae with outsiders. These—"

But Annabel wasn't allowing an explanation. "Tell me what's happened, Esther."

"Come. Let us speak in the sitting room. I must introduce ye to our visitors, and then I'll tell ye of our outing."

Annabel looked briefly in our direction, swallowing hard. She nodded curtly before following Esther down the hallway, fussing over her pallor and if she might need a "wee tincture" after encountering the unruly villagers. Esther calmly deflected as Hamish muttered unintelligibly under his breath.

I steeled myself for the delicate battle ahead as we stepped into the bright light of the sitting room. We were greeted by a roaring fire, and I could have wept for joy at the prospect of warming my icy feet near the hearth.

"Fitz, Hadley… I am pleased to introduce ye to my aunt, Annabel McAlpine."

Fitz and I nodded in acknowledgment.

"We're so pleased to finally meet you," I said.

Annabel's eyes widened at my speech, and her head snapped back to Esther, who narrowed her bright eyes in warning.

Annabel cleared her throat before turning back to us. "Ye are most welcome here."

Both her tone and her energy suggested otherwise.

"Thank ye," Fitz said. "It is an honor."

"Ye are a nephew of mine, as I come to understand."

"Aye. Many generations separate us, but we are blood just the same."

Annabel's eyes softened for mere seconds before she regained her carefully placed cynicism. "Pray, tell me what ye think of this wee encounter—meeting yer ancestors that ye shouldnae ken."

"Aunt," Esther warned.

"It is all right," Fitz said.

Annabel stood and crossed her arms before walking nearer to the fire. Esther took the opportunity to relay the events of the afternoon. Though Annabel was concerned, she had little to worry over, especially considering that Esther left out the more alarming details.

The door creaked open, revealing Millie and then Isla. They carried wooden trays filled with refreshments, but it was Millie's tray that truly caught my attention. She placed it on the table nearest the sofa where Fitz and I sat.

"I took the liberty—that is, I thought perhaps ye might be in need of yer tea," she said softly.

"You are too good to us," I said warmly.

Millie smiled as she poured the tea. Over her shoulder, I caught sight of Annabel's gaze fixed upon us. I didn't know her well enough to guess at her feelings, but if her energy was any indication, she was both skeptical of and annoyed by our presence.

After Millie secured the refreshments, Esther said, "Dinnae forget to take yer herbal tea for the cough."

Millie nodded with a bow and left the room.

"Ye asked of my experience earlier," Fitz began, reaching for his teacup. "It is sobering."

The question on Annabel's face was encouragement enough.

"It's a perilous time to be what we are."

Annabel nodded. "Then why place yerself in a dangerous time such as this?"

"This time might be dangerous, but we have our reasons," he said.

"It is dangerous in our time as well," I said.

"Aye, and what do ye ken of danger?" Annabel said.

Esther set her teacup onto the platter with a thud. The room fell silent as all eyes turned to her.

"I have seen much of yer time," Esther said. "The evil is different, to be sure, but 'tis there, all the same."

Just how much had Esther seen of us before we arrived in Forfar?

"Ye have seen battle… and death."

"Unfortunately, we have," I said, recalling the Opimaeans who had needlessly lost their lives at Lorenzo's hands, recalling Ian and Keoni.

Our sadness permeated the air, and I wondered if it was as stifling to the others in the room as it was to me. Fitz's gaze tingled along my skin, but I didn't meet his eyes. I couldn't.

"Is that why ye have left yer time? Surely, ye dinnae seek refuge in times as dangerous as these," Annabel said.

"No," Fitz said. "It isnae easier, nor did we expect it to be."

"Ye dinnae belong here—from the manner in which ye carry yerselves to yer strange speech, 'tis plain to see. This is madness. Why have ye come?"

Fitz opened his mouth to speak, but he was cut off by Esther.

"'Tis nae business of yers," she said tersely.

"Aye? And whose is it?" Annabel countered. "They seek refuge in yer hame, do they no? Their presence will bear consequences on us all, aye? And I have nae right to ask why they have journeyed to our time? Come now, Esther."

"Aye. They are guests in *my* hame. They are under *my* protection. And as such, they shall be treated with dignity and respect. I willnae have ye chasing our family away before I even have the time to ken them."

"I made nae such effort to do so," Annabel countered.

Esther scoffed before her features softened. "Will this be taken from me as well?"

The room fell silent, and no one dared even the slightest movement. I was puzzled by Esther. She had been warm and welcoming, but she was keeping information from us as well. I wasn't sure what to make of her.

"I want to ken my family," Esther continued.

"And so ye shall," Hamish said sternly as he entered the room. I started at his voice.

"I only mean to protect this family. There is danger in them being here," Annabel countered.

"Danger to Esther, you mean?" I asked.

"Aye. Humans in this burgh are jealous of her charm and beauty. Fraternizing with a widow like Katherine already increases her likelihood of being called to testify before the minister, and now two distant relatives have arrived from another time. Mark my words, ye will only increase the size of the target on Esther's back."

"Aunt…." Esther said.

"Nae, Esther. I willnae force them away, but I willnae hold my tongue when it comes to yer well-being either."

Esther's mouth pulled into a hard line, but she didn't argue.

"The witch hunters will suspect something of ye, and soon."

"You don't think our stories are enough?"

Annabel scoffed. "The people of this burgh are suspicious of even their own families. The priest has planted seeds of fear and distrust amongst the villagers, and they are prepared to turn on anyone, especially if it keeps themselves out of the tolbooth."

"Och, dinnae call him that," Hamish said sarcastically to Annabel.

Annabel only rolled her eyes.

I met Fitz's eyes. "What are we missing?" I asked.

"He wishes to be called 'minister,' so we dinnae confuse the Anglicans with the Catholics," Esther said.

"God forbid we be on the wrong side of their religious war," Hamish said.

Annabel sighed, and Esther took a sip of tea, her eyes distant.

"I thought King Charles was tolerant of both Catholics and Protestants?" I asked.

"And he may be," Hamish said. "But it doesnae make it so for the rest of the country."

I nodded. "What can we do to prevent the villagers' suspicions?" I asked, pulling the conversation back on track.

"Leave," Annabel said flatly.

Esther sat up straighter in her chair, her lips parting as she found her response to Annabel's suggestion.

"I willnae force ye to do so—at least, I willnae command it in Esther's hame," she said glancing at Esther. "But 'tis the plain truth."

"We willnae be doing that—not yet," Fitz argued. "We have business here. But we will show our hosts the courtesy of discussing it first with them."

Annabel's cheeks reddened. Hamish bit at his lip, seemingly hiding a smirk.

"The longer ye wait, the more danger ye cast on each of us," Annabel spat.

"Enough, Aunt," Esther said.

"What did ye witness today in the market?" Annabel continued, ignoring Esther's warning. "Helen's fate will be the fate of many if the minister has his way, but I willnae allow it to be Esther's. She might tolerate yer ignorance of our ways, but I willnae allow it."

Annabel's eyes were resolute, but even so, they misted, and her energy only further weighted the melancholy atmosphere of the room.

It was in that moment that I truly realized how difficult our objective would be. I had known Annabel was willing to risk everything to save Esther, but it was increasingly apparent with every tick of the clock how deeply Annabel's love for her niece ran. Just like Helen Guthrie with her daughter, Annabel would trudge through the depths of hell to protect Esther to the bitter end.

"Why do they hate us?" I asked, my voice barely audible.

"They are frightened of anything that challenges their beliefs," Esther said softly. "They fear anything new."

"Humans are weak," Annabel said. "In groups, they grow bold, but alone, they cower in fear."

"A self-righteous lot," Fitz said. "I wish I could say they improve with time."

"Perhaps ye will turn the tides in yer time," Esther said.

"I'm afraid they still fear what they dinnae understand, but we'll still fight for their freedom—even if they use that freedom to hate us."

"If ye are to remain in the past, I trust ye willnae stand in our way as we continue our own fight against the injustices of our day," Annabel said.

I met Fitz's gaze, deciding how best to respond. Esther sensed our hesitation and broke the silence.

"Perhaps we will revisit this conversation another day. Our guests have only just arrived and much has happened. Shall ye visit us again in a few days' time to continue our conversations, Aunt?"

Annabel met Esther's gaze warily. She knew Esther was managing the situation, and Esther clearly wanted to speak with me and Fitz before conversations continued any further. For everything this group said aloud, there was far more that passed silently between our stolen glances.

Annabel finally nodded and gathered herself for departure. "John and I have business in Kingsmuir to soon attend to. I'll call on ye once that's settled."

Annabel quitted the room, leaving us quietly at the fireside contemplating all that had been said—and even more that had not.

"Well, Annabel is our biggest fan," I said once Fitz had closed our bedroom door.

We'd had a quiet and awkward dinner with Esther and Hamish. Hamish's concern for Esther's well-being and his disdain for our arrival had turned to sullen anger, curating a specific tone for dinner, which was set to somber expressions and the clinking of forks against dinner plates. The scene would haunt me for all of eternity.

Fitz pinched the bridge of his nose before looking up to face me. "It'll be divine intervention if she'll even tolerate us by the end of all this."

Even with the discord, I couldn't help but be envious of Fitz's position. We clearly were experiencing the mixed reception we'd anticipated, but we were still meeting Fitz's ancestors. He still knew exactly where he came from—now more than ever—and the hollow pit in my stomach grew. I *was* glad Fitz was able to have this experience, but as far away from familial ties and as unmoored as I was, it made me long for my own.

I fell onto the end of the bed before wincing and immediately standing again. "Can you get me out of this dress? I can't even think anymore in this prison."

Fitz, who was unbuttoning his own vest, nodded. He pushed the sleeves of his shift up to his elbows and crossed the room.

I removed my waistcoat and twirled around for Fitz to work on my stays. I could almost envision his fingers at work as I felt the pop of the laces relaxing.

Fitz sighed. "This willnae do," he said, his tone determined.

Before I could ask what he was up to, his magic surged into the air around me. I glanced over my shoulder and found his fingertips motioning through the air as the laces seemingly untied themselves.

"Having fun?" I asked.

"If only," he said.

I sighed, an unconscious action that I quickly regretted.

"What's the matter, Hads?" Fitz asked.

"I'm just tired."

Fitz pulled the stays off of me and tossed it onto the chair. I took a long, deep breath, my body finally free. I turned to face him, and his eyes narrowed.

"What?" I asked skeptically.

"Oh, nothing much. Pushing back against the weight of the air—a fib has weighed it down."

I was caught off guard. I didn't think my deflection would be enough to alert Fitz that I wasn't being completely forthcoming.

"Fine," I said. "I'm tired, worried about Annabel and the ring, reeling from the hatred of this burgh, feeling odd about how we're supposed to just bow to Fate and let Esther die, and you know... just wearing the weight of the world right now."

Fitz's cheek twitched. He didn't smile, but I knew he was fighting against it. He'd always found it endearing when I was snarky, God love him.

"But most of all," I continued, "I wish I knew how you were feeling right now."

"You summed it up pretty well," he said.

I held his gaze for a few seconds, but I let it go.

I'm sorry I pushed us to continue to Lorenzo's fortress and your father died, I wanted to say.

"What's your take on Annabel?" I asked instead.

"Angry, highly protective of Esther, suspicious of our motives."

"I think she genuinely believes she can save Esther."

"Aye. And punish those who stand with the government."

"Now that one I can understand," I said.

Fitz pulled his shift over his head, revealing his lean, sculpted abdomen. My focus momentarily wavered.

"We'll be lucky if we can convince her of a damn thing," Fitz said.

"You think we'll have to go around her after all?"

"I hope not. I dinnae feel good about that option, but I dinnae think she'll be reasonable. Do you?"

I thought through her words and actions from earlier in the day. "No," I finally said. "She's not going to give up on her plan to save Esther with this ring."

"But perhaps that could be a braw strategy—focusing her attention on all possible options for saving Esther, not only utilizing the ring."

"It's worth trying. But if Annabel doesn't agree to hand over the ring at the… right time, then I think we have to take it?" I asked.

"I dinnae know if that will anger Fate or not," Fitz said. "And it's not only that."

"Betraying your family… I know."

Fitz's lips pulled tight.

"I don't want you to have to do that either, but we should know what our breaking point is—a week, a month? This could last forever."

"Based on that crowd's hunger for blood this afternoon and the timeline we know from our future, I'm certain Esther has little time left," Fitz said softly.

The thought was sobering.

"Perhaps we need to find our way closer to the council," Fitz said.

"This council might be the most corrupt yet. I'm not sure if speaking to them would help our mission or make everything worse."

"Aye, you have a point there."

"I'm concerned about the council's leader."

"Aye, the key to all this might just lie with Malcolm. Why is he willing to betray his own kind—and allow innocent humans to die? What's he after?"

"Do you want to get close to the council to help Esther or to satiate your thirst for research?" I asked. Fitz was a historian after all, and he'd spent enough time attempting to solve this mystery that his research might be clouding his judgment.

"That's a bit unfair, dinnae ye think?" he asked.

"Is it? I'm not making some sort of accusation here. I just know how much time you've spent on this and imagine that your curiosity is high."

"My curiosity isnae high enough to put us or Esther at further risk."

I raised my hands in surrender.

"The councils we've come to know in our day always stand to gain something from their action or inaction," Fitz said. "If it's the same in this time, as I suspect it is, it is worth investigating. If we find what Malcolm is truly after, perhaps it could turn the tides for Esther."

"You're ready to tempt Fate like that?" I asked.

"I cannae yet say… but I'll know my opinion on it once we have the facts."

"If making any change to the past is going to be even a consideration, we need to figure out where that ring is—just in case anything goes awry and we need to grab it fast."

Fitz nodded, his eyes distant.

I continued, "Esther hasn't worn the ring the last couple days, so perhaps it's just stashed away in her room for now."

"Esther seems reasonable. Perhaps we'll make some headway there." Fitz walked toward the tub. "Help me fill the bath?"

Fitz rolled the water from the large holding buckets toward the tub, and I worked with my fire magic to heat the water before he deposited it directly into the wooden bath.

"Esther *is* reasonable," I said, "but I'm not sure Hamish is. I don't want to be unfair because I'd be the same way if it were you in Esther's shoes." I blanched at the thought. "But he's another complicating factor."

Fitz shed the last of his clothes and lowered himself into the tub.

"And will ye be joining me, or cleaning your delicate bits by sponge later?"

I rolled my eyes, though I couldn't withhold my smile. I pulled my chemise over my head, stepped into the warm water across from Fitz, and lowered my legs onto his.

"Are we to bathe together every night?" I asked.

"Well, I dinnae much like your tone, Ms. Weston," he said. "Do you wish it otherwise?"

I laughed. "You better not let Millie hear you call me that."

"Have I lost all my charms in the past?" he continued.

I splashed water in his direction, and he grinned the boyish smile that had always made me weak.

Silence fell, and I tilted my head back onto the edge of the tub.

"I'd pay any price to ensure your safety," Fitz said, his tone shifting to utter sincerity. "Hamish will do the same when it comes to Esther. I'm certain of it."

I leaned forward, holding his gaze. "The entire world is at stake, but to Hamish, Esther *is* the world."

"Aye. Let's keep our focus for the next couple of days on spending time with them—observing, learning, building rapport. Fate will reveal her truths to us."

I nodded.

"I was thinking of calling on Annabel tomorrow," Fitz said. "If I can convince her we mean well, perhaps we can start earning her trust."

"I could stay with Esther and try the same with her. She and Hamish are keeping secrets."

"A braw plan. She knows more than I expected. To even know of our time in Opimae...." Fitz's brows knit together. "I knew she was powerful, but this—she's a marvel."

I didn't disagree. "With that being the case, I think we do some reconnaissance first. We need to catch up."

Fitz's features grew pensive. "Ye want to start looking for the ring now."

"…yeah."

Perhaps I was pushing a bit too hard, but I worried we'd lose sight of the true objective of this mission otherwise. I didn't want to be insensitive to Fitz's emotional tie to his ancestors, but I couldn't allow us to falter with the ring just because it lay with Fitz's family.

Fitz released a deep sigh. "I still feel a bit mixed up about that—snooping around."

"I understand. We've spent so much time debating this, and I've tried to give you as much space as I can. But now that we're here… Fitz, we have to make a decision."

Silence fell, and my nerves prickled. Finally, he nodded.

"I dinnae know that I like it, but… I can acknowledge that it's a braw idea."

"Good," I said, relieved. "So, where do we start looking?"

"According to Annabel's accounts and your previous spirit-travel, the ring has been given to Esther, though we don't know if Esther has kept it at this point."

"True. It could be at Annabel's."

"Aye," he said. "Esther is observant, so we'll need to be careful here."

"Hamish clearly doesn't trust us at all, and their staff is always moving around the house."

"You'll use your spirit-travel?"

"We could just try the spell, but what if we call it up while someone has it in their possession? What if they realize someone has taken it?"

"We would inadvertently cause a wee crisis."

"But I'm not sure of the alternative. A seasoned witch might recognize my spirit form is in the room with them," I said, thinking of Lorenzo. "There's risk with both plans."

"I wonder…" Fitz said, his eyes growing distant. "I wonder if you recited the summoning spell again, would you summon the ring or would it summon you?"

I thought long and hard about it. "I don't know. I'm not sure if my spirit-travel happened because of Lorenzo's protection on the ring, or if it had more to do with my connection to you and the ring itself," I said.

"Aye, because Annabel's protection is bound by blood," he recalled. "If only her bloodline can summon it, but it recognized our connection…."

"Then perhaps it would do the same here in the past. It could summon my spirit to it again."

"The spell shouldn't work that way," Fitz said. "It must have called you forth because it couldn't escape Lorenzo's protection spell."

"But Annabel probably has it under protection as well, so would the answer to her spell be the same?"

Fitz let out a loud sigh. "For my part, Hads, I'm not certain."

"Ugh, and if it does, then I would have to break Annabel's protection spell." I rubbed my temples. "I think my brain actually hurts."

Fitz chuckled lightly.

"Lorenzo does complicate this," I continued. "But truthfully… I don't know that he had anything to do with what happened between me and the ring. I was thinking about my loophole power with him. I find my way around his spells, so I think the ring pulled me to it because of our connection and your bloodline, but my loophole allowed me to pass through Lorenzo's protection."

"It's a plausible theory." Fitz nodded slowly. "But we cannae be certain."

"True. But does it make enough sense for us to test the theory?" I asked.

"If we find a time frame with the lowest risk, then I'd be comfortable with it."

"At night?" I suggested.

"It seems a braw idea, but we don't know anything about Annabel's sleep patterns—and as we learned earlier, Esther isnae sleeping well."

"You're right. This is a rough time for both of them."

"However," he continued, "if we attempt this while Esther and Annabel are visiting in Esther's sitting room, then there's a much lower risk."

"Since Annabel is due for a visit soon, we just wait for the first opportunity and excuse ourselves."

"Then we come back to our room, and I'll guard the door while ye try the spell."

"Fitz… I think this will work."

"Aye, it just might."

"That leaves one big question though," I said. "What we do with it once we've located the darn thing?"

"There is endless risk attached to every possible course of action."

"God, I hate this."

"It's all right, Hads. As we've said, we dinnae have to sort this just yet. Let's not worry with the council just yet and focus on these relationships with Esther and Annabel while we locate the ring. Once we sort that bit, we'll decide what comes next."

CHAPTER NINE

Esther

The dark-haired man turned his head. Even through the foggy lens of my broken vision, I kenned it was him. He'd infiltrated both my visions and my dreams in recent months. Though his face was familiar, I couldnae be certain why he returned to my visions as oft as he did. He spoke in riddles that I couldnae make sense of. What message was it that Fate sent? I couldnae seem to grasp it. And so, the dark-haired man continued to vex me.

His lips moved, but his voice was muffled and his lips too obscured. *Curse these muddled visions.*

The man tilted his head, his dark eyes piercing through mine despite the veil that seemingly hung betwixt us.

He raised something to his line of sight. Gold glimmered in the soft rays of sunlight that poured through the window beside him. The charm of a necklace perhaps.

No—*a ring.*

I shook my head, attempting to clear my vision.

"She's the key," he whispered.

My breath grew shaky, and the vision dissipated into darkness as though I'd tripped and fallen right into the depths of the mysterious man's eyes.

Only the glowing embers from Millie's fire remained, and I wasnae certain if that granted comfort or no. Though it wasnae flames that would lick my flesh when the witch hunters came for me, the faces of my sisters who had met their fates by fire haunted my thoughts. Their deaths were in my memories as though I had stood in the crowds and borne witness to their pain, as if their cries for help had graced my own ears.

Hamish stirred but didnae wake, and I was glad of that. He had always slept poorly, e'er since the cursed night I had witnessed my own fate. I hadnae wished to plague his mind, but there was nae keeping what I had seen from him. It had been many years since the vision had vexed me, and Hamish had remained consistent in his concern. There had been brief respites at our most joyous occasions—our wedding, the birth of our weans—but the weight hadnae left his shoulders since we ourselves had been bairns. I traced the air just above Hamish's face, following the lines that had been carved by his worry. He rarely spoke of it, but it was apparent how it had afflicted him. I worried most for Hamish after my death. He would be irrevocably altered, but Callum, Archie, Elsie, and Ainsley—our sweet bairns—would rely on him more than e'er.

The embers dimmed. If I was to leave my bed, the time was now. I pushed the blanket away timidly and pivoted away from Hamish.

My shoes were cold against my feet, and I hastened across the room to toss another log on the fire. I opened the door quietly and moved quickly through the hallway. A strange energy set the house on edge tonight. E'er since Helen's capture, all hadnae been right with the world. Katherine's withering away had laid a heavy burden on my spirit, as had Agnes's arrest. But it was more than that on this eve. I couldnae account for it, but the air was thick with trouble.

I hastened down the hallway, regretting that I hadnae thought to bring my heavier dressing gown. But all of that was forgotten as I passed Fitz and Hadley's quarters. A scream pierced the air, and energy spilled forth as violent as the winter wind. I halted, uncertain if I should intrude. Another scream penetrated my soul, and I walked to the door, hesitating only a moment before striking the door several times with my fist.

"Aye?" Fitz's voice called.

I opened the door but didnae dare to step inside. "Pardon the interruption. I heard Hadley's cries and only wanted to be useful."

"Esther," he said. "One moment."

The sounds in the room were familiar—they were ensuring their decency for my intrusion.

"Come in," he called.

Fitz had busied himself stoking the fire, and it burst to life as I entered the room, although Fitz couldnae claim the achievement as his own. Hadley had sent fire blazing red across the room, deftly igniting the wood in the fireplace.

"I foresaw yer powers in my visions," I began, "but to witness yer fire in such a way is remarkable."

"You haven't seen fire magic worked before?" Hadley asked.

"Ne'er."

"Never? How can that be?"

"Fire witches are rare, even in my time. 'Tis a marvel. *Ye* are a marvel," I said.

Hadley nodded, though her energy did not seem in agreement.

"What troubles ye tonight?" I asked.

Hadley looked down, and even in the candlelight, the tears on her face were visible. "I had a night terror."

"A night terror? I dinnae take yer meaning."

Hadley sighed. I didnae think her impertinent, but rather, burdened by her troubles.

"I hope I dinnae trouble ye. I only seek to understand."

"I know," she said quickly. "I'm trying to decide where to begin."

I nodded. "Take all the time ye deem necessary."

"The place where we were before we came here...."

"Opimae," I said.

"Do you know much about it?"

"Aye, I... I considered seeking refuge amongst its inhabitants once before."

"If ye dinnae mind my asking, why have ye not done so?" Fitz asked.

"'Tis forbidden. The council doesnae wish to arouse further suspicion, so they have declared nae witch shall leave the burgh at this time. 'Tis punishable by death for all who defy the councils. Along with anyone who offers us aid."

"Oh," Hadley said. "Hamish, your children."

Fitz shook his head.

"Please continue, Hadley," I said.

"An evil witch has sought refuge there, and he's created a mess. We were sent to remedy it." Hadley paused. "But it's taken a lot from us."

I swallowed hard. "Lorenzo, ye mean?"

"You know about him?" Hadley asked.

"I've seen bits and pieces. I've connected to others, but I cannae see enough to make sense of it all. I cannae see that planet's future plainly."

"We were sent to defeat Lorenzo, but he has a powerful army. We've experienced battles, war crimes, betrayal, death…."

She looked to Fitz at the last word, but his eyes remained carefully fixed on the fire. I wouldnae pry tonight.

"And these memories… they haunt yer dreams?"

"It just started recently, but yeah… each time it happens, I'm back in Opimae and in battle. It all comes rushing back."

I nodded. They had more resilience than I had first suspected. Perhaps they would survive this time yet. "I dinnae ken that it helps to say this, but yer condition is normal. The men who fought in the civil war—many of them experienced the same."

"I just… I want to make it stop."

Her voice shook, and Fitz walked quickly to her side. She clung to him like he would save her from drowning.

"In my experience…" I cleared my throat, thinking of all that plagued my mind. "'Tis best to discuss the matters that trouble ye."

"That's what Izzy tells me." Hadley tilted her head while studying me. "Izzy is Fitz's sister. She looks just like you."

"What a thought," I said, my chest swelling with emotion.

"She told me I should talk to you."

"Yer conversation is most welcome," I said. "If I may be of service to ye, I am pleased to do it."

"Thank you, Esther."

"Dinnae mention it."

"Would you like to go back to sleep?" Fitz asked Hadley.

She shook her head.

"We can warm a bit of milk," I suggested. "I ken how to do it just so."

Hadley smiled. "I'd love that," she said.

"There's a chill about," I said, "if ye'd rather I fetch the milk."

"No, that's okay," Hadley said. "I could use the change of scenery."

She stood, reaching for the woolen dressing gown Millie had sewn her.

"Then, it's settled," Fitz said. He kissed her quickly. "I'll be right here."

Perhaps it was the dream or the late hour, but there was a frankness to Hadley this evening that I hadnae yet seen, and I hoped verra much that it was the whispered promise of more to come.

Hadley

We descended several steps into the kitchen; we must have been mostly below ground. The fires had burned out long ago, but the old stone room wasn't as uncomfortable as I'd expected. A worn wooden table was tucked into a corner to the right of the doorway. A bowl of dried herbs sat at its center, and sturdy wooden chairs flanked its sides. Heavy wool curtains were pulled across the eye-level windows, and I suspected they were expertly shuttered, just as they were in the rest of the house.

"Isla insisted," Esther said, following my gaze. "The kitchen is a full oven itself most days, and Isla makes the most of it in the winter months. She takes the curtains down every morning to keep them clean and fetches them every evening before she leaves."

Esther smiled warmly.

"Isla runs a tight ship," I said.

"A tight ship?"

Too modern, I realized. "She manages the kitchen very well."

"Och aye. We are grateful she found us. I hope when I'm gone—" Esther paused and then waved her hand dismissively. "Weel, it does nae good to speak of it."

Esther pulled a tin pot from the wooden cupboard before tugging the curtains open at the far side of the room. She stepped on a small stool, drew the shutters open, and lifted a wooden door. After reaching far into the hole, her hand emerged with a jar of milk.

"I'm sorry for the trouble," I said as she handed me the jar and pulled everything back into place.

Esther's brow furrowed. "Trouble?" she asked. "Is this trouble?"

I laughed lightly. "I suppose not."

"How do ye store yer milk?"

"In a refrigerator."

"I dinnae reckon I've seen that in my visions."

"You've seen electric lights?" I asked.

"The lights that have nae flame?"

"Yes."

"Aye, I've seen those."

"Well, they are powered by electricity. And electricity also gives power to a refrigerator. You put it in your kitchen, and it keeps your food cold. But you just open and close the door."

"And a fireplace to cook yer meals? I suppose ye dinnae have that?" She pointed to the large stone fireplace. It took up much of the far wall and had an open hearth.

"We have an oven. You don't need to start a fire to use it."

"Weel," she drawled out. "I do like the sound of that."

"Speaking of which, should I?" I asked, pointing to the fireplace.

"If ye dinnae mind."

I grabbed the fresh wood stacked nearby.

"For the morning fire," Esther said. "We'll be sure to replace it."

I called my fire magic to the surface, and my fingertips glowed red. Esther's eyes widened, a slow smile gracing her lips. I spouted fire from each of my fingertips, one by one, allowing Esther to take in the sight of a full fire display. Then, I tossed the fire onto the wood, and it roared to life. I tended the flames until it was a "proper" one, as Fitz would say.

Esther chuckled. "I've ne'er witnessed such a thing."

"It still doesn't seem real to me."

"This power hasnae been with ye always?" she asked as she poured the milk into the pot and placed it on the stove.

Esther listened intently, stirring the milk as I told her of my journey, how I had never understood myself until Fitz had come into my life.

She pulled honey from the cupboard and added a bit to the milk. "Ye felt strange as a bairn?" she asked. "Alone?"

"I know what it is to carry a burden by yourself, Esther," I said. "I know it isn't the same, but I understand feeling alone."

Esther kept her eyes fixed on the milk, but she nodded.

"If you ever need to talk, I'm here."

"I thank ye, Hadley."

Esther procured two glasses from the cupboard and poured the milk, steam swirling from their depths. Though Esther had heated the milk for quite a while, I wasn't sure if it was technically pasteurized. I didn't want to get sick. But it was such a small amount, and I didn't want to be rude. I hesitated for only a moment before I took a tentative sip. The milk was certainly different, but I was surprised to find that I enjoyed the taste, and the sweetness was just right.

"This is good," I said.

Esther smiled and pointed to the nearby table. Its wooden surface held many scratches and dings, a testament to its usefulness. We pulled out two chairs and sat across from each other. I took another sip of milk, stalling. I didn't want to push Esther to talk at such a late hour, but we knew she wasn't sleeping well anyway, and this was a good opportunity… I just didn't know where to start.

"Ye carry a great weight," Esther said, finally breaking the silence.

I nodded. "So do you."

"Aye. That I do."

"The villagers watch you closely," I said.

She nodded.

"They haven't accused you of anything even though they suspect you as a witch?" I asked.

"There have long been rumors about me, about many of us witches in the burgh—mostly women, of course."

"Of course," I said, rolling my eyes.

"But the hunt only began recently. The villagers might have suspected us, but they didnae fear us, not until Father Evans arrived."

"How did this all start?" I asked.

"It began with Isobell Shyrie. She found herself in argument with George Wood. He died, and villagers suspected it was because she cursed him."

"Ridiculous."

"Aye, 'tis. Isobell was nae witch. Ne'ertheless, it was enough to rouse suspicion." Esther took a sip of milk. "Then Helen was arrested. Everything grew much worse after that."

"Because Helen has been compromising others?"

"She has indeed."

"And the villagers haven't come for you or any of the other witches because…?"

"Because Helen hasnae implicated us. The villagers make claims, but Father Evans appears to trust Helen's word. That will only last for so long—'tis a matter of time."

"I'm surprised Father Evans listens to her."

"Aye, I cannae see the reason. Helen is notoriously ill-behaved. Killed her half-sister when they were bairns, that one."

I nearly choked on my milk.

"Are ye well, Hadley?" Esther asked, leaning forward.

"Yeah, it's just—she *what?*"

"Och aye. I cannae recall the particulars—said it was an accident of sorts, I believe—but 'tis true."

Silence passed as we sipped our beverages. My mind raced with Esther's information. When a croaky meow disrupted the quiet, I jumped, pulling a soft chuckle from Esther.

"'Tis only Freya," Esther said. She called to the feline, who promptly jumped on top of the table. Large and lean, Freya was solid black with a pair of striking hazel eyes. "She keeps the mice from the food, and me from loneliness during these dark, sleepless nights."

I nodded before greeting the cat. She gave another hoarse meow before meandering my way.

"I do love that wee beastie," Esther said smiling. "She has been a great comfort."

"People don't give cats enough credit," I said. "They're wonderful companions."

"Intuitive lot, they are," she said.

Freya headbutted my hand, and I ran my fingertips down her neck before scratching under her chin. She lifted her head and leaned into my fingers, clearly enjoying the attention. A spark jolted through me, and I paused.

"Is anything the matter?" Esther asked.

"I'm… not sure? It just felt like something odd blew through me—a burst of energy, I think."

Esther nodded. "'Tis the same for me. Freya appears to spark my visions on occasion."

I raised my eyebrow.

"It seems odd, but 'tis so."

I nodded. "I've seen stranger things."

Esther laughed.

"I guess that's pretty clear, isn't it? I wouldn't be sitting here right now in your kitchen if strange things weren't normal for me."

Esther nodded, her eyes growing distant.

"Being here is harder than I thought," I admitted, changing the subject. "I knew the witch trials would have already begun, but this is truly sickening."

"'Tis a difficult time to be what we are."

"They hate us so much. I know this is being stirred up by Father Evans, but I don't understand how all these villagers can go along with this."

"Hamish says they are sheep, but 'tis more than that." My pleading eyes pushed her forward. "The men of this burgh fear strong women because they cannae control them. The thought of a witch—a woman with that much power? Weel, that's intolerable, indeed."

"Where I come from, we like to think we've made progress. And perhaps the formal trials are over, but still, hate is thinly veiled and the battle for power continues."

After a brief pause, Esther asked, "What is it that ye have seen in yer *night terrors* to trouble ye so?"

I paused.

"Ye say 'tis remembrances of yer time in Opimae, but I—" Esther was speaking quickly, smoothing out her skirts without meeting my eyes. "Perhaps I shouldnae speak of it. I dinnae mean to offend by speaking plainly. I am sorry if I have done so."

"You haven't offended me. You took us in during a very dangerous time, and now you've just heard my screams echoing down your hallways. You have a right to ask questions."

Esther hesitated still.

"I think my night terrors haunt me as your visions haunt you. They aren't the same, but I have a feeling we understand each other better than we think."

Finally, Esther nodded. "It stems from battle? The things ye see when ye close yer eyes?"

"Yes. And loss."

I couldn't expect Esther to share with me if I was unwilling to do the same with her, but the thought of saying this out loud was difficult.

"We lost Fitz's father, Ian." I paused. "Another great-grandson of yours. He was murdered by Lorenzo in Opimae."

"I beg yer pardon for asking. I share in yer grief, Hadley. I am sorry."

"Don't be sorry." I slid my hands around the warm glass, finding comfort in it. "We'll never know each other if we don't talk about these things."

Esther nodded. "Is Fitz all right?"

I sighed. "Truthfully, I don't know. He hasn't talked about it since it happened. I mean, not really. He hasn't shared how he's coping. I think talking about it just reminds him more that his dad is gone. But I've been there—I lost my dad a couple years ago—and clamming up is a bad move." I shook my head. "I'm worried for him."

"Aye," Esther said, nearly a whisper.

Something in her energy stirred. I thought I'd perhaps struck a nerve.

"And yer companions?" she continued.

"I've tried not to dwell on it since we left Opimae, but I think of them every day. I'm scared for them, Esther."

"I cannae see Opimae or the inhabitants of that land clearly, but I ken well enough that yer crusade is dangerous. I've seen glimpses."

"Do you see glimpses through us, or is it like you're watching from in the room?"

"A bit of both," Esther said. "Though I sometimes connect directly to Gabriella."

I leaned forward. Gabriella was a member of Lorenzo's staff in his fortress, but she had helped us on more than one occasion, proving herself to be an ally.

"What have you seen?"

"Nothing that hasnae already come to pass for ye," she said.

"You haven't connected to her again?"

"Nae."

I sighed, my mind spinning wildly. "Each morning, I wake up wondering if our little family is okay." My voice faltered, and I took a beat before continuing. "I wonder if I'll return to my time to find I've lost them forever. Esther, what if Fitz and I led them to their deaths? I couldn't... I couldn't bear it."

Esther leaned forward, speaking earnestly. "Nae. Ye cannae think of it in such a way. Ye didnae force them to go, aye?"

"Of course not," I said lowly.

"They each journeyed to Opimae of their own accord. They've each decided to fight these battles because they ken 'tis the proper thing to do. Hmm?"

I nodded.

"Then ye cannae shoulder blame. Ye were born to a grave task— as were they. Ye cannae cast the blame on yerself for what Fate has commanded."

"In my clearest moments, I feel that. In my darkest ones… I don't know. My fear for their safety grows so loud."

Esther nodded slowly. "If only my visions would grant me another glimpse. My visions of Opimae have dissipated since ye've left."

"You haven't seen anything at all?" I said, hoping she had at least some crumb to offer.

"I've attempted it countless times. I…." She paused. "I grew quite proficient while ye remained in that place. I longed to ken that ye and Fitz were safe."

It hit me then, and my magic hummed with my epiphany. "Even across the ages… across universes and time, you and I longed for the same thing. I've thought of you often, Esther. I've hoped for better for you."

Esther smiled sadly.

Thinking of Opimae and seeking a bit of comfort, I reached for the chain around my neck and pulled it over my head. I slid Jess's black tourmaline first from the necklace. Jess had stalked me in Edinburgh, and even in Opimae, causing a fair amount of trouble—especially with Fitz. But the longer I'd known him, the more I had questioned what was true, especially after he had saved my life and given me this protection charm.

I then pulled Marina's amulet from the chain. I ran my fingers across the amulet, welcoming both the comfort of the protective energies and the connection to Opimae—to my team.

"How bonnie," Esther said. "The energy is… strange."

"This was given to me by the queen of the water witch nation in Opimae—Queen Marina."

"'Tis little wonder it feels strange, then."

And lastly, I slid my moonstone ring from the chain and onto my finger, wondering what Esther's response might be. My pulse slowed with the comforting energy of the ring passing through my system.

I was just about to offer the amulet to Esther for further inspection when I looked up to find her expression muddled.

"Hadley…" Esther began.

"What is it?"

"Yer ring," she said.

I instinctively flexed my hand, the moonstone shimmering in the flickering candlelight.

"It cannae be?"

It was time for us to acknowledge it, then.

"No," I said, gathering my courage. "This is a replica of yours."

Esther pursed her lips.

"What's troubling you?" I asked.

"'Tis only… I wish to understand, but I am afraid to ask."

"About where the ring is in my time?"

"Aye."

I took a deep breath, exhaling slowly, as I parsed through my thoughts. I couldn't discuss the full details of our mission with Esther—Fitz wasn't here. But with the world quiet as we sat across the table from each other cast in soft firelight, I felt an honesty between Esther and me that wanted to bloom.

"Well," I began, "Fitz and I didn't come here to alter the past. We came to set it right… if we can."

"What has happened?"

What hasn't happened, I wanted to say. But instead, I sipped the warmed milk and wondered exactly how much I should share. I'd thought about this time and time again, and yet… I still had no idea what to do. I barely registered how the honey's sweetness curbed the sour taste of the milk, or its thick texture on my tongue, or the fact that I was sitting in a seventeenth-century kitchen with one of Fitz's ancestors. How sweet the moment might have been if not for Lorenzo or Lucio and their carnage—their names bitter on my tongue.

Giving Esther context for the things she had already seen seemed like a good place to start. "Well," I began, a bit timidly. "You've clearly seen some of our future. Maybe we should start there."

I told her what Fitz and I were trying to accomplish in Opimae, what Lorenzo had in his possession, and why we feared for our futures. Esther's eyes filled with tears as I told her of the troubles of our time. The room fell to silence after I related our situation. Finally, Esther disturbed the quiet with the question I had most dreaded.

"How did Lorenzo come by the ring?" she asked.

My gaze dropped to the table.

"Hadley," Esther began. "I ken my fate… I ken I shall die at the hands of the villagers. Ye need no trouble yerself."

I met her gaze, tears obscuring my vision. "I'm sorry," I whispered. "I don't mean to be emotional. It's just… I feel like I've known you for a long time now. Your story has always been more than that—more than just a story—to me. Fitz and I, we've spent countless hours learning about you, reading Annabel's records, discussing what your life might have been like, finding sorrow in your death. To sit here across from you like this? It's overwhelming, Esther."

The tears spilled from both our lashes. Esther reached across the table and grasped my hand. We held onto each other as our tears eased the weight we carried for just a moment.

"What is it that ye mean to do in the past?" Esther asked. "Do ye mean to destroy Annabel's ring?"

"No," I said, sniffling. "I think Fate would consider us changing the past like that too brazen."

"Aye, with that I agree."

I took another sip of milk. It had begun to cool, but it was still warm enough to soothe a bit of my anxiety. I closed my eyes at the sensation.

"If ye dinnae mean to destroy the ring, what is yer plan, then?" Esther prompted.

I opened my eyes and found her studying me.

"Would you mind if we continued this discussion with Fitz? I don't feel right talking through it all without him."

"Och aye," Esther said. "I understand."

"This has been his search far longer than mine, and this is *his* family matter." I shrugged.

Esther nodded. Her curiosity nipped at the air, but even so, she seemed resolved to be satisfied for the moment. Her eyes flickered to mine. "We shall speak more of it soon, but perhaps… if ye dinnae mind… I long to ken of yer life. Ye learned much of my story, but I ken so little about ye and Fitz. 'Tis yer most dangerous moments that often come to me."

I laid my other hand on hers. She gripped it softly.

"Now, I'm an open book with you, Esther. Tell me where to begin."

CHAPTER TEN

Esther

Hadley and I had passed the deep of night in conversation, finding solace in the company of each other until the candles burned low. The cover of night had encouraged our openness, but now the sun's dim light seemed to have quieted her. The weight of Fitz and Hadley's troubles hung heavily in the air this morning.

Hamish was equally troubled.

On typical mornings, Hamish meticulously buttered his bread in ornate patterns and drizzled honey across it, savoring every bite. But today, he couldnae have even tasted it before kissing me quickly and departing for his office. I hoped he would find means to release his fear and welcome Fitz and Hadley into our home before he lost his only chance to ken them.

Once we had taken our breakfast, we retired to the sitting room. The breakfast room was comfortable, but it ne'er seemed warm enough despite Millie's best efforts tending the fire. Before Hamish and I had sent the bairns away in the summer, Elsie and I spent many an afternoon on the chaise by the window while I taught her to read. I situated myself near the fire and wiped a tear from my cheek, hoping it would go unnoticed, before taking up my needlework. Hadley settled herself on that verra chaise and reached for Hamish's copy of *Beowulf*. Fitz busied himself with the paper, or so it seemed, but upon closer observance, he seemed to be watching Hadley. His eyes held a sadness that was plain to see, but his features bore another look I couldnae quite place. And though I didnae often pry, I longed to understand what it was that I found in his expression.

"I think I'll take a turn in the park," Fitz finally said.

He crossed the room, kissed Hadley's forehead, and swiftly departed. I waited for Hadley to look over to me, but instead, she restored her focus to her account of fierce monsters and a hero of old. Quite abruptly, she closed the book and stood.

"If you'll excuse me, I'll be back in just a minute."

I hardly had time to nod before she had gone. I set my needlework down, which showed verra little sign of progress, and stood to take a turn about the room. I moved nearer to the fire. A chill had crept deep into my bones, and I couldnae quite seem to rid myself of it. Movement on the opposite side of the windowpanes drew my attention, and as I moved closer to the window, the cold air radiating from the glass nipped at my skin. Fitz and Hadley spoke with each other near the garden gate, their expressions grim. I thought perhaps Fitz spoke Annabel's name. I turned from the window, granting them privacy. Perhaps my aunt's visit had unsettled them.

I rubbed my aching temples as my thoughts shifted to my aunt. Her fear had sat so long with us that Hamish and I were accustomed to her bouts of anger, but for Fitz and Hadley, perhaps it had been too much. I would speak to Annabel at my first opportunity. My spirits sank as I considered her last visit. If only I could find a way to quiet her fears.

I had little time to consider it as Millie threw open the door to announce a visitor. "'Tis Mistress Sampson."

"Please, show her in."

I straightened my posture and smoothed my skirts. Katherine was one of my dearest friends, but still, I had to gather myself up and find strength to maintain my spirits while she was about the house. Her melancholy energy was nearly too weighted to bear.

The door again opened, this time to admit Katherine. Her blonde hair was winning its battle to escape the bun that had been swept atop her head. Katherine had always been a bit unkempt—there was a wildness to her that stretched back to our youth—and she had ne'er much cared for a pristine presentation. Och, how I longed to see that wild girl once more instead of the broken woman who moved to greet me.

Katherine and I clasped hands, and a wave of grief coursed through me.

"Yer wee travelers havenae left already, Esther?" Katherine asked.

"Nae, they've only stepped out," I said. "I expect Hadley back at any moment."

Katherine looked about the room as if she hoped Hadley would materialize from the elements. "I wish to visit with them."

I nodded.

"Have yer visions restored themselves since they've arrived?"

"Nae. I mean to ask the coven's help."

Katherine took a long breath in.

"Ye think it madness," I said.

Katherine's eyes flitted to the fire as she pondered my question.

"I dinnae ken what it would take to bring the coven back into accord," she finally said.

"I thought perhaps sharing that my descendants have time-walked here from the future might do the trick."

Katherine smiled.

"Perhaps it willnae work, but I will attempt it just the same."

"And what will ye ask of us once we are gathered?" Katherine asked. "Channeling our powers to enhance yer visions of Fitz and Hadley's futures didnae work before."

"But now that they have arrived, Katherine… I believe Fate may favor us."

"Our connection to the future grows with their presence… 'tis worth another attempt." Katherine's eyes narrowed as her thoughts surely churned. "Have ye considered speaking with the faeries? Their magic differs from ours to be sure, but—"

Katherine paused as the door opened.

"Hadley," I said, "Katherine has come to call on us."

Hadley's smile was wide, and she moved quickly to Katherine's side, taking her hand in greeting. She seemed genuinely pleased to see Katherine, and Katherine's energy lightened around Hadley. It did my heart good. Millie entered with steaming mugs and short-bread cookies—one of my favorites from Isla's kitchen.

"Ye ken, I am pleased to see ye, Katherine, but what else brings ye here?" I asked.

"Is seeking my friend's company no reason enough?"

"Aye, though I ken ye far too well to believe that," I quipped. "If ye're visiting betwixt our weekly visits, ye have business to tend to."

Katherine's blue eyes grew serious. "May I speak plainly?"

"Och aye." I gazed at Hadley. "She willnae betray our secrets."

I was surprised by how firmly I believed that to be true.

"I'd never share your secrets," Hadley said earnestly. "You have my word… for whatever that's worth."

Katherine nodded, looking around to ensure we were alone. "I believe my time is nearly gone. Elspeth heard rumors on the streets today. Helen has spoken of me to Father Evans, and I believe—" She paused, swallowing. "It has been suggested to me that I will be called into his interrogation."

I set my teacup down with a clank, startling even myself. "Nae," I said simply. "They cannae take ye to the tolbooth."

"We both ken that they can. What law exists to prevent it?" Katherine clasped her hands tightly together. "I dinnae ken what I mean to do when they take me away. I dinnae think I'll return from the tolbooth, and I… weel, I cannae stomach the thought of what awaits me in that dark place."

I laid my hand on her forearm. "Dinnae speak of such. I cannae accept that, Katherine."

"We have nae choice in the matter," Katherine said. "Helen has implicated half the village in some manner or the other. The villagers are keen to lay the blame at one another's feet. Nae loyalty exists amid the minister's search for blood. He means to make a spectacle out of us, Esther, show the burgh what happens to witches. Neither blood nor the bonds of friendship are thick enough to coat the villagers' desire to direct the minister's eyes away from them."

"Helen will condemn us all," I whispered. There was nae malice in my statement. How could I begrudge her for attempting to save Janet's life?

Hadley took a long sip of tea, closing her eyes momentarily.

"If they arrest you," Hadley said to Katherine, "would it be the first time they've arrested a witch?"

"Aye, twelve women dead and many others tortured—and all have been human," I said.

"At long last, they would be doing what they set out to do, but the fools dinnae have the sense to ken it."

"If they arrest ye," I said quietly, "then Malcolm has truly failed."

"He has failed already, Esther. He's had the power to stop this nonsense all along."

"Ye dinnae ken that."

"Ye must tread carefully," Katherine said, turning to Hadley. "They will show nae mercy to ye. Being an outsider isnae enough to save ye, but 'tis plenty to condemn ye. Compassion isnae often shown by the leaders of this burgh. If a villager decides ye're a witch and speaks it, ye're as good as condemned. Law and reason are of nae value to these villagers."

Hadley opened her mouth but paused, her lips tugging down in thought. Something flashed through her eyes, and when she began speaking, I kenned it wasnae what she first meant to say.

"You haven't asked why we're here—Fitz and I," she said to Katherine.

"Ye willnae find me impertinent. Yer business isnae mine unless ye make it so," she said plainly.

"I appreciate that," Hadley said. "I know we'll be the talk of the village soon enough."

"Nae," Katherine said. "The villagers have talked much of ye already. Being an outsider who sought shelter in this hame... weel, it was enough to raise an eyebrow or two. And that is all it takes in this godforsaken village. The humans already speak of ye with suspicion."

"Is there really no convincing the local coven to help things settle down?" Hadley asked.

"Even if we convince Neilina—our coven lead—'tis right to do so, she willnae stand against Malcolm," I said.

"Perhaps we *should* seek council with her again," Katherine said with a light in her eyes I had no seen for some time. "Perhaps she will feel differently now that Helen has implicated a member of the coven."

I sipped my tea, considering. "Neilina hasnae favored me since Annabel forged the ring."

Katherine huffed. "Ye ne'er asked for the wee ring, and Neilina kens it."

"And yet, 'tis so. I will ask for her council to aid in my visions, but I dinnae see a path where Neilina stands against Malcolm or the witch hunters."

"Then perhaps we do so ourselves," Katherine said.

My heart sank. This conversation only grew more difficult with each passing day.

"I'd take my stand against them if no for my bairns," I said.

"I understand," Katherine said. "Of course I do."

I longed to ask after Máirín, but Katherine ne'er spoke of her daughter unless we were alone, hoping the burgh's memories of her would dissolve in the mist. She feared for Máirín's well-being just as I feared for my own bairns. Though Máirín was grown and married to a fisherman from Inverness, she'd ne'er be far enough away for Katherine to be assured of her safety—no with her ties to Forfar. Máirín had written many times attempting to persuade Katherine to leave for Inverness, but Katherine's reasons for declining were the same as my own. Neither of us would place our bairns in harm's way, our own fates be damned.

"You're sure they'd be able to find them?" Hadley asked.

"Aye. We've done our best in concealing their location, but Malcolm has his ways."

"So, the alternative is just walk straight to the gallows and put up no fight?" Hadley asked.

"We willnae survive them either way," I said.

Katherine turned to Hadley. "I have an advantage, ye ken. They believe me to be weak because the strength of my body wanes, but what do they ken? Surely, nothing of my power or they would truly ken fear."

Hadley's blue eyes met Katherine's. I hadnae realized until that verra moment that their large eyes were the same—blue as storm clouds raging over a dark, tumultuous sea. They smiled at each other, and I saw it then—their smiles were tinged with danger. Their energies yet held fear, but their determination was apparent. Katherine wasnae the only witch in this room ready for a fight.

"Out of the frying pan and into the fire," Hadley said.

"What do ye mean?" Katherine asked.

"Where I come from is dangerous," Hadley said, her eyes flickering to mine.

I nodded. She was safe to continue with Katherine.

"I knew there would be dangers here, but I don't know which is worse. The magic of this world is strange to me. Your burgh is a frightening place."

"Aye. It should frighten ye—if it were otherwise, then I'd ken ye didnae understand the truth of it."

Hadley twirled the gold band on her ring finger.

"This place ye've come from," Katherine began.

"Yes?"

"How are the dangers different than our world?"

Hadley looked to me.

"Katherine kens of my attempts to trace ye and Fitz," I said. "Opimae isnae spoken of much even in our time, but 'tis no unheard of."

She nodded.

Katherine leaned forward, eager to ken more, but Hadley's eyes settled on the fire and remained there for some time. Katherine's lips parted, but I raised my hand to prevent her from speaking.

"Grant her time," I said, speaking to Katherine's mind.

A tight smile was the only answer I received from Katherine. She held her tongue and settled back into the sofa.

At last, Hadley found what she wanted to say. She didnae tell Katherine all she had told me, but she spoke of Opimae, of battle and honor, loss and hope. Even so, her fear and her pain settled inside my chest, burying itself in such a way that I thought I might ne'er root it out. It was a part of me now.

The more expediently she and Fitz completed their mission, the sooner they could return to their time. I wasnae certain of their task—what exactly did they want with the wee ring? If only I could see more of Opimae. If only I kenned what the dark-haired man wanted. If only Annabel could be brought to reason.

Our web was a tangled mess I couldnae sort. The longer Fitz and Hadley remained in our time, the more muddled the timeline would become, and the more dangerous our dance with Fate grew.

My vision twitched, sending the world sputtering from light to darkness. I took a deep breath.

"Esther, is anything amiss?" Katherine asked.

I waved my hand. "'Tis only a vision attempting to come through."

"Is there anything we can do?" Hadley asked, moving closer.

"Nae," I said, unable to say more.

"This has always been her way," Katherine said. "E'er since we were weans. Give her time."

Hadley remained silent, but she watched me with great concern. I closed my eyes, hoping the vision would surface. My senses were confused, much like my mind. Something *was* amiss. I moved closer to the fire. Perhaps the elements would pull the vision to the surface.

The flames danced, calling to my mind, bidding it to produce the images that sought to surface, but it wouldnae come through. I steadied my breathing, pulling the air in and pushing it away. The energy that coursed through me was strange, unfamiliar. And I kenned it then—all these threads would tie themselves together and grant us our answers, whether we were prepared or no.

Hadley

After dinner that evening, we retired to the sitting room with Esther and Hamish. The meal had been both quiet and unnerving, a pattern that I longed to end. Fitz had called on Annabel while I'd stayed with Esther and Katherine. I hadn't anticipated progress quite this quickly, but I wasn't complaining. Between my conversation with Esther after my night terror and chatting with her and Katherine at tea, I felt like I might be finding my footing… at least a little bit.

I wished I could say the same for Fitz with Annabel. When I'd asked Fitz about his time with her, his face contorted into exaggerated desperation. According to Fitz, she'd been quiet and combative in equal measure—just as we'd expected. But she hadn't chased him away from the house *and* she'd offered him some of her famous wellness tea steeped from local herbs, so I considered that progress.

We settled on the furniture near the warmth of the hearth. The fire crackled, and Esther reached for a book as Hamish poured drams of whisky.

I looked to Fitz. *"I know they aren't very chatty tonight, but I think we should still discuss the ring."*

I'd told Fitz about my conversation with Esther, and after an invitation like that, we knew we should discuss the ring soon.

"We dinnae have much time," he began. *"If we wait for Hamish to return to braw humor, we'll be waiting a very long time. However... I dinnae much like the timing."*

"The longer we wait, the more tangled this all becomes."

Fitz's energy wavered—his uncertainty trickled through my veins threatening to ignite my anxiety. My foot tapped the floor, and I steadied myself as Fitz's eyes flickered to his ancestors. I wondered if he feared pushing them away before he'd had the chance to truly know them.

"If you're not ready, we don't have to do this tonight," I added quickly. *"It's your call."*

A beat.

"It's fine," he finally said. *"Nothing is ideal about any of this. This is no different, I suppose."*

When I returned my gaze to Esther, I found her studying me intently. I smiled, and she set the book down.

"Is anything the matter, Hadley?"

I met Esther's gaze and found her bright eyes troubled. I stole a glance at Hamish, who was studying me as he passed a glass of whisky to Fitz.

I attempted a brave smile. "I just have a lot on my mind."

"Dinnae ye mind Hamish. I wish to ken what ails ye."

Hamish pursed his lips, but he remained silent. I didn't want this conversation to lead to a fight with Hamish, but perhaps we'd have to take that risk. My conflicting desires fought against one another, but I found the presence of mind to begin.

"From all that's been foretold and what we know to be true from our present..." I paused, gauging the mood of my audience. "I'm worried about the fate of Annabel's ring."

"There's nae need to concern yerself with that," Hamish said, passing a glass of whisky to me. "The ring is our responsibility, and we'll see that the wee thing is destroyed."

"History tells us that isn't the case," Fitz said.

Hamish's brows knit.

"In fact, it falls into the hands of evil."

"How can that be?" Hamish asked.

"Hamish," Esther began, "the visions I've had of Hadley and Fitz in their time—this is their mission. They've been fighting to retrieve the ring from Lorenzo."

Hamish paced near the fireside.

"Ye've come for the wee ring, then. What do ye mean to do with it?" he asked.

"We wish to see it destroyed once it's served its purpose," Fitz said. "Or to bring it into the future with us in the hopes that it disappears from Lorenzo's possession."

"And ye're certain he has it?" Hamish asked.

"I'm afraid so."

"What would ye have us do?" Esther asked. "I suppose what I mean to ask is what do ye believe to be the proper course of action?"

"Fate complicates this mission," I said. "We want to set things right—to see the ring destroyed as soon as we all see fit—but we're also worried about staying in the past that long… about displeasing Fate."

Hamish nodded. "Ye're wise to consider that."

"Aye," Esther agreed. "But ye dinnae think Fate will be angered by yer involvement?"

"We can't know that for sure," I said. "But we believe Fate will view it as us trying to set things right, restore the chain of events to their original order."

"The ring is stolen from this time and brought into the future," Fitz added. "It was never meant to happen, so we hope Fate will aid us in restoring events to their natural course."

Hamish let out a long, low whistle. "It appears there isnae a clear path before ye."

"Should I consider destroying it?" Esther asked.

"The ring has already been forged, and the magic currently resides within it, correct?" Fitz was wise to ask. Of course, we already knew the answer to that, but we didn't want to arouse suspicion.

Esther nodded.

"Destroying it now would be unwise. Fate willnae like us meddling at this time, I think."

"I agree. I think the ring has to serve its purpose—complete its intended journey," I said. "Fitz and I have debated back and forth, but we believe sticking as closely as possible to the intended course of events is our best bet at not angering Fate."

"Do ye have any opposition to destroying the ring once you're finished with it?" Fitz asked.

"Nae. I've ne'er been keen on the wee thing. I've told Annabel I willnae use it. The risks are far too great." Esther sighed. "However, I *do* wish for the power to be released properly."

"Of course," I said.

"I may no agree with my parents, but I willnae dishonor them. Their power must be respected."

Everyone nodded in agreement.

"What does this Lorenzo intend to do with the ring?" Hamish asked.

"He's planning a rebellion against the witchkind government of our time—on both Opimae *and* Earth. He believes they oppress us by not allowing us to live openly as witches and rule over the humans."

"Is the government in the wrong?" Hamish asked.

"In some ways… of course," I answered. "But his solution isn't right, either."

"I thought as much," Esther said. "I havenae seen him often, but I've seen enough. Gabriella detests him."

"I was pleased to hear you've seen Gabriella," Fitz said. "She has offered us aid, but it is difficult to know who we can trust."

"So, Lorenzo wishes to fight yer councils with the ring?" Hamish asked, bringing us back to the point.

"Yes, and to place himself in a position of power. He's already murdered countless innocent citizens in Opimae," I said.

Fitz's eyes were troubled. "Currently, he's committing these horrors with his own power and influence, but if he accesses the power of that ring, we've lost all hope."

"Then we cannae allow that to come to pass," Esther said.

"Utilize the power of the ring, Esther," Hamish said. "And once ye're free from these villagers, we'll destroy it."

Esther held his gaze, but she didn't respond.

"'Tis the only way. We need ye," he said softly.

Esther dropped her gaze to her fingers, and she twisted them nervously. After a moment, she looked to me, then to Fitz.

"What would ye have me do?" she asked.

I shook my head.

"Esther, we cannae advise ye," Fitz said. "It isnae our place."

Esther frowned but nodded.

"I can't imagine how difficult this is," I said, "but if we advise you, then we're directly altering the course of the past."

"Fate would consider ye to be meddling, and that might worsen our circumstances."

"Aye," Fitz said.

"Is the ring still with Annabel?" I asked, hoping to garner more information with the question than we already knew.

"Aye," Hamish answered. "She brought it to Esther, but when ye arrived, Annabel asked to keep it in her hame."

"She said she would return it to me when the time has come," Esther said.

"She didn't trust us to be around the ring," I said.

"Perhaps she sensed ye'd be after it," Esther said. "Or perhaps the thought of outsiders in our hame was too much for her to bear."

"If we speak to her about this…" I began.

"It will go poorly," Esther finished.

"You're certain of that?"

"Quite," Esther said. "Annabel willnae hear of this ring going anywhere but on my finger."

"Esther attempted to reject the ring," Hamish said. "Annabel wouldnae hear of it. If ye tell her of this, she'll be convinced ye'll take the ring before Esther can use it."

"We'd never alter the course of time like that, let alone compromise Esther's chances," I said indignantly.

"Still, Annabel… she willnae be made to see reason. Of that much I am certain."

"Is there no chance of us gaining Annabel's trust?" Fitz inquired.
Hamish scoffed.

Esther looked reproachfully at Hamish. "I dinnae consider anything to be impossible. But I will warn ye that Annabel is suspicious of everyone and everything. She willnae be easily swayed."

"We'll accept a challenge," Fitz said. "It will hardly be the first impossible hurdle we've attempted."

"There's one other wee problem. Annabel is the only one who kens how to destroy the ring," Esther said. Our curious glances pulled more from Esther. "The vast power within the ring protects it, along with Annabel's own protections spells. She willnae teach me how to release the power properly until I've satisfied her by using the ring."

Fitz dropped his head in his hands. "This cannae be," he said, barely above a whisper.

"Annabel risks nothing," Hamish said.

"If you don't mind me asking," I said, "what are you meant to do with the ring?"

"Esther didnae utilize its power in yer version of history?" Hamish asked.

I looked to Fitz. That was a question for him to answer.

"Nae," he said softly. "She refused."

"And what happened to her?" Hamish asked. His eyes grew narrow, his jaw set.

Fitz hesitated.

Hamish drew in a deep breath. "Aye, I thought as much."

"Hamish," Esther said.

Hamish stared at the floor, refusing to meet her gaze.

Finally, Esther answered my question. "Annabel's first plan she brought to me was to simply defy orders and leave. Take Hamish and the bairns and leave for Opimae or some such place. She says with the ring's power, our councils would be nae match for me. She believes we could leave this place and live in peace."

"'Tis a fine plan," Hamish said, eyeing Esther meaningfully.

"First plan," Fitz said. "So, there's another?"

Esther met his gaze, her eyes troubled. "Aye."

"We won't like this one," I guessed.

"It too is a fine plan," Hamish said, the slightest smile tugging at the corners of his lips. "But no verra peaceful."

Esther cleared her throat. "The second plan is to use the ring's power to overthrow both the government leadership and the coven leadership."

"Malcolm, Neilina, and all," I said.

"That would be quite the fight," Fitz said.

"'Tis a fine plan, and more than likely, a necessary one, but I willnae be the one to do it."

"You don't feel up to it?" I asked.

"I have fight in me, to be sure, but that? That is quite another thing altogether. It would cause chaos amongst all the witches, and I fear it would create more division than unity, which is what I wish to promote amongst the coven."

"And what would that mean anyway?" I asked. "To overthrow someone like Malcolm… that would be his death, yes?"

Esther nodded, scarcely meeting my eyes.

"Ye dinnae need to trouble yourself," Fitz said. "Hadley and I have been to battle. We hardly think less of Annabel for suggesting ye overthrow a corrupt government official."

Hamish raised a rather approving eyebrow at that.

The look in Esther's eyes surprised me. It was one of understanding.

"Annabel's thought was to kill Malcolm—cut off the head of the local council, as it were. The minister and the magistrate were on the same list."

"Remove each head of the two organizations spearheading the witch trials—and the leader of the council who isnae doing enough to stop them," Fitz said.

"The government, the church, and aye, even the local council," Esther said. "Then make a motion to remove Neilina as head of coven."

"I don't know that you need the ring's power for all that. You're pretty powerful yourself, and if you were in league with Annabel…." I trailed off.

"Perhaps, but the ring ensures victory, aye?" she said. "And 'tis impossible to ken how the rest of the coven might respond."

"Makes sense."

"She has selected the replacements for each seat, and I do believe they would be improvements; however, the church is a stretch—I dinnae think even she can be persuasive enough to have much say in that replacement."

The room fell silent for a few moments as the new information soaked in. I thought back to Annabel's first plan.

"Esther," I began. "I want to be very clear before I say what I'm about to say: I am not suggesting anything here…."

Esther nodded for me to continue.

"But have you seriously considered leaving Forfar for Opimae? In our time, the border was closed until very recently, but it's open in this time. You mentioned it briefly the other night… have you truly considered seeking refuge there?"

Esther looked to Hamish, who gave her a long, knowing look. When she turned back to face us, her eyes were distant.

"Aye. The plan has been thoroughly debated. I cannae bring myself to do it."

"Why?"

"Another universe appears safe, but that couldnae be further from the truth. The witches who have forbidden us from leaving are more than capable of finding us in Opimae. I cannae risk the safety of my family."

"Unless you use the ring," I said.

Esther bit her lip. "I cannae do that. I just… I dinnae think it to be right."

"She worries about the power corrupting her," Hamish said. "But Esther is too pure of heart for that to happen."

"Ye dinnae ken for certain," she argued.

Chloe had spoken of the same thing when we discussed our options back in Opimae. *That amount of power takes on a life of its own,* she had told us. Even the purest of heart could be compromised by the magic of so many witches at their fingertips.

"I understand the fear," I said.

"Aye," Fitz agreed. "But even without the ring, there is the option of slipping through time in order to lose the council."

"Are we any safer in time? Would Fate allow it? Would we land in unrest like yer time?" Esther asked. Her brow furrowed as her lips pulled into a frown, and her pained energy grew uncomfortable in the air, heavy and unsettling. "I'd rather meet my fate at the gallows than endanger my family."

I nodded, understanding her hesitation perfectly. I wouldn't have risked Fate's anger against Fitz if our roles were reversed. I'd accept my fate to keep him from harm.

"What if ye only left for a bit? Come back to Scotland when everything blows over," Fitz suggested.

"The risks remain the same," Esther said.

"We cannae be certain of that," Hamish said.

"We've been over this."

"Aye, and we cannae seem to agree."

Esther nodded. "The risks outweigh the possible reward. I am thankful for yer concern, but I willnae risk the fate of my family. That is my final say on the matter."

Though Esther's words were certain, the flicker in her eyes and the feel of her energy seemed to disagree. Was there still a chance Esther would change her mind?

CHAPTER ELEVEN

Esther

Each evening, Hamish and I talked of a great many things as we readied ourselves for bed: the latest shipments Hamish had received, idle—and sometimes no so idle—hearsay our staff collected from other households, Annabel's latest concerns, and countless other things. Some of the information was troubling, while other bits were humorous, leaving us in fits of laughter. Whatever it was, we brought it to our evening conversations, one of the few times we were truly alone. While some nights were joyous and others were somber, they were *ours*.

But on this eve, Hamish was quiet as we cleaned ourselves, slipped into our night clothing, and prepared ourselves for the following morning.

Hamish climbed into bed while I sat at my vanity, combing my hair. I caught sight of him in the mirror, his sturdy chest visible above the quilts. My eyes lingered as I poised my brush near the crown of my head. He discovered me mid-act. Our eyes met, but he held his tongue, granting me nae glimpse into his thoughts. I pulled the brush down slowly as it found resistance in my auburn strands, ne'er breaking my gaze. I held the pattern for a moment more before my decision was made. I set the brush on the table and turned to Hamish.

"Will ye no simply say it?"

"What is that?"

"Whatever it is ye mean to say."

Hamish sighed.

"Out with it, Hamish. This quiet is troubling me."

"Ye willnae be pleased about it."

I raised my eyebrows.

"Hadley was right to bring up Opimae."

"We've discussed this far too much already," I said sternly.

"I ken, but ye ne'er listened—no truly."

"'Tis a dangerous option for ye and our bairns."

"Aye, and this current arrangement—it isnae right either."

"This arrangement offers them protection," I said.

Hamish scoffed.

"What?" I asked plainly. "Ye cannae well argue that fact."

"I can, and I will," he said. "Ainsley isnae yet seven. Will she recall the way ye quiet her fears when she wakes from a troublesome vision in the dark of night? She has yer foresight, Esther. Who will train her?"

I ground my teeth, determined no to greet.

"And Elsie," Hamish continued, "she glows with magic after tending the soil by yer side. How will she face her wee plants without her mother, the only one she's e'er content to confide in? Archie might follow me about the house asking a hundred questions, but when I teach him any new thing, he runs to show *ye* what he's learned. And Callum?" Hamish shook his head. "He is old enough to ken just what's amiss. I had word from him only yesterday, begging for news of ye. He lives in fear of the day a letter arrives with news of yer death." Hamish's voice broke at the last word. He breathed for a moment before continuing. "Bairns need their mother. And if ye're still hellbent on the gallows, then they're losing the last bit of time they could have with ye."

"Ye think I havenae considered that?" I asked, tears falling down my face. "Ye think I havenae mourned the loss of this time with our bairns?"

"Esther—"

"Naw," I said forcefully. "I am suffering, Hamish. I miss them at every moment of every day. I worry for their safety. I worry for their futures. I ken they will miss the love of their mother!"

My voice wavered, and I swallowed back my grief.

Hamish opened his mouth to speak, but I raised my hand, cutting him off.

"I think of them. I think of ye. I think of Annabel. I think of everyone *except* myself. Hamish, I am dying, even now. Each day, another piece of my soul withers away."

Hamish sat forward, his eyes softening.

"The darkness is slipping in, and I cannae stop it. My death grows closer, and each tick of the clock signals another second lost."

"Esther," he whispered, "I am sorry."

"Ye have fought bravely, *mo ghaol*. I wish nae more of ye except…" I paused, searching for the words. "Weel, except for yer tenderness in these last days."

"Nae. I havenae done enough." His voice was hollow.

"Ye have such fight in ye, but it isnae fight that I need at present. I need ye to hear me. I cannae continue in this way. We must accept what is."

Hamish dropped his gaze, his breath coming low and deep in an effort to calm himself. When he looked to me again, his eyes were misted.

"I relish in every small victory, even as I ken it willnae be enough to save ye. I believe we can win this because I must. I cannae think otherwise. I'm… I fear I dinnae have that strength."

A heartbeat passed before I found my response. "And what was yer victory today?"

"Our guests dinnae yet bring trouble to our doorstep. The witch hunters are still distracted elsewhere. It isnae much, but 'tis what we have."

"Why will ye no give our family a chance?" I asked. "Fitz is yer own blood, Hamish."

"They increase the threat against ye."

"The threat will come to pass whether they remain here or return to their time."

"We'll continue to disagree on that wee fact. But it isnae only that." Hamish cleared his throat, his eyes shifting to the fire.

"Out with it, Hamish. I willnae have secrets betwixt us."

He sighed. "Why make such an effort with them? They'll soon be gone."

They would leave him, same as me. My breath caught at Hamish's near confession.

I wiped my eyes while I found my words. "The purpose is that ye may ken yer family for a time. Better than nae time at all."

"It isnae right."

"I sense my aunt's faulty logic seeping into yer mind."

Hamish frowned.

"Ye have a chance to ken yer family—yer descendant. What a gift Fate has granted us."

"Esther," Hamish began.

I shook my head. "Dinnae squander the time we have left."

Hamish's eyes burned into mine.

"Unburden yerself," I said simply.

"I know ye say ye cannae think of a different future, but… if ye would only consider Opimae… our victory might be enough to guarantee yer safety for the rest of our lives. Think of it, Esther… the two of us with our wee family, beginning a new life in a place where 'tis safe to be as we are."

I smiled softly. It was madness, it was fool's play, but it was an escape nonetheless. I had fought with myself to be practical, but Hamish's words were like wildflower honey, and I longed to taste their sweetness.

"We could practice magic openly. The bairns could live free lives, be MacGregors without persecution. Think of it, Esther. Can ye imagine such a thing? To nae longer fear for our safety simply because we exist?"

Hamish's eyes were pleading, and in his energy, I found something no so unlike hope. He was wild with it, and after a moment, I understood. For the first time, he was allowing himself to truly believe we could win.

"This is foolish speech, Hamish."

"Call me foolish if ye must, but I believe my wife can persist against all odds if only she would believe in herself. The small victories might no matter much, but a grand one…."

"Hamish," I whispered, closing my eyes.

"Nae, Esther. Dinnae do that."

"Do what?"

"Squander all hope. Refuse to try. I believe in ye. I believe in *us*. I only need ye to do the same."

"*Mo ghaol*… I do. Of course, I do. I only fear for the safety of our wee ones."

"They are more capable than ye realize. Ye have decided for them… and that *isnae* fair. They dinnae want to navigate all the years of their lives without ye. For once, please consider it. Give me nae answer tonight."

I thought of each of them. My heart shattered at the thought of Callum's worry. I kenned my death would hurt them, but the fear of my actions bringing harm to them was louder.

"I dinnae wish to raise yer hopes above what is reasonable."

"And what is reasonable, do ye reckon?" Hamish asked, his voice falling to a deep rumble.

"Hamish," I warned.

"Is it no reasonable for me to expect my wife to live? To fight for the life we built? Is it no reasonable for me to ask the mother of my bairns to live? To no fold as the heather in the north wind? Come now."

"That is no what this is."

"Is it no reasonable for me to expect a bit of fight from ye?" Hamish's voice grew louder, his speech heavy with anger. When he spoke again, his words were those of a broken man. "Fight, Esther! For God's sake, fight."

My spirit crumbled at the sound of his plea. He was equal parts sadness, anger, fear, and want, and I couldnae bear it. "This is madness."

"Esther, this is my hame. I am forged of this land. But I will forsake it all for ye if ye'll just fight, *mo ghaol*. I'll leave on the morrow and collect the bairns. We could be free of this fate."

I sighed.

"We go round in circles as though we're caught on old Stuart's water wheel, ne'er finding rest. I beg of ye… be loud. Dinnae walk to the gallows and die obediently by the hands of yer captors."

Quiet fell. To respond would be to lose control of my emotions, and I had vowed to temper my grief before my loved ones. A few moments more, and I was ready.

"Perhaps this will all come to naught. Perhaps Fitz and Hadley's presence will alter the future yet."

"Nae, ye cannae help what others decide or what they alter—but ye can decide yer own path."

"As comforting as it is to dream, I believe my fate to be inevitable," I said flatly.

"I dinnae understand the things ye say sometimes."

"'Tis of little matter."

Hamish pinched the bridge of his nose.

"Ye might as well just say it," I said.

"Ye concern yerself with our safety, but ye dinnae see how this is affecting those who love ye. I suppose ye cannae understand because ye're no in our shoes."

I paused, unsure how to respond. Anger lingered in my bones, ready to consume me at my first allowance. But I couldnae blame Hamish for his feelings, nor could I risk his safety. He might be willing to risk himself, but I wasnae.

Before I could argue his point, the air rippled throughout the room. The fire danced about strangely, shifting in and out of focus until finally, it held. A city was burning—a city I didnae ken. The hearth faded as the vision grew stronger. Hamish was already near and supported my weight so I might lose myself freely to the call of Fate.

The structures were unlike ours; I kenned the city wasnae in Scotland. The edges of my vision blurred and sputtered, and I understood then—this was Opimae. And by the looks of it, the future. Magical beings ran through the streets, and I focused with all my might, searching for any face I might ken. Crumbling stone fell from nearby buildings, ash floating like snow and screams saturating the air. I steeled myself against the onslaught of emotion.

A witch came into sight who tugged at my memory. He was tall and handsome. His light eyes were clouded, his face determined. It was then I recalled—I had seen him in visions with Hadley and Fitz in Opimae. The witch ran down the smoke-filled streets, and my witch's eye nipped at my mind, signaling it was important to follow his path.

Everything fell to darkness, and a rush of air filled my lungs.

"Nae," I whispered. "Hamish, guide me closer to the fire."

The heat grew uncomfortably warm on my exposed skin, and I answered the element by pushing my energy toward it. In turn, I pulled my energy again to me, bringing the vibrancy of the flames along with it. The vision resurfaced, and I breathed deeply, willing it to settle within my mind.

The man moved quickly, and I hardly kenned what was falling away in my periphery as I focused on him, determined no to lose sight of him again. Flames leapt brilliantly toward the gray heavens… the sheer loss would be staggering. My heart beat so hard that I thought it would certainly leap from my chest as my senses mingled with the man's. Finally, he stepped around the corner of a large gate. The stone walls rose high above us, the largest barrier I had ever seen. He looked up and froze.

"No!" he cried, his lament settling deeply within my own chest. "We're too late."

He ran through the gate nonetheless, and the sight took my hope with it.

Countless stoic soldiers dressed in black, a dark sea with rippling waves that wouldnae cease, stared ahead, marching through a stone archway. The portal to Earth.

The man's horror buzzed through the air as he fell to his knees. His face crumpled, and a tear rolled down his face. As the tear reached his jaw, movement from within it called to me, and I was pulled toward it like a moth to flame. Darkness fell. When light again dawned, I was in another place entirely.

A stone fortress rose overhead, and snow lay thick in every direction. A tall man with raven hair walked down a line of magical beings who were shoved to their knees in the cold powder. I didnae need to step closer to ken it was Lorenzo, nor did I need to hear the voice of the woman at the center to know it belonged to Hadley.

"This isn't finished," she said. "Not by a long shot. We'll never give up. This will never be over."

Lorenzo laughed. "Still so much fight in you, even after such defeat."

He dropped to one knee in front of her and took her jaw in his hand. Fitz swore and launched himself toward Lorenzo, but between his tied hands and the guards gripping him, there was little he could do. Hadley attempted to pull away, but her hands, too, were bound, and the guard behind her held her steady.

"Such courage, such power." Lorenzo frowned as he stood. "Such a tragedy," he added as he walked away. "Take them to the holding cells."

My vision dissipated, leaving me in darkness. The shift in atmosphere left my body shaking.

"These are the things that shall come to pass if the scales of justice should waver," a woman said, her wispy voice echoing through my mind. I couldnae sort who she was.

The air was thick with strange energy that pecked at my skin, taunting my senses and my heart with dread. I drew in large gulps of air in hopes that it would dispel the feeling that gripped me. I needed the fire's energy to release me, and I sought to anchor myself to anything that would pull me back to myself.

Recalling that Hamish held me in his grasp, I croaked, "Hamish, hold onto me tightly."

His arms tightened around my body.

I fell into his energy, reaching for our bond, concentrating on the rise and fall of his chest, his tenderness. The world shifted. My breath came evenly, and the heat of the flames grew distant. Hamish had picked me up, and by the time he set me on the bed, my sight had restored itself.

Hamish climbed onto the bed and slipped behind me. He pulled me onto his lap, and I leaned against his solid chest. The pressure from his arms calmed me further.

"What did ye see?" he finally asked.

"A possible future for Fitz, Hadley, and their folk. It wasnae a braw scene, Hamish," I said. "They have a greater fight ahead of them than we can imagine."

"Hmph."

"There's something else," I said, pulling myself up to face him.

I told Hamish of the woman's voice in my vision.

"Ye've ne'er heard such before?"

"Nae, Hamish. It was strange."

"I suppose it wasnae anyone from the vision."

I considered the vision once more, but I was certain. "I dinnae ken whose voice it was."

"'Tis strange, indeed. Perhaps ye'll come to understand it soon."

Perhaps that was true, but I dreaded the answer. Might this be a sign of trouble to come?

CHAPTER TWELVE

Hadley

Opportunity to search for the ring presented itself faster than I thought it would. Annabel called on Esther the following day, likely owing both to Fitz's visit and to Annabel's fear that we'd compromise her plan with Esther. But no matter the reason, Fitz and I scurried to our bedroom. When I turned from the door, I found Fitz sitting on the edge of the bed, smiling.

"What?" I asked suspiciously. His smiles had been in rather short supply.

"Our espionage reminds me of simpler times."

"Back when we thought this whole thing was just a family mystery." I leaned against the door, returning his smile.

"Aye. Our fear of the councils seems like child's play after everything that's happened since."

"That honestly feels like a lifetime ago."

"It was. Several, in fact."

I made a face, pulling a chuckle from him.

"You know, I was scared when we faced the councils, but I believed in us. I still do."

"Come to me, *mo chridhe*."

I did so, and he wrapped his arms around my waist as I stood before him.

"What does that mean?" I asked.

"It means *my heart*."

Mine warmed. His grief still lay thickly between us, but maybe we were turning a corner.

Fitz tugged at my neck, and I bent forward, meeting him in a tender kiss. When he pulled back, his face was resolute. "Right. Well, we'd better get on with it before Annabel leaves."

I nodded once and closed my eyes. I focused my mind and began.

"That which was lost

Soon shall be found"

My body reacted in a new way to the spell, buzzing with excitement.

"Desire in your heart

Ignite with the fire"

The fireplace burst with renewed life.

"Bring the ring

Here and now"

The world went dark, and when it revealed itself again, a familiar room lay before me.

Annabel's bedroom. The ring had summoned me once more.

The small bedroom was well lit, the light cloud coverage not enough to prevent the bright morning sunlight from filtering through the windows along the east-facing wall. The lofty four-poster bed sat just where I remembered, and instinct pushed me toward the worn oak desk that sat in the far corner of the room. The last time I'd spirit-traveled here, Annabel had sat at the desk, and her husband John had stalked out of the room after what had clearly been an argument. Today, the room was vacant, and I heaved a sigh of relief.

I stood in front of the desk, recalling the first time I'd seen it—the first time I had successfully spirit-traveled on my own, using a grimoire and a spell as my guides. Now, I was fully in the past on an impossible journey. I shook the thought from my mind, refocusing on my task at hand. Annabel hadn't sensed my spirit before, but she had been distracted from the argument, and I feared this time might be different if she returned home to my spirit in her room.

I closed my eyes, feeling out the energy in the space, where Annabel's magical presence lingered heavily. I'd come to know it well while studying her grimoire and journal, and I was sure I would have recognized it anywhere. It was an odd thing, to feel as though I knew Annabel and to care so deeply about her story, while she did not know of me nor care for me at all. So many strange dynamics of this sort had played out over the last couple years, and I now understood how Henry and Isaac must have felt while protecting Fitz and me from harm before I ever knew them.

Past Annabel's energy, the room was quite still. That was until I found the faint hum of another energy in the room. It was muddled, but even through whatever spell Annabel had cast to dim its energetic presence, the combined power of multiple witches called to me.

The path of energy brought me closer to Annabel's desk. I extended my hand, feeling along the wooden edge, searching for the precise spot where the energy seemed most potent. About halfway across the desk, I found what I sought. From there, I traced the energy to the middle drawer and pulled. However, I couldn't connect to the handle. Spirit-travelers moved objects in their spirit form through intention and energy, and this task with the drawer was no different.

Come on, Hadley. There might not be much time.

I sighed and settled my mind.

I tried again, and the drawer tugged open, releasing a wild current of energy. A stack of papers were tucked into the small space, and I tugged them out of the way and laid them carefully on the desk to keep them in order. If I was careless, Annabel would surely discover it, meticulous as she was. It was the little things that tipped other witches off.

A shallow box of crystals first caught my eye, and I sifted through them quickly but found no ring. I pulled out a second box, which was wooden and rectangular. Curious, I removed the lid and found only a spare quill pen. I set it aside and reached for the next one. I opened the large square box to find a wax seal kit.

I was growing impatient.

When my fingertips met the wood grain of the next box, magical energy pulsed into my hand. My heart beat wildly as I reached inside and pulled out a small burlap bag. I tugged it open and pulled the magical ring from its depths. An astonished laugh escaped my lips as the ring glimmered in the sunlight. My triumph was cut short as a voice sounded on the other side of the door.

I scrambled to piece everything back together, but it was no use—I abandoned my task as the door swung open and bolted under the bed, ring still in hand. Footsteps echoed amid the squeaky protests of the worn wooden floors, stopping just short of the desk. If the other occupant of the room was specially attuned to magical energies, they might notice my spirit form, but I took the risk, extending my head just far enough to catch a glimpse of the intruder.

The woman standing near me looked familiar. She was middle-aged and dressed in working clothes, resting her hands on her hips. She released a dissatisfied sigh. The woman muttered under her breath, and though I couldn't make out her words, I thought I caught the word "mess," and her tone suggested she wasn't happy with what she found.

I released a deep breath with my realization that it wasn't Annabel. Perhaps this little venture would work out after all. The woman tidied up quickly before walking over to the wardrobe to do the same. I thought of Murdina tidying up in the kitchen on my first spirit-travel to Annabel's and recalled where I had seen this woman before. She had stood past the open doorway calling to Murdina that day. *Alannah.*

After completing her business, Alannah exited the room and closed the door, leaving me to remove any trace of my presence. I shimmied out from under the bed and raced to the window. I threw it open and tried to pass the hand that held the ring though the opening. A burst of energy seared through me, and I dropped the ring, clutching my hand.

As suspected, Annabel had placed a spell on the ring, preventing anyone from removing it from her room. I might be able to break the spell, but that was a task for another day. I closed the window and scooped the ring from the floor, returning it to its rightful place.

I closed my eyes and focused on my energetic footprint in the room. I tightened my hold on my energy and asked the elements to pull it back to me. I couldn't remove it all, but hopefully I wouldn't leave enough for Annabel to notice it. With my business tidied up, I thought of the bedchamber at Esther's house. I thought of Fitz's warmth, the feel of his sturdy arms, and as Annabel's room faded,

Fitz's strong jawline and his emerald eyes welcomed me back to safety as I awoke in my body.

"Welcome back, my wee spirit-traveler."

I couldn't help but giggle. I tried to sit up, but my body wasn't quite ready for that.

"Not so fast," he said, grinning.

"You're enjoying my discomposure just a little too much."

"*Me?* Never," he said, rather gallant.

I rolled my eyes.

"What did ye discover?" he asked.

"I found the ring in Annabel's middle desk drawer. At the back in a dark wooden box with a sprig of heather carved in the top. There's a small burlap bag, and the ring is just inside."

"Nice work," Fitz said.

"It's enchanted. I was able to retrieve it from the bag, but it can't leave Annabel's room unless the spell is broken."

"I figured as much. Could ye break it, ye think?"

"I'm not sure. I didn't want to chance the timing of Annabel's visit, especially after her lady's maid Alannah walked in on me mid-investigation. I'd have to go back to really feel out the spell."

A question lingered on Fitz's face, his eyebrows raised.

"Oh, it was fine. She assumed Annabel left it in that state and tidied it up."

"Close call," he said.

I rose slowly and sat up on the bed next to Fitz. "It's unusual for me to be disoriented like this for such a short distance. I didn't even travel to a different time."

Fitz considered the situation for a moment. "Annabel is thorough. Perhaps she has new protections placed on her house and around the desk that meddled with ye a bit."

"I didn't meet anything that was an outright barrier except for whatever is holding the ring in that house, but I guess that doesn't mean there weren't protections around that I didn't feel."

Fitz shrugged.

"Well," I began, "we know where it's located. Now, if I can just go back and assess the protection spell, we might have that option open to us."

I blanched at the thought of stealing the ring. The more I got to know Esther, the more difficult this mission became.

"Now it is time to make a decision, and here I am asking myself the same questions," Fitz said. "Am I willing to sacrifice the whole world to protect my honor? To preserve my family's?"

"Some would call it dishonor to give into your family's wishes."

Anger flashed through Fitz's eyes, but he looked away toward the fire. After a moment, he responded, his voice rough. "And they might be right."

"But I understand what that means. Annabel will be a wreck once she loses Esther..." A lump formed in my throat at the very thought of Esther's death. I had only just begun to know her, and I was already mourning her loss.

Fitz's eyes were closed.

"If we take the ring from Esther before her..." Fitz stumbled on the word. "Her death, then I think we'd change the timeline too much."

"So, we take it right after." I winced at my own words. This was hell.

"Aye, since Hamish was meant to collect the ring then anyway, it seems the proper course."

"Since you're of her bloodline, you have the best chance at releasing the power back to its rightful place—with or without Annabel's guidance. It's the easiest path too—keeps us from relying on the council for any of it."

"That plan alters the chain of events the least."

"So, this is what we do regardless of whether Annabel is on board or not."

Fitz finally met my gaze once more. He nodded.

My mouth pulled into a hard line. It was decided then.

"I hate all of this, Hadley."

"I know," I said simply. "I do too."

We fell silent. The rain started, and its patter against the window paired with the crackle of the fireplace to form the soundtrack to our consideration.

"You're certain ye heard Katherine correctly yesterday?" Fitz asked. "About the faeries."

"Yeah, I'm sure. Did you know there were faeries here this long after The Great Passage?" We'd learned about the mass migration of mythical beings to Opimae while we were there, but we hadn't heard about any staying behind.

"Scotland is famous for our folklore, and faeries play a big role in that. But I'd always considered it myth—stories passed down from the generations who would've lived here at the same time as the faeries. So, if they're really here, they're potentially another resource."

"Or another obstacle," I countered.

"Yet another factor for us to assess."

"I'll ask Esther about them when I find the chance?"

"Aye. I might ask Hamish as well."

"If the faeries are still here, I'm curious if they're playing any part in all this," I said.

"We do know they notoriously keep to themselves, or at least they did in Opimae."

"There's something else Esther and Katherine mentioned," I said.

Fitz cocked his head in question.

I told him of their conversation about Neilina and how I wondered about the state of the coven.

"I'd like to speak with Neilina myself," I said.

"Hadley, dinnae go meddling in the coven's affairs."

"I'm not trying to meddle," I said, affronted. "But if we're planning to be thorough on our research, Neilina and the coven are a factor we need to understand."

"I'm not saying we shouldnae learn more, but that is a hornet's nest if I've ever seen one. Let that lie, at least for a bit, aye?"

I couldn't agree to that—not if a chance presented itself—so I changed the subject instead.

"I thought I would feel clearer after locating the ring," I said. "But I don't."

"I think ye should speak with Esther again."

"To what end this time?"

"To find out what Annabel spoke of today." Fitz's eyes swirled with storm clouds, and his energy wasn't any less turbulent. This mission would consume him if we didn't find a way to ease his mind.

"Okay, I'll ask her about it."

The echo of my promise resounded through me. This had all begun with a family mystery, and perhaps, a family mystery was exactly where it would all end.

CHAPTER THIRTEEN

Opimae
Present Day

A strange light shed a pale glow across two linked hands. One complexion was dark, the other light. The lighter hand gripped the other tightly, refusing to release it.

"No," a man's voice whispered. "I willnae leave you behind."

"Henry, you have to. You *have* to make it out of here." The woman's voice was forceful, desperate. "I don't know what happened to Gustavo. Please—find him."

Her slender, deep-brown hand pulled Henry's closer, revealing dark iron bars on either side of their linked hands. Prison bars, perhaps?

No… a gate.

A loud thud caused the two witches to duck down, coming more clearly into view.

"They're closing the rest of the gates. You have to go right now."

The woman tilted her face toward the only source of light, her bright amber eyes sweeping upward. "It's the only way."

Henry followed her gaze to the opening above the large stone walls.

"I willnae leave you, lass!" he said, his voice growing angry. "We need to channel enough energy to blast through these bars, that's all."

"We've already tried that. There's no time. I'll go this way and see if I can find another way out."

Henry released his grip on her hands and grabbed the iron bars, shaking. "Why will magic no work on these?"

She scanned the barrier. "I don't know. A spell?" She ran her hands along the bars and whispered, "Hadley would know just how to break it."

Shouting sounded on her side of the gate.

She turned and extended her hands, and suddenly, her palms were covered in an icy blue hue. Water danced and swirled around her palms, which was charged with magical energy that sputtered and sparked in warning.

"Jordan!" Henry called.

She turned back and leaned toward the gate. "I'll meet you in the trees just south of the fortress."

Henry's hazel eyes darted across her face.

"We have no choice. *Please*."

Henry nodded, his chiseled jawline clenched hard. "Aye, I'll work my way around. I'll find you. Perhaps I'll meet Gustavo along the way."

Tears filled Jordan's eyes, but her face grew determined, set in stone. "I'll see you soon."

"Be careful, lass. Fate be with you."

He reached his hand through the gate and rested it on her shoulder.

She nodded once, turned, and ran toward the commotion, hands blazing blue.

Esther

I gasped, rising from the comfort of our bed. Hamish started, jumping from under the blankets, crouching as though he were prepared for battle.

"All is well, *mo ghaol.* Come back to bed."

Chest still heaving, he followed my instruction, sliding himself tightly against me. He kissed me tenderly, stroking the hair that had escaped my braid.

"A vision?"

"I—Hamish, I dinnae ken."

"What are ye saying?"

"It came to me much like a vision, but it was… strange, as if I was peering through a hazy windowpane. I dinnae ken if it was a vision, or if I'm"—I recalled two coven members whose powers had enmeshed once before—"connecting to Hadley's night terrors somehow."

"What a strange thought."

"Aye, but this isnae right, Hamish. That much I well ken."

"What did ye see?"

"Fitz and Hadley's companions, I think. Their wee family they've left in Opimae."

"And it wasnae a braw scene?"

"Nae. I couldnae make it out, but it seemed that Hadley's dearest friend was left in danger, and Fitz's friend—Henry, the one I've told ye of—was attempting to help her."

I closed my eyes and clasped my trembling hands.

"*Mo ghaol*," he said softly. "Dinnae fash."

"This is all too great a burden," I said.

I had held my tongue many times over with Hamish. He knew what I carried, but I didnae speak of it often. There was nae reason to trouble him further when it would do us nae good.

"We will sort this, Esther. I still believe that."

"I dinnae wish to trouble them if this is only a dream."

"Ye may ask in the morning if Hadley's had a dream."

"I dinnae want to face this," I said softly.

"Och, Esther, I ken. Ye are safe tonight, and nae decisions must yet be reached."

Hamish took me in his arms protectively. I looked at him—my lover, my protector, my friend. I kissed him then. Love, fear, exhaustion… it all flowed across our bond, and I kenned, even with the weight of it all, Hamish was strong enough to bear it.

He sighed, his energy half-contented, half-concerned, and he kissed me deeper still. His lips moved longingly, seeking the reprieve only we could grant to each other. When he dipped his head back, opening his eyes, the love I found in them set my chest heavy with want.

"Hamish," I whispered.

"Aye, Esther. I want ye badly, but I dinnae ken what ye've seen tonight. Wish me away until I return to myself, *mo ghaol*, for otherwise, I am lost in ye."

I traced his lips with my fingertips, falling deeply into the bond betwixt us.

"I cannae be strong enough for the both of us against such desire, Esther. Ye must tell me what ye seek. I am yer ear if ye will it. But I am waiting to pull ye under, if that is what ye wish."

"Aye, Hamish," I whispered, my voice wavering. "Make me forget."

Hadley

I shuffled into the breakfast room in search of tea. Fatigue held me in its grasp after my night terrors about our team back in Opimae.

Hamish nodded to me over his usual bowl of porridge. It might not have seemed like much, but it was progress.

"How do ye fare this morning?" Esther asked, her eyes lingering across my face.

Fitz kissed my forehead before pouring a cup of tea for me.

"Tired." Truthfully, my mind was muddled, and I feared for Jordan, Henry, and the rest of our team after what I had seen.

Are they in danger or was it all a dream? The question was on a loop through my mind.

"How about you?" I asked.

She smiled. "Much the same as ye it seems."

I had expected to enjoy Esther's company, but it still surprised me how much. I would truly mourn her loss when we returned to our time.

Hamish set his napkin on the table. "Ready?"

"Aye," Fitz said. He turned to me. "Hamish has asked me to join him at the warehouse today. He has a new shipment of imports coming in and could use an extra hand."

"A fine shipment from the docks at Arbroath. New spices from the east, and more of yer tea, I'd imagine."

I nodded, smiling. I was thrilled to see Hamish making an effort with Fitz, and the gleam in Fitz's eyes told me he was happy to connect with his family. It must mean more now than ever after the loss of Ian.

Fitz kissed me quickly as Hamish took his leave of Esther. Hamish nodded once in my direction before heading for the door.

"If ye have the energy for it today," Esther said once they'd left, "I was thinking of walking up in the hillside after breakfast. I need to collect a bit of willow bark and thistle on the northwest side of the loch."

"That sounds lovely," I confirmed and excused myself to get ready for our outing.

The burgh roared with life in the late morning hour as we made our way toward the main thoroughfare. I thought perhaps we would avoid the area, but Esther wanted to remain steady in her daily habits, not wishing to arouse suspicion by seemingly disappearing altogether. I tried my best to remain present. Though I was haunted by what I had seen last night, I had to trust that my team was trained well enough to persevere without us.

"Ye seem troubled this morning," Esther said.

"I couldn't sleep."

"Was it a—what did ye call it?"

"Night terror," I said. "Yeah, I think so."

Esther's face was pensive, and her energy crackled through the air.

"What aren't you telling me?" I asked.

"A scene came to me in dreams, but I dinnae ken if it was dream or vision."

Our pace slowed as Esther set up the story, explaining that what she had seen was different than how visions usually came to her. She accounted for the difference of planets, though she claimed her previous Opimaean visions hadn't felt like this.

I remained decidedly quiet as she explained it all, allowing every detail to sink in. It aligned with what I had seen.

"I wonder if I am seeing yer night terrors."

"Does that happen?"

"On occasion. Magic betwixt witches can sometimes connect in this manner. Ye might see my visions, and I might experience yer night terrors."

"Does that feel true to you? In your heart, do you feel like this is a vision?"

"I truly dinnae ken. I can only say for certain that it didnae feel like a usual vision. Take that as ye will."

My heart sank. I wanted so badly to understand what was real.

"Did any of this happen before—what I saw?"

"No, but my night terrors aren't true memories. They're bits and pieces, but some of the things that happen in them didn't occur in real life."

Esther grew quiet as we passed a few villagers on our side of the lane, resuming once we'd turned the corner into an empty alleyway. "My visions of ye in Opimae… they were cloudy, but they didnae appear like this."

"What else could it be?" I asked.

"Ye dinnae have foresight." It was both a statement and a question.

"I don't."

"Has anything of this sort come to pass—before ye came to the past, that is?"

"Once. I had a dream about my friend, Tanner. I don't know if it was a vision, but I feel it was. It was like… maybe Fate shared it with me for some reason?"

"Did it come to a seer, or did ye alone see this vision of Tanner?"

It was strange to hear Tanner's name on her tongue.

"I don't think what I saw was tied to a seer, but maybe… I do read minds, so perhaps it has something to do with that."

Esther paused.

"My mind reading is under control. I'm not listening."

Esther gave a soft smile. "Perhaps I am only seeing yer night terrors. For my part, Hadley, I dinnae ken. I've ne'er been so uncertain in my life as I have been in recent weeks."

"I think I agree with you," I said. "Or maybe I just want to believe this is a nightmare and not real."

Esther gave a tight smile and left me to my thoughts as we wandered into the heart of Forfar. This burgh was truly on edge. Even with the hum of conversation and the clatter of carts trudging through the mud, the energy was the most distracting—a constant reminder of the fear, prejudice, and suspicion that swept through it. The villagers followed our path with their eyes as they had before, and I did my best to ignore their curious glances. One set of eyes, however, seemed surprisingly sympathetic. A storefront sat to my right, comprised of stone, and it held two small windows to the left of the doorway. Fiona was standing in the threshold of a small shop, a simple broom in hand as she watched our progress.

Fiona looked around before nodding in greeting. I was taken aback by her gesture, but I returned her acknowledgement, which caught Esther's eye.

"Ah, Fiona's in her new shop, then."

"Oh? She's graduated from the stalls?"

"Aye, I heard it just yesterday from Millie—the housemaids boast the real gossip of the burgh, aye?" she whispered.

I laughed at that but nodded. I had always seen it portrayed as such in period pieces, and it didn't shock me to learn that this bit of the culture was true.

We grew closer to Fiona, and I smiled brightly at her. Her eyes met mine and then darted around. The villagers all seemed to have returned their focus to their daily tasks, except for a group of middle-aged women who were gathered on the far side of the building that held Fiona's shop. They glanced between the two of us and whispered to one another. At this, Fiona's brow furrowed, and she stepped inside.

My mouth opened, but Esther cut me off. "Too brazen, I'm afraid."

"The smile?"

"Aye, ye brought attention to her—the one thing these villagers avoid like the plague."

"I didn't think a smile would be a big deal," I said, realizing how naïve that sounded.

"'Tis all right, Hadley," Esther said. "Simply refrain next time. We dinnae wish to implicate her. Ye are under suspicion—Fiona cannae risk the same fate."

I swore under my breath. One small act of kindness gone wrong, and now I was second-guessing everything I might say, every action I might take. A few moments of silence fell, but as we passed Elspeth and Thomas's shop, a question rose to my lips—one I couldn't stifle.

"Is Thomas kind to Elspeth?" I asked quietly.

Esther's gait slowed, and she turned her head to face me, her eyes filled with an emotion I couldn't name. "Why do ye ask?"

I focused on meandering around a large puddle, stalling on my answer. I didn't wish to offend Esther, but in my gut, I knew something was wrong. "Elspeth just seemed—I don't know—uncertain around him?"

Esther made no response, but her eyes lit in recognition.

"I mean, they're married, but she didn't seem comfortable with him. And he just acted like everything was perfectly normal, and then I thought… perhaps things *are* normal for Thomas, but their normal might be painful for Elspeth."

Esther tugged on her right sleeve nervously before looking straight ahead.

"I dinnae ken," she said finally. "They have always made a braw couple—their love was palpable since we were bairns." Esther sighed. "Lately, 'tis though Thomas isnae himself, and aye, Elspeth doesnae act as she normally does around him. 'Tis a difficult time to be what we are… the trials have affected us all."

"You don't think… would he hurt her?"

"I cannae say for certain—Hamish and I have seen little of them the last few months. My intuition says nae, it isnae… that."

"What else could it be?"

Esther glanced at me, her eyes narrowing. My pulse quickened.

"I don't mean to press, or to seem nosey, but seeing another woman like that…." I trailed off. "Esther, I need to know she's safe."

"Thomas pressed Elspeth to keep her distance from us for a time. I have long considered Elspeth a dear friend, but with the state of the coven and her husband's urging, she and I havenae found our footing," Esther said.

I nodded for her to continue.

"I ne'er expected such a winter betwixt them, or us. Perhaps now that Thomas has had a change of heart, we might make an effort to socialize with her more frequently."

"I think that would be wise."

"'Tis settled then. Perhaps I'll ask her to tea this week, and we'll better examine her."

I smiled.

We continued on, and when we'd made it to the far side of the burgh, a familiar figure approached us, a scowl blanketing her features. I thought perhaps that was a permanent expression for Annabel.

"What is the matter, Aunt?" Esther asked.

"The butcher sent his laddie to my kitchen just this morn advising Murdina to accompany me to his shop to see a fine prized chicken. A *chicken*. Weel, I told yer Uncle John this was certainly a waste of my time, but considering the fine day," she said, pointing toward the sun, "I thought I may as well humor the wee gowk."

Esther subtly covered her mouth, fighting against the smirk on her face. I fought against my own. Had I stumbled into the humorous account with the butcher that Fitz and I had read about in Annabel's journal?

"So here I come, dragging Murdina along—begrudgingly, might I add—and ye well ken she complains aplenty at even a mention of poultry. We enter the shop, and old Fraser grins like the fool he is and runs to the stockroom. Weel, and what do ye suppose but he comes running up with a live chicken!"

Esther loses her hard-fought battle with composure. Her laughter is deep and unguarded, and I couldn't help but join her. Annabel didn't seem to mind, continuing straight-faced with her story.

"'Tis a wee beastie, and I said weel, what do ye reckon we do with that? And he tells us it lays the finest eggs he's e'er tasted. So, it wasnae even for dinner."

"So, ye didnae buy it?"

"I told him I didnae ken how a sickly-looking thing such as that could lay anything worth paying for. He was mighty sore at that, and we set to arguing, so then Murdina gave him a piece of her mind, and next thing we ken, the chicken was loose in the store! Clucking and flying about, and Fraser couldnae catch the wee thing. Murdina was running about one way, and Fraser was running the other, and I couldnae stand it another minute, so I stepped outside."

A man's voice floated across the air. "Get yerself in this bag, or ye'll find yerself on my supper table tonight!"

At that, even Annabel had to smile, though she huffed.

"I reckon I *will* help. If I catch the wee beastie, I might yet take it hame to roost with the others. It does have *spirit*."

She smirked and took her leave. I couldn't wait to tell Fitz.

Esther and I continued our trek, laughing the whole way from the village, until we were winding through the tree line outside of town. The air of the surrounding country was the cleanest I'd ever tasted, and I took a deep breath, filling my lungs with air not yet polluted or tainted by humanity. The wind blew steadily across the billowing grass, falling deeper into cold as the sun hid behind the clouds, but I couldn't find a reason to be bothered by it today. The last few days had already been filled with excitement, fear, and anger, and though I probably should have attempted to talk more with Esther, it seemed we were both enjoying the unbridled elements and a few moments' peace.

Esther worked her way along the tree line, looking for this and that. I held the satchel open, and as she scratched or pulled at bark and weeds, she dropped them into the bag. Esther was clearly at home in the natural world, and as her cheeks flushed with the sting of the wind, she grew more beautiful by the second. Hair fell from her bun and she tugged it behind her ear, leaving bits of soil on her face. She was every bit an earth witch. Even separated by many generations, Fitz and Izzy both derived their powers from the earth, just like Esther.

Isaac had once told me that the MacGregor magical lineage was distinguished, and though I had never doubted him, I saw that so plainly as I spent more time around Esther. I didn't know Hamish's relatives, but Esther was extraordinarily powerful. A great deal of the magical prowess in their bloodline must have been owed to her.

Esther continued to remind me of Izzy. They shared a love for the outdoors and an aptitude for medicinal work. Though it saddened me to think that Esther couldn't practice her tinctures openly for fear of condemning herself as a witch, it made me smile to consider how her gifts would be passed along her bloodline, living defiantly in Izzy long after the witch hunters had torn Esther from her home. Though they were trying to rid themselves of us in this time, it filled me with an irreverent joy to stand amongst them as the living proof that the witch hunters would fail. And beyond that… it gave me comfort to think of how our loved ones live on in us, that we didn't die completely with our earthly bodies, that those of us living could honor our ancestors with the gifts they passed along to us.

Esther worked lovingly in the earth as she uprooted a particularly difficult plant—a thistle, I thought. Her hands were firm in their work but precise in their movements as she treated the source of her power with reverence.

We passed the time happily, though the same strange energy I sensed when Fitz and I had first landed in the past still lingered amongst the trees. Esther paid it no mind, and I thought perhaps it was only the feel of these woods. But the longer I sat with the energy, the more I was certain it was magical. When Esther had nearly completed her mission, the energy grew too strong for me to dismiss.

"Esther… why do the woods feel strange here?" I asked.

A curious wind whipped through the trees, carrying the softest hum on its wings. It rustled the tendrils of hair that escaped my braid, and my skin tingled with warmth. The balmy breeze clearly wasn't the work of Mother Nature, and as it mixed with the frigid afternoon air, it sent chills rippling through me. Esther dropped the thistle from her hands and stood, her eyes fixed on the growing depths of the forest.

Katherine's words from the other day hung freshly in my mind.

"Is this the work of faeries?" I asked.

Esther's emerald eyes met mine, bright above her rosy cheeks. She had just begun to speak when footsteps crunched through the lingering autumn leaves. Esther's energy tightened, and I held my breath as a nearby tree rustled. Then, a woman emerged from around a tree.

"Och, Marjorie!" Esther exclaimed.

"Aye! Good afternoon to ye."

"I am glad to see ye. Come and meet Hadley."

"Och, I'd be delighted!"

Marjorie was eye level to me—rather tall for a woman of the time, I thought. Her eyes were whisky brown and set in a fair face beneath a strong brow. Her chocolate hair was swept into a braid much like my own.

"I am fair chuffed to make yer acquaintance, Hadley! The coven has longed to meet ye."

"The coven wants to meet me?" I asked Esther.

"We spoke much of ye and Fitz before our meetings ceased."

"Still, we have waited—watching for signs of ye," Marjorie said. "We were pleased to hear ye'd arrived safely."

"Thank you. It's nice to be here."

"Perhaps we can convince Neilina to call the coven to order while ye are with us. It would be a delight for us all."

I looked to Esther for guidance, and she smiled, nodding once.

"I'd be honored by the invitation."

A whoosh of flapping wings disturbed the air to our left, and the hair at the back of my neck bristled as a chill crept all the way through me. A murder of crows, black as night, flew above us, cawing with an urgency that was not lost on the three witches standing beneath them.

"I dinnae much care for that," Marjorie said.

"Aye, something has certainly upset the wee beasties. Bad tidings to be sure."

One crow broke from the others and swooped in my direction. I held perfectly still, my witch's eye finding no ill intention from the bird. It turned parallel to me, its eye gleaming in the muted light of the cloudy afternoon. A soft energy poured from the crow, probing against my skin, and it paused maybe a foot away from me, flapping its wings to remain suspended beside me. The crow cawed so lowly I thought I'd imagined it, but as the bird ceased its call, a scene took hold of my mind.

A fireplace roared toward the far end of a wooden desk. A large, pale hand with thick, stubby fingers pulled a quill pen across a sheet of paper, writing the date: November 20, 1662.

A little more than a week away.

The scene flashed to the next.

Helen Guthrie sat in a worn wooden chair. Across from her sat a group of men who were scattered across a long pew. Helen's fear gripped me, and I yelped at the charge of energy that blew through my system and fell to the ground. A middle-aged man in a black robe pointed a finger, waving it disapprovingly at her. Though I couldn't hear her, her lips were quite clear when she mouthed "*Esther MacGregor*," making eye contact with me as she did. I shook my head and whispered in protest.

No. Or at least, I tried. *My* voice seemed to be stuck at the back of my throat.

The same men flanked Esther's sides, pulling her arms into their firm grasps and dragging her toward the tolbooth. Esther's eyes were troubled, scared, pleading… but she made no sound of protest, no cries of pain. The scene was consumed by flames, and a man poked Esther mercilessly in her back with a stick, prodding her to climb the stairs toward a hanging rope.

I released a bloodcurdling scream, which I was certain was heard all across the hillside. I tore at my hair and slapped at my face, hoping to dispel the vision. Esther moved closer to the rope. I screamed again in protest. She reached the site of her demise. I blinked hard. A man placed a rope around her neck. I slapped the ground.

Esther's eyes met mine, and the vision dissipated.

When my sight cleared, I found Esther also on the ground, her head resting in her hands. Marjorie knelt beside her, running her hands across her back. She stole a glance at me, her eyes wild, but as soon as she registered that I was conscious, her eyes turned pleading.

"What has happened?" Marjorie whispered.

"I—" I paused, sorting through my thoughts. What the hell *had* happened? "I don't know."

"What did ye see?" she prompted.

"I saw…." I choked on my words, my eyes clouding.

"She saw my fate," Esther said softly, running her hands through her hair to tame the wild flyaways.

"Are ye certain?" Marjorie asked.

"Aye. It was just as I'd seen it before." Esther finally met my gaze. "*This* was a vision. Nae doubt."

"It was so clear. It felt… *real.*"

"I am sorry, Hadley," she whispered.

I wiped the tears that fell from my lashes. "No. Please don't apologize."

I crawled nearer, not yet trusting my legs to stand. My body shook violently, though more with fear or anger, I was unsure. I pulled Esther into an embrace, and we sat there, suspended in time.

"How did this happen?" I finally asked, pulling away. "How did I see your vision?"

"I reckon Fate wished ye to see it. Animals are often her messengers."

"This hasnae occurred to ye in the past?" Marjorie asked.

My shoulder ached, pulling my attention. I must have irritated it during the vision. I massaged the injury and found my response. "Before Fitz and I arrived here, a crow crossed our path, and we suspected it was an omen of some kind. But there was no vision."

"Ye dinnae possess this gift, then?" Marjorie asked.

"Receiving visions from animals?" I shook my head. "No."

"This is a curious case, then. Perhaps ye might consult other coven members," Marjorie proposed.

The leaves rustled a second time, tearing our focus from one another, but I had a sinking feeling our visitor wouldn't be quite as cordial as Marjorie. The energy shifted around us as a man stepped into view. He was dressed in warm wool, and his red beard shone in the sunlight. His hair was cropped, his jaw clenched.

He emerged from the tree line, his eyes scanning across the three of us. His gaze lingered, and as his eyes narrowed, his violent energy peppered my skin. The sun reflected from a piece of metal, and it was then that I realized the man carried a firearm.

"No, come *on*," I muttered.

Esther eyed me.

The man stepped closer, raising his firearm in our direction. He gripped the barrel with his left hand, the stock of the gun pressing into his right shoulder.

I steadied my mind, calming my nervous system as much as I could, before standing—refusing to meet our opponent in any way that showed weakness.

"I don't think so," I said, dropping into battle posture as the villager stepped uncomfortably close. Anger coursed through me with every breath, the deep pulse of it humming through me.

"Hadley, nae," Esther whispered urgently.

"'Tis Duncan Maxwell," Marjorie said, placing her hand on my arm. "He'll kill ye in an instant, and our government will raise nae questions about it.

"Why?" I asked incredulously.

"He is called 'The Witchkiller,'" Marjorie said. "The minister believes in him steadfastly, and everyone is too frightened of Father Evans to question him."

Perhaps I should have heeded their warnings, but with Esther's fate fresh in my mind, I saw no other path forward. Rage consumed me, steady and true, as I thought of him murdering women in cold blood.

"Let's see how he fares when his victims aren't human."

"Three for the price of one," Duncan said. "Father Evans will be mighty pleased."

Esther's fearful energy ran around me, but I pushed it back, recalling my training from Opimae.

I took another step forward.

"That's close enough, witch!" Duncan called, resting his finger near the trigger.

"Why do you suppose me to be a witch?" I asked, pausing my progress toward him.

"Dinnae play coy with me. It willnae serve ye well."

"I'm not sure what offense I've given you."

"Weel, yer presence in Forfar, for one. The time has come to send ye back to hellfire where the devil made ye." Duncan sneered. He was proud of himself. His eyes were filled with conceit and superiority, and his energy felt like I'd dragged my nails across a chalkboard.

He was repulsive.

"I don't think my presence is the one causing problems in Forfar. I hear you make a habit of harassing innocent women in this burgh. You say you'll send me back to Hell? I'll meet you in its fires then."

An intake of air was all that betrayed Esther's surprise. Marjorie mumbled something in Gaelic. A prayer, I hoped. I might need divine intervention to prevent me from killing the bastard.

It happened so fast.

Duncan took a step forward, steadying himself as he tightened his shoulders into a position with better aim. I called forth my fire magic and shot flames at Duncan before he could pull the trigger on his firearm. He flew backward into a tree with a thud before sinking to the damp earth. His head drooped, and his body was still.

Esther and Marjorie ran to me. Marjorie appeared a bit shell-shocked, her eyes wide and her breathing labored. But Esther wore a smug smile on her lips.

"We must sort this carefully. This was reckless, Hadley." Esther paused. "But it was a most welcome sight. He has harassed many of our sisters, and several human women werenae fortunate enough to survive him." Her eyes shifted to the limp figure at the base of the tree.

"Aye," Marjorie said, finding her footing once more. "'Tis too bad we cannae send the bastard back to Hell where *he* came from."

My fingers twitched at the idea. Esther must have followed my train of thought, and she pulled my nearest hand into hers.

"We cannae kill him," Esther said, her eyes meeting mine meaningfully. "This isnae Opimae, Hadley. If he's killed, it will rouse suspicion for all our sisters."

That was the last thing I wanted. I closed my eyes for a few seconds, suppressing my instincts.

"I understand. A missing villager is asking for trouble," I said, looking again to Esther. "Is it possible… for us to take his memories?"

I hated the words even as they ran across my tongue. The threat of having my own memories erased was still too fresh in my past for the suggestion not to raise complicated feelings, but there was no other choice.

"Aye, we must, but 'tis a risk," Marjorie said. "Sometimes, the person doesnae survive. And sometimes the memory isn't removed entirely."

"Too much potency, and you'll kill them. Not enough, and it won't be effective," I concluded.

"Aye, that's it."

"My vote is to kill him," a man's voice sounded through the nearby trees.

Marjorie flinched, and I jumped, wincing at my stupidity. I should never have dropped my guard—not after what had just happened.

"Thomas Tailyour, ye frightened us half to death," Esther said disapprovingly.

"How can ye say such a thing?" Marjorie asked.

"Verra easily, in fact," Thomas said, moving nearer. "His life isnae worth sparing."

"And the witch hunt that would ensue?"

"Couldnae be worse than our current state of affairs."

Esther shifted uncomfortably.

"Ye ken what Esther has seen. Dinnae tempt Fate," Marjorie said.

"Perhaps this would help her cause. Did ye consider that?" Thomas turned to Duncan. "We've passed countless hours agonizing over the fates of humans. Their lives are fleeting, and yet we hide ourselves and our true nature to avoid their persecution." He raised his eyebrows. "Little good that's done."

"You speak as though their lives are less important than ours," I said.

"And would I be amiss in that opinion?" Thomas challenged. "They bring naught but destruction."

A muffled groan came from behind us, and we turned to find Duncan rousing from unconsciousness. He rubbed his head and looked around, confused.

"We must take his memories. 'Tis the only way," Marjorie said.

"I've never done this," I said.

"Dinnae fash, Hadley," Esther said. "Rest yer powers. Marjorie and I will perform the spell."

Duncan was just beginning his next round of verbal assaults against us when Esther raised her hands, and he went slack. His head tilted back, his hands falling limp to his sides. Marjorie whispered in Scots Gaelic, which prompted Duncan to lie flat and close his eyes.

It was Esther who spoke next, and I longed to understand Gaelic more than ever. The act of taking memories had plagued me for well over a year, and I couldn't help but feel the pang of anger rush through me as I considered how many humans the council had subjected to this… and witches too. This very act might have been my own fate had Fitz and I not been careful before my powers surfaced. I pushed against the rising pain and focused on the villager before me. This man didn't deserve my sympathy.

A steady stream of energy poured from both Esther and Marjorie as their powers intermingled in their path to Duncan, each fueling and magnifying the effects of the other. A dim light glowed around

The Witchkiller as his memories were pulled from his mind. Finally, the light disappeared, and Esther and Marjorie lowered their hands.

"Is it done?" I asked. "How do we know if it worked?"

"Ye'll ken soon enough with that one," Thomas said, rolling his eyes.

"We willnae ken for some measure of time," Marjorie said, casting a disapproving look toward Thomas. "But aye, once he returns to the village, we'll ken the damage."

"Aye," Esther said. "We'll ken if he recalls anything of importance."

"He is a proud man. I dinnae think he will talk of waking in the woods and suffering at the hands of three women," Marjorie said. "He will keep quiet."

"We cannae risk him waking with us nearby," Esther said. "We must go."

We gathered our belongings quickly and made our way down the hillside. I ventured one last look at Duncan before he was out of sight. He lay perfectly still, and I tore my gaze away unwillingly.

We walked as though a spell had been cast over us. Thomas fell into step beside me, and I stole glances in his direction as I was able, my curiosity raging.

"Where's Elspeth today?" I asked, striving for normal conversation.

"Collecting her wee plants for a salve," he said. "She's just on the other side of this wood. I took the opportunity to scout the area for other useful ingredients for her tinctures."

"You don't worry about her out here?"

Esther looked ever so slightly over her shoulder, clearly tuning into our conversation.

"No with the faeries about these woods," he said, shrugging. "I find it strange they didnae intervene with Duncan."

Faeries.

"The faeries dinnae laze about hoping to bag such a prize as Duncan Maxwell," Marjorie said rather dryly. "They do have other business to attend to."

"So, there *are* faeries here," I said to myself.

"Certainly," Thomas said. "Esther, have ye no been educating yer charge about such important matters?"

"Och aye. I've been schooling her without cease over the last few days since she's arrived. We're covering the wee redcaps this evening."

Marjorie chuckled at Esther's sarcasm.

Thomas's brow furrowed. "Weel, there's nae need for that. It was a simple question, ye ken?"

Just then, the wind blew warm and strange, just as before.

My skin tingled once more, and I turned to Esther, my eyes questioning.

She nodded. "Aye, 'tis them, to be sure."

"I must be going," Thomas said rather abruptly, his eyes darting around uncomfortably.

"Are ye well?" Esther asked, her brows knitting.

"Och aye. 'Tis only Elspeth will be missing me. I cannae be delayed any longer."

Thomas's energy stirred, and a thread formed above his head. Not quite the truth, then.

"If ye'll excuse me, ladies." Thomas bowed and quickly departed.

"All isnae well with him," Marjorie said. "Elspeth claims it is, but I cannae see it."

Esther met Marjorie's gaze. Her eyes were weighted, troubled by many unspoken things, but her lips were silent.

Suddenly, the air rippled near a large willow tree, and a leg glided into view seemingly born from the foliage. It was clad in warm woolen trousers, which were synched at the waist with a brown leather belt. An arm materialized, and the sleeves of the blouse were fine linen, though much of it was covered by a thick gray cape, which was secured around the neck by a gold brooch in the shape of a tree. Finally, the woman fully materialized, a grim expression resting on her features.

"Aladia," Esther said. "I am pleased to see ye again."

Aladia swept her dark brown eyes over the three of us.

"Your companion was keen to leave," she observed. Her accent wasn't Scottish, but I couldn't quite place it. It sounded a bit… Nordic?

"He wished to return to Elspeth," Marjorie said.

Aladia raised an eyebrow.

"Ye dinnae believe him to be in truth," Esther said.

"He continues to gather plants and herbs here with Elspeth, at the queen's allowance, but he is much changed since the summer."

As Aladia came closer, it was clear she was neither witch nor human. Her dark brown skin shimmered with the faint glow of faerie magic, and the feel of her power was warm, fluttering like butterfly wings along my skin. Her hair was braided and pulled into a low ponytail, and daggers were strapped at both her thigh and waist.

A scout, I realized.

"And who is this?" she asked, nodding to me.

"I'm Hadley."

"A guest of mine," Esther said.

"Your witch from the future," Aladia said.

Esther nodded.

"We don't want trouble here," she said.

"Nor do we."

She eyed me suspiciously. "Queen Tarron will desire an audience."

"For what reason?" Esther asked, her voice defensive.

"Reason? That is our accord."

"I havenae heard of such a thing."

"The queen attends your coven meetings when a new member is introduced, yes?" Aladia asked.

Esther paused, her eyes dropping. "Aye, 'tis so."

"And that is the purpose."

"The coven nae longer convenes," Marjorie said.

"Then your guests will come to these woods and be shown to the queen's hall."

My breath caught. I wasn't sure if I was more nervous or excited.

Esther paused, and I nodded to her. I didn't want to anger the faeries. We might need every ally we could muster by the end of this all.

"Fine," Esther said.

"Meet at the path at dusk in two days' time," she said before nodding and disappearing from our sight.

CHAPTER FOURTEEN

Rain poured from the dark skies, casting an appropriate mood for our journey. Villagers scattered about, their boots splashing as the rain washed over the muddy streets. Distracted as I was by the chaos, I nearly stepped right into a large puddle. I staggered to the right and bumped into a man with a menacing scowl dressed in dark wool. His ruddy cheeks matched his heaving chest, and he clutched what must have been several yards of fabric halfway under his coat in an attempt to keep his new purchase dry.

"Mind where ye're stepping, wi—" he trailed off as he met my gaze. I wasn't sure what he found in my features, but it was enough to quiet his temper. His eyes flickered with something—fear, I decided. He quickly gathered himself up and continued on.

My fingertips stung, my fire power anticipating its necessity, and I swore under my breath. Had he seen flames in my eyes? I willed my fire power dormant, and pushed forward.

When Esther and I entered the sitting room, Fitz and Hamish were seated near the fire, whisky glasses in hand. For the first time, I saw a genuine smile on Hamish's face as Fitz toasted and took a sip. They rose as Esther and I entered the room, offering us a dram, when Fitz's face grew pensive. Hamish's eyes narrowed.

"What's happened?" Fitz asked.

Esther and I looked to each other. Lying would do us no good—and Fitz would detect the lie anyway. There was no way forward but to share the truth.

"We went up the hillside near town to collect some ingredients for Esther's tinctures."

I paused. Esther motioned toward the furniture, and we all found our seats.

"A villager pursued our path and attacked us." Esther looked to Hamish. "Duncan Maxwell."

"The Witchkiller." Hamish's massive hand gripped the whisky glass tightly. I couldn't help but wonder if he had the strength to shatter it with his bare hands.

"The *Witchkiller*?" Fitz asked. "Anyone care to expand on that?"

"He has murdered innocent women in this burgh believing them to be witches doing the devil's bidding," Hamish said. "He's sanctioned by the minister, and the villagers dinnae even attempt to fight him for fear of being next." Hamish turned his head to Fitz. "He's ruthless."

When Fitz turned back to me, his eyes were wild. My encounter with Duncan would be a larger problem than I'd realized.

"What happened?" Fitz asked.

Esther and I were forthcoming with the details. When we reached the part about the faeries, Fitz stood.

"So faeries *are* here?"

"Aye," Esther said. "No all crossed during The Great Passage."

"We've been summoned to an audience with the queen," I said.

"When?"

"Two days' time."

Fitz's eyes instinctively shifted to Esther, who nodded as if he needed reassurance.

Though Esther and I had inadvertently gone on quite the adventure, we had handled it. Still, both Fitz and Hamish were fuming. The room fell silent until Hamish burst out in emotion.

"Ye cannae do this anymore, Esther. Ye cannae tempt Fate in this manner!" he bellowed.

"*Me?* Tempting Fate?" She tensed. "I cannae believe ye'd say such a thing."

Hamish met her gaze defiantly.

"Now ye wish for me to relinquish all my freedom? Is that it? I've lost far too much already."

Esther's eyes clouded, but she remained in control of her emotions.

"Nae," she whispered. "Ye wish me to live inside this wee box and pray my fate will alter?" She drew herself upright, shoulders squared. "Naw, Hamish. I can give ye a great many things, but I cannae give ye that."

She met his eyes firmly before moving to the door.

"I beg yer pardon," she said softly over her shoulder, before slipping through the door.

I turned to Hamish, who stood, shoulders squared in open challenge of Esther's words. His chest heaved, and his neck broke out in red splotches. He pushed hard against the wooden mantlepiece, gripping it tightly, and when he pulled back, his hands were red. He met my gaze.

"Will ye no just say it, Hadley?" he growled.

Fitz sat up a bit taller beside me. "Hamish," he warned.

I shook my head dismissively, my eyes fixed on Hamish.

"If ye wish to say it, now is the time," Hamish said.

"I don't have anything to say."

Hamish raised his eyebrows.

"Fine, I'll say it. This must be horrible for Esther—to stifle her powers when she must want to use them more than ever to protect herself."

Hamish sighed, but he offered no other response.

"There has to be another way," I said.

"Ye think there is a path I havenae considered?"

"No. I'm not saying that at all."

"Ye think I havenae tried everything under the sun to keep my wife alive?" he bellowed.

"Hamish," Fitz said again. This time, the grumble in his tone marked a clear warning.

"What would ye have me do?" Hamish yelled, ignoring the warning.

Fitz slid forward on the sofa, but I laid my hand on his. Now wasn't the time for a challenge.

"Enough, Hamish," Fitz said. "Ye have every right to be upset, but it willnae serve ye well to shout at Hadley. I willnae have it."

Hamish paced toward the window before coming back to the fire and dropping into a nearby chair.

"What would ye have me do?" he asked again, barely above a whisper. He turned to face us, tears welling in his eyes. "There isnae an answer."

We held still, as though even the tiniest movement would break us all.

Hamish looked through the windowpanes. "I'm as lost as the snowflakes that blow about in our winter winds. If I fight the council alone, 'tis certain death for Esther. But who will stand with me?

Annabel? We cannae overpower them on our own. Esther refuses to use Annabel's ring." He raised his hands in exasperation. "Esther refuses our plan to leave for Opimae. So, I've sent our bairns away. The villagers will ne'er find them, but the witches on the council… weel, we're tempting Fate there, aye?"

Hamish drained his cup and set it down with a thud.

"If I save my bairns, I lose Esther. And if I save Esther, I may lose my bairns." He sighed. "That alone would kill her, and then I've lost everyone dear to me." His restless hands fiddled with one another. "But I cannae lose Esther."

The tears slid down his cheeks.

"So tell me, what would ye have me do?"

I dropped my head in my hands, overcome by the weight on Hamish's shoulders.

"Aye, I thought as much. The future doesnae bode well for me."

Hamish stood and paced to the doorway, but he paused, turning back toward us.

"There's a wee hame across from my office. The man is an apprentice at a shop on the other side of the burgh. Even on the days I arrive at my shop well before dawn, he's already gone, hard at work. Each afternoon his wife meets him at the door, their youngest bairn in her arms. He kisses his wife and takes their wean from her, cradling him gently. They're poor, but they laugh together every evening as I walk down the steps to make my way hame."

Hamish paused, looking down.

"Their life is hard, but I envy that man. If Esther willnae listen to reason, my spirit will die with her at the gallows. But that man's wife willnae be taken from him and tried as a witch. He will go on loving her long after I've become a ghost."

Hamish cleared his throat.

"I cannae force ye to take yer leave, but this I will say: dinnae make this harder for us than it already is." His eyes pierced mine. "Show us this mercy, at least."

We'd barely shut the door to our bedroom before Fitz set the tone for the rest of the evening. He walked wordlessly toward the fireplace, unbuttoning his vest as he moved, and tossed the garment on the bed. He raked his hands through his hair, and my breath hitched as energy crackled wildly through our connection.

"Ye should've waited for me to come back. Or Hamish. Ye should have never gone to the hillside alone." Fitz's accent grew thicker, his voice deeper. His anger caught me off guard.

"Are you… mad?"

"Aye, I'm angry," he said, turning to face me.

"Why?"

"Because I cannae believe ye've done this!" Fitz bellowed.

"Me?" I yelled back. "What on earth have *I* done?"

"Ye put yerself in a dangerous position."

"By gathering plants with Esther?" I asked incredulously.

Fitz's nostrils flared. "Ye know damn well what I mean, and it doesnae have a thing to do with her wee tinctures." His voice was icy, eerily calm, and my eyes narrowed at his anger.

"How dare you take that tone with me?"

"What do ye even mean? I'm *no* yelling, Hadley."

"I know how mad you are right now, and it's completely unfounded."

"Oh, is it now?"

I raised my arms in exasperation. "How were we supposed to know some angry villager was going to follow us up the hillside?"

"Ye're serious? Ye think the villager is my main concern right now?"

I dropped my gaze. Of course I didn't, but the villager was easier to talk about than the faeries.

"Maybe the scout was truthful—maybe the queen just wants to meet us."

Fitz looked at me with disdain. Now wasn't the time to reason with him.

"Look, the faerie surprised me. I certainly wasn't expecting her. But the villager is what worries me. The humans are getting brazen."

"Of course they are. More arrests will happen by the end of this week, Hadley. Esther has a target on her back. Why would ye no think someone might do her harm?"

I flinched at his words, but it was more than that. I thought of the vision I'd had only hours before, and my blood turned to ice.

"This has been going on for a while. I just didn't realize things were shifting so quickly, I guess," I finally said.

"Aye. And now we've come to visit. We've stirred up interest around this little burgh—ye know we have."

His tone was clear. He was daring me to contradict him. But I wouldn't. I couldn't. I sighed instead.

"Dinnae start that."

"I know you're angry, but it's not like I got into a fight with a villager on purpose."

"I didnae say ye did. What I *am* saying is that ye have to start thinking, Hadley. This isnae Opimae. Ye cannae do as ye please and rely on yer magic to help ye sort it."

"You think I don't know that?" I asked, affronted.

"I'm no quite sure what ye're thinking right now because ye're smarter than this. This was foolish."

I rolled my eyes. It had been a bad move, but it had happened before I could stop myself.

"Did ye just roll yer eyes at me?" Fitz's volume rose.

I ignored his quip. "I didn't mean for this to happen, Fitz."

"Every move ye make causes a ripple. What if the villager had died? Did ye even consider what Fate might do?"

"Of course I did!"

Fitz's eyebrows rose. "Sometimes, I still dinnae think ye understand. This web is delicate."

"Don't do that," I said, fuming. "Maybe back in Paris I didn't understand this world, but you know I do now. I didn't go all the way to hell and back in Opimae without being crystal clear."

Fitz ran a hand over his face, stopping to pinch the bridge of his nose.

"Look, I get that you're mad, but I need you to listen to me, Fitz. Esther does this all the time—picking herbs outside town, meeting with the coven in the trees on the hillside, walking in the park. She's never had an issue before. It did occur to us that someone might follow us, and we were careful. There weren't any signs…" I sank into the chair by the fireside. "We handled it."

Fitz leaned back against the wall, resting his right foot against it. He nodded slowly. "Aye, ye handled it this time. But ye'll no go back alone. Do ye understand?"

My eyes must have doubled in size. Fitz had warned me against many dangers and shielded me from many more. He'd asked me countless times to be careful. But he'd always fought for me to have agency in my own decisions. He'd changed his entire life to protect me so I could make my own choices. He'd explained this witchy world to me so I could understand its dangers. Of course, he'd been angry in the past when I'd put myself in danger, but this was the first time he'd ever looked me in my eyes and given me an order, a command to obey.

"Are you kidding me?" I said through gritted teeth, rising from my seat. "I don't take orders from you!"

"Ye will this time." His eyes pierced through me.

I marched across the room to face him. He remained perfectly still, only his eyes shifting to fall to my face.

"I'll make that decision for myself," I spat.

Fitz exhaled before crossing his arms. The thin fabric of his shift pulled tautly against the muscles in his arms, and against my will, my pulse quickened. Fitz's chest continued to rise and fall, and I was hardly calmer. Anger burned through his emerald eyes, and the energy crackling across our connection was heated, decidedly uncomfortable.

My indignation burned through me, my fingertips tingling with warmth, but my mind was spinning in its attempt to make sense of this. Why was he acting like this? I'd gone to battle and fought against one of the most dangerous witches either of us had known. Why was this situation with a human bothering him so much? When I asked, Fitz looked away.

"No," I said, reaching for his chin and pulling his focus back to me. "Why, Fitz?"

"Have ye really no considered the last few months? Aye, I've stood beside ye in battle. I've seen ye fell yer enemies, but Hadley… I lost my father. One of the strongest, most sure, steadfast figures in my life. He's gone. This period of time in Forfar is *dangerous*. These humans are bloodthirsty. Hads, if I were to lose ye…."

His words were a balm to my anger. He was still displeased—the rage had not yet left his eyes, nor were his brows any less furrowed—but his words were honest and sincere.

I simply nodded.

He pursed his lips, seemingly in thought, and I studied them. The odd energy lingering across our magical bond filled me with deep desire. I wanted to set things right between us, and that desire was physical just as much as it was emotional.

I stepped toward him.

"Ye dinnae want to do that just now," Fitz said.

A rush of energy sent a thrill through me, and my belly ached with longing.

I swept my thumb gently across his lips. "Yes, I do."

I ran my hands along his chest, and he gripped them with his own. Then, he gripped my waist and flipped us around. I gasped as he pushed me against the wall and pinned my hands above my head. He pressed his lips hard against mine. An urgency flowed through us that refused to be repressed. Fitz's free hand roamed my body, running across my hips, the top of my stays, and coming to rest at my neck. He pulled back, his eyes smoldering and his hand rubbing against the base of my throat.

"I cannae—" he broke off, his chest heaving. "I'm right angry, Hadley. I dinnae think I can be…." He stopped himself, his lips still parted, his eyes darting about as they searched mine.

"It's not tenderness I seek tonight, Fitz," I whispered roughly.

We held perfectly still except for the rise and fall of our chests. We were suspended somewhere in time, feeling the onslaught of everything we had said—and everything we had held back. The love that channeled between us was pure and true, but the anger that encircled it was searing hot, just like the desire bubbling through me, threatening to consume me from the inside out. I struggled against the hand that pinned mine to the wall, and he pushed them back with force before moving against me and kissing me again, his decision made. I moved with him, but my skirts were inconveniently full, and my breathing grew too labored with my restrictive clothing.

"The stays…" I murmured against his lips. "It's hard to breathe."

Fitz pulled back, his gaze dropping to the garment in question. He nodded and spun me around. He worked quickly, and I sighed with the release. Fitz tugged the stays loose and threw it to the floor. His lips were on the back of my neck as his hands explored the newly freed territory. I placed my palms against the wall, and he loosened my skirts. They fell with a whoosh, and I arched into him as he explored further.

He was right—he wasn't gentle. But neither was I.

I turned and tugged his shift from his body, raking my fingertips across his back. He tilted his head back, breathing hard, and I pulled him closer to me, forcing my lips against his. He pushed my chemise upward, bringing our skin blissfully into contact. He lifted me against the wall, gripping my thighs, and I wrapped my arms behind his neck for support. I kissed him hungrily, our energies mingling wildly through our connection.

And through a mix of urgent hands and forceful movements, we made our way along our path to atonement, relentless in our pursuit of the gentle arms of euphoria.

The following morning, I woke tangled in the sheets next to Fitz and lay there for some time, unwilling to disturb our quiet moments in the soft light of dawn. Angry as we had been, we'd found our reprieve in each other, and overnight, our bodies had fallen into their familiar pattern—as though we sought each other even in dreams. Autumn's muted sunlight filtered through a gap in the curtains, and I realized that Millie hadn't woken us at our normal time. My heart fluttered, wondering if anything was amiss, before realizing Esther had probably told her to leave us be this morning.

I tilted my head up slowly, careful not to disturb Fitz's slumber. I moved my finger through the air, tracing the length of the scar on his chin. He'd made it clear that he hated the proof of battle that stretched around his chin and under his jawline, but I couldn't feel the same way. If this scar was a part of Fitz, then I was destined to love it because I loved its bearer—even through our spells of anger and darkness.

Fitz stirred, but I held still, studying his energy. It had been peaceful once he'd fallen asleep, but I wasn't sure what to expect once he awoke. Fitz rolled his head in my direction, blinking back the lingering sleep. His emerald eyes tilted to mine, but I found them unreadable. Fitz pulled himself up to his elbow, and I did the same. For a moment, we held each other's gaze, but Fitz restarted time when he reached for my hand.

"I didnae intend to be so cross last night."

"You were scared."

"Aye. I still am. The thought of losing ye…" He trailed off. "Well, ye know very well how that feels."

I nodded. It was an excruciating pain that settled deep into our bones. To lose our mates would be to lose a part of ourselves. Everything from our minds to our bodies to our magic felt the effects of that fear acutely.

"I do think your grief over Ian has muddled your judgment though."

Fitz's features clouded.

"Just a bit," I added, realizing my words sounded a little harsh.

"My feelings are heightened. That's plain enough to see, and I willnae dispute that," Fitz said. "But what ye did was dangerous, whether ye realized it or no, so let's no downplay that wee fact."

I winced at his directness, but there was no malice in his tone.

"We'll be more careful now that we know the danger has increased. But not because we can't handle ourselves," I added indignantly. "Only because I don't want to tempt Fate too much, and I know having to truly silence a human, even in self-defense, would anger her."

Fitz nodded. "Hadley…"

"What?" I asked.

"I am nae only fearful for ye. Anger still burns in me, and I dinnae much know what to do about it."

I exhaled raggedly. I didn't know where to start.

"I see your wheels spinning—it'll do ye no good. This anger runs deeper than it did yesterday, and I must sort this on my own."

I bit at my lip as I sunk deeper into my own thoughts. What did me no good was not being able to be useful to him.

"Hadley, if ye place yourself in danger again… ye realize I will burn this burgh to the ground for ye, aye?"

I held his stare, unmoving, barely breathing.

"If these villagers cry for your death, if this Witchkiller even so much as looks at ye again, if Malcolm and his wee council make moves against ye… I'll kill them."

"Fitz…."

He shook his head. "Keep yourself out of trouble. I mean it. I willnae lose ye to these godforsaken humans, the councils be damned, and if ye think I willnae make good on my word, then ye dinnae know me quite so well as ye think."

Fitz's gaze was resolute, daring me to contradict him.

"I've already lost my father to this crusade. I willnae lose my mate to it, and I'll tell ye that till my body draws its last breath."

I slid my hand along his neck, my thumb trailing along his jawline. My blood hummed as I searched the face of the man who had sworn again and again to protect me, even when I had fought against it, even when he burned all the way through with anger.

"Why do they have to hate us so much?"

"I cannae give ye an answer that will make sense," he said. "Hadley, when we traveled to Opimae, we were in awe. We couldnae have ever dreamed of a planet so filled with magic. Rather than meeting that world with hate and fear, we embraced it. These humans do the opposite. We arnae the same, and we will never understand their fear-driven hate."

I sighed discontentedly. He was right.

"These villagers are growing more restless by the day," I said. "Clearly, it won't get better, but you can't very well go out and slaughter half the town."

"If they lay siege to this doorstep thinking they'll haul ye off to your death, they've very well earned it."

How could I argue when I knew I'd do the same for him?

"Ye think you'll talk me down this time, but you're mistaken, Hadley. I'll tear the door hinges off Hell's gates to keep ye from harm."

Fitz's energy swirled around me, differently than normal—rougher, more resolute than ever. I knew it then with every fiber of my being. He meant every word he said.

There we sat, two bruised warriors who'd battle the devil himself for the sake of the other.

"I know, Fitz."

A stillness took hold of us as we took in the gravity of what Fitz had said. When his eyes met mine, my breath caught in my throat. The intensity in them took me off guard, but it wasn't unwanted. I longed to fall so deeply into our streams that there was no beginning nor end between us. My eyes flickered to the growing rise and fall of Fitz's chest. When I found his eyes again, it was decided. I wasn't sure if I moved of my own accord or if he pulled me to him, but I was pressed against him. Energy flowed through our connection, sending a euphoric rush through my body. I tilted my head back and parted my lips, allowing instinct to take the reins.

Fitz traced his lips along my neck before planting a kiss at my jawline. He slid his hand behind my neck and pulled my gaze back to his.

"Call me reckless if ye must, but I am your sword for all of eternity."

PART TWO

CHAPTER FIFTEEN

I smoothed my overcoat as we neared the edge of the forest, nerves settling deep inside me. Fitz and I were meant to meet Esther and Hamish on the far side of the woods just before dusk. They had set out thirty minutes ahead of us so we weren't seen walking together as we left town. As such, Fitz and I trudged through the damp, browned grass of the beginnings of the Scottish winterscape alone.

I stole a glance at him, his chiseled jaw clenched and his emerald eyes narrowed as the mist peppered our eyes. Fitz's anger had ebbed while in our bed, but once we had left Esther's, he'd grown aloof. His emotions were muddled, and I wasn't quite sure if it was anger that quieted him, or if it was something else. While studying him, I miscalculated a step and my boot sunk into a small patch of dense mud.

"Seriously?" I muttered.

Fitz looked over his shoulder, assessing my situation, and turned back to assist me. Fitz wasn't sullen nor pouty—it wasn't his nature—

but he did grow quiet when he was troubled. And when he was angry, it was as though a raging river formed between us, restricting our flow of energy and comfort. Navigating those tumultuous waters sometimes felt like we'd never land safely back on shore. Of course, I knew that wasn't true, but being out of step with Fitz often felt like a punishment. Whether he meant it to be or not mattered little in these moments. They were miserable all the same.

I tugged at my foot, but it didn't budge. I tugged harder, and my boot slid free with such momentum that I fell back into Fitz's arms.

"There now. I've got ye," he said. His tone wasn't soft, but it wasn't harsh either. He sounded distracted. Distant.

His conflicted emotions swirled inside me, and as my anxiety rose with his discomfort, I focused on pushing back against my racing thoughts.

I looked intently at the man I loved so dearly, and his eyes searched mine. Perhaps he needed the same comfort from me that I sought from him. I held his gaze for a few seconds too long, and our magical connection grew so intense it almost pulled me under.

Fitz set me upright, and I inspected the damage.

"Blast," I said, turning my foot to each side. "I wanted to look presentable for the queen."

I slid my boot across the grass, attempting to remove some of the mud.

Fitz raised an eyebrow. "Ye thought after traipsing through the countryside in this weather, you'd arrive in fashion?"

"Your sarcasm stings, Dr. MacGregor."

A wry smile formed at his lips. "Ye havenae called me that in some time."

I laughed lightly. "It pleases you, I see."

He shrugged.

"Well, let's get on with it, shall we? We'll be soaked to the bone by the time we find the path Esther told us about... wherever that is."

We trudged on, and I clung to Fitz's arm as we set out again on our mission. We fell silent while searching for our companions, but it was more comfortable than it had been at the beginning of our journey.

"Esther offered Annabel as a guide for us," I finally said.

"Was that meant to be a comfort?" he asked, his face contorted.

"Oddly enough, I think so. I told her I thought we'd find our way just fine on our own."

After what seemed like an eternity, three figures came into view. Esther and Hamish had made it safely, but I was surprised to see a woman I didn't recognize.

"Hadley, Fitz, we're so glad ye made it safely. Come meet Neilina, our head of coven," Esther said.

From the woman's wary dark eyes to her crossed arms to her set jaw, it was clear she was not in good humor.

"Lovely to meet ye," Fitz said, bowing his head to acknowledge the presence of a lady.

Neilina hesitated, but Fitz held her gaze firmly, refusing to release her without an acknowledgment. I studied her curiously, awaiting her response.

"Neilina," Esther said, her voice soft but her warning clear.

I studied Neilina, curious if Esther's censure would matter. Neilina cleared her throat and eyed Esther with annoyance, but she took a step forward and curtsied to me and Fitz. I met her in equal gesture.

"Ye have traveled from afar, as I understand it."

"Aye," Fitz said.

Neilina nodded once. "I dinnae think there's need of me sharing my apprehension, but I'll do so anyway. Yer presence places each of us in even more danger than before."

"We aren't here to make things more difficult for you. We're here to remedy a situation that's placed our world in danger," I said.

Fitz cut his eyes at me, his energy fluttering with displeasure. I understood if he had some apprehension with me being direct with Neilina—I did too—but what good would it do to be coy? Neilina would know the truth soon enough, and her displeasure with Annabel's ring had already been made clear. Perhaps that would be common ground enough.

"I dinnae wish ill for ye, but I willnae have ye making trouble for us here."

I stared at her plainly. Perhaps it was unfair, but I was tired of hearing the same argument from everyone. They couldn't even handle their own affairs; they had no right to make accusations at us. My fire magic sparked in my veins, and it was too late to hide it.

Neilina's breath caught in her throat as her eyes searched mine. She then turned to Esther and to Hamish.

"I have ne'er seen such," she said.

"I can't help what I am," I said. "Nor would I want to change it."

"Ye cannae be seen like this!"

"I don't plan on it, but occasionally, my anger gets the best of me."

"What angers ye today, Hadley?" Esther asked.

I hesitated, looking to Fitz. He shrugged, and I saw it then—he was resigned to watch how this scene played out. It was unlike him to just let go, and that worried me far more than his anger.

"I'm tired of being told what we're going to do. If I've heard once that we're going to place everyone in danger, I've heard it a hundred times. The reality is," I said, turning to Neilina, "the leaders of your time are clearly the danger here. Their inaction has led to absolute chaos in this burgh. How dare you say that Fitz and I are going to be a problem when you can't even solve your own."

Fitz raised an eyebrow. There was exasperation in his eyes, but at the same time, a hint of a smile tugged at the corners of his lips.

"*I beg yer pardon?*" Neilina said, her eyes wide. "Ye've only just arrived and ye're already making allegations?"

"Fitz has studied this period in Forfar extensively, and I've reviewed his research. If anyone standing here today knows the outcome, it's the two of us." My voice rose. "If anyone understands the implications of your inaction, it's us. So don't sit there and tell me that I'm the danger. You have blood on your hands, Neilina."

"How dare ye speak to me this way?" she demanded. "If this is how ye intend to behave, ye may return to yer own time."

"Ye hold nae authority over us, and we will do nae such thing. What Hadley has said may no be easy to accept, but it *is* the truth," Fitz said.

"We're taking action as best we are able!"

"Nae," Fitz said. "I cannae tell ye what to do, but it's quite another thing to listen to your lies."

"*Lies?*"

She meant to say more, but Fitz cut her off. "Aye, *lies,*" he said, taking a step closer.

I observed carefully as he continued.

"*Ye* are the reason yer coven members will die. I understand being frightened, but as a leader, it is yer responsibility to protect yer coven. They have entrusted ye, and ye will betray that trust by the end of it all."

Neilina's eyes misted. She stared back defiantly, but her energy betrayed her. It grew ripe with uncertainty.

"Ye took an oath, aye?"

She gave no answer.

"It would serve ye well to uphold that oath rather than fold at the first sign of trouble."

Esther took a step forward, placing her hand gently on Fitz's arm.

"We must go," she said, nodding toward the forest.

Aladia stood at the edge of the forest, where the trees opened just enough to admit our passage.

"If you're done arguing amongst yourselves, we should go before you're late to see Queen Tarron," she called.

Neilina took a step forward.

"Just the four of you," Aladia said, eyeing our family group.

"But I am head of coven."

"And?"

"I must accompany them."

"Not into the hall of the faeries. This isn't one of your coven gatherings. You have not been called here."

Neilina looked shell-shocked, but Aladia turned without awaiting her response. Fitz and I exchanged a wary glance, but we moved toward the forest just behind Esther and Hamish.

There was no denying that something strange lay in the woods. A chill lingered deep inside my bones as we neared the trailhead, and the energy that channeled through me was dark and ominous. I couldn't say it was overtly negative, but I hoped this wall of energy was in place to ward off unwanted visitors. Regardless, it was unlike anything I had experienced—different even from the energy of the faeries of Opimae.

We approached the opening, and my heart skipped a beat. The air was permeated by a strange, musky scent. The empty branches gnarled into a canopy, and even the bright light of the rising moon did not penetrate the darkness that clung to the forest.

"Should I?" I asked, raising my hands.

"Nae," Esther said. "The faeries will light our path."

I had never cared much for the dark. But no sooner had I taken my first step than a faint glow grew until my eyes were able to make something of the space. In addition to Aladia glowing from head to foot, she also carried a magically lit lantern. The very sight took me back to Opimae.

My mind eased slightly at the memory, and I took another step forward.

Soon, we were enveloped by the deep cover of trees, which had turned from the bare branches into luscious evergreens. The forest floor was decorated with verdant moss, ferns, shrubs, and countless flowers. The air grew warmer with each passing step, and we shed our outer layers. The forest seemed to be a greenhouse of sorts, meant to grow what could not naturally survive the harsh environment of Scotland.

Eventually, we came to a wall of trees. But just ahead of us, the branches crafted an arched opening, and within it, a glowing oval swirled like the water underneath ocean waves.

"Think of the queen as you pass through this portal," Aladia said.

Fitz looked unsure, his posture tense. I cleared my mind and thought of Queen Tarron, whoever she might be, and stepped forward.

With a bright flash of light, I stepped onto a bed of lush, green grass. We had entered a room of sorts. At the far end, two beings were huddled over a raised bed of flowers, and one of them spoke softly with the other, hands gesturing excitedly. To their left, two large trees grew next to each other, and under their canopy sat two thrones crafted from dark wood. Vines with dark green leaves entangled the thrones in a whimsical web. The high, arched ceiling was stone, and a doorway lay at the far corner. Pale sunlight filtered through, casting a soft glow across the space. The light was familiar. It was almost like…

"Fitz…" I whispered.

"Aye, Opimaean light."

When I turned to face him, his eyes were narrowed as they swept the area. I took a deep breath, steadying my nerves, and returned to my assessment. Aladia stepped to the side and extended her arm, motioning us toward the thrones, which were flanked by guards. One sat empty, but the other held quite the ethereal scene.

The queen studied us from her seat, poised to hold an audience. Half her raven hair was swept onto her head while the rest spilled down her neck and shoulders. A golden crown of vines sat atop her head, and a sage dress covered much of her dark, bronzed skin. Her dress wasn't of the 1600s, and her style vastly contrasted ours. The neckline of her garment scooped just below her collarbone, though the sleeves covered the length of her arms. She stood to greet us, revealing two slits at the front of her skirt. It was when she worked her way down the steps that I understood the design of the dress. A dagger was strapped to her thigh. Beautiful but functional for battle—a style worthy of a warrior queen.

Her dark eyes studied us intently, but a diplomatic smile spread to her features.

"You are most welcome here," she said, clasping her hands together at her waist.

"We are honored by yer invitation," Esther said.

"My apologies for my sibling not receiving you properly." She smiled tightly. Her speech, as controlled as it was, still betrayed her annoyance. "They are currently quite taken with their *flowers*."

"Oh yes! Forgive my manners."

Her sibling strode across the space, their forest-colored robes billowing in their wake. They extended their hand, shaking both mine and Fitz's. It was strange for the time, and I guessed Fitz felt the same, considering the quick look he gave me.

"My sibling—Prince Faolán of Cadhla."

The prince bowed their head, a bright grin rising to their features. Their hair was as dark as the night sky, just like their sister's, and their skin was the same deep bronze. They wore a crown of dark vines, and their golden faerie light shimmered all around them.

"My apologies if the glimmer is distracting. Pierre and I have quite possibly just created a masterpiece. A flower like you've never seen before," they said, smiling. "I am so pleased, I can't seem to tone myself down."

I took the opportunity to look around the space while Esther remarked on the prince's green thumb. We were surrounded by stone walls, but they were practically hidden behind shrubs, plants, vines, and flowers. The greenery hung from the ceiling, stretched across the walls, and was planted all around the space.

"Come," the queen said, pointing to the stone walkway.

"Pierre just finished the walkway. Isn't it magnificent?" the prince asked.

"Lovely," I said.

"The last one was so bland. I wanted a more inviting space."

Their sister sent an exasperated smile in their direction, but it only seemed to humor the prince further. The pair looked no more than thirty, but I wondered if their appearance was any true reflection of their age. Faeries had longer life spans than humans, just like witches, but as I thumbed through my mental rolodex, I couldn't recall just how long they typically lived.

As we neared their thrones, the prince took their rightful place next to their sister, and we each showed our respect through bows and curtsies.

"You have journeyed from afar. From the future?" Queen Tarron asked, her dark eyes sweeping across Fitz and me.

"Aye," Fitz said.

"Tell me, what is the purpose of your travels here?"

Fitz and I exchanged a quick glance.

"Could we not meet somewhere less fussy, Tarron?" Prince Faolán asked.

The queen slowly turned her head to her sibling, her mouth firmly set as her eyes narrowed. "That is not appropriate."

"And are these not our guests? Really, Tarron, I think they'd be more apt to answer your questions if they were comfortably seated. Jennings must have a bit of mead at the ready."

It looked like steam would escape Queen Tarron's ears at any moment. Her mouth opened slightly, but she corrected herself before it fell agape.

"We're meant to be collecting information for Fate, not hosting a tea party, Faolán."

My breath hitched at the very words… *for Fate.* I had hoped relentlessly that Fate would be our ally in this endeavor. Perhaps we were about to discover the extent of her grace—or the lack thereof.

"And can we not do both? When have we ever declined the opportunity to host a gathering?" the prince pressed.

Queen Tarron held the prince's gaze steadily, their silent exchange leaving the rest of us in suspense. Finally, the prince grinned, and the queen rolled her eyes.

Prince Faolán stood. "Please, do follow me."

As we rounded the thrones, a small opening in the trees denoted a passageway. I was unsure if I should be nervous, if we were in danger, but my body tingled in anticipation. We were traveling further into the faerie realm, and I could barely contain my excitement. Esther looped her arm through mine, her emerald eyes nearly glowing in the dim light. Fitz and Hamish glanced around, searching for any signs of danger.

We emerged from the tunnel of trees into a room with earthen floors. A few guards moved into position around the edges of the room, which was comprised of evergreens grown so thickly together, their branches were like walls. Lanterns hung from a wooden grid above us, the magical light burning brightly. Prince Faolán motioned us toward a long wooden table at the center of the clearing with two benches flanking either side. Candelabras lined the center of its surface, and with the soft lighting, the room was ethereal.

We stood near the benches, waiting for the queen to take her seat. She stood at one end of the table while the prince positioned themself at the other. Both beings glowed in the dimly lit room. A group of faeries emerged from a second opening in the foliage with two large wooden chairs and set them into place. The royals took their seats, and we followed suit.

"Now, I hope everyone is comfortable," Queen Tarron said.

"Quite," Esther said. "We are indebted to yer hospitality."

The queen gave a slight smile.

"Would you care for refreshments?" the prince asked. "Jennings, what do we have to offer?"

A tall faerie approached the table. He looked middle-aged and wore a formal robe.

"Water, mead, wine, tea, and coffee are ready at present, my lord."

"*Coffee?*" I asked.

"'Tis new to Scotland," Hamish said. "'Tis a bit strange. Might want to stick to yer tea."

I stifled a smile.

"It's not widely traded—or accepted—just yet," Prince Faolán said.

My head turned at their words. "*Yet?*"

Fitz tensed, clearly concerned about my curiosity.

"Yes," the prince replied casually.

"But you know that it will be."

Queen Tarron tilted her head. "We're meant to be the ones quizzing you."

She could hardly expect us not to wonder at Prince Faolán's words. "I apologize if I'm being too inquisitive," I said tactfully.

"Not at all," the prince said before the queen could respond. "You're observant."

I hesitated before nodding.

"I imagine that won't make you many friends in the burgh," the prince said, their face looking as though they'd tasted something sour. "But it will serve you well on your mission."

"I'm glad to hear you think so," I said, stifling my surprise at his knowledge.

We settled on tea, and Jennings departed quickly to fetch the tea service.

"And to answer your question," Prince Faolán said, "I do know that coffee will catch on. Coffee shops will sweep the world, though it doesn't quite live up to Etain's London Fog, does it?"

My stomach flipped, and Fitz took my hand under the table. "How do you know that?"

"You may ask your questions, but we may choose not to answer them," the queen said.

Smarting off to the queen was surely frowned upon, but that was precisely what I longed to do. I ground my teeth in my effort to keep quiet.

"Her majesty might not allow my answer to *that* question in particular, but perhaps you can try again."

Prince Faolán raised an eyebrow, and I cleared my throat, thinking through my next question.

"May I ask where we find ourselves?" I looked around. "Clearly, we are in your kingdom, but I don't know where your kingdom lies."

"You're not quite anywhere," the queen said. "You're nowhere."

"Are we no in the kingdom of Cadhla?" Fitz asked, his face scrunched in confusion.

"Indeed, you are," Queen Tarron said.

"But the kingdom is nowhere?" I asked.

What was I missing?

The prince stole a glance at their sister, who nodded.

"You are somewhere in time, though where, we cannot say."

We stared blankly.

"We are commanded by Fate," the queen said. "We carry out work for her on Earth."

"On Earth…" I said.

"Our brothers and sisters in Opimae take care of that world's business, but we are bound to Earth to do Fate's bidding. You are neither in Earth nor in Opimae. You do not exist currently in the past, nor are you in the future."

I frowned, confused. The queen might as well have been speaking riddles, and I was growing tired of this word game.

"This doesnae make good sense," Hamish said.

"You are correct about that," the prince said, "but it is true. We exist somewhere between time and space when we are not actively carrying out our work on Earth. Time passes, but we do not comprehend it."

My heart raced. This was madness… and I longed to know more.

"Do you mean to say you do not age in this place?" I asked.

"We do not, and neither do you. You will return to Earth the very moment that you left on your journey to Cadhla."

"Are ye… immortal?" Hamish asked.

"We do not live forever, but we do live for a long time—especially if we spend extensive time in this place," the queen answered.

"A gift from Fate," the prince said, though their eyes were distant and their tone tinged with sadness.

"And your entire kingdom rests in this in-between?" Fitz asked.

The prince sighed. "Not exactly. Those of us who are bound to Earth return to this place and know it as home. But those of us bound to Opimae call *that* planet home. But we are all children of Fate, none of us more so than Tarron and me. One thing I know with certainty is that Fate will bid her children do as she pleases."

"Might we enquire what type of work ye do?" Fitz asked.

"We restore balance when it is warranted. We often are assigned to work with human situations. But sometimes magical beings overstep. Perhaps they speak too freely with humans, the witches fall into discord with humanity or someone practices dark magic," they said. "The list goes on. Someone must assist Fate in her many endeavors."

"Now," Queen Tarron said, changing the subject abruptly, "why have you come?"

She looked pointedly at Fitz and me.

"I feel like she's asking a question she already knows the answer to," I said to Fitz's mind.

"What if they dinnae already know of the ring?" Fitz asked. *"What if we answer their question, and we're betraying my family?"*

"You may stall all you wish, but I'll have my answer," Queen Tarron said.

Her gaze made me squirm and angered me in equal measure. She may have been an agent of Fate, but she didn't have to treat us like suspects being questioned by her court.

"They're messengers of Fate. If they don't know, it's just a matter of time."

Fitz took a deep breath. "Are ye aware of a magical ring in…." He paused before sweeping his hand toward Esther and Hamish. "A ring in their time?"

"The one created by Annabel McAlpine?"

This ring was not so secretive as Fitz and I had believed it to be.

"Yes, we have been made aware of its existence."

Fitz nodded. "We have come to ensure it doesnae fall into the wrong hands."

Prince Faolán raised an eyebrow at Fitz's response.

"And why do you suppose that is your right?" the queen asked.

"I dinnae see it as our right, but rather, our duty. The ring had a natural course charted, but another witch will travel from the future to steal the ring for his own gain."

The prince sat forward in their seat.

"Hadley and I have traveled from our time to prevent him from doing so."

The queen's brow furrowed, and her eyes flitted around. Finally, she met our gaze. "Fate has not shared this with us."

"Perhaps Fate does not find that detail to be our business," Prince Faolán said pointedly to their sister. "She does not often share the full picture with us."

The queen shook her head. "You're certain of this?"

"Aye."

"Fate must know. Perhaps she allowed it to occur for a reason," the queen said.

"But Fate does not control our every action," the prince answered. "She sends us signs, warnings. She charts *some* courses, but she does not control us. Perhaps she did not stop him the first time because she did not believe it right to intervene. That doesn't mean she condoned it."

Queen Tarron nodded distractedly. "I suppose so. It's never quite straightforward with Fate."

"To be sure," the prince answered. "But their intention here seems to be an attempt to restore balance, not to disrupt it."

"Whatever their intention, it might not change the outcome," she said.

"We are trying not to alter the past in any significant way," I said.

"We will consider your efforts and consult with Fate before taking a stance on your mission," said the queen. "But I implore you to act with caution. Do not make an enemy out of us… or out of Fate."

"We appreciate your efforts," I said in an attempt at diplomacy.

"You speak to royalty with considerable ease," Queen Tarron said.

"Hadley and I were assigned as crusade leaders on a mission in our time. We have worked with many powerful leaders such as yourselves."

"We have heard rumblings of some sort of mission, but it was not ours to consider—at least, until now."

"You have contact with the future?" I asked.

"You truly do not know your place, do you?" the queen asked.

Fitz opened his mouth to speak before thinking better of it.

"I believe my place is advocating for what's right," I said. "I do not mean offense, but I won't allow the entire world to suffer for the sake of propriety."

The prince stifled a laugh. The queen sighed, but a slight smile formed at her lips.

"I know another of your opinion," she said glancing at her sibling. "But do not let the humans see it or you will find yourself in line at the gallows."

"So I am told," I said.

"And wise advice that is—ye must take heed of it before it's too late," Hamish said.

"It *is* risky, especially for a woman in their time," the queen said, nodding to Esther and Hamish.

"Does this ring you seek have something to do with the current issues in Opimae?" the prince asked.

"So, you do spend time in the future," I said, smiling.

"God, you *are* infuriating," Queen Tarron said.

The prince laughed heartily. "Yes, but she *is* right, Tarron." They turned back to me. "Yes, the Opimae we know is not the one of the past. At the moment, we live between seventeenth-century Scotland and twenty-first-century Opimae," Prince Faolán said. "Now, your turn."

I looked to Fitz.

"Aye," he said. "This ring cannae fall into the hands of Lucio Belmonte. The carnage in Opimae's future will be even greater than it is now if his son Lorenzo is able to utilize the ring."

"Unbelievable," the queen muttered.

"If you spend time in our present, how is it that you don't already know this? Or know who we are?" I asked.

"We are twenty-first-century beings," the queen said. "But as we've said, faeries are agents of Fate. She sent us here to monitor the balance of good and evil. We remain wherever we are needed most until Fate assigns us our next mission—in whatever time that may be. We see little of our own time."

"Even when we are in our proper time, it is difficult to learn of all current affairs," the prince added.

"Is Kevardhu your home, then?" I asked.

"It is our turn," the queen said, cocking her head to the side.

"Of course," I said, forcing a careful smile to my lips. She was not nearly the first difficult leader I'd faced, but after being forced off the crusade, I was tired of these delicate dances.

"What do you wish to do with the ring once you've obtained it?"

"We wish to destroy it," Fitz said.

Queen Tarron's head snapped to the side. She hadn't anticipated that answer.

"We dinnae wish to alter the past by taking the ring too soon, but we are here to ensure it is destroyed at the proper time."

The siblings exchanged a surprised look.

"And the trials? You have no desire to intervene?" the queen asked.

"Kevardhu," I said before Fitz could answer their question.

"I should dismiss you for contempt of court," the queen said.

"Sure, we can leave if you'd like," I said, standing.

"Wait," the royals said in unison.

I paused.

"We have more to discuss," the queen said firmly.

"Queen Tarron, I am honored by your invitation today. I have enjoyed my visit to your realm, and it has been my extreme pleasure to meet you both." I smiled. "However, I am no fae, and I do not fall under your jurisdiction. Though I wish to honor you, especially while I am your guest, I do have a right to ask questions."

"Hadley," Fitz said softly.

But I would not be censored.

"Though I do not wish to offend, I do not wish to *be* offended either. I have been through far more than you can imagine, I am sure, and I have learned a lot. I have a voice, and it deserves to be heard. I have questions that need to be answered… because Fitz and I have a big role to play in preserving the peace on Opimae and beyond. I am certain you love your kingdom, so let me help you."

The queen's expression was firm, but her eyes danced about as she listened. "You are truly the crusade leaders against Lorenzo Belmonte and his army?"

We were, I thought tartly.

"Aye," Fitz answered.

"Then there's the prophecy to consider," Prince Faolán said.

"I will ask you again—and I intend to hear the truth—why are you here in the past? There is more than what you have shared. Tell us of your time in Opimae. If you are honest, we will be the same to you." The queen nodded. "You have my word."

"*Faeries are famously true to their word,*" Fitz said to me.

"*Still, I'm nervous.*"

"*Aye, so am I, but we need them to remain quiet so they don't tip off the Opimaean officials—that means the leaders of Kevardhu as well.*"

"*Shit,*" I said.

"*Aye… we should be honest and ask for their partnership.*"

I took a deep breath and began.

"Holy shit," Prince Faolán said when we finished relating our history.

Queen Tarron was too preoccupied to comment on their improper remark. She bit her lip, her eyes distant. Finally, she found her response.

"The faeries have been persecuted for as long as history has been recorded. The humans accuse us of malefice, blaming us for all their misery. Other magical beings resent our connection to Fate and our duty to her, so they keep their distance from us. They believe us to be the cause of their trouble, when we are only following our orders. It has caused…."

"Strife," the prince said.

"Strife," she agreed. "Because of this, the faeries have kept to themselves, and over the years, our relationship with other beings has become minimal."

This was a different tale than we'd been told in Opimae. When I had asked about the faeries, I'd been told they kept to themselves… but we hadn't been provided this context.

"We do not often agree with the councils of Opimae. You can be certain of our silence regarding your current mission."

Relief flooded through me.

"But I cannot say what I think Fate will do with this—she is unpredictable."

"Do you have influence with Fate?" I asked. "Are you able to advocate for those you believe to be right?"

"We work for Fate, not the other way around," said the prince.

"She willnae help us with the witch hunts in Forfar?" Esther asked.

"I doubt it," Queen Tarron said. "If she hasn't intervened yet, I do not expect she will."

"We want to fight against this evil, but the leaders have forbidden it," Esther said. "Would ye be willing to assist us?" Her eyes were pleading.

"What is happening in your burgh is horrific," Prince Faolán said. "However, we are not allowed to intervene in human affairs unless directed by Fate."

"And what about intervening in witch affairs?" Hamish asked.

"What you ask would still require us to intervene in human affairs," the prince said. "As much as we'd like to help, we would be punished. Our entire kingdom would be punished."

"What would happen?" I asked.

"Likely death for the two of us," the queen said, motioning toward her sibling. "For our subjects? Perhaps the same. Some sort of natural disaster, war… whatever you can imagine, it might come to pass."

My heart fell.

"I cannot emphasize this enough: *we are devices of Fate*," the prince said. Sorrow hung in their voice. "My life is not my own. We work for our subjects, but we are ruled by Fate."

I nodded, my brows knit as I processed the heavy truth.

"We have been chosen to maintain balance, to do the work of Fate, and whether we want that or not, it is our duty."

Queen Tarron eyed her sibling, clearly unhappy with their transparency. "There is nothing to be done except the work given to us," the queen said, regret lingering in her tone.

"We do assist when we can, when it's appropriate," the prince said. "But our hands are tied here. I am truly sorry."

"And what about…" I paused, gathering my courage.

"Yes?" the queen prompted.

"What about your portal into Opimae? Would it be possible for us to cross over?"

The queen's disapproval was clear. "Absolutely not."

My disappointment was clear.

"Hadley only wishes for us to hear some bit of news about our crusaders… our wee family," Fitz said.

"I do not forbid it to be cruel," she said. "Only those ordained to carry out the business of Fate may cross this portal. Trust me when I tell you that Fate's consequences would be severe."

Disappointed as I was, I didn't want to further tempt Fate.

With our business concluded, we took our leave, and the guards moved closer to escort us back to Scotland.

The prince approached us and extended their open palm. A small bouquet of flowers materialized in the glow. The green stalks were precisely the color of the dimly lit evergreens, and the flowers were a dark purple at their base, slowly fading to lavender at the edges of the petals.

"My new varietal," they said. "When crushed, the leaves will slow bleeding in any species, and the faerie magic within them will assist in healing."

"A proper gift for this time," Fitz said.

I smiled before taking the bouquet and passing them to Esther.

"Esther is a healer," I explained.

The prince smiled and bowed their head.

The queen rose to take her leave. "Though I do not know Fate's opinion," she said, "I do know she is unforgiving. Proceed with great caution. Do not test her. Until we meet again."

CHAPTER SIXTEEN

The following morning, Fitz and I retired to the sitting room with Esther after breakfast to await a visit from her fiery aunt. I fought to get my thoughts in order before Annabel's visit, but Fitz's odd disposition and subdued energy worried me. He paced near a far window, book in hand, while Esther knit. Perhaps he was retreating inward as he processed the last few months, or perhaps he didn't know what to do with the fear that I could be tried as a witch. Seeking an extra boost of its calming presence, I removed the moonstone ring from the chain around my neck. There'd be no need to conceal it from Annabel after this conversation anyway.

Annabel's entrance shattered my thoughts. She greeted Esther warmly before nodding in mine and Fitz's direction, offering a crisp hello.

"Aunt, there is something we have a mind to speak with ye about." Esther studied her as she motioned for us all to sit. "'Tis important," she added, her voice firm.

Annabel eyed Esther, suspicion dripping from her pursed lips and narrowed eyes. "And what might that be?"

"'Tis about the wee ring," Esther said.

Annabel's posture went rigid. "What of it?"

Esther looked to me, and I nodded in encouragement.

"The ring has fallen into the hands of evil in Hadley and Fitz's time. Earth *and* Opimae are in danger."

Annabel's narrowed gaze shifted to Fitz, then to me, and back to Esther. "What do ye mean by *danger*?"

"The ring has fallen into the hands of a witch—Lorenzo Belmonte—who is threatening the balance between witch and humankind," Fitz answered. "He's already responsible for countless deaths, and he means to utilize the ring."

"How did he come by the ring?" Annabel asked.

Fitz's jaw tightened, so I jumped into the conversation to share the burden.

"After the ring falls out of Esther's possession, no one releases its power, and it's stolen from your time by Lucio, Lorenzo's father. He time-walks here… in a few weeks, in fact."

"Nae, this cannae be." Annabel looked to Esther, her eyes wild.

Esther nodded. "'Tis true."

"Och. Esther and I will release the power once the trials end. Dinnae fash—we'll see to it."

"That might be your plan, but that isnae what comes to pass," Fitz said softly.

"Dinnae vex us with any more of these lies."

"Aunt," Esther snapped.

"These are falsehoods, Esther. We will release the power as we decided."

"*Ye* decided, and yet… my fate doesnae alter from my vision."

"Nae!" Annabel said, her voice breaking. She stood hurriedly, and placed her hands on her hips.

"Ye must accept what Fate has decided."

"I willnae do that, and neither should ye. Esther, this isnae proper."

Tears welled in Esther's eyes, but when she spoke again, her voice was strong. "How many times must I say this? Pray, Aunt. Let this be the last time: I willnae risk my bairns' safety for my own. Be cross with me if ye must, but I am resolute. I shall no be prevailed upon to choose a different path."

"We have cultivated the type of power that other witches only dream of," Annabel said sternly, her voice rising. "We have thought and planned and lived only to protect ye. Ye dinnae think we havenae done the same for yer bairns? This willnae do, Esther."

"I ne'er asked any of this from ye," Esther said, her voice low and filled with venom.

Fitz raised his eyebrows. We hadn't yet witnessed this side of Esther. It was unnerving.

"I didnae mean—"

Esther held her hand up, signaling Annabel to stop. "I willnae discuss it further."

"Ye need to *fight*, lass," Annabel said, ignoring her wishes. "These other women in the burgh may no have the means to stand and fight, but ye do. Set an example. Knock the doors right off the tolbooth."

Esther sighed.

"Ye ken I am right. Ye've felt the power in the wee ring, and ye ken it's enough to silence this minister and this burgh of small-minded humans. Ye have the power to serve justice."

"That isnae my concern. It isnae my place."

"And whose is it if no ours?" Annabel asked. "Ye have the power to improve matters here—no only for yerself and yer family, but also for the poor women of this burgh."

Esther closed her eyes.

"Please, Esther," Annabel said, her voice barely a whisper. "Ye and yer Uncle John are all I hold dear in this world."

Esther looked at Annabel. "I cannae use that ring. It isnae right for me to do so, and I ken Fate will deliver punishment for it. I cannae risk it. I cannae risk us all to save my own neck—and if it displeases Fate, I'd be better served to discard the wee ring now."

Annabel hesitated in her answer, and it was just enough time for me to test the waters with Annabel on another potential plan.

"There is still Opimae to consider," I said.

Fitz's energy stirred, and his eyes closed briefly—in exasperation, I thought. Esther's eyes flashed to me, her warning clear.

Annabel's energy fluttered. The atmosphere was saturated with her fear and anger, but at my suggestion, the air danced differently— lightly—against my skin.

"Have ye considered it at last?" Annabel asked.

"Nae." Esther cocked her head, her eyes distant.

Annabel's gaze fluttered to me and Fitz, and he gave her a tight smile. His eyes pleaded, *give her a moment.* Annabel nodded, and surprisingly, she sat quietly until Esther spoke again.

"I considered Opimae as a possible path, but we cannae be certain of its success—it isnae a foolproof plan. I tossed it aside, but Hadley mentioned it again in recent conversation. Hamish is pushing me to reconsider."

"Aye, a fine route it would be. Ye'd be safe in Opimae," Annabel said.

"We dinnae ken that." Esther fumbled with her hands.

"Child," Annabel said, her voice softening. "Nothing is certain. None of us are promised our next breath." She broke off, and the looks they exchanged told me there was more to Annabel's statement than we knew. "Every choice in life is a risk. Are we meant to sit home and worry? Nae, we make our choices and pursue our paths without apology or fear. 'Tis the only way, Esther."

Esther nodded. "I long for the woman I once was. I long for the witch who wasnae frightened of every path forward."

"Dinnae allow these witch hunters a victory over ye," Annabel said. "Take yer wee family and leave for Opimae."

"And if we were to go? Would ye and Uncle John no travel with us? Ye'd remain here in Forfar?"

"Aye, it would be best for us to remain here."

"Why?" Esther demanded.

"These thoughts cloud yer head," Annabel said. "It would be too conspicuous if we all left. The key is to change as little as possible, so the witch hunters dinnae grow too angry and punish the village for our act of defiance."

"But how could I leave ye behind?"

"Ye are every bit a daughter to me, Esther." Annabel paused, taking her seat beside Esther. "I will keep ye safe until the bitter end, and I care no for how I am punished."

Esther clasped her fingers together, running her thumb nervously against her opposing palm.

"I've lived a long time," Annabel continued. "It hasnae been an easy life, but it was braw enough. I can meet my fate without qualm—as long as I ken ye're safe."

"I dinnae wish to make this more difficult for everyone. I ken ye mean to help me."

Annabel took Esther's hands in hers. "Dinnae go apologizing."

Quiet fell, marked only by the patter of rain and the crackle of a roaring fire.

"Maybe it isn't as difficult on everyone as you think, Esther." I looked to Annabel. "How would this work?"

Fitz's attention remained fixed on Annabel, even though he must have felt my gaze as I attempted to gauge his reaction. He didn't speak.

"Esther should travel to Opimae with the ring. The witch hunters will assume she fled," Annabel said. "What would they do in such a case? Search for her, but if we plan properly, they wouldnae locate her. Doesnae sound like a bad plan to me."

"And they'd be expending their efforts on a fruitless search, which would tie up resources that would otherwise be spent in harassing the women of this burgh."

"A fine point," Annabel said, nodding curtly.

It wasn't much, but it was progress.

"But it wasn't what Esther chose to do originally," Fitz said. "This plan might anger Fate—and change the entire future."

Esther pursed her lips.

"Oh," I whispered. "You'd have to return to Scotland, or else your lineage could change significantly."

"Aye, it could result in me… no longer existing."

My pulse thumped heavily in my throat. Whatever wrong we might have done, whatever mistakes we might have made, I would never allow this outcome.

I took a deep breath, attempting to steady myself.

"Another wee thought to consider is we might… break the timeline?"

I swore.

Annabel sat quietly, but the look on her face was revealing. She didn't know the answers either. From the contents of her grimoire to the vast spells she worked, I had always seen her as a source of knowledge. The fact that she was unsure made me feel worse.

My stomach twisted.

"If you didn't exist…." A chill rippled through me, and suddenly, it was difficult to breathe.

"Nae, Hadley," Fitz whispered as he moved to my side. "Let's take some deep breaths?"

I nodded, but those breaths weren't coming easy.

"It's all right. Listen to my voice. Ye are safe, and we are gonnae sort this. I promise."

I focused on Fitz's eyes, how they flooded with concern for me. I listened to his heartbeat, felt it thumping against my body, and longed for my own to match. I panted until my breaths became deeper. As the air rushed through my system, I grew calmer. Fitz wrapped his arms around me, applying just the right amount of pressure. Soon enough, my system was much closer to normal.

Fitz pulled back, though he kept his arm draped around my shoulder.

"Does that happen often?" Annabel asked.

"Not anymore," I said. "I've gained better equilibrium with my mind and body, but sometimes…." I shook my head. "The thought of something horrible like Fitz not—well, that'll bring the panic through me."

Annabel nodded.

"How are ye feeling? Need a bit of tea?" Esther asked.

I nodded sheepishly. "Please."

Esther called for Millie, and we fell quiet.

"We need to talk through this," I said.

"Are ye ready for that, *mo chridhe*?" Fitz asked. "Dinnae overtax yourself."

I searched his emerald eyes, taking comfort in these moments with him that felt normal.

"It'll help if we talk through it. I need to find solutions and rationalize."

Fitz kissed the top of my head. "If Esther guarantees her bairns will return to Scotland once the witch trials have ended, then nothing would be disturbed. History says Hamish, Annabel, and John do move away from Forfar to Glenstrae to be with Hamish's family and the children. If ye returned from Opimae and resided there instead, that might be enough to set things right."

"How do we know they'd meet their spouses and whatnot?" I asked.

"I think if they move to the area where they're meant to be, Fate would take care of the rest... dinnae ye reckon?"

"I do," Annabel said. "I think it would be enough for her."

"Aye," Esther said. "I dinnae think ye need to worry, Hadley."

"Why?"

"Because she doesnae intend to go," Annabel said.

Esther's lips tightened into a straight line.

"Well, it's good to talk everything out anyway," I said, hoping to avoid another conflict between aunt and niece.

"All right then. So, if I run off to Opimae, I must come back to Scotland to ensure Fitz's lineage is secured."

Sarcasm lingered in Esther's tone, but at least she was discussing the plan.

"And for many other reasons," Fitz said. "Perhaps the ring traveling to Opimae that early could alter the timeline as well. What if Lucio gets his hands on it at the wrong time? What if things are different—worse?"

"We can't chance that," I said.

"Perhaps the ring should remain with ye," Esther said to Annabel.

"Nae. The ring isnae meant for me."

"'Tis the same argument always."

"Why couldn't you use the ring?" I asked Annabel.

"Besides the wee fact that my heart isnae as pure as Esther's," she began, "the elements didnae bless my course with the ring in the same way. The power is meant for Esther."

I didn't have a firm enough grasp on spell work to truly comprehend it, but I understood Annabel's meaning.

"I dinnae care for being the reason ye fail in yer mission," Esther said. "I take that responsibility quite seriously."

"Thank you," I said.

Esther gave a humorless smile. We were all trying, and that was all we could ask for.

"What else have ye thought of?" Fitz asked.

"A direct appeal to the witchkind council," Esther said.

"Even if we were granted an audience," Annabel said. "Malcolm is nae friend to the witches he represents."

"So we've heard," I said.

"Even if it wasnae so, the council would sort ye immediately," Esther said.

"You mean, knowing we're from the future?"

"Aye," Annabel said. "There would be nae concealing it from them."

Fitz rose from the sofa to pace again near the fireplace. "It would add another level of urgency to the situation. They'd want to deal with us quickly."

"'Deal' is the correct word," I said. "They might want to punish us."

"Maybe," Fitz said. "But I think they'd rather us return to our time. They wouldn't want to keep us here."

"That is the most likely course of action. They'd command ye return to yer time," Esther said.

"It still catches their attention," I said. "We believe Malcolm is doing wrong, but what about the others?"

"Difficult to say," Annabel said.

I twisted the ring on my finger absentmindedly. Such a curious little object that had brought us all together. I rubbed my thumb across the stone, finding solace in Fitz's warm energy buzzing around the moonstone.

"Show yer ring to me, lass," Annabel said, extending her hand.

This was it. I moved to the chaise where Annabel sat and laid my hand on her open palm.

"This looks just like…."

"The ring you made for Esther? Yes."

"Why?"

"Fitz had it made for me. It was his symbol of protection. Just like you with Esther, he would go through any trial to keep me safe."

Annabel's eyes softened. She ran her thumb across the smooth surface of the moonstone. "I dinnae ken what to make of all this."

Her honesty shocked me, though I did my best to keep my features even. It was a welcome change. Annabel didn't trust us yet, but being cordial was a step in the right direction.

"This witch…"

"Lorenzo," I said.

"Aye, Lorenzo. What has he done to make ye fear his possession of the ring so?"

"He's attacked villages, and he has countless murders on his hands because of it."

"Perhaps carrying that shame will be punishment itself."

"I don't think he cares who or what he has to cut down to achieve his goals."

"Lorenzo is consumed with a lust for power that overshadows his moral compass," Fitz said. "We must win against him—defeat is no an option if we wish for our worlds to remain intact. If he taps into the power of that ring, it's over."

"Then we'll ensure the ring doesnae fall into his hands."

"If we dinnae succeed in our plans—"

"Nae. Dinnae say the words, Fitz." Annabel shook her head, her features filling with anger. "I cannae speak of this."

"Ye must," Fitz said.

"Aye? And who are ye to tell me that?"

Esther opened her mouth to speak, but Fitz was faster.

"I am yer nephew. I am yer blood who holds knowledge of the future. I am yer family who has traveled across time to help." He nodded once, his eyes wild. "We must speak plainly, Annabel. If we cannae be thorough, it will be our downfall."

Annabel sighed.

"The ring is meant to be destroyed by ye and Hamish," Fitz said. "If the past repeats itself and that doesnae happen, I want to ensure I can handle it myself."

Annabel scoffed.

"I willnae fail," Fitz said, determined. "Ye have my word."

"I dinnae trust that ye willnae destroy the ring before its purpose is served."

"I wouldnae dishonor ye nor Esther in that way, and I wouldnae take such brazen action against the natural course of the ring," he said. "This timing is delicate, and I recognize that."

Annabel nodded, though she didn't look convinced. "It isnae an easy task."

"I didnae expect it to be."

"And if Esther chooses to travel to Opimae?"

"Then we must sort what the right timing is," he said. "When do we agree that the ring has served its purpose? Before she crosses over? Just after?"

"Or when she returns to Scotland and the trials are truly over."

"If this is what Esther chooses, we'll find an agreement," I said, sensing another argument brewing.

"The ring must be destroyed through blood magic, aye?"

Annabel raised an eyebrow.

"Your grimoire has been passed down to me," Fitz said. "Hadley and I have studied it."

"We tried summoning the ring," I said.

"And did it work?"

Fitz looked at me from the corner of his eyes. So, Annabel *had* already placed the spell in her grimoire. It wasn't something she'd done after the ring had been stolen.

Fitz and I explained our encounter with her spell and Lorenzo's protections. We talked of my loophole magic and how Lorenzo's power was still blocking us from obtaining the ring.

"I recognized your blood spell," Fitz said. "It's how I located the page regarding the ring. Your blood recognized me hundreds of years in the future, even if ye refuse to do so now."

Esther's face fell, and though Annabel attempted to remain stoic, her energy wavered.

"Why did ye work your magic through blood?" he asked. "Why leave that page for your future kin?"

"I have planned for all possibilities," she said simply.

Annabel pushed against exploring a reality where we failed, but she had done her due diligence in private. She had a reasonable side to her.

"So dinnae stop now," Fitz said.

The air around Annabel stirred, but she sat quietly for a minute more. Finally—"When is Esther meant to be captured? Ye ken the answer to that, aye?"

"Aye," Fitz hesitated, looking to Esther.

"Nae," Esther said. "I dinnae wish to ken."

"Nor do I, but it will tell us how long we have to change yer future," Annabel said.

"There's no guarantee it will happen the same way now," I said.

Annabel sighed. "Aye, because ye've come to the past."

"Anything could change," Fitz said.

"So we wouldnae take this date as truth set in stone, but rather a loose timeline."

"Allow me to think about this," Esther said.

"Of course," I said, racing to speak before Annabel had the chance to argue. "Nothing should change in a day or two. Perhaps we should all think on this and reconvene."

"Aye, nothing major has changed since we've come to the past, and we havenae had any substantial influence on the natural course of events yet. This decision would mark the first. We have a bit of time."

I opened my mouth to speak but thought the better of it.

"What is it, Hadley?" Fitz asked.

"It's... well, I have a suggestion, but in light of this discussion about us altering the past..."

The room was still, as though someone had let all the air out. Finally, it was Annabel who spoke. "Say what's on yer mind, Hadley."

My mind raced, wondering if I should speak, as I shifted my focus to Fitz.

Fitz raised his hands. "We're in murky waters now."

"Let me start by asking a question, then. What's really going on with Malcolm?"

Esther and Annabel locked eyes.

"See, something's there. I'd like to know who we're truly up against."

"The truth is we dinnae ken," Annabel said. "'Tis widely believed he works against us—his own kind—but nae one speaks freely about what has come to pass."

"The details are… sparse, at best," Esther said. "Perhaps we could ask members of the coven."

"Now you're on to something," I said. "Besides Fitz and I wanting to understand who we have to contend with while here, it's beneficial for you to know as well."

"If he's actively working against other witches, investigating him would help all our causes," Fitz said. "Perhaps this is an overstep, but I am uncertain."

"I have a mind to agree with ye—on both parts," Annabel said. "I'll risk the consequences. Let me speak with a few members of the coven."

"Fitz and I could help."

"Nae," Annabel said. "That would raise suspicion. I'll handle this bit."

"Hamish will want to help ye," Esther said.

Annabel's eyes narrowed ever so slightly, but she agreed.

"Katherine seemed to know more than she shared the other day," I said. "Perhaps begin with her?"

Annabel sighed, but before she could respond, Esther stood. "If ye'll pardon me."

She left the room quickly, and we all exchanged wary glances at the thud of door closing.

"There's one other point I'd like for us all to consider," Fitz said. "We cannae wait for Lucio's first move. Perhaps we can sort if he's here."

"I have a locator spell that rarely fails," Annabel said.

"Neither of us are too keen on spell work, so we'd be grateful for your guidance," I said.

Annabel nodded. "Ye both possess immense power. Ye should be proficient in spell work as well as yer elemental skills. 'Tis vital."

Fitz's eyes clouded, and I could almost hear his internal groan, but he recovered quickly. I'd learned early in our relationship that he hated spell work.

"The spell works best with a few coven members. Might I include Marjorie and Elspeth in our work?"

Fitz and I exchanged a wary glance.

"I dinnae trust many, but I can vouch for them."

I wanted to believe Annabel, and I wanted to trust the women of this coven, but Opimae had left a scar that went further than my night terrors. I didn't know if I could trust new team members. Not after Keoni's betrayal. We had found an ally in Esther, but beyond that, I wasn't sure.

"I think we have to take a leap of faith here," I said to Fitz's mind.

"Aye, though I dinnae much like it."

"Aye, include them then. We'll need whatever edge we can muster," he said.

"There is one condition, though," I said. "Only Marjorie and Elspeth. I don't know how I feel about Thomas."

Annabel raised her eyebrow. "That makes two of us, then. I dinnae ken what's amiss, but... weel, he was seen at the tavern with Malcolm last week. It wasnae the first time either."

"Ye suspect they might be working together?" Fitz asked.

"I didnae say that, but I wonder if he might be playing at some game. Perhaps he wouldnae mind passing time in Malcolm's company to ensure Elspeth's safety, ye ken?"

"Let's hope your research will yield some answers about Thomas and his ties to Malcolm," I said.

"Then it's settled," Fitz said. "We leave Thomas out of the invite. We should set a time to meet. The sooner, the better."

"Lucio is dangerous to us all," I said. "There's no guarantee he won't steal the ring before Esther needs it if he sees the opportunity."

"Then we'll do what we can to find him," Annabel said resolutely.

"We knew the past so well, but nothing is certain now," I lamented.

"I ken the future is uncertain now, but for my part, I am glad. Regardless of what Esther has said today, her energy has changed. I ken her well enough to ken she's considering another plan."

"You really think so?" I asked.

"Aye, I do. For the first time, I'm allowing myself to hope."

CHAPTER SEVENTEEN

After learning about our plan to locate Lucio, Esther invited Katherine to join us. Annabel would be displeased, but Fitz and I kept quiet. It wasn't our business, after all. Besides, there was something about Katherine—she possessed a calmness about her that I found soothing, and she had proven to be an ally thus far. I was growing quite fond of her.

Considering our upcoming spell work, I decided to work on my craft as we awaited Annabel's arrival. I had just added a new line to my spell in progress when Millie announced our visitors.

Annabel strode into the room flanked by Elspeth and Marjorie. Her face fell briefly when she registered Katherine's presence, but after a slight delay, she nodded in Katherine's direction. I didn't think Annabel truly held ill will toward Esther's friend, but she certainly wasn't warm with her either. Whatever the case, I was happy to find everyone at least civil as we gathered in a circle near the hearth.

"This locator has ne'er failed me," Annabel said. "It has the most precision of any locator spell I have used—mine or otherwise."

"What is our price?" Elspeth asked.

"It will claim a wee bit of yer energy, but we are many. With seven of us, the tax will be light."

"I dinnae mean to overstep," Marjorie began, "but is Katherine strong enough for spell work right now?"

The room fell quiet, and all eyes turned to Katherine.

"Ye dinnae think so, it seems," Katherine said.

"I said nae such thing. I was merely asking. Ye've grown frail, Katherine. Ye cannae deny it."

Katherine looked as though she wished to do just that, her brows furrowing and her mouth set tight, but before she could answer, Esther interrupted.

"She'll do fine," Esther said. "I've worked this spell with Annabel before, and it wasnae taxing even for the two of us."

"As ye say," Marjorie returned.

"I ken we usually dinnae allow men to partake in these wee spells of ours, but Fitz isnae only a powerful earth witch from Esther's bloodline," Annabel said. "He also holds a connection to Lucio, and I believe he will increase our odds of a precise location."

Annabel paused, allowing time for any objections, but none came. She then motioned for Fitz to move in closer. He settled into place at my left and shared a warm smile with Esther, who stood to my right, her eyes bright. We then moved to the floor and shimmied ourselves until we formed a perfect circle.

The significance of the moment wasn't lost on me. Fitz was about to cast a spell alongside his ancestors, something I would never be able to do. Though I was glad Fitz knew exactly where he came from and that he had grown up in a magical household, I was pained that I couldn't have the same experience. I thought of Gram. Where were my magical ancestors in this time period?

"Since we are in agreement, let us begin," Annabel said, pulling my focus back to the group.

At her statement, Fitz's eyes filled with wonder, and his energy hummed excitedly through me. My own nerves tingled at the thought of our task. If we located Lucio—assuming he was already here—it made our task with the ring feel that much more real. Fitz turned to me and smiled, and the warmth between us fluttered.

Annabel led us through meditation to steady our minds, bringing us into the proper stream of consciousness. She then pulled open a map of Forfar and rolled it onto the floor in the center of the circle. She set four wooden candle holders on the corners of the map, then rummaged through her bag for four white candles, setting them in the holders before glancing in my direction. She was testing me, I thought, but this was a test I would ace. I called a flickering flame to my pointer finger and lit the first candle. A soft intake of air rushed through Elspeth's lips, while Marjorie and Annabel sat silently, transfixed. After lighting all four candles, I extinguished my flame and looked at Annabel, a bit smug.

Annabel pulled a juniper branch from her bag and handed it to Esther, who leaned toward the fire and lit the branch. Once it caught, a steady stream of smoke poured from it. The room filled uncomfortably with heavy smoke, and just as it grew almost unbearable, Esther tossed the branch into the fire and opened the nearest windows. Annabel passed a bottle of whisky around the circle, and we each took a swig.

"A restorative after cleansing the negative energy from the space," Esther explained.

Cold air drifted through the room, and I breathed easier again.

Annabel then picked up the candle nearest to her.

"Let yer thoughts turn to Lucio," she said. "This spell works only if we are of one mind."

She held the candle out in front of her and began muttering unintelligibly. As Annabel spoke to the elements, I thought of Lucio. I imagined every detail I could, everything I knew about him. I envisioned his face, his movements, the sound of his voice, pulling his energy closer to me and to the elements surrounding us.

Still chanting, Annabel tipped the candle, spilling melted wax onto the map. Instead of hardening, the wax remained liquid. Annabel set the candle down and moved her hands over the board, hovering just above it. The wax followed her path until the last words of the spell left her lips. I held my breath as the pool moved around the map, seeking its resting spot. Finally, the wax ceased its movement, but something was wrong. The wax wasn't at rest. Rather, it seemed as though it was meeting an invisible barrier.

Annabel grimaced, perspiration gathering at her hairline.

"What is the matter, Aunt?" Esther asked.

"The wax, 'tis fighting me."

"What can we do?" Marjorie asked.

"I dinnae ken. I've ne'er seen this before."

I leaned forward, and Marjorie was quick to place her hand in front of me.

"Careful, Hadley. We dinnae ken what might be amiss."

I felt my way forward slowly, and sure enough, I was met by a protective energy. My pulse quickened.

"Are ye all right?" Fitz asked, his brow furrowing.

"This energy… Fitz, it's him—Lucio."

Annabel's spell was true. Lucio was here. I knew it in the depths of my soul.

"He has a powerful protection spell masking his energy. Your spell is butting up against it."

"Aye," Fitz agreed. "It feels like an elemental protection."

Annabel frowned. "I dinnae ken how to break it."

"Hadley?" Fitz asked. "Can your loophole magic sort this one?"

I closed my eyes and placed my hands just above the map, feeling for the edges of the protection. Sure enough, just like his son's, Lucio's spell would be straightforward enough for me to unravel.

"Yeah, I can do it."

I looked to Fitz, and he understood instantly. The group's magical energy was crackling around the space at full throttle, distracting me. It would also skew my results.

Fitz asked that everyone focus their magic to supporting me in my task, and I set to work. I found the tingling ends of the spell nipping at my fingertips and connected to them. Everything from my fingertips to my torso burned with the initial impact.

"Take a few deep breaths before continuing," Fitz said, monitoring my progress.

I nodded and followed his instruction.

"Exhale and release his energy."

The sound of his voice was soothing, and I allowed my senses to sink into that rather than the pain of Lucio's energy. Soon, I broke my threshold, and the pain dulled. With the extra boost of energy from my magical sisters, I tugged hard at the edges of his protection.

It unraveled.

Fitz placed his hand protectively on my back and rubbed gently until my energy returned to its former state.

I nodded to Annabel. "Let's try that spell again."

This time, it worked.

I smiled with pride as the wax rolled around the map's surface. Finally, it stopped over one of the headings, but as the seconds ticked by, the wax refused to harden.

"Is this normal?" Fitz asked.

"Nae," Annabel said. "It hardens quick."

The wax split in two, and each half crawled across the map. The crinkling of the map and the crackle of the fireplace were all that stirred. Everyone was silent, hoping for the best.

Finally, the original bit of wax came to a halt.

"Oh god," I said. "There he is."

"Just to the southwest of the burgh," Esther said.

"He must be encamped there—there are nae hames in that area," Annabel said. A spark lit in her eyes. "*But* there was an old settlement in those woods. It has fallen to ruins now."

"The Bruce homestead," Marjorie said. "It belonged to my ancestors."

The last of the wax rolled to a halt.

"Nae!" Elspeth exclaimed.

"What's wrong?" I asked.

"The wax," Elspeth said, her voice faltering.

Esther leaned closer. "It appears to have stopped…." Esther paused, her eyes locking with mine. "'Tis stopped over Elspeth's hame."

"Nae," Elspeth whispered. "I must go! Oh, what if something has happened to Thomas?"

"Ye must wait!" Esther exclaimed.

"Aye, give this a moment," Annabel said.

Elspeth didn't look convinced, but when Katherine made a fuss in her attempt to stand up from the floor, Elspeth rushed back to the circle.

"What are ye doing?" Elspeth asked. "Sit still!"

"Ye cannae rush to yer hame just yet," Katherine said. "We dinnae even ken that this is correct, and ye'll need our power if Thomas is in danger."

Elspeth seemed torn, and when she met my gaze, I nodded. She then focused on the map, her eyes wild with fear. Maybe I was wrong about Thomas. Maybe it truly was circumstance that had driven his behavior—and the distance between him and Elspeth.

Finally, the wax hardened.

"This cannae be right," Annabel said. "He cannae be in both places."

"He can if he's a spirit-traveler," I said.

All eyes turned to me. Magic still crackled intensely around the space, and with everyone's focus shifting to me, it was overstimulating. I dropped my eyes to the map and focused my senses there before continuing. "That's one of my gifts. His body and his spirit could be separated."

"Aye," Fitz said. "That makes good sense, but we cannae count on that—this is only one theory."

"But what would he want at my hame?" Elspeth asked.

"If he's here—if he's truly in Forfar right now—he's collecting information," I said, turning to Annabel. "He's searching for details about the ring."

Marjorie stood. "If this man is as dangerous as ye've said, then we're sitting ducks! He'll have us all sorted soon enough."

Esther's face grew stern.

"Now, cease this noise, Marjorie," Annabel said. "*We'll* be the ones to sort this mess, and I'll hear nae other opinion on the matter."

"Should we tell Neilina?" Elspeth asked, her energy frantic.

Katherine looked to her disapprovingly. "Nae! She needs no ken what's amiss here. Calm yerself," Katherine said to Elspeth. "I am inclined to believe Hadley's theory. Thomas is fine. Let us solve this ourselves."

"I need to ken it—now," Elspeth said, her eyes pleading.

"Then let's go find out," I said.

"I'll ask Hamish to accompany us," Esther said.

Dusk had fallen. We dashed over the dark streets of Forfar, the illumination of lanterns and the waxing crescent moon our only sources of light. We stumbled over potholes, and our boots sunk into the fresh mud as we closed the distance to Elspeth's home.

We snuck up the old cobblestone path, and Elspeth pushed open the wooden door. The house was quiet, the silence loud in the dim light. Elspeth bid us wait in the foyer as she followed the flicker of firelight into the nearby sitting room. I grew restless as we awaited her return, and I focused instead on the energy of the house. I recognized Thomas's immediately, distinct, unsettling. Beyond it was the faint tremor of magic from the other witches in the home, but I had little time to consider it before she returned, Thomas at her heels.

"I thank ye for accompanying Elspeth hame," Thomas said, his breath labored.

"What is amiss?" Esther asked.

"I dinnae ken. I fell to sleep while reading in the sitting room, and when I awoke it was with a sense of dread." Thomas looked around the room. "I ken it sounds mad, but I feel with certainty that I was under watch."

"By someone in the room, you mean?" I asked.

Thomas's eyes grew distant in thought. "Aye. The energy of another was strong about the room. They must have been near."

Elspeth covered her mouth, her eyes troubled.

"Shall we take a wee look about?" Hamish asked.

"Please," Elspeth said before looking to Thomas.

He nodded. "I think it best we do."

Thomas had searched part of the downstairs area already, but we broke into groups of two and combed every inch of the house. The energy had mostly dissipated, but Thomas was right—another witch had certainly been in their home, at least in some form.

"We are no verra familiar with spirit-travel," Elspeth said to me. "Do ye reckon the witch was in spirit form or nae?"

"It's difficult to say, especially since the magical footprint had already faded so much. I'd keep an eye out, though," I said. "With spirit-travel, you *can* perceive their energy, but it's difficult. Be vigilant, Elspeth."

"Aye," Elspeth said. "Thank ye kindly, Hadley."

"Should someone remain with ye this eve?" Marjorie asked.

Elspeth and Thomas looked to one another.

His brow was furrowed in thought. "I dinnae ken. This witch has left, but I suppose they might return."

"We could work a stronger protection around the house," Annabel suggested.

"Aye, that's just the thing," Marjorie said.

The spell was quick—and quite strong with a group of our size. Even Elspeth's worry eased at the feel of our collective magic.

"Shall we reconvene tomorrow?" Katherine asked. "Will ye track Lucio?"

All eyes turned to me and Fitz.

"We'll visit the ruins tomorrow and investigate," Fitz said. "Hopefully, we'll find something useful."

"I'll accompany ye, if ye'd like? I am familiar with the area," Esther asked. "Hamish too."

"A braw idea," Fitz said. "If we do happen upon him, I dinnae know how he might respond."

"I'll join ye," Annabel said.

"Are ye certain?" Esther asked. "Ye're no worried about yer knee?"

"What's the matter with your knee?" I asked Annabel.

"'Tis nothing to concern anyone," Annabel said, shrugging off Esther's concern.

"Her right knee gives her trouble sometimes," Esther said. "I only worry about an injury."

"Quit yer fussing. I'll be fine."

Esther didn't argue further, though her eyes narrowed. She wasn't pleased.

"Let's talk strategy this evening and plan from there," Fitz said. "Tomorrow, we'll find ourselves a thief."

CHAPTER EIGHTEEN

A couple of days had passed since our encounter in the woods with The Witchkiller, and we thought it was well past time for us to make an appearance in town, lest the witch hunters grow suspicious at Esther's absence. We wouldn't search for Lucio until the evening. The MacGregor staff had kept their ears to the ground, but no mention of The Witchkiller had surfaced. No one was spreading wild tales about a scuffle in the woods with a bunch of witches, and no word had been whispered that Duncan had hurt himself. Perhaps he was laying low until his wounds healed.

Esther and I had just readied ourselves for departure when a knock sounded on the door. Millie's hand was already resting on the handle, and she laughed at herself for jumping. She opened the door to Marjorie Bruce.

"Good, ye're both here," Marjorie said. "Thomas and Elspeth have had a bit of news about Duncan this morn, and I thought ye'd like to accompany me to the shop to hear of it yerselves."

Esther and I eyed each other pointedly. "Aye," she said, turning to Marjorie.

"Let's be on our way, then."

Town was quieter than normal, perhaps due to the icy conditions of the day. Sleet fell from the sky, and a heavy downpour overnight had left the ground muddy and perilous. We trudged along slowly, holding our skirts as best we could while avoiding the larger puddles. Soon enough, we found our way to the old shop filled with tinctures and dried herbs. Smoke rolled from the chimney, a promise of warmth.

We were standing under the small awning, shaking the excess precipitation from our clothes, when the door opened. Elspeth's face lit at the sight of us.

"In with all of ye. Quickly!" she said.

We followed her instruction, and Elspeth locked the door behind us. She placed an arm around me as she guided me toward the fireplace at the back of the shop. "I thank ye once more for yer assistance yesternight."

I smiled broadly. "I take it there were no further disturbances?"

"Nae. I tossed and turned all night, but all is well."

Esther's friends had all been kind to me, but Elspeth's quiet demeanor was especially endearing. She radiated warmth, even amid the uncertainty with Thomas, and that had a calming effect on my anxiety.

Thomas motioned to a table near the fireplace. As we took our seats and exchanged pleasantries, Thomas's energy prickled on my skin, and despite her concern for him the previous evening, Elspeth's distance with him continued to pique my suspicion. It was easy to observe him once everyone was settled, as it was Thomas who began our conversation.

"We've finally had word of Duncan. He sent for Harris this morn—the physician," Thomas said, turning to me at the last bit.

"Old Harris was in the shop just this morn in search of a wee salve of ours. Something to aid in treating burns." Elspeth raised an eyebrow before grinning. "I shouldnae be pleased with it, but this man has been a blight on us for far too long."

"It must be pretty bad if he's calling for a doctor," I guessed.

"Aye. Harris said his wound is mighty angry—red and swollen—and the sickness has spread through his chest. He said Duncan should have called him sooner. He isnae certain he can save him."

I swore before covering my mouth.

Elspeth placed a hand on my forearm. "Dinnae feel bad, lass. Ye were only defending yerself."

Esther eyed me, but it was Marjorie who spoke first. "Hadley has seen battle, as I understand it. I dinnae think she is displeased, Elspeth."

Elspeth blushed but clicked her tongue at Marjorie, pulling a mischievous grin from her.

"I'm not upset about him being wounded. This burgh is better off without him."

"Then what is the matter?" Thomas asked.

"Fate," Esther said. "If he dies, then she's altered the past significantly."

All eyes at the table darted to me.

I nodded, my mouth pulled into a hard line. "There's nothing I can do about that now. Nothing but wait and see if he heals."

"So, he wasnae meant to die before?" Esther asked.

"I don't know. I've seen nothing about him in our research, but I can ask Fitz if he recalls anything. He didn't seem to know him by name, but perhaps something might spark his memory."

"If he *was* meant to die, Hadley saved us from dealing the death blow," Marjorie said distantly. When she noticed us all looking at her, her eyes widened. "I beg yer pardon," she said to me. "I didnae intend to say that aloud."

I waved off her apology. "I'm not sensitive to the truth… not after the journey I've been on this past year."

Elspeth eyed me sympathetically, but it wasn't pity I sought. I only meant to ease Marjorie's mind.

"Was it difficult?" Marjorie asked. "The first time, I mean."

"Yes," I said simply. "It was horrible."

"I am sorry," she said. "But I must confess I am pleased Duncan will take our secrets to his grave."

"I hope he doesnae begin talking as he nears death," Esther said. "I have heard that often occurs."

"The physician would normally believe 'tis only death's delusions, but with the burgh being as it is now…" Elspeth trailed off.

"He might report it to the minister," I finished.

"Aye," Thomas said.

"We cannae risk that," Marjorie said simply, her eyes on the floor.

"The more I think of it, the more confident I am that we were successful in erasing his memories," Esther said. "This worry is all for naught."

"Did the physician share how Duncan claims he hurt himself?" I asked.

"Aye, said he was tending a fire and fell."

"And the man believed him?" Esther asked.

"Och aye. He went on about the importance of safety around open flames and warned me to be mindful of myself around the hearth here."

"That's a good sign, at least," I said.

A booming knock sounded at the door. We all rose to our feet.

"Open the door, Thomas!" a man's voice shouted.

Thomas halted, and when he turned back to us, the blood had drained from his face.

"What is it? What's the matter?" Elspeth asked, her eyes filled with fear.

"'Tis the minister."

My heart dropped straight into my stomach.

"He has nae business with us," Elspeth said firmly. Her energy went from warm to furious.

"We know you're in there!" the minister called. "Open the door, or we will open it ourselves."

Thomas swore, but he moved to the door and unlocked it.

The door swung open violently, and the minister strode into the room flanked by several large men. A crowd of people perched underneath the awning.

"What is the meaning of all this?" Thomas asked.

"Elijah here has some concerns we must address."

"Och, does he now?"

The look Thomas gave Elijah was piercing, but Elijah refused to look away, glaring back at Thomas. "Aye, and yer wee meeting here is suspicious."

"Why is that?"

"A group of witches meeting in broad daylight on Main Street! Ye dinnae even attempt to hide it."

"How dare ye come into my shop and make these accusations!" Thomas fired back.

"Ye've become quite brazen, but we have remedy for that." Elijah's lips pulled back tightly, showing his scattered teeth. He was seething.

"Elijah believes ye to be consorting with the devil," the minister said.

"Och aye? Just now, in broad daylight, in front of the market for the whole burgh to see?" Thomas returned mockingly. "Weel, we'd be brazen indeed were any of this true. More idle lies from this one," he said, nodding his head in Elijah's direction.

"How dare ye speak to me that way, witch!"

Elijah launched himself at Thomas, but Thomas clocked the move just in time. He hunched to block the initial assault, and the two of them fell to the floor, wrestling. Our entire party cried out, and I nearly broke from the other women, but Esther held my arm.

"Show them ye ken how to fight and they'll have ye in the tolbooth by the next chime of the clock. And ye'll lose yer upper hand before ye need it most."

I stared blankly at Esther, wondering what her last words meant, but my focus was pulled back to Thomas and Elijah as the guards tugged them apart. My fingertips tingled with magical desire, my pulse racing. I wanted nothing more than to obliterate every human man standing in the room. I breathed deeply, extinguishing the flames that threatened to spill over.

"Keep your wits about you!" the minister called, pulling my attention to him. His accent was undoubtedly English, and I realized he'd been sent by the Anglican Church to have a presence in this heavily Catholic community. As Hamish had said, King Charles might have been tolerant, but the unrest and vitriol hadn't simply died with the previous monarchs.

Father Evans stood out, not only because of his accent, his dialect, or his pretentious air, but because his presence was completely out of place. This burgh was mostly comprised of working-class Scots. These people were *real,* and a bit rough around the edges. But the minister was clearly of "good" English breeding, expensively educated, and thoroughly indoctrinated by the king's church to ensure allegiance from the Scots. He would follow a preset plan to provoke fear, and then "save" the burgh from disorder and evil. It was brilliant, really.

"Elijah, please present your evidence to us."

"I was walking hame one eve through the old trees to the west of the burgh when I happened upon a strange scene. Fire raged about twenty feet down the tree line, and women were dancing about it. I kenned it was witchcraft, so I didnae move close for fear of being cursed."

Mutters and nods sounded across our small audience.

"I saw Helen Guthrie, Janet Stout, Agnes Cameron," he continued. He snapped his gaze to Marjorie. "And Marjorie Bruce."

"*No,*" I whispered.

Gasps echoed through the room.

"I saw it plain as I see each of ye!" Elijah said, making eye contact with his fellow villagers. "She was dancing with the devil himself!"

"Ye should be ashamed of yerself!" Elspeth yelled. "How dare ye make these false claims!"

"Mind yer tongue, witch, or I'll cut it out!" Elijah spat.

Thomas broke from the crowd, clearly set on another scuffle with Elijah, but he was subdued quickly by the guards.

"You'll cease this violence now unless you wish to spend time in the tolbooth yourself," the minister said. He then looked to Marjorie. "And you'll come with us for questioning."

"Nae!" Elspeth yelled. "Ye willnae take her. She's done nae wrong."

"Guards," the minister said calmly.

The guards had Marjorie quickly by the arms, and Elspeth was just before them, grabbing at their hands in a feeble attempt to free Marjorie.

"Someone subdue this woman before she earns herself a stay in the tolbooth!"

Esther and I pulled Elspeth away from Marjorie. She struggled against us, but we overpowered her. Elspeth shook violently as she sobbed, and as she sank to the ground, we supported her, lowering ourselves with her.

"All will be well, sister!" Marjorie yelled above the noise of the crowd. "Ye'll see. I have done nae wrong!"

The crowd jeered and hurled insults, but Marjorie held her head high. The guards removed her from the shop and made their way slowly toward the tolbooth. The minister swept his eyes across the rest of us before silently passing through the doorway. This was it— the first witch captured. The clock was ticking. How long before our time ran out?

CHAPTER NINETEEN

With Marjorie's arrest, we delayed our expedition to Lucio's potential hideout. Esther was in no shape to accompany us, and truthfully, I wasn't in much better condition. The agony that gripped me brought with it intense moments of rage, and then sadness. I was humbled beyond hope after hiding my power and allowing the witch hunters to take Marjorie to the tolbooth. Hate had won.

To add to the mess, Fitz and I wondered about the timing of the arrest. Fitz hadn't brought his notes with us into the past, but as we worked through the timeline, he concluded Marjorie hadn't been arrested quite this early. The question arose: was this a result of our meddling?

I lay in bed the following evening, staring at the warm woolen canopy as I imagined what the rest of Marjorie's story might have looked like had the witch hunters spared her. It was pointless, but it gave me some small measure of peace to imagine her anywhere other than the prison cells of the tolbooth. Finally, my nerves eased, and the call of sleep beckoned me. The edges of my mind grew fuzzy, my pulse slowed, and darkness pulled me under.

Pale sunlight cast itself across the worn wooden floors of the massive room. The light was strange, but I recognized it instantly—it wasn't the glow of Earth's sun, but rather of Opimae's two suns. Rows of long tables and chairs stretched up a steady incline, like a large lecture hall at a university. A podium and small opening sat at the front of the room, which was unoccupied except for a group scattered across the first few rows. Most of our team members were in discussion with several Opimaean leaders. Their voices were low and even, but their tone betrayed their urgency.

"Saoirse says the troops have made little progress. She thinks we'll lose a great many beings if we don't pull back by sunset," Lana said. She removed her jacket, exposing pale arms littered with bruises. Dried blood was caked in her honey-colored hair. Lana had been our head of security in Opimae, and her mate, Saoirse, was a military scout. Lana was a warrior through and through, but even so, it pained me to see such a kindhearted and ethereal elf in such a state.

The Opimaean leader, Charles, swore, dropping his head in his hands.

"We haven't won in battle since Hadley and Fitz were sent away," Molly said. "Fate is against us."

My breath caught; she hardly looked better than Lana. Her umber eyes were troubled, and a large bruise covered most of her right cheek. Blood was smeared on her neck, though it was questionable whether it belonged to her.

"There is no doubt in my mind that the chamber has made an egregious error," Prime Minister Bakari said. "Look at where we are now."

The prime minister of Thalassa—and confidant of Queen Marina—looked pointedly at King Alden, the leader of a large Druid kingdom.

"I thought we were acting with caution and wisdom—removing the biggest risk by reassigning Fitz and Hadley—but now I fear we've made a mistake," King Alden of Bain said, his voice heavy with regret.

"I won't waste time saying I told you so," Charles began. "You allowed your prejudice against the Earth team to cloud your judgment. I do hope the chamber will learn from its mistake. Sending our crusade leaders back to Earth has only set us back."

King Alden nodded.

"Fate is certainly angered," Queen Marina said.

"Aye," Henry said. "Just look at what happened today."

He pushed a lock of hair out of his face and winced. Isaac leaned over to inspect the damage and fished a handkerchief from his pocket to blot at the wound. My heart tightened at the sight of Fitz's best mates.

"Far too many beings have lost their lives. This is a tragedy," James said, shaking his head. "And ye must have that wound inspected immediately."

Henry waved off his concern, but the look James and Isaac exchanged showed he was outnumbered. James wasn't always right, but his experience was vast. I'd learned to heed his knowledge—both in witchkind matters and at the castle, where he'd been my manager before the chaos of the crusade took over our lives.

"We're losing ground," Molly said. "Good soldiers fell to take back Adamo, but we're one setback away from losing our footing again."

"Everything we sacrificed will be for naught," James agreed. "We cannae afford another loss like the one at the old lookout."

"And let us speak plainly about the crusade leaders," Prime Minister Bakari said. "Lorenzo will become reckless if he realizes where they've gone. His desire for their power and allegiance will result in catastrophe."

"We need Hadley's loophole power. That's how we gained intelligence that helped us before," Molly said.

"And both Fitz's power and intuition with strategy is sorely missed," Isaac said.

The team grew quiet, exchanging meaningful glances.

"Do you think the chamber will vote to bring them back?" Henry asked.

"The chamber recognizes we will fail if we remain on our current course," Charles said. "If we reconvene, I believe they could be made to see reason."

"If we fall back this evening, it'll require another session anyway," Prime Minister Bakari said.

"Let's put it to a vote," Charles said. "Each of you has sacrificed heavily during this crusade and has proven yourselves as leaders. Every being in this room has a right to have their voice heard."

Charles paused, but no opposition was raised. Gazes were cast in King Alden's direction, but he only nodded.

"All those in favor of continuing today's battle, raise your hand."

No one stirred.

"All those opposed."

The room rippled with movement.

"It is decided then. Lana, will you give the order?"

"Gladly," she said, rising from her seat and exiting the room.

"I don't see how anyone could vote against bringing Hadley and Fitz back," Molly said, breaking the silence. "Any chance to regain Fate's favor is worth it."

"We must move swiftly," King Alden said. "If we call for Fitz and Hadley in the coming days, how quickly might we have them back on Opimaean soil?"

Henry met Charles's gaze, his eyebrows raised. Charles leaned forward and nodded.

"This will be interesting," Prime Minister Bakari said.

"Aye."

"You all seem to share in a secret that I have no knowledge of," King Alden said. "Enlighten me."

The beings around the room met one another's gazes warily. Charles looked to Queen Marina, who nodded, then to James. Their silent exchange ended with Charles clearing his throat.

"Aye," Henry said. "We'll tell you of what's happened, but prepare yourself. You willnae like it."

CHAPTER TWENTY

I was in ill humor after tossing and turning for much of the night.

Fitz and I trudged to the edge of the burgh in silence, dodging mud puddles and ignoring wary glances. The rain had stopped, and I hoped that would remain the case for a bit longer—at least until we had the chance to find the Bruce settlement.

For the millionth time, I pondered: had last night's scene been a dream or vision? If it *was* a vision, were the crusaders reaping the consequences of the Opimaean chamber's decisions—or had we made everything worse for them as well?

Finally, I unburdened my mind to Fitz.

"Did ye speak with Esther? Did she see the same?"

"She has no memory of a vision nor a dream last night." The disappointment in my tone was clear.

"It was likely a dream, then," he said.

"I don't know. It didn't feel like a dream, and Esther's visions haven't been normal lately. She said so herself."

Fitz didn't respond.

"Fitz," I said, my voice shaking.

He stopped and turned to me. "What's the matter?"

"I'm scared."

His face fell, and he took me by the hand. "I understand," he said. "But ye cannae keep with this worry. Perhaps it will help to keep in mind that the more focused ye are here, the sooner we'll return to our time—to help our crusaders."

I nodded. He was right, of course, but it wasn't that simple.

Fitz didn't look convinced, but we resumed our path, keeping our hands linked. Fitz's energy was again distant, and I stifled the urge to ask him what was bothering him. We didn't need to keep Esther and Hamish waiting.

To avoid drawing attention to ourselves, we'd broken into two groups. Esther and Hamish took one path, and Fitz and I took another. After Marjorie's arrest, Annabel and Hamish set their focus on Malcolm, so she decided to forego the outing to the Bruce settlement in lieu of an interview with Katherine.

As we neared our exit from the village, a man walked toward us on the opposite side of the street. He was familiar, but I couldn't seem to place him. As we grew closer, he looked up, noticing me for the first time, and the horror in his eyes was discernible even from a distance.

"I know this man," I said to Fitz. *"I ran into him that day after the ordeal with Duncan. I think he might have seen flames in my eyes."*

Fitz paused and turned to me, dropping my hand.

"We'll have to take his memories before he reports ye," Fitz whispered, his features stormy.

"Another ripple," I said.

"Would it be better to wait for him to tell the whole burgh ye're a witch? Ye know very well what would be required of me then."

"Well, you can't kill him," I said matter of factly.

"If ye dinnae want him harmed, then ye best find a solution that agrees with ye."

My blood was boiling, but I knew if I lost my patience, everything would fall into utter chaos.

"Someone might see us…"

"We cannae very well help it, now can we? We'll have to manage." Fitz's jaw was set tight, and I knew there was no reaching him now.

I didn't see anyone around, but that didn't mean we weren't being watched. Houses lined the street, and countless windows stretched for a fair distance.

I reached for Fitz's hand, acting as though we didn't see the man and were only preoccupied with each other. Fitz ran his fingertips down my jawline, and between my nerves and Fitz's touch, my pulse quickened. Fitz's gaze dropped to the side, carefully watching the man's progress. The villager stopped maybe ten feet away and studied us.

"Pardon me," Fitz said. "We're searching for the old Bruce homestead. Do ye ken it?"

"Aye, I ken it."

Fitz pointed toward the woods. "Are we taking the proper path traveling just this way here?"

"What business do ye have there?" he asked.

"Our business is our own."

The man huffed, but he didn't respond. Silence fell for just a moment, but Fitz held eye contact with the villager. It was a good tactic—people tended to start talking if you made things slightly uncomfortable.

"Nae one has called it hame for many years."

"Aye, we understand it is in disrepair, but my wife longs to see it."

"And what business does a witch have there?" he asked.

"A witch?" I asked, feigning ignorance.

"Dinnae be coy," he said. "It willnae get ye far with me."

"Why would you think I'm a witch?" I asked.

"Yer eyes… they're unnatural."

I scoffed. "There's nothing—"

"Flames danced in yer eyes," the man said, cutting me off.

"What? That's ridiculous."

"I ken what I saw, and ye willnae talk me out of it."

"Why would ye claim falsehoods about my wife?" Fitz asked.

Despite the danger, my heart fluttered at the sound of Fitz calling me his wife. I groaned internally, annoyed with myself for it.

"'Tis nae falsehood!" he exclaimed. "I saw it with my own two eyes. She's a witch, and she'll pay for it."

A deep rumble disturbed the quiet. It was more energy than anything else, but it confirmed what I already knew. Fitz would kill this man if that was what it took.

I moved closer to the villager, and he took a step back.

"Smart man," I said, flashing him a devious smile.

The man recoiled.

"Do I make you nervous?" I asked. "Good. That's very good."

His eyes grew desperate as they darted around the empty street.

"Why haven't you reported me?" I asked.

"I did. Father Evans hasnae taken action."

I stole a glance at Fitz, who looked warily to me.

"I find that hard to believe," I said.

"He questioned Helen. She said ye were nae witch." The man's lips curled in disgust. "He places too much faith in her."

The surprise must have registered on my face.

"Aye, a mistake on his part," the man said. "'Tis little matter—in time, ye will be crushed under our heels."

I took another step forward, but this time, the man grasped at my forearm.

I laughed at his attempt. "It'll take more than that to stop me, sir."

Fitz, however, found no amusement in the man's actions. His energy permeated the air. I squirmed under its weight, so strong as it was. He took a step forward and gripped the man's hand.

"Keep yer hands off *my wife*," he said sternly.

"Or what?" the man asked, though his gaze flickered to Fitz's hand.

I saw it in Fitz's eyes, felt it in his energy, breathed it in my lungs. His anger burned hot.

"Attempt to touch her again, and I'll kill ye," Though Fitz spoke through gritted teeth, his voice was low and calm. "Maybe I will do so anyway."

Fitz moved so he was maybe a foot away from the villager and looked him square in the eyes.

Time suspended. Fitz knocked the man unconscious, and we dragged him in to the tree line, praying no one had seen.

"Blast, he's heavy," Fitz said, his voice strained as we approached a good spot to pause and regroup.

"Anything I can do to help?" I asked.

"Aye, stay focused on Esther's energy so we dinnae lose our path. I dinnae want to tote the bloke further than necessary."

"Do you want to transport over, and I'll meet you there? I think it's safe now that we're out of the village."

"I willnae leave ye."

"Have it your way," I said and pressed on.

When we stepped into sight of the Bruce settlement, Esther and Hamish were seated on old stones that had fallen from a large crumbling structure.

"Och, ye brought a gift," Hamish said, his features falling to annoyance.

"What happened to him?" Esther asked, rushing over.

"We need to take a memory from him. He saw Hadley's irises in flames."

Hamish raised his eyebrows. "How many times do I have to ask ye to no make a spectacle out of yerself?"

"Oh, for God's sake, Hamish. Lay off," I said. "It's not like I did it on purpose."

Hamish almost responded, but the look on Esther's face silenced him. He raised his hands in mock surrender.

"Hadley and I haven't erased memories before. It's a skill only used by the councils in our time."

"Yer councils have too much power," Hamish said.

"I agree," Fitz returned.

"What do we do?" I asked Esther, returning our focus to the issue at hand. She had bid me rest the last time, but I wouldn't sit this one out.

"This magical act is only performed by witches with power of the mind." Esther turned to me. "This should be an easy task for ye."

Finally, some good news.

Esther looked to Fitz. "Do ye have abilities of the mind?"

"Aye, I control memories. I can bring any memory to the surface and recreate the scene in yer mind as though ye're reliving it."

Hamish let out a slow, deep whistle.

"Then ye'll have the strongest connection of us all. Hadley, Hamish, and I will focus our energy to support ye so 'tis a quick process."

Fitz nodded.

"The easiest method will be this: find the memory and allow it to run through his mind, and then ye'll sink yer magic deeply into the threads of that memory. Instead of pulling it forward as ye would for recreation, ye'll envision the scene as ye'd like him to remember it and plant that into his mind instead. That memory will stick and the other will fall away. Ye only need to command it to be so."

"Understood."

Fitz closed his eyes, and his magic burst to life, golden sparks sputtering all around him.

Esther smiled and nodded to me.

We channeled our magic toward Fitz, and his face scrunched as the energy coursed through him. A strange pop sounded through our connection. Dread filled my senses, but he set my mind at ease.

"I'm in," he said.

His power rose and fell as he navigated the man's memories, but we held steady to our stream of magic. After a few moments, his energy dropped, and he opened his eyes.

"Done?" I asked.

"Done," he confirmed.

"A braw job. Now we must return him to the village," Esther said, as though we were returning a library book.

"I'll sort it," Fitz said.

"You're fine to do that?" I asked. "Your power, I mean."

"The additional energy surge was enough. I'm fine."

"I'll keep an eye out," Hamish said to Fitz, his gaze falling in my direction.

"You know I'm a trained warrior, right?" I asked.

Hamish smirked before jumping into action. He pulled the man into a sitting position, and Fitz slid into place. In the blink of an eye, he was gone.

Esther shook her head lightly.

"What is it?" I asked.

"Ye and Fitz… truly, ye are marvels."

In less than a minute, Fitz reappeared.

"Ye didnae leave him at the bottom of a well, did ye?" Hamish asked.

Fitz smirked. "Thought about it."

Hamish chuckled. His amusement caught me off guard. I hadn't expected him to make light of the situation.

I turned toward the settlement and took a step closer. Something lurked in the elements, nipping uncomfortably at my skin. It was as though the air was angry. I shuddered at the sensation.

"What's with this strange energy here?" I asked.

Esther and Hamish exchanged a knowing look.

"What is it?" Fitz asked.

"The Bruce family that once called this verra place hame was murdered here, along with several families that settled on this homestead alongside them," Hamish said.

"A man came to ask for work around the place. Said it was eerily quiet, save for the sound of a crying wean. He found several bairns huddled in one of the hames, and he ran to the village to ask for help," Esther said. "None of the parents survived, but the bairns were spared."

A deep melancholy settled inside of me.

"The children didn't see anything?" Fitz asked.

"By all accounts, the bairns refused to speak. They were so young that as they grew older, they couldnae recall what had happened."

"We didnae think to mention it. It happened so long ago," Hamish said.

"We havenae come to this place since we were quite young—we'd forgotten how strongly the energy lingered."

"It's really unsettling," I said.

"Aye. Best no to linger more than we must. Let's get on with it?" Esther asked, nodding toward the ruins. "I dinnae *need* to say this to the two of ye, I am sure, but be safe—this is a strange place," she said over her shoulder.

"Aye, why woudnae it be?" Fitz said in his most sarcastic tone.

The settlement was comprised of eight separate buildings in various states of ruin. Esther was concerned about disturbing the dead, so we split up to avoid lingering in the strange place for longer than necessary.

Fitz motioned to our right, and I swallowed hard as we set off toward our first building.

"Do you feel that?" I asked.

The eerie sensation grew stronger, almost unbearably heavy on my skin.

"Aye, isnae a braw feeling. I think Esther was right in her warning. We should be vigilant," he said. "The spirits of those who lived in these buildings might no be pleased we're here."

"Angry spirits… great."

We pressed on, and despite the strange energy, the old structures were beautiful in their wild states. The crumbling stones were decorated with hanging vines and patches of green moss. Fitz pushed aside the vines draping the entrance so I could pass through. The door was still intact, though it looked precarious. I pushed timidly against the aged wood, and it fell with a clatter that shattered the silence. I winced and turned to a grimacing Fitz. We held perfectly still for a moment before my breath returned to my body.

The energy of the building was different. Though it remained unsettling, it wasn't as heavy as what had lingered outside. I realized quickly that it did not stem from Lucio, but rather, from the previous occupants. The stone structure must have been vacated hundreds of years ago, and yet, the energy was as strong today as if they'd only just stepped outside to gather fresh water from the stream. I moved across the floor that had been reclaimed by nature and found an old pan lying in the corner. I dropped down and touched my fingertips to the discarded item, inexplicably drawn to the old object.

A myriad of memories flashed before my eyes—mostly of a young woman with a baby at her hip. She'd cooked countless meals in the pan for her young boy and her husband who returned to the house every evening, kissed her, and took the baby into his arms, occupying the child while his mother finished preparing dinner.

My eyes misted. Did their spirits still roam the homestead after their violent end? Or had they found peace? I feared the answer wasn't a happy one.

I resurfaced from the vision and found Fitz eyeing me.

I waved him off. "Nothing helpful. I'll tell you later."

The space wasn't large, and soon enough, we were walking toward the exit. The remnants of some kind of markings were around the door, and we paused to study them.

"Can you make anything out?" I asked.

Fitz's eyes narrowed, straining. "Time has faded them beyond recognition. This area of the home isn't directly exposed to the elements, but…." He trailed off, shrugging.

I summoned fire to give us additional light, but even so, it was a lost cause.

We moved on to the next structure. This one looked promising— even though it displayed some of the ravages of time, its roof was mostly intact. And if my senses weren't betraying me, the scent of a recent fire floated on the cool northern breeze.

Fitz and I entered warily, ready to strike. This space was darker than the last, in both light and energy, so I ignited my fire magic again. This structure was larger, boasting several rooms instead of one open space. Though nature was making its best efforts to reclaim the stone floor, its progress was slower than with the last building. We moved carefully, mindful of the many tripping hazards. By the time we entered the second room, the lingering energy took hold of me, and I paused, attempting to steady my trembling hands.

"I feel… *ill.*"

"Something extraordinarily dark happened here. The pain…" Fitz choked out. "These people suffered greatly."

I nodded, my breath coming too short to respond.

"Push against it," Fitz said. "Release as much energy as you comfortably can."

We did so in tandem, and our breathing grew less labored, though it wasn't enough to make either of us comfortable.

"Let's get out of this room," I panted.

The atmosphere in the next room was less severe. It nudged at my face, and the sensation was familiar. I swept my flames toward the right side of the space and stumbled upon a few candles. I lit two and handed one to Fitz.

We worked our way around the room. A hole in the ceiling had resulted in water damage, and consequently, moss and ferns grew from the floor. We found nothing of value in the nearest corners, but I knew resolutely that we were on the right track. Finally, we made it to the back corner of the room, which held more promise. The ground had been disturbed, and I stumbled upon the charred remains of a recent fire.

Fitz and I used our candles to scan the area in hopes of any information that might be useful. Finally, after a thorough search, Fitz lifted a newspaper clipping from a fern growing in the far end of the room.

"What does it say?" I asked.

Fitz squinted. "It's just the date and the name of the newspaper— *The London Times.* May 3, 1998."

I thought of the last time I'd seen that periodical, gripped in Henry's hands. It was the small things that reminded me how much I missed our little family.

Another item lay at the base of the fern where the newspaper clipping had been. I reached for it and pulled a book through the leafy blades of the fern.

The Hound of the Baskervilles. The binding was distinct, and I realized I had seen this volume recently.

"What's the matter, Hadley?" Fitz's eyes were troubled.

"I saw this in Lorenzo's office. On the day of the fortress raid. It's the same book," I said. "It's just… Fitz, I think it's important."

"You want to take it."

I nodded.

Fitz sighed. "Well, I dinnae suppose a displaced book is likely to anger Fate. But if it's important…"

My heart sank. If it really was important, that might not be true. "I know."

"Ye're the one who recognized the book. Ye're the one who has the feeling it's important. This is yer call, Hadley."

I hadn't expected that answer.

"Let's take it. We can always return it, but I'd like to look through it—see if there's a reason it caught my attention."

We did one more sweep of the room before heading outside to meet Esther and Hamish.

"Any luck?" I asked them.

"Nothing," Hamish said. "Did ye find anything?"

"We found this wee clipping from a newspaper," Fitz said, holding it up for them to see.

"And this book."

"And ye think they belong to Lucio?" Hamish asked.

"The clipping is dated from the future, and the energy on the paper does feel familiar. And this book—I'm confident I saw it in Lorenzo's office in our time."

Esther and Hamish gathered closer, eagerly scanning both the clipping and the book. Esther covered her mouth with her hand.

"Are ye well, Esther?" Hamish asked.

"Aye. 'Tis only… I've seen much of the future, but I've ne'er…."

"Aye," Hamish said, his eyes returning to the items. "I can hardly believe it myself."

"Ye've encountered this energy before?" she asked, returning our focus to Lucio.

"Only briefly," Fitz said. "We ran across Lucio only once before, so we cannae be certain. Either way… it's a lead."

Hamish nodded. "Let's bring these with us, but we should go. Darkness falls soon, and we dinnae want to be here when it does."

Hamish pointed to a path, and we began our walk home.

"Did the town ever discover what happened to the people who lived here?" I asked. "They must have had theories."

"Och aye. The murders were brutal, so it couldnae have been any of the fallen. Countless motivations were considered, but none that would warrant all of the deaths," Esther said. "Several of the buildings have fallen completely now, but it was a large settlement at one time."

"This lot is superstitious," Hamish said, "but even the witches couldnae account for it."

Shapes wavered in the dim light of the forest, and a shiver ran down my spine. It didn't take much imagination to be superstitious in a place like this.

"One woman—a witch—claimed she had seen a banshee roaming the woods the day prior, but I dinnae think a banshee would care much about leaving the weans alive," Hamish said.

"What a comforting thought," I said.

The light grew dimmer with each circle of the clock, and I wanted nothing more than to leave the strange woods. Since we now walked Esther and Hamish's path back to the burgh, I wasn't sure how long we had to go. The dense trees spreading in every direction gave no indication that we were nearing the exit. The distant rush of water caught my ear. Some sort of stream, I thought.

"Have ye made any progress with Malcolm?" Fitz asked Hamish.

"Verra little," Hamish said. "Elspeth had much to say about him, but confirming these accounts will take time. I hope Annabel learns something useful from Katherine."

We finally reached a small clearing, where splashing water caught our attention as it bubbled and rushed down a particularly rocky path. Hamish slowed his gait, and Fitz gave a questioning glance.

"The water… it wasnae this high or untamed when Esther and I passed through."

Esther froze.

"What's wrong?" I whispered.

Esther pointed in the distance. "The Bean Nighe."

"The *what?*" I recalled Fitz saying it was some sort of malevolent spirit, and my nerves prickled at the thought.

"Get down!" Hamish whispered urgently.

We followed his instruction and lay on our stomachs behind some small shrubs.

"Someone better start talking," I whispered, my hands smarting from their impact against the sharp rocks.

"She's… an omen of death," Esther said.

My blood ran cold.

I carefully peered around the shrubs. The woman had moved closer, stopping just across the stream from us. Her face held the signs of age, and her dark hair was mixed with gray. She was dressed in simple clothing and wore no shoes that I could see. She was bent over the stream, washing a garment that was stained red.

"Is that…"

"Blood," Fitz finished. "Aye. She's also known as the washing woman. She washes the blood from the garments of those who are doomed to die."

"We must take her by surprise," Hamish said.

"What do you mean? We're going to capture her?" I asked. The woman had a long, drawn face with a disproportioned mouth. Her arms were sinewy, granting her a non-human appearance that looked poised to attack. Everything about her seemed a warning.

"We're certainly gonnae try—if ye capture a Bean Nighe, then she must tell ye of yer upcoming fate and grant ye three wishes. Some say she wields the power to change a being's fate."

"'Tis useless," Esther said. "She will tell us nothing we dinnae ken, and she cannae save me."

"Aye, right. Especially if we dinnae even try."

Esther sighed, and Hamish fully ignored her annoyance, focusing his energy back onto the Bean Nighe.

We rose from the ground as Hamish broke from the rocks and ran stealthily down the stream. He crossed the frigid waters slowly and sneaked up the opposite bank. Just before he reached the woman, she turned and extended her hand, bidding him to stop.

Hamish froze. The Bean Nighe looked to us and pointed. Understanding her silent request, we moved slowly until we reached Hamish.

"Ye wish to ken yer fate and make yer wishes, but I cannae give that to ye," she said in a raspy voice.

"Why no?" Hamish asked.

"Fate would be displeased with me."

"I dinnae understand," Esther said.

"She has given orders. We cannae change yer destiny."

"There must be something ye can do," Hamish said, his voice pleading.

"I am bound to roam this land until the day shall pass when I was meant to die. Nae person prevented my untimely death, and I cannae prevent yers. I cannae help what Fate has decided."

She swept her sunken eyes to mine. "Mark my words. If ye dinnae change course, ye both will hang."

My knees grew weak, and Esther's head snapped to me.

"Change yer course," she said, "and ye yet may be free. Change nothing, and share in the fates of Esther MacGregor, Elspeth Taily-our, Marjorie Bruce, Katherine Sampson, and many more."

"No," I whispered in horror.

"Many shall meet their end at the hands of the witch hunters. A reckoning is coming."

At this, the spirit fell to her knees and wailed.

"Let's go," Fitz said. He took me by the hand and pulled me toward the path home. When he realized neither Hamish nor Esther had moved, he called to them.

Nothing.

Fitz grabbed Hamish by his arms and shook him. Hamish startled back to life and quickly moved to Esther's side, guiding her behind us. We rushed home silently.

When we reached the foyer, I took Esther's hands in mine.

"There is still time to change your future," I said. "The Bean Nighe might lack that ability, but never forget that *you* have that power."

CHAPTER TWENTY-ONE

The following day, I found Esther in the kitchen at the center table, reading from a grimoire and giving orders, while Millie fussed about, fetching this and that. Esther's eyes narrowed as she clicked her tongue.

"What's wrong?" I asked.

She sighed. "This is one of my more complex tinctures, and I seem to have run out of a few ingredients."

"I could go retrieve whatever you need."

"I would be much obliged, but Millie can fetch them for me."

Millie's lips fell into a hard line, and it was apparent that she wasn't pleased by the prospect. After the previous days' events, I imagined it had mostly to do with leaving Esther.

Though Millie would complete the task in half the time, I needed to walk off a bit of my excess energy, and I couldn't exactly be spotted running through the park.

"I'd like to go for a walk, and this is about the only excuse I have," I said.

"Walking about the burgh alone doesnae seem a braw idea."

"It's just to Elspeth's and straight back. I'll be fine, I promise."

Esther's lips tugged up in thought.

"Esther, I have to get out of this house. My magic is dying to get out, and the only way I can subdue this energy is to exercise a bit. A walk will do the trick."

"Fine. I dinnae ken that I can face the Tailyours this morning."

I'd been so wrapped up in our journey to the homestead, I had almost forgotten about the altercation from two days before.

"How are you holding up?"

Esther had been busying her hands with grinding herbs and stirring the contents of a large bowl for the last two days, not allowing much space to grieve. I couldn't blame her.

"I am as well as I can be," she said, looking up. "Thank ye for asking."

Though her response was polite, she clearly sought solitude, so I excused myself to prepare for my outing.

I stood near the foyer, pulling on my gloves, when Millie and Isla emerged from the far side of the room. Millie was buttoning her overcoat as Isla slipped on her gloves.

"You're not staying with Esther?" I asked Millie.

"She bid me join ye at the market," she answered, her features falling.

I nodded. "She'll be okay."

"Aye," Millie said, though her tone seemed less certain.

"Will you be joining us, Isla?" I asked.

"Aye, ma'am, if it suits. I have need of a few items in the market. It willnae delay us long—only a few minutes, in fact."

"Of course," I said warmly. Isla kept us all well fed, and the last thing in the world I'd do was prevent her from collecting whatever she needed for her delicious meals.

"Thank ye, ma'am. I'll be serving haggis this evening with dinner, and if I dinnae have the proper herbs and spices, it tastes… weel, it tastes like sheep's intestines."

I laughed, taken off guard.

"Weel, nae wonder," Millie said, a wry smile forming at her lips.

The burgh was busier than it had been the day prior. I couldn't decide if that was better or worse for us. The villagers seemed mostly preoccupied with their usual business, and I relaxed a bit as I realized I wasn't the center of attention today.

When we entered their shop, Elspeth was hunched over the counter, grinding a bit of herb in her mortar and pestle, and Thomas was at the far corner assisting a customer. Elspeth stood, stretching her back as she reached toward the ceiling, and when she caught sight of me, she smiled sadly.

"I am glad to see ye," she said, removing her apron as she walked around the counter.

We met in a warm embrace, but when she pulled back, I couldn't ignore the pain in her eyes nor the sadness marking her face. If I knew anything at all, she'd spent the better part of the last few nights in tears, leaving her eyes red and her face puffy.

"Are ye well?" she asked. "How is Esther?"

"We are well. Esther has been staying busy. She's thrown herself into her work."

"Just as I suspected. She's always been braw at busying herself, but e'er since her bairns were sent away…" Elspeth paused. "Weel, she hasnae been the same, ye ken?"

I nodded. Of course she wasn't. How could she be?

"And how are you faring?" I asked.

"I fear for Marjorie. I dinnae think she'll see the sunlight unless they mean to…" she trailed off.

"Is it truly hopeless?"

"Nae, it isnae. Others have been questioned and set free, but it isnae likely on this occasion. The evidence is strong against her."

"I am sorry," I said. "Marjorie seems like a wonderful woman."

"The verra best," she said. "Even when we were bairns. I've ne'er kenned another being who was so full of light and kindness. She's been a caretaker in our group for as long as I can recall. We dinnae deserve her."

"This town seems to hate women," I said.

"These leaders have diminished our worth in the eyes of this burgh," she said softly, her expression falling. "Women were once celebrated in this land, but now we are treated with suspicion and contempt. We are persecuted, in truth."

"Has suspicion been thrown onto any men?" I asked.

"Aye, but the bulk of it has fallen on women—helpless women, at that. It has mostly been widows or poor women with little defense. Now, if a man stands in the way of the witch hunters' path, that is when he is captured—though ne'er killed. That is a distinction saved only for women."

My heart felt heavy. I had known this, but watching it happen in real time was another thing entirely.

"An absolute tragedy," I said. "We have to do what we can for Marjorie. There must be something."

"Aye," she said. "We'll sort what might be done."

I glanced around. "It looks like customers haven't been too deterred by the events of the other day?"

Elspeth shook her head. "These villagers cannae help but cast stones at their neighbors, and they've spoken ill of us plenty. Still, they'll step into our shop and purchase just what they need with nae qualms. They dinnae wish to dine at our table, but that is quite all right. I dinnae care to spend more time with them on any account."

I laughed lightly. "A fine outlook."

"Weel, ye didnae come here to listen to me prattle on, so tell me what it is Esther has need of."

My spirits were high when we departed from Elspeth and Thomas's shop. Though we were all troubled by the events of the other day, and Elspeth was clearly devastated by Marjorie's imprisonment, we had found a bit of sorely needed solace in each other. And something had been different about Thomas today—Elspeth had seemed much more comfortable with his presence and his touch, and his energy was vastly improved from my previous encounters with him. Maybe we were wrong about his ties to Malcolm. Maybe all would be well between the two of them.

Isla led us toward a market vender. We meandered behind a row of stalls when Millie paused, falling into a coughing fit. Esther had mentioned she'd fallen ill during the early fall.

Millie waved off my suggestion to rest for a moment, citing her desire to get back to Esther. When I turned to continue through the market, two men stepped in our path, preventing our passage. "May I help you, gentlemen?" I asked casually.

"I dinnae need any help from ye, witch," one of them spat. Gray streaked from his temples and peppered through his bright red locks.

"Then perhaps we'll continue on," I said firmly.

"I dinnae think so. Do ye?" the older man asked his companion.

"Nae, listen to her strange speech," the younger answered, sneering. From his red hair to the hazel eyes that perfectly matched his companion's, I surmised they were father and son. "I think she's due for a bit of questioning."

"I'm afraid I don't have time to talk with you today."

I stepped to my right, intending to walk around them, but they took a step in tandem.

"I'm afraid ye dinnae have a choice."

My pulse quickened. "If you don't need anything from me, I have to wonder why you'd keep me from moving on."

"Wonder all ye'd like, witch. Doesnae matter to us."

I sighed. I was going to lose my patience with these two quickly, and I couldn't afford to do that in the middle of the town square.

"Allow us to pass. We have done nae wrong to ye," Millie said.

The men looked to one another, chuckling.

"Och. Is that so, Millie? Yer nothing more than a common servant. Ye think ye can order us about?"

"A common servant?" the younger man said. "She's thrown her lot in with these witch whores. She's nae better than the verra dirt on our shoes."

My fingers twitched at the derogatory term, and fire ignited deep within my chest. Elspeth was right. Being female was as good as committing a crime in this town.

The men seemed amused by the change in my expression, but their misogyny only fueled my flames. They had no idea I could end their lives quicker than they could take their next breath, and even with the frustration that accompanied the fact that I couldn't blast them halfway across town, I was smug in the knowledge that I *could*.

My smugness seemed to enrage them further.

The younger man strode forward and gripped me by my shoulders. Before I could react, Neilina appeared beside me and removed the man's hands from my body.

"I wouldnae do that if I were ye," she said, her voice like ice.

"And why no?" the man returned, rather proudly.

"Because if ye do, I'll slit yer throat right here in broad daylight. And then I'll gut yer father."

"Your hatred of women has no dominion here," I said.

The men laughed, and lost in my anger as I was, my eyes blazed to life, my irises dancing with flames.

I didn't understand their exclamations in Gaelic, but their shock was palpable—as was Neilina's disapproval. She scowled as she stole a glance at me. Unfortunately for her, I didn't much care about the scene I was causing anymore. I wanted these men to be frightened to their very cores… and based on the looks on their faces? I was succeeding.

Neilina took another step forward, and the men took a wary step back, their eyes darting between the two of us.

"That's right," I whispered. "Run scared, you stupid bastards."

Neilina's eyes narrowed, and her jaw was set tight, prepared for whatever fight might ensue. There was something wild in her demeanor. She was filled to the brim with power. Regardless of her intentions or her carefully placed normalcy, there was no such thing when it came to Neilina. She was formidable.

The duo departed, glancing over their shoulders as they rushed off through the crowd.

"Ye must be more careful," Neilina said lowly to me once the men were out of sight.

"You're one to talk," I said. "You can censure me all you like, but we don't blend—especially not you."

Neilina scoffed.

"Believe whatever gives you comfort, but it's the truth. You stand out, Neilina, whether you want to or not."

"Ye should get home to Esther."

"Perhaps you'll accompany us?" I asked, eyeing Millie and Isla.

Neilina hesitated, but finally, she nodded.

The path seemed longer on the return than on our outset, and I suspected we owed that to Neilina's presence. I was more curious than uncomfortable, and I decided to make the most of our time together.

"What do you know of Annabel's magical ring?" I asked.

Neilina's eyes widened for a few seconds before she regained her carefully placed composure. "Not as much as I'd like."

I nodded.

"What do ye ken of it?" she asked.

"A great deal, though I don't know the one thing I wish I did."

I'd taken Neilina by surprise, but I hoped my honesty would loosen her tongue.

"Why are ye speaking candidly with me? This is yer family, aye?"

"It is," I said. "But this ring shouldn't exist, and family or not, nothing changes that."

"Then we are in agreement on something."

"I want the women of this burgh to live, Neilina. I want peace for you and your coven."

She walked silently for several heartbeats. I came as close to intruding into her mind as I ever had, desperate to know her thoughts.

Finally, she responded. "I wish to believe ye, Hadley. But these are dangerous times, and I cannae trust anyone."

"I understand. I've not been able to trust many beings in my lifetime either."

"This, I have heard," she said.

"I want to do what I can to ease the burden in your time. Then I want to return home… more than anything."

I hated the way my voice broke at the end, but there was no helping it. I longed for *our* Scotland. I longed for my normal life that had only just budded when we'd left for the crusade. I had tired of the political intrigue in Opimae, and the past was no better. Between Malcolm and the council and Neilina and the coven, this was equally delicate. Only now, I was tired of feeling confused and homesick.

Neilina's energy lightened ever so slightly as she spoke again. "I want the ring destroyed."

"Fitz and I want the same—ultimately. We won't alter the past as far as the ring's natural progression goes, but we are here to ensure that it's properly disposed of at the right time."

"And this is because its natural course will be altered?"

"Aye." The word slipped from my tongue naturally, but my whole body tensed at the sound. I'd been in the past too long if I was taking on the dialect of the people around me.

We neared Esther's door, and Neilina stopped, eyeing the facade.

"This is where we part ways," Neilina said. "Perhaps we'll meet again soon? I share in yer interests, Hadley."

CHAPTER TWENTY-TWO

The rain poured from the sky the next evening as I readied myself for bed, resulting in a peaceful atmosphere despite the tension in our room. The flickering candles and the raging fire sent light and shadows dancing across the space. Fitz was tucked into an armchair near the fire, intent on making out the words of a new book, the volume in question poised carefully against his knees as he made the most of the dim light. His brow furrowed as his lips pursed. I studied him closely, suppressing the urge to ask him about what he was reading. He'd been displeased about my outing to the shop, which had led to a painfully quiet day between us—with many pointed looks and unspoken words hanging heavily in the air.

Curiosity nipped at the corners of my mind, and I fought against the words that rose in my throat, wanting to ask him why he continued to be so distant. It wasn't my way to simply let things go. I wasn't patient by nature, but I was doing my best to grant Fitz the space he needed. His voice startled me after the intense quiet.

"Nae, Hadley," he said, never pulling his eyes from the page.

"How do you even know what I was going to say?"

"I dinnae know for certain… but by the feel of yer energy alone, I have a braw idea."

I stared wordlessly at the fire, keeping my promise that I wouldn't push him, and turned my thoughts toward a useful distraction. Realizing I had left my spell book in the sitting room, I sighed and shrugged into my heavier dressing gown before taking a candle from the nightstand.

I had passed a portion of the afternoon flipping through *The Hound of the Baskervilles*, feeling around for any traces of magic and attempting to work rudimentary spells to find anything of importance. When it all came to nothing, I had turned my sights to improving my craft. With all the recent talk of spell work and partnering with my witchy sisters, I had used my time that afternoon to work on creating spells. I had spent little time on that part of the craft since I'd discovered I was a witch. Having gone from power training to preparing for battle, a new career and a new home to a new planet, spell work had fallen to the wayside.

"Where are ye going?" Fitz asked, his tone crisp as he finally looked at me.

"I left my spell book in the sitting room. I'll be right back."

"I can fetch it for ye," he said.

Though I was glad he offered, it felt like an automatic response.

I shook my head. "I know just where it is. I'll be back before you know it."

"All right then."

The hallways were already drafty, and as I padded across the worn wooden floors, I wondered if I'd made a mistake turning down Fitz's offer. The sitting room, however, was still warm from the evening fire, which burned dimly in the hearth. It had little life left in it but enough to illuminate the spell book on the nearest table. I scooped the linen-bound volume into my arms.

I had just picked up the book when I was startled by something thudding onto the floor. I turned quickly, searching into the darkness with the candle. The light wasn't enough, and I set the candle down before calling my fire magic to the surface to look again.

Something dark moved in the corner, and my flames sputtered while I strained my eyes to study the abyss. When a creature launched itself across the sofa, I released the deep breath I'd been holding.

"Freya," I said in exasperation. "You scared me to death."

Freya came nearer, arching her back and offering a chattering meow in response.

"Come here," I said crouching down. "Aren't you supposed to be in the kitchen this time of night?"

I extended my hand, but when Freya made contact, my vision blurred. For a couple of seconds, I was confused, but as my startled mind caught up, I breathed deeply and welcomed the vision to the surface of my mind. Perhaps I couldn't be sure of the validity of my dreams, but the crow had brought a vision for sure. I had the distinct feeling this was the same.

The scene that unfolded before me was clear.

Despite the sizable window lined with burgundy curtains, the room was dim. Storm clouds blanketed the sky with a dark gray that was so deep, it was tinged with blue. Magic-fueled torches flickered in sconces along the stone walls, and a fine dark wood dining table lay at the center of the room. A young servant opened a massive mahogany door at the far side of the space, admitting a captivating woman whose magic swirled ominously around her.

Her skin was a fine porcelain, which contrasted greatly with her raven hair. Her eyes were pale as a winter's sky, and her lips were painted a deep red. Her cheeks held a rosy hue, and though her features clung to her youth, her magic was seasoned enough to tell me that she was older than she looked.

Lorenzo Belmonte sat at the table, perfectly still as though the woman would strike like a panther at the slightest movement, and though she slowed her pace as she neared him, she moved with ease and confidence. Her fingers were long and slim, and her red nails were shaped to complement them. She slid her fingers around the delicate stem of a wine glass and pulled it from the table. Her gaze fell across Lorenzo, who still sat motionless, his body tense.

"Mother." Lorenzo's thick Italian accent bit through the air, his tone as cool as the snowflakes fluttering on the other side of the windowpanes. "Why are you here?"

Mother. Why would Fate show me a glimpse of Lorenzo's past?

Lorenzo stood before she could answer, walking toward a wooden cart at the opposite side of the room.

A servant stood nearby, his eyes wide. "Signore, may I help you?"

Lorenzo raised his hand in dismissal, his eyes smoldering. He took a wine glass and turned back to his mother. He raised his eyebrows, seemingly tired of awaiting her response.

"Must I have a reason?" she asked, her accent vaguely Germanic. She took a slow sip of wine, watching her son warily. "Can a mother not miss her son?"

Lorenzo returned to his seat and poured a fresh glass before raising his gaze to his mother.

"I'm sure she can," he answered. "But you? I am not so sure."

Adelina ran the fingertips of her free hand through Lorenzo's hair, smoothing it into place. He gently pulled back, tilting his head away from her.

Adelina smirked. "Still not forgiven, I see."

Lorenzo turned to face her then. His dark eyes held a contempt that made me shudder.

"Forgive you?" he said icily, gripping the stem of the glass. "What gave you the impression that I would ever do that?"

"You'll understand that it was necessary once this is all done."

"There was no necessity in it. I need not choose one over the other."

Adelina scoffed as she dropped onto a dining room chair. Lorenzo observed her, still radiating anger.

Adelina's gaze fell, and I followed her focus to a sight that made my stomach turn. Lorenzo's sleeves were rolled, exposing his forearms. Tattoos in familiar patterns snaked their way along his skin—moving with the aid of magic.

Lorenzo caught her glare and laughed. "Still sore?"

"Still proud?" Adelina shot back.

"Does it anger you that I lack gratitude? That I cannot thank you for what I've lost?"

"I've never asked for your gratitude, and you have certainly never bestowed it. But this is not a good look, my son. I will say it again: it *was* necessary."

Lorenzo's gaze turned to the window, seemingly watching the merciless snow fall outside. The pair sat in silence, neither rushing to break the quiet.

"Why do I have this connection to Hadley?" he finally asked.

A flurry of nerves traveled through me. This didn't make sense. Lorenzo couldn't have already known about me when Adelina was alive.

Adelina held the wine glass in both hands, her fingertips entwined and her elbows rested on the table. She had positioned herself so the glass hung from her fingertips and obscured her mouth, but even so, it was clear she was smiling.

"Do not torment me today, Mother," he said, waving his hand dismissively.

"You have no patience, Lorenzo. That has always been your greatest fault. Your father and I wanted the best for you, and you shall know all in good time."

How did *she* know about me? She was dead… wasn't she? My witch's eye prickled. I considered the countless pages of government intelligence I had been given by the councils, the chamber, Jordan.

Had I only assumed Adelina's fate?

Could she still be alive?

Lorenzo leaned back in his chair. It was clear he didn't like being told what to do, nor did he appreciate information being withheld from him. "I fear she has the power to unravel me, yet you play your games. Trust you? It seems you wish for my demise."

At that, Adelina's smirk faded. "How dare you question me?" she demanded, her voice rising. "Do you have any idea what I have sacrificed for this? For you?"

The world began to fade.

"No," I whispered. I focused with all my might, giving my best effort not to lose the vision, but it was useless.

"Why would you leave me so vulnerable?" Lorenzo asked, his voice growing distant. His dark eyes were all I could see.

"You still do not understand," she said.

It was the last thing I heard before the darkness pulled me under.

Strong hands gripped my body, and a familiar voice called my name.

"Come on, Hadley. Come back to me," the voice called.

"Fitz!"

"I'm here."

After a few deep breaths, I thought the world might have come back into focus, though I couldn't be sure.

"I'm not going to lie. I hate how dark it is at night around here," I said, my breathing still labored.

"Aye, it's an adjustment." An edge lingered in his voice. How long would his anger burn?

"Opimaean magical lighting would do a world of good right now," I said.

"If I didn't fear the household staff talking out of doors, I'd risk it," Fitz said. "But for my part, I dinnae much trust anyone right now."

"You and your practicality."

A small, breathy laugh escaped Fitz's mouth, but I knew I wouldn't gain much further ground—not yet.

As my eyesight adjusted, I found the fire had gone out, as had the candle I'd brought with me. Only the one flickering candle Fitz had with him offered the glimmer of light near us. I was lying on the ground, but I had been crouched down to pet Freya when the vision took control. I must have fallen.

"Care to tell me what's happened?" he asked.

"It was a vision… but I don't know where it came from."

"What do ye mean?"

"I told you about the vision that came to me near the trees with Esther, the one that was brought on by the crow. This was the same— Freya found me here, and when I petted her, the vision took hold of me."

"I've never heard of such," Fitz said. "Animals bringing visions to a witch who doesnae have the earth witch connection in them nor the gift of foresight."

My heart beat quickly. What was happening? I was shaking, though from the nerves or from the cold, I couldn't say.

"Here, let's get ye to bed."

"Wait… I need just a moment."

"What's the matter?"

"My legs feel weak."

Fitz placed his hand softly on my cheek. "I've got ye."

I grabbed my spellbook and candle before he helped me to my feet, and then he swiftly scooped me into his arms. He cradled me tightly against him and carried me to our room.

Once he'd placed me in bed and crawled in beside me, I shared the details of the vision with him, careful to include every detail I could recall. He held me tightly as I filled him in, his warmth and the pressure calming my nerves. By the time I'd related all the particulars, the shaking had ceased.

"The tattoos…." Fitz said.

"Yeah, they're what you're thinking… just like Charles's."

I recalled the way Charles's white tattoos had snaked across his dark skin, moving about as if they were as alive as their bearer.

"I dinnae recall us ever discussing their meaning," Fitz said.

"Me neither, so I have no idea. There weren't any clues in the vision, unless… maybe Esther saw it too. I'll check with her tomorrow. Maybe she saw more than I did."

"Hadley, this cannae be a coincidence."

"I agree, but if Charles has a connection to Lorenzo…."

"Aye, my mind wants to go there too, but it may come to nothing." Fitz sighed. "Of course, we willnae know until we return to our time."

"It's difficult to learn information that we can't do anything with yet," I said. "Do you recall Adelina being alive?"

"We've spoken of her so little," he said. "Always in past tense. We've assumed her death, but if this is truly a vision, then it's likely current since Lorenzo spoke of ye."

Fitz's energy tightened with the statement, and the shift coursing through our connection was unnerving.

"Questioning if Lorenzo's mother is still alive in our time was not where I saw this trip into the past going."

Fitz's eyes were hard when they met mine, but his touch was gentle as he continued to soothe my nerves.

"I know you're still mad at me. Thank you for being softer than I know you want to be right now."

"Hadley, I might be angry, but it's because I care an unfathomable amount about yer safety. I am yer sword and shield… whether ye want it or no, remember?" He found my hand in the darkness. "When ye need me, it is always so."

I nestled closer to him, and even with the edge in his energy, I found comfort in his proximity.

I wondered if Esther was awake. If the vision had any correlation to her foresight, Esther would be in the kitchen by now—but I didn't want to leave. I felt guilty potentially leaving Esther to her own thoughts, but I couldn't quit this moment with Fitz. Tomorrow would bring its fresh share of trouble, and I was certain Fitz wouldn't be as soft as he was right now. The promise of it lingered in his energy. But tonight, he was calm and comforting, gentle and open, and I couldn't help but linger in the warmth of these stolen moments.

Fitz flipped over to his back and pulled me with him. I looped my leg around his, and his arms cradled me protectively as I laid my head against his chest. The last thing I recalled was the feel of his hands rubbing my back soothingly as I sank deeply into a safe and warm peace.

CHAPTER TWENTY-THREE

Esther had also seen the exchange between Lorenzo and Adelina, and she and I felt that it had truly been a vision from Fate. That only strengthened Esther's opinion that her visions and my night terrors were mingling between the two of us through some sort of connection.

When Katherine entered the sitting room the next morning, her gait was slow and unsteady. I wasn't the only one to notice.

"Are ye well?" Esther asked as she spotted Katherine to her seat.

"Aye. Dinnae bother with me."

"What is troubling ye today?" Esther asked anyway.

"I'm tired is all. A bit of pain in my back and my side." Katherine pointed to her left side.

"Have ye spoken with the physician once more?" Esther asked.

"Nae. He avoids me still."

My blood boiled at the thought. "Because he suspects you're a witch?"

Katherine nodded. "Isnae fond of us, that one."

"Isnae fond of women," Esther said. "He's found companionship with Duncan for far too long to have any tolerance for us."

Millie entered with the tea service, and after thanking her warmly, Katherine turned to me. "Where might Fitz be this morning—learning to be a tradesman?"

I laughed lightly.

"Trying to bond with his ancestor, I suspect," I said. "He's probably making about as much progress with that as he is with learning to be a tradesman."

Esther chuckled, but she followed up quickly with, "Dinnae let Hamish fool ye. He's gruff, but he's taken a liking to Fitz whether he says so or no."

I smiled.

"I think it has helped him… with our bairns being gone, I mean."

My heart softened. "I think it's helped Fitz with the loss of his father… to be *here* with family."

Esther nodded, her eyes betraying her emotion.

"So much loss," Katherine said, shaking her head. "Far too much in recent months."

She must have been thinking of her husband.

"All is well with ye, Hadley?" Katherine asked. "Ye dinnae seem yerself."

"I hardly know," I said honestly. "With the events of the last few days, what's to come with the trials… Even—" I shook my head. "Never mind."

"What's the matter?" Esther asked.

I knew I was safe with Esther, and my intuition thought the same of Katherine, but it felt too personal to say the rest.

"Each woman in this room kens what it is to have a mate… what it is to be a wife," Katherine said knowingly.

My expression betrayed me.

"Just as I suspected. Share yer burden, Hadley. None of us should carry our troubles alone. Sisterhood is sacred."

I wanted to tell them more than I'd realized. I wanted to know if I had pushed Fitz too far or if I was being unreasonable. I'd trusted my gut always, but… Fitz was different than I was. Was his grief different than mine too?

"It's just that Fitz lost his father in Opimae, and on top of everything else we went through in that *hell*, we're out of step. He's so angry. Maybe he really doesn't need to talk about his loss, but I feel he does. Or that he needs to do something to work through the grief, because right now, it's eating at him day and night."

"It doesnae help that ye've come to a time where danger lurks around every corner—especially for a young woman who doesnae quite blend with the townsfolk," Katherine said.

I nodded. "He's worried for my safety, and he's told me that he couldn't bear losing me too. I just want to help him, and I don't know how."

"But ye are," Katherine said. "Simply stand by his side as he sorts his grief. He'll talk when he feels 'tis time."

"So you don't think I should push him at all?" I asked.

"I dinnae ken. If this continues for a long measure of time, then aye. When did he lose his father?"

"Maybe a month ago? I'm not sure if that's right. I don't even know anymore."

Esther smiled. "Time must be a mess to ye."

I nodded again.

"It hasnae been long," Katherine said. "If ye've let him ken ye wish to discuss when he is ready, then give him a bit of time. Enough that he may make sense of it all. Dinnae fash until then."

She was right, of course. I was worried and anxious because he was distant, but of course he was. How could he not be? What I sought was reassurance, but that was a selfish request.

"Things between us ebb and flow. I know that's normal. But the current underneath his energy is constant. The only time I feel true normal connection between us is—" I cleared my throat, my neck coloring.

"'Tis no unusual for a man," Katherine said. "They dinnae often ken how to express their feelings, aye?"

I nodded, smiling softly.

"That hasnae changed in a few hundred years, I see."

"Not enough," I said. "Fitz and I have talked about expressing ourselves, but we've bounced from one mission to the next...."

"That doesnae leave much time to progress in such matters," Esther guessed.

"Maybe one day we'll have that opportunity."

"I am certain of it," Esther said. "Fitz is a braw man."

"Thank you for the advice."

Silence fell.

"Weel," Katherine said, "I've gotten distracted, but I did bring news with me—'tis all over the burgh this morning."

I slid forward in my seat.

"Cameron Blair—the other man whose memories ye took—is dead."

"*Dead?*" Esther and I asked in unison.

"Aye. Found at his hame this morn. The family sent for the physician, but it was too late."

"Do they know what happened to him?"

"They dinnae ken *who* happened to him, but they ken it was a wound to his head."

Esther sat back in her seat, her eyes distant.

"Well, that certainly wasn't from us," I said, eyeing Esther.

"Of course no," Katherine said. "I ken ye'd only act in self-defense."

But perhaps she'd given us more credit than we deserved. I'd have to speak with Fitz.

Esther leaned forward, clutching her head, and I rushed to her side.

"Esther, what's wrong?"

"A vision," she panted out. "It isnae proper. 'Tis flashing before my eyes… but 'tis blurry and bright and I dinnae ken—'tis all wrong."

"Breathe for me," I said. "Nice deep breaths if you can."

"Aye, I can manage that," she said. She followed my instruction, pulling the air in and out. I met Katherine's eye and found determination in them. She moved herself over on the sofa closer to us and closed her eyes, whispering in Scots Gaelic.

Esther's heart rate slowed, and her energy calmed—though it still felt troubled, wrong.

"Talk to me," I said.

"The vision is slowing, but 'tis still blurred. Katherine's energy is helping me focus, but the vision still isnae right." She paused, her lips still parted, and I waited. "'Tis over."

"Could you make anything out?" I asked.

"Movement—beings were fighting, I believe, but I dinnae ken who. I saw Lorenzo, but I dinnae ken who he spoke with."

"The dark-haired man?" Katherine asked.

"Who?"

Esther's eyelids fluttered, and she fidgeted in her seat.

"Who is this?" I asked again.

"I dinnae ken," she said. "I havnae mentioned him because I cannae see his face nor can I understand the visions."

"Lucio, perhaps?"

"Perhaps." She pursed her lips.

I reached for Lucio's book and the newspaper clipping, piquing Katherine's interest. I explained their significance and my failure to identify what had nipped at my witch's eye. "I just feel like there's something here that I'm missing."

"May I?" she asked, her tone bordering on something like reverence.

I handed them over, and her eyes widened as she ran her fingertips along the spine of the book.

"Aye, my witch's eye agrees with ye. A strange energy lingers within these pages." She gently thumbed through the center. "In a way, 'tis familiar."

Esther's brow furrowed. When I'd asked her to examine the book, she hadn't perceived anything magical or out of the ordinary.

"I have a mind to take this hame for further examination, if it wouldnae vex ye," Katherine said. "I have a spell in mind that might reveal the book's secrets."

I mulled over her proposal, slightly nervous to part with the book. But Katherine was an ally, and I wanted answers.

"I'd be grateful for any information you can find in it. Once you've finished your review, we need to return it to the homestead, though."

Katherine nodded. "Give me a day—two, at most. In the meantime, I think the time has come to speak with the coven about yer visions, Esther. I didnae think it wise, but now… we have nae choice."

"Will they be… okay with what's going on here?"

"Weel, they all ken ye're here, and none have outright forced ye to return to yer time," Katherine said. "Perhaps that is enough."

"Aye, I think the same. Neilina doesnae seem against ye, and Katherine has advocated greatly on yer behalf."

"You have?" I asked.

"Aye. Neilina has been far too narrow-minded this last year. She cannae see the truth through her fear."

"Thank you," I said softly. "Has Neilina made any moves to bring the coven back together? I haven't heard any rumblings of it."

"Aye, just this morning, word is being dispatched. She means to call the coven to order this evening to discuss the recent events and bring the coven to some kind of accord."

"Even Esther?" I asked.

"Nae," Esther answered. "She bade Annabel, Hamish, and I refrain from attending so they may discuss our conundrum with the ring."

My nerves prickled at the very thought.

"Once they reach an accord… perhaps they might help us understand what's happening betwixt ye and I," she said to me.

"What is happening?" Katherine asked.

"We arenae sure. We dinnae ken if I'm seeing her dreams, or her my visions."

"Maybe it truly is Fate at play," I said.

"Ye may well be right about that. The coven might have record of this occurring before—surely Neilina will ken better than anyone," Katherine said.

"Before Neilina became head of coven, she kept our records for twenty years," Esther said, as if anticipating my next question.

"If additional power is required to assist Esther in receiving these visions, other seers in the coven would be quite useful," Katherine said. "They might ease some of Esther's burden."

I exhaled deeply. "I do want to help Esther. If you two think it's the best next step, then let's do this."

"If the coven doesnae rule in yer favor, next we approach Queen Tarron," Katherine said. "She, too, might be able to offer some assistance."

"Going outside of our kind and seeking help from the fair folk would be a radical act," Esther said.

"Ye cannae well help it. If the coven willnae aid ye, I implore ye to consider it. If our sisters willnae unite and protect one another from the humans, we might be forced to seek refuge amongst the fair folk."

Esther hesitated, her energy stirring wildly. Finally, she nodded.

"Let us await the outcome of this evening," Katherine added. "I'll send word as soon as I'm able."

Esther nodded. "In the meantime—Hadley, would ye be open to a mission while the coven is distracted this evening?"

"What did you have in mind?"

"We couldnae tell Hamish nor Fitz."

"You have my full attention," I said.

"I'd like to pay a visit to The Witchkiller."

Guilt tugged at my conscience as I slid out of bed later that night. I thought about waking Fitz as my feet met the ground, but his face was relaxed and peaceful, something I hadn't seen enough of lately. I couldn't find it in me to disturb him. Perhaps it was only an excuse I clung to so I would feel better about participating in Esther's plot, but either way, I moved quietly across our room, slid into my petticoat and overcoat, and I slipped through the door.

Esther was waiting for me at the foyer.

"I feel so guilty," I whispered at the sight of her.

"Would ye prefer we didnae go?"

"No… I need to do this as much as you, and Fitz and Hamish would crowd us. Maybe I don't feel as guilty as I thought."

Esther laughed before covering her mouth. "I'll wake the entire house."

I stifled a giggle.

"Did ye tighten yer streams?" she asked.

Henry had once taught me about restricting the flow of a mate's connection, and Esther had thought that would be best tonight. We could easily reverse it if we found ourselves in trouble.

"Yes, just a few minutes ago."

"Let's get on with it, then."

The streets of Forfar would have been eerily silent if not for the rain, and I was grateful that it drowned out the sound of our footsteps. We brought lanterns with us, but decided against using them unless we found ourselves in a dire situation—even the slightest flame would draw attention to us with the widespread lack of light. Luckily for us, many of the villagers had purchased lanterns from Hamish after he'd bought a surplus of them by accident. The shipping agent in London had been a "wee gowk," according to Hamish. He'd sold them cheaply to the villagers to decrease his inventory, who'd left them burning into the evening as their fear of witches increased, unknowingly benefitting two of the very beings they feared. The flickering flames guided us without casting enough light into the streets to blow our cover.

When we turned the corner on High Street, two figures moved near the tolbooth, and Esther and I darted behind an empty market stall. As they approached, one of the voices was familiar, and Esther covered her mouth. I was about to ask her what was wrong when the voice registered.

Thomas.

"*Who is he with?*" I asked.

"*Malcolm.*"

Her energy danced through me.

"I appreciate yer attention to this matter," Thomas said.

"Aye," Malcolm returned. "I share in yer interest. All will be well—in good time."

Thomas nodded, and the two shook hands before breaking for the evening and disappearing into the night.

Once we were certain they were gone, Esther and I walked briskly down the lane. Once we were a few minutes down the road, I broke the silence.

"I want to know what those two were discussing."

"Aye, I dinnae ken what Thomas is playing at."

"We'll have to update Hamish and Annabel tomorrow. We *have* to find out, Esther."

Finally, we came to the edge of the south side of town.

"Where do we go from here?" I whispered.

"Up that wee hill just there. There's a path we follow for a bit."

"He's further away than I thought," I said as we labored up the hill.

Esther grinned slyly. "Aye, 'tis a real shame neither of us are able to transport."

After another ten minutes or so, we came to an opening in the thick tree line, and Esther signaled that we'd arrived. We crept along the trees as we neared Duncan's house, assessing the perimeter. His windows were shuttered, though one was slightly ajar, allowing us a limited view inside. No light shone through the cracked shutter, but that wasn't something we could guarantee.

"*Do ye sense more than one energy in the house?*" Esther asked.

I paused and followed the subtle wisps inside. Though a human's energy wasn't as strong as a witch's, they were palpable enough to discern. After a moment's work, I was decided.

"Another's energy lingers, but it isn't fresh. They've been gone awhile."

"Likely the physician," Esther said.

"I agree. I think we'll only find Duncan."

We proceeded to the back door of the house, hoping it led into the kitchen. Esther tugged on the door, but it was locked.

"Weel, I suppose I expected that," she said. *"If we use our magic, we must first work a privacy spell to prevent the lock from giving us away."*

"Give me a moment. I'll investigate," I said.

I sat on the ground and leaned against the house before closing my eyes and allowing my spirit to leave my body. I turned toward Duncan's home and stepped through the back door. The room was dark, and I was grateful I didn't need to be concerned with stubbing a toe or knocking items over. I paused briefly, assessing the man's energy and determining it was stronger to my right.

A door in that direction entered the main part of the home, and from what I could make out, the rest of the structure was one large room. The remnants of a fire still smoked, though any chance of it emitting light was long past. I was nearing the source of Duncan's energy when a noise from behind me pulled my focus.

My heart dropped. In my body. Which was still outside. I moved swiftly toward the kitchen and realized the noise had come from someone unlocking the door. I got closer just as the person in question crossed the threshold. Even with the torch illuminating their face, I couldn't make out their identity, but a masculine hand set a bag on the nearby counter before shutting and locking the door behind them.

When the man turned, I was certain I didn't know him, but I suspected I had just found myself face to face with the local physician. He seemed to look right through me as he reached for his bag and fumbled at the clasp, never taking his eyes from me. I recognized his energy as the second one from earlier. He wasn't a witch, then. He reached inside the bag, his other hand still holding the candle, and pulled out a silver crucifix, holding it out in my general direction.

"Strange spirits arnae welcome here. Be gone with ye!"

I hesitated for just a moment, equal parts surprised and annoyed. He held the torch forward as though it would help him see my spirit, and it cast light and shadows across his face, toying with my vision just enough to drive me mad. His brow was furrowed—that much I could see—but behind the flames and under his wide hat brim, he remained mostly obscured.

I considered channeling my energy to knock over a pan or wave a knife, ridiculous as the circumstances already were. But the responsible side of my brain reminded me that mass hysteria would break out across the burgh by sunrise. Instead, I moved around him and out the door. When I stepped outside, I looked to my right, foolishly concerned I'd find my limp body where I'd left it. If that had been the case, the physician wouldn't have entered the house so casually. I swept the woods, looking for a sign in vain. I paused and focused on my connection to my body, and sure enough, it led me straight home. I awakened in the woods, damp moss cradling my head.

"I apologize," Esther whispered. "Ye'll be lucky if ye dinnae catch cold in this dampness, but I didnae have much time."

"How did you get me out of the way in time?"

"The rain had slowed, and I heard him approaching just down the path. I made short work of pulling ye into the trees—though I dinnae ken how he didnae hear all the fuss. I didnae have time to work a privacy spell."

"Nice work, Esther."

"Perhaps I am yet meant for secret work."

"You'd make a fine crusader, I'm sure." I laughed, but my breath was still short.

"Are ye well?" Esther asked.

"Just need to steady my heart rate," I said.

I told Esther of my panic over my body after my encounter with whom I assumed was the physician.

"Aye, it was him all right."

"He must be worried to be here at this time of night."

"They are dear friends," Esther said. "Dinnae forget—they've cozied up quite nicely to Father Evans."

"The three musketeers from Hell," I said.

"I dinnae understand."

The book would come out centuries later, I realized. "Nothing. Too early in time to be understood."

My teeth were beginning to chatter by the time the physician left. He double checked the door behind him. We didn't breathe easily until we finally heard his footsteps fade into the distance. I nodded toward the door, and Esther moved slowly in its direction.

"One more time," I said, before resuming my previous position.

I exited my body back to spirit form, and stepped through the door, turning and channeling my energy into my right hand. I pushed the lock upward slowly and cautiously, and the door opened with the softest click. I swung it open and found Esther's smiling face.

After readjusting to my body, Esther and I moved into the house, closing the door behind us. Esther followed my lead as we tiptoed through the kitchen and into the larger room. The physician had stoked the fire, and it blazed warmly in the hearth.

Duncan was propped up in bed at the far side of the room, his eyes closed and his hands resting on his chest. I paused and watched for the rise and fall of his breathing, hardly knowing if I wished to see movement or not. When he inhaled again, it was labored, and I found I was disappointed. If he was still alive, then he was still a liability to us—and a threat to our sisters.

We were nearing the foot of his bed when his eyes popped open. We froze.

"The angels have come," he muttered. "My time draws near."

"*Hallucinations*," I said to Esther.

"Why have ye come? Do ye mean to take my spirit away from this place?" he asked, his eyes distant.

"We've come to see if you've done right by your neighbors," I said aloud.

"I have done what I could. I have slain the witches, just as King James instructed in *Daemonologie*."

"You've procured their confessions?" I asked.

"It wasnae done so easily," he said, his voice growing stronger. "But in the end, they always confess."

"It's no wonder they confessed. Torture has a way of getting the answer you wish to receive."

"Nae," he said. "They were witches. They said it was so. What good did their allegiance to the devil do them? They were so easily felled."

"That's because they were human, you idiot," I said, calling to my fire magic so it sparked just beneath the surface.

Duncan pulled himself straighter. His eyes seemed to focus for the first time.

"Nae, I havenae killed any humans—only witches. Yer games willnae work with me, *witch*."

"You're right about one thing," I said. "I *am* a witch."

"Then meet yer death."

It all happened very fast.

He pulled his musket from under the covers and pointed it toward me, his finger moving to squeeze the trigger. Though I knew muskets were notoriously unreliable at a distance, we were standing at close range. I hurled fire, fully charged, at Duncan's chest. It met its mark, but not before Duncan's finger pulled the trigger.

"Down!" I yelled to Esther as I released a burst of energy to alter the bullet's course. Esther simultaneously grabbed my arm, tugging me down to the floor. The bullet missed, sending something clattering to the floor on the other side of Esther.

"Are you okay?" I asked.

"Aye, whit about ye?"

"I'm fine," I said. "Stay down until I tell you."

It would take Duncan more time than he had to load another shot, but I couldn't be certain he didn't have another weapon nearby. Sure enough, he was reaching for another firearm under the bed. His breathing grew even more labored, and even at the odd angle, his burnt flesh was visible through the singed fabric of his shift. I wondered if he even had the strength to pull himself upright once more.

My question was answered quickly when he sat up and pulled his firearm into position. I called my fire magic forward again and discharged it. Duncan dropped his weapon as my fire met his chest. His eyes grew wide, and he grunted at the impact.

Duncan squeezed his eyes shut tightly, his face scrunched, and then his body slumped forward, dead.

Esther rose from the ground, her face carefully stoic. But even in the dim light, she couldn't hide the wildness of her eyes. I meant to take a step toward Esther, but I stumbled backward, my knees weakening with a burst of energy burning through my body. I fumbled my way to the floor, my breath growing shallow.

"Hadley!" Esther said, kneeling beside me. "What is the matter?"

Her eyes scanned across me, searching for damage.

"I'm okay," I said. "It just felt so strange. This energy blew through me once he was… gone. It was like his death released something. I don't know."

"Aye, the energy was familiar. I think perhaps it was a curse from our sisters."

I nodded.

"He meant to kill us," Esther said flatly. "Ye saved my life."

"We saved each other," I said weakly.

Esther sat back on her heels.

My brain finally made sense of the entire series of events, and I recalled the clatter from earlier. "Did you hurt yourself?"

"Perhaps a wee scratch. Nothing to concern ourselves with."

I narrowed my eyes. I'd have to double check once we left Duncan's.

"Can ye walk?" she asked. "We mustn't tarry."

"I'll manage."

Esther helped me up from the floor, and my legs steadied. The blast of energy had left me shaking, but I would be able to make it home.

We found the clouds had parted, granting an unobstructed view of a first quarter moon. We walked through the city streets by the moonlight, and there was something poetic about that simple fact. After the energy had fled Duncan's body, it seemed no accident that the moon smiled upon us. Perhaps neither God nor Fate would hold it against us that we had removed such evil from the burgh.

Only time would tell if I was right.

When we were halfway back to Esther's home, a prickle worked up my spine. The curious energy wasn't foreign, though I couldn't immediately place it. I paused, looking around, and though the moonlight lit our path, it didn't reveal the source of the witch's stare. Though it wasn't my first time being tracked, it didn't ease the tension building within me.

"*Ye feel it as well? The energy?*" Esther asked.

"*Does it feel familiar to you?*"

"*Nae, I dinnae—*" Esther stopped.

"*What is it?*"

"*I am mistaken. 'Tis familiar.*" Her eyes widened. "*'Tis the same energy as that of the Bruce homestead.*"

I swallowed hard. "*Let's get moving.*"

Eventually, we made it home. Even after we locked the door, warm adrenaline still sang through my veins. I thought of Fitz and Hamish. Surely in numbers, we were safe.

We tiptoed to the kitchen, hopeful that no one had missed us. The warmth of the kitchen was welcome, and I was glad to set the wood in the fireplace ablaze. Freya was waiting patiently near the hearth for her evening treat, and when I sat, she jumped into my lap. She purred as she curled up where she could monitor Esther's progress. Esther smiled before fetching the jar of milk.

"Are ye well?" she asked. "Are ye upset that ye had to…"

"Kill him?" I asked. "No."

I searched my heart and found that I truly meant it. I didn't regret what I had done. Perhaps that made me ruthless, but I couldn't mourn the loss of a wicked soul like Duncan.

"Unfortunately," I continued, "Opimae taught me self-preservation."

Esther paused for only a second before resuming her task, a motion that might have been overlooked by others.

"You find me brutal," I said. There was no malice in my voice, no hope that she'd contradict me. Rather, it was simply an observation.

"Nae," she said. "I cannae understand what ye've experienced in battle, though I've seen enough to ken ye've done what ye must to survive."

Esther poured a large spoonful of milk into a small bowl before ladling out a healthy serving of honey and adding it to the cauldron of milk hanging over the flames. She set the small bowl on the ground, and Freya leaped from my lap and trotted to her treat.

Esther stood near the hearth, stirring the milk. "Was it difficult—the first time ye had to defend yerself in this way?"

"Yes," I said simply. "I went into shock."

"Shock…" Esther repeated.

"When something traumatic happens and your mind kind of moves slowly?"

"Och aye. I ken the feeling. It was the same for me when I first saw the vision of my death."

"Yeah, that would do it," I said.

Our conversation was interrupted by footsteps. Soon, Fitz strode through the door.

"I thought perhaps I'd find ye in here. I woke with yer nerves…" he trailed off, registering my overcoat.

"Esther and I have been out."

"*Out?*"

I met his gaze defiantly, though I held my tongue.

"Hadley." His voice was barely above a whisper, though his eyes pierced mine. "What have ye done?"

"The Witchkiller is dead," I said flatly.

"Did he harm ye?" Fitz's eyes studied me quickly, his heart rate increasing.

"No."

Then it hit me.

"Esther, I'm so sorry. I forgot," I said, standing.

Her brow furrowed.

"I want to make sure you aren't injured."

Esther waved me off.

"Seriously," I said, pointing to my recently vacated seat.

Esther sighed, removing the milk from the fire before trudging across the kitchen and taking a seat. She lifted her skirts modestly, and sure enough, there was a large cut visible through her torn stockings.

"It isn't too deep," I said, inspecting it. "Still, we should dress the wound to avoid infection."

Esther eyed me through her narrowed gaze.

"Yes, I know you're a healer," I said. "I'm still giving you instructions, so I know you'll actually take care of this in a timely manner."

"Fitz, would ye fetch the honey from that cupboard just there?" she asked, pointing to the far side of the room.

Fitz rummaged through the cabinet in question, emerging after a few seconds with a jar. Esther then directed me to the linen closet, and once I reemerged, I dampened the cloth and handed it off to her, along with soap. Esther cleaned the wound before looking to Fitz. He moved to her side and held the jar while she scooped out a healthy serving of honey and slathered it across the cut.

She wrapped her leg expertly before looking to me. "Pleased?"

"Very," I answered.

She gave a wry smile before returning to the fireside, where she set the milk back to warm.

"Now, I need ye to help me understand what's happened. I woke with yer nerves in my chest. I cannae believe I didnae wake sooner—" Fitz's eyes narrowed. "Are ye gonnae remove yer wee spell from our connection, or are ye trying to tell me something?"

I pointed to the table. Fitz's expression was sour, but after a second's hesitation, we took our seats out of Esther's way. I set things right in our connection, and the rush of his anger was overwhelming. I cleared my throat and organized my thoughts before walking him through the evening. He sat quietly, allowing me to share the tale without interruption.

That was, until I reached the part where Duncan pulled his musket.

"Are ye serious, then? He could have killed ye both!" he exclaimed, rising from his seat.

"Yes… but he didn't. You know I'm trained better than that. We had things under control."

"Oh aye?" he said. I knew we were in dangerous territory when he pulled that line out. "Is that why ye were almost discovered by the town physician?"

"I'll admit, that was careless on my part."

"Aye, right. Ye think?"

"But in my defense, it was past midnight and pouring rain. No one was stirring."

"Except for the physician."

"Okay, can we not get hung up on this?"

Though Fitz's features remained tart, I decided to ignore his attitude.

"And that's it."

"Oh, that's it? That's all of yer wee tale?" he asked, his accent thickening.

I shot Esther a look.

"*Now is a good time for you to escape,*" I said to her.

"Fitz, this is my doing," Esther said, ignoring me. "I worried about Duncan's condition. I worried he would recall our encounter and condemn us to the minister. So, I devised this wee plan and pulled Hadley into it."

"If there's one thing I ken about Hadley, 'tis that nae one pulled her into anything. She does just as she damn well pleases, this one."

I winced at his delivery, knowing full well he didn't mean it as a compliment. I decided to get the rest of the story out. It was only a matter of time before I needed to share it.

"One last thing," I said. "That strange energy from the Bruce homestead—we felt it on the way home tonight."

"The energy just… lingered?" Fitz asked.

"It felt like someone or… *something* was tracking us."

There had likely been a better delivery, but the words hung so heavily in my mind, they just tumbled out.

Fitz's face grew stormy. "And ye had our streams restricted? Nice, Hadley."

"I just wanted you to know, so we can be on our guard. Nothing happened."

"This time. Whether that energy belongs to a spirit or another being, it likely kens what ye've done," Fitz said, dropping back into his chair. His exasperation hung in the air.

"We didn't notice it at Duncan's."

"Hadley, that doesnae mean it wasnae there! Ye cannae perceive everything at once when ye're fighting for yer life!"

"The fault for this plan is mine," Esther said. "Dinnae be cross with Hadley. If ye must be angry, let it be directed at me."

"Ye should have told me. Does Hamish ken?"

"Do ye think I would've made it three feet out the door without my shadow had he kenned? Nae. Hamish is many things, but subtle isnae one of them."

"Someone should have known. It could have gone horribly wrong."

"But it didn't," I said.

"Aye, and ye're lucky for that. But ye may no be so lucky next time."

"I dinnae think there will be a need for another time. The old fool has been silenced."

"And Fate may have loads to say about that wee fact very soon," Fitz countered.

"It was worth it," I said. "He can't hurt any more of us."

I felt my eyes misting, and I blinked hard. The thought of the women who hadn't survived Duncan flooded my senses.

Fitz's energy softened. "I'm angry but no unfeeling. I wish ye had told me, but I understand why ye've done it."

I looked down at my hands, which were fumbling with each other. Fitz took them in his.

"I love ye, my brave witch. I worry because I cannae do without ye."

I wrapped my arms around him, and he hugged me tightly. The tears spilled over, cleansing my spirit as they washed away the events of the evening.

He pulled back and studied me. His eyes had cooled, but the same angry energy still simmered underneath his carefully checked exterior.

"I *am* angry with ye."

"I know."

He nodded once. "I am glad ye're safe—both of ye."

I glanced over at Esther and found a smile rising to her lips.

"Ye'll tell Hamish of yer wee adventure?" Fitz asked.

"Aye. Duncan's death will be much talked of. I cannae well avoid it."

"Aye. This will stir up the villagers, Father Evans, and God only kens who else. And that doesnae even consider Fate."

I grimaced.

"But we'll save that trouble for the morning light," Fitz said. "It's late. Come on—off to bed with ye."

"One moment," Esther said.

She turned to the fireplace and ladled milk into two cups before handing them off to us.

I hugged her fiercely.

"Ye did well tonight, Hadley. I am proud of ye."

CHAPTER TWENTY-FOUR

Fitz leaned against the wall near the fireplace while I buttoned my waistcoat. I intended to pay a solo visit to Annabel to hear of her latest progress and he insisted on accompanying me, citing my lack of judgment. I rolled my eyes but didn't argue. However, that was enough to piss him right off.

"Damn it, Hadley. Ye're gonnae have to be reasonable."

I pulled my overcoat from the wooden peg near the door and laid it on the bed, turning to Fitz. "What are you talking about?"

"Ye run headfirst into danger, and then ye act like I'm unreasonable for being concerned."

"That's not what I'm—"

Fitz put his hand up to stop me. "Dinnae even think about arguing with me right now. Ye do this, and ye ken I'm right about it. 'Tis always been yer way."

I crossed my arms.

"And if ye roll yer eyes at me one more time...."

"You'll what?" I asked, glaring.

He ground his jaw.

I walked across our bedroom until we were mere inches apart. "I'm not nearly as unreasonable as you make me out to be."

I wasn't sure if he was more amused or angered by my statement. It was his turn to roll his eyes, but he met my gaze, unyielding. We stood there, soft shadows dancing across our faces from the wind-blown trees just beyond our window, each of us refusing to release the other.

Our energy crackled through the room, and as our tension grew, I grew a bit lightheaded. His eyes dipped to my mouth, and I could think of nothing but pressing my lips to his.

And yet, neither of us made a move.

My eyes flicked to his neck, where a blood vessel beat against his skin, strained with his anger. I felt his eyes on me as I studied him.

But still, we held firm.

Our eyes finally met, our labored breathing mingling in the space between us. Just when I thought he meant to end my torment and press his lips against mine, he turned and made his way to the door.

"I'll be in the foyer," he said over his shoulder as he left the room.

I gripped the nearby chair for support and breathed deeply until I was composed enough to grab my overcoat from the bed and follow.

Our trek to Annabel's doorstep was quicker than I'd expected and far quieter than was comfortable. Silence marked the entirety of our trek. Once we reached the front door, I exhaled the morning's anger and prepared for whatever fresh fight lay ahead.

Annabel's lady's maid, Alannah, swung open the door. Her face fell at the sight of us.

"This way," she said. "If she'll see ye."

Fitz and I exchanged a wary glance before stepping through the doorway, attempting to match the woman's brisk pace. Alannah announced us, nodded for us to enter, and strode out in short order. She'd barely closed the sitting room door before Annabel started in on me.

"Have ye gone mad, then?" she yelled. "What is the matter with ye?"

"And which charge is it that we're discussing now?"

"The wee fact that ye're running around the burgh killing humans conspicuously!"

"It was *one* human, and it was hardly conspicuous."

Fitz pinched the bridge of his nose, eyes closed, and Annabel's face reddened.

"'Tis only a matter of time before a villager accuses ye! *Think*, lass. My god, think!"

I sat quietly but held her gaze.

"And then ye speak openly to Neilina about the ring. Ye say ye long to find a solution, but I cannae see the truth in that. No when ye're behaving so."

Annabel continued on, but my mind was too preoccupied replaying the events to listen to much of it.

"Hadley!" Annabel yelled.

"Yes?" I asked, returning my focus to her.

"I asked ye a question."

"Could you repeat it?"

Annabel threw her hands in the air. "Can ye no do something about this?" she asked Fitz.

"Believe me, I've tried," he said, raising his hands in surrender.

She sighed heavily. "I asked what had ye so preoccupied."

I hesitated for only a moment before I decided. "We felt strange energy last night. Someone was watching us."

"Have ye considered that if ye didnae draw attention to yerself, ye might no have that problem?"

"We need to figure out who it was."

"Ye're certain it was the energy that lingers around the homestead and no the energy of another we found evidence of there?" Fitz asked, eyeing me meaningfully.

He suspected Lucio. I considered the thought. But then I remembered what Gabriella had said as she double-crossed Lorenzo to help us.

"Wouldn't Lucio try to kill us if he knew we were here? Why would he just watch us?"

"Perhaps, but it makes little sense that a spirit would track ye and take nae action," Fitz said.

He was right. Unfortunately, neither option added up. At least, not based on what we knew.

"Spirits are strange creatures. Perhaps all isnae as it seems," Annabel said. "Be mindful. I dinnae much like ye poking about in this manner."

"She'll proceed with caution," Fitz said. "Will ye no, Hadley?"

I groaned inwardly and forced a less than convincing smile to my face. I was tired of being told what to do.

"And while we're discussing important matters—dinnae trust Neilina. I dinnae mean to find out again that ye've spoken to her about the ring. Or Esther."

"I was only trying to help. You said that if I found another way for Esther to be saved, you would hear it."

"What have ye found out, lass? Out with it."

There were so many tangled webs: Lucio, Malcolm and Father Evans, Esther and the coven… and Annabel with her ring. Fate and all of us, for that matter. I hardly knew what I should share with anyone.

"Nothing concrete—not yet."

"And ye willnae either. No with that one."

"Can you just let me try?" I said, louder than intended. "I am trying my best to find another path for Esther!"

Annabel sat back in her seat, her eyebrows raised.

"Everything is far more complicated than we're at liberty to say," Fitz said. "We dinnae wish to be cross, but we are trying to do right by everyone—and the pressure is immense."

Finally, Annabel nodded.

"I can't forge another path for Esther," I said. "Only she can do that. But I'll be damned if I'm going to just sit by as she walks to the gallows. We want the same thing, Annabel. I know we do. Just give me a bit of space."

"Fine," she said, a bit crisp. "I'll likely live to regret it. Ye have nae subtlety about ye, but... aye. I'll give ye until the end of the week, and then?" Annabel's features grew grim. "Then, we'll do this my way."

I was hesitant to agree, but I finally nodded.

"Now that that's settled, we did come to talk to you about something. Have you made any progress with Malcolm?" I asked.

Annabel stood and paced to the fire. "What I've learned is troubling. I dinnae ken if I believe it to be true. Malcolm may be doing just what we suspected. Actually, I am late to call on a coven member who has evidence—or so they claim."

Finally. Maybe this would make a difference in the way the upcoming events would unfold.

"I mustn't tarry any longer, but I'll pay ye a visit in the morn."

The following day, Hamish and Fitz hung around the house rather than heading to Hamish's shop, which cast a bit of a shadow. Neither were unkind, but concern and anger burned in their energies. It would take time for them to forgive me and Esther for sneaking out on them, but with everything happening, I hoped Hamish didn't waste his time with Esther being angry.

Katherine turned up just after breakfast, and her visit was a welcome distraction. We retired to the sitting room while Fitz and Hamish excused themselves to Hamish's office.

I'd thought recounting the entire saga of our visit to Duncan's house would be tiresome, but it turned out to be a well-needed release. Katherine leaned forward in her seat with widened eyes, fully engrossed in the tale Esther and I took turns narrating in minute detail.

"Perhaps I shouldnae be pleased that he is gone," Esther said, "but he has taken far too many lives for me to regret his end."

"Ye both have done a service to this burgh," Katherine said, eyeing me pointedly. "Dinnae fash. Ye have restored at least a wee bit of balance at a time 'tis sorely needed. Darkness has plagued us for too long, and today, the whispers on the breeze are lighter. Perhaps the tides shall turn for the better."

"I hope Hadley willnae see consequences from Fate for this," Esther said.

I studied Katherine closely as Esther spoke. She lifted her teacup to her lips, and it shook in her slender fingers. She was deteriorating. Her frailty was even more apparent in today's dress, which sagged from her weight loss. Her collarbones protruded from her body, and the square neckline of her dress did nothing to hide it. The concern in Esther's eyes was undeniable.

After a while, Fitz and Hamish entered the room and settled near the fireside with books in hand. Their entrance shifted the conversation, and we chattered about Esther's latest tincture until Millie announced Annabel's arrival.

"Aunt! We are so pleased ye've arrived."

"I thank ye for the kind welcome," Annabel said, grasping Esther's hand.

"Och, yer hands. Ye're chilled to the bone, I'd reckon. Please, have a seat by the fire."

Hamish vacated his seat for her. "Ye bring news?" Hamish asked, settling onto the sofa.

"Aye," Annabel said, though she paused, looking pointedly at Katherine.

"Katherine kens all," Esther said.

Annabel nodded in her usual way. Her expression wasn't quite as sour as it typically was around Katherine.

"The news I bring is quite troubling. Matters are far worse than I first realized." She turned to Hamish. "Hamish spoke with several coven members on the first of the week."

"Aye," Hamish said, "and in speaking with Katherine and Elspeth, I learned of Malcolm's early years just after his apprenticeship."

"I recall ye once mentioning his father died while in London," Esther said to Katherine, her face puzzled.

"More than that—he died in prison," Katherine said.

"Why was he in prison?" I asked, leaning forward in my seat.

"It was a dark time for this country," Katherine said. "King Charles the First had found himself in a bit of trouble. He was bleeding funds for his wee war with Spain, so he forced loans upon many of his subjects."

Hamish glanced at Esther. "We were in MacGregor country at the time, and we passed through the conflicts mostly unscathed, but Malcolm and his family met quite a different fate."

"His father refused to offer a loan when asked by the crown, and Charles made him an example," Katherine added, her face grim.

"Aye, and so his father was executed while imprisoned in the Tower of London. It angered many a Scot, which led to many in this wee burgh joining the fight against Charles once the civil war began," Hamish said. He ran a hand through his hair, smoothing back a few loose strands. His eyes were distant, like his mind was traveling elsewhere, and I wondered if any of his own family might have fought in the wars.

"How does this wee bit of history connect to Malcolm today?" Fitz asked.

"Malcolm traveled to London to retrieve his father's remains. A guard was appointed to travel with him, and they fastened his father's body atop a cart—it was the condition to bring him hame to Scotland," Annabel said.

The thought soured my stomach, and I covered my mouth with my hand.

"This was common after the Jacobite Rising of '45. It was meant to demonstrate what becomes of those who oppose the crown," Fitz said lowly to me. I thought back. The Jacobite conflict wouldn't yet occur for almost another eighty-five years.

Esther cleared her throat uncomfortably. Though the others were distracted in conversation, Esther's head was tilted in our direction.

"Are ye well, *mo ghaol?*"

"Aye," she said softly, though her gaze shifted from the floor to Fitz and me.

"*She knows,*" I said to Fitz.

Fitz nodded subtly before returning the conversation back on track. "And when Malcolm returned?"

"He told the burgh of the impending civil war. He had learned much from the witches of London."

Charles I had allegedly been loyal to the Catholic Church, which many in Britain decided would result in subjugation to Rome. Coupled with his thirst for the war with Spain, his relentless spending of the country's funds, his dismissal of Parliament when they wouldn't give him whatever he wanted, and his belief that God spoke directly to him and that he should not be questioned, Charles had become quite unpopular with many of his subjects.

"It seems that when the war began, Malcolm joined the fighting, and he met a young minister who remains his faithful ally even to this day," Annabel said, her tone bordering on sarcasm.

"Father Evans," Fitz said.

"Father Evans," Annabel confirmed.

"So, why keep that secret?" I asked. "What would it matter to the villagers if they were friends?"

"It doesnae matter," Hamish said. "Unless ye wish to hide yer true objectives."

Fitz rose from his seat and walked toward the fire. When he turned, his hand ran absentmindedly through his chestnut hair, a sign that he was deep in thought. "It confirms our suspicions that something is amiss with the trials. They're planning something we cannae see in plain sight."

"Aye, just what I think," Annabel said.

"Why would Malcolm want a bloodthirsty, witch-hunting minister in this burgh?" I asked. "And for that matter, why would he want to befriend someone like that in the first place?"

"That is what we mean to find out," Hamish said.

"If the hysteria benefits his cause, then I hope we are all prepared for the fight ahead," Katherine said. "To betray his own kind... his cause must be dear to him indeed."

"There's more." Annabel paused, clearing her throat. "Several have said he works a strange and concerning magic."

"Dark magic?" Fitz asked.

Dark magic? Fitz and I had never discussed that before.

"None have been so bold as to say it plainly, or to confirm it when I asked."

"Fearing for their safety, most likely," Hamish said.

"What exactly is dark magic?" I asked.

"The wild claims the villagers make about us," Katherine said, turning to me. "Consorting with the devil or evil spirits to cause harm to others—'tis precisely that."

"Summoning a spirit to do yer bidding is one example," Fitz said. "It can even be as simple as breaking our witches' code—using every-day magic for harm."

"No in self-defense," Esther clarified. "Only unprovoked."

I recalled our conversation with Katherine, Esther, and Hamish when we'd first arrived, how Fitz and I suspected they were hiding something about Malcolm. I was certain Katherine had spoken to Annabel and Hamish about it, but Fitz and I knew nothing of the real details.

"You mentioned something about the woman he silenced—allegedly—but you never mentioned how he did so," I said.

Katherine looked to Esther and raised her eyebrows.

"Och, all right," Esther said.

"It has long been rumored that he uses dark magic to do his bidding—against even his own kind," Katherine said. "When they recovered the poor lass, the only word that was pulled from her mouth was *fuath*."

A fuath.

"A fuath is a malevolent spirit?" I asked.

"Aye, or so 'tis said," Katherine said. "'Tis said to roam near the rivers and lochs, ready to make ye their prey. I havenae encountered one myself."

"The *only* way to command a fuath would be through dark magic," Fitz said as he paced the room. "Ethically, I dinnae think we can call it anything else."

"Aye, ye are perfectly right," Katherine said.

We all took a beat. My stomach turned at the thought of what we might be up against, what type of carnage dark magic might cause.

"Do ye have any proof?" Fitz asked, taking a seat once more.

"I spoke with Neilina after Katherine and I discussed the unfortunate woman," Annabel said.

I looked tartly at Annabel, who paid me no mind. I was censured for speaking plainly to Neilina, but apparently, Annabel had free rein.

Esther gasped.

"Aye, it wasnae pleasant," Annabel said, raising her eyebrows. "But we found our way."

"What did she say?" Esther asked.

"She was hesitant at first, likely fearing for her own safety. But said she has long heard the same—that he practices the dark arts."

Esther sat back in her chair, her lips pursed.

"Perhaps he works the dark arts, perhaps no. But much of the coven is frightened by him," Katherine said. "None have stood against him, and with reason."

One man stood between the women of this burgh and their safety. Dark magic or not, it pained me to know Malcolm was the reason we continued to suffer.

"What do Malcolm and Father Evans want?" I wondered.

"It isnae plain to me, but I ken one who might have answers," Katherine said.

"Helen," Esther said.

"Perhaps we should find a way to speak with her," Hamish said.

I sat forward in my seat, eager for others' reactions.

"Soon," Annabel said. "Helen will die once she is nae longer useful at the hands of that fear-mongering blight of a *minister*." She shook her head. "And all endorsed by the crown of England."

Annabel's resentment filled the air, adding heavily to the weight of our intermingled anger, frustration, doubt, and fear.

"The coven still won't do anything to quiet the witch hunts now that they've turned toward actual witches?" I asked. "I understand the fear of dark magic, but we're already being persecuted."

"I dare say, Neilina will ne'er allow the coven to break Malcolm's orders," Annabel said. "We have suggested intervening many times in the past already kenning where this would all lead—a wish that was ne'er granted."

It must have been nearly unbearable to watch the persecution of their neighbors, knowing they could put an end to it but were prevented by their leadership. I was beginning to know something about how that felt.

"They wish to cut us all—humans and witches—down like the summer's hay until they are left with nothing but uniformity. They care only to control the subjects of the crown so they may use us as they see fit. Beings like the lot of us dinnae fit into the minister's plans." Annabel turned to Fitz and me. "And might I remind ye that he will cut ye both down on his path to conformity, but no before ye widen the target on Esther's back."

Great. Now we were back to this.

"I willnae have more of this talk," Esther said. "We must focus on the issue at hand."

"Ye willnae solve it with yer wee family in such discord." Katherine's quiet grief grew stronger, and the entire room stilled at the feel of it.

"If Ailean were still alive," she whispered, her words breaking at the end. Tears poured down her cheeks as she hung her head. "Nae—I beg yer pardon. This does nae good."

"Nonsense," Esther replied. "There is nae need for apologies here."

I timidly reached my hand toward Katherine's. It may have been too forward a gesture, but I hoped it would send a signal of support. Katherine gripped my hand firmly, and a spark sounded through me. Her energy was as comforting as it was strange.

Katherine's eyes studied mine carefully, but she then smiled, patted my hand with her free one, and shifted her gaze to Esther.

I stole a glance at Fitz, who wore a tight smile.

"Ye MacGregors will sort it in the end," Katherine said. She then turned to me and to Fitz. "And ye'll have many years of marital felicity, I am sure, once ye are wed."

Her pointed message wasn't lost on me, and based on the shift in his energy, it wasn't lost on Fitz either.

Before we could speak, Hamish's head jerked toward us. "Ye arnae *married*?"

"We haven't had time for a ceremony," I explained.

"That matters little here," he countered. "This must be remedied… immediately. I dinnae ken what madness passes in yer time, but this willnae do here."

"In witchkind, a formal mating is considered as braw as wed," Fitz said. "The humans need no be the wiser of the details of our union."

"Aye," Esther agreed. "Our unions are more binding than the human ceremony. However, the humans dinnae understand that. If they kenned the truth, we'd all hang." Hamish winced at Esther's words, but she continued. "I ken Hadley wears that ring, but if anyone questions it, ye dinnae have proof of yer union. There is risk."

"They'd think us impure," Fitz said.

"Aye. They'd despise ye for it. More importantly, it would draw more attention to this house than we could bear." Esther's expression was pained. "I am sorry 'tis so… I wouldnae mention it but for the Bean Nighe. Her prophecy concerns me—for *ye*."

"It would make things worse for you too," I said, filling in the final blank.

"Aye." Hamish's eyes were desperate.

"Then we have to remedy this," I said.

"A simple ceremony will suffice. Ye may celebrate in any grand fashion ye wish when ye return to yer time," Hamish said.

I looked to Esther. Her eyes were filled with emotion. "I am truly sorry."

"There's nothing for you to apologize for," I said.

"We'd do this to protect ye alone, but it also seems to be in Hadley's best interest," Fitz said.

I couldn't read his feelings. Did he truly want to marry me right now?

"So ye dinnae mind?" she asked.

A small, breathy laugh escaped Fitz's lips. "Our wedding might look different than we anticipated, but this is important. We'd have already celebrated our union if the crusade allowed the time."

Our eyes met, and a tender warmth flowed through our connection. After the last few weeks, this energy was a lifeblood channeling through me, warming me to my very core.

"I think it best," Katherine finally said. "There is nae harm in having the ceremony. It will bring ye closer even yet. Dinnae stand by as precious time passes away."

Katherine's grief seized my soul. She was right. We were wasting time when we should have long since married.

"I love Fitz more than anything," I said, never releasing his gaze. "We'll celebrate with the rest of our family and friends when we can, but for now… it'll be special to celebrate with all of you."

Raised voices interrupted from outside the sitting room door.

Something wasn't right.

Hamish rose from his seat, and Esther crossed the room. She threw open the door and mumbled in Gaelic, but even as she did, the energy in the room shifted, leaving me dumbfounded. I looked back at Fitz, my eyes wide, and his expression rivaled mine.

This was energy we recognized.

"Nae, it cannae be," he whispered.

"What is the matter?" Hamish demanded gruffly.

"I think we have visitors," I said. "Visitors from our time."

Hamish's eyes narrowed just as Esther stepped aside, revealing Ann and Izzy MacGregor.

CHAPTER TWENTY-FIVE

I raced into Izzy's arms, her warm energy enveloping me like a cozy blanket. The familiar scent of evergreens and ripe strawberries mingled with ancient herbs brought tears to my eyes.

"How on earth are you here?"

Izzy pulled back, and the trouble in her eyes set my nerves on end.

Ann was in raptures over seeing Fitz alive and well.

"And you," Ann said softly, turning toward me. She placed her hands on either side of my face. "Have these villagers been unkind to you?"

"Nothing I haven't been able to handle," I said.

Ann hugged me tightly, and I melted into her maternal embrace. The edges of my heart that had been so tight with anxiety softened ever so slightly.

"That's my girl."

Fitz took a step closer. "Mum, I'm glad to see ye—both of ye. But what *are* ye doing here?"

Ann and Izzy looked to each other, and anxiety quickly reclaimed what Ann had just softened.

"We wouldnae have risked Fate's displeasure if it werenae urgent," Ann said. "You ken that, I'm certain."

"Is the team okay? Has anything happened in Opimae?" I asked, my heart racing.

"All is well with the team," Izzy answered. "It is *you* we've come for."

"Me?" I asked, confused. Fitz and I exchanged a wary glance.

"What's happened?" Fitz asked.

Ann hesitated, looking to our audience. Having been so distracted by Izzy and Ann, I hadn't noticed that the rest of the room had stood and were watching the four of us cautiously. Esther had grasped Katherine's arm, and the pallor of her face sobered me. Hamish eyed Izzy warily as Annabel gripped the chair next to her.

"We've been rude. My apologies," Fitz said, turning toward his ancestors.

"How… how can this be?" Annabel said, looking at Izzy.

Esther cleared her throat and adjusted her stance, standing tall.

"I might as well be looking in a mirror," she said, her voice holding the slightest strain.

Izzy laughed softly, her cheeks blushing.

Hamish stepped closer, mesmerized. "'Tis strange, is it no?"

"'Tis strange times, aye?" Katherine retorted.

Fitz took a step closer to Izzy.

"Mum, Izzy, I'm pleased to introduce ye to our hosts, Hamish and Esther MacGregor. This is Annabel McAlpine, Esther's aunt. And this is a dear friend of Esther's, Katherine Sampson."

Esther had recovered enough to clasp hands with Izzy, and Katherine spoke to Ann. Izzy's eyes filled with wonder as she talked to Esther for the first time, but I couldn't focus on the pleasantries, not with the worry that had gripped me. What could have prompted Ann and Izzy's journey?

"Please, do make yerselves comfortable by the fireside," Esther said, motioning toward our usual seats. "Millie, fetch a bit of tea for our guests?"

Millie nodded and closed the door behind her.

I studied Ann and Izzy, attempting to keep my mind occupied. They were dressed head to toe in the council's idea of seventeenth-century fashion—loud fabrics, puffy sleeves, and all—but I was sure we could pull together a few less conspicuous garments to help them blend in. Though it would be near impossible with their bright auburn hair, emerald eyes, and milky skin. They practically screamed *witch*.

Hamish's eyes darted around curiously, clearly taken aback by Izzy's likeness to his own wife, differentiated by only the slightest influence of Ann's features on Izzy's face. I'd often noticed Izzy's similarities to her mother, but seeing Izzy and Esther in the same room was striking.

Esther bore the situation more casually than Hamish as the initial shock faded, sitting tall with a smile resting on her face. Her eyes were lively, and though she had to be curious, delight currently seemed to be winning the fight for her strongest emotion.

"I'm sorry to interrupt," I said at my first opportunity, "but what's brought you here?"

Ann looked to Fitz.

"'Tis all right. Everyone present is an ally."

"A few days ago, we received a small parcel in the post," Izzy began. "No return address was given, but it was posted to both Mum and me."

"The contents were… concerning," Ann said, looking from me to Fitz.

Millie returned with the tea service, and I nearly screamed. She was quick with her duties, but one more delay might actually kill me. I jumped when Millie shut the door a little too loudly.

"A threat of some kind?" Fitz asked.

"It was a warning," Ann said. She sat her teacup on the table and turned squarely to face us. "This parcel contained a book that was published in 1891, and it contained countless facts and references related to the Forfar witch trials."

My witch's eye prickled at her words, and I instinctively took Fitz's hand in mine.

Ann looked to Izzy, and I knew another silent conversation was taking place. Izzy cleared her throat before taking over the story.

"The book had a comprehensive list of those persecuted during the trials. Even with the vast research that was done by both our family and the councils, there was nothing quite so detailed as this. It's a rare, out-of-print book. Until it arrived, there was but one known to be in existence—in the British Museum.

"We were curious why it was sent to us. Mum and I studied the text closely, and as we read the list of names of those persecuted, the reason grew horrifyingly clear. One of the names listed was 'Hadley MacGregor.'"

The world tilted out of focus, and Fitz's grip tightened on my hand. Izzy vacated her seat and was kneeling on the ground in front of me before I could blink.

"Breathe, Hadley," she said lowly.

Fitz's arm slid protectively around me, and he pulled me closer, knowing a bit of pressure would help me feel safe.

"Do ye need assistance?" he asked.

I had declined his offer the last few times I'd teetered on the edge of a panic attack, wanting to deal with them on my own, but in that moment, with all eyes on me and in the wake of earth-shattering news, I thought that might be just what I needed. Unable to find my voice just yet, I nodded shakily. My pulse beat rapidly as hysteria bubbled through me, threatening to destroy every last bit of my equilibrium.

Fitz turned his body to mine and nodded to Izzy. They were communicating a plan, I realized, though I could barely process it as I clung to myself. The air was growing thin by the time the first surge of calm entered my bloodstream. Soft, warm energy poured from my connection with Fitz and nestled around me. My pulse slowed as my breathing grew less labored, and soon, I was calm enough for Izzy to squeeze my hand and resume her place on the sofa.

"Thank you," I whispered to my fiancé and his sister.

"Are ye well, Hadley?" Esther asked.

"Well enough. Thank you for asking."

Esther nodded, and Ann gave me an encouraging smile.

"When you say persecuted..." I began. "Are there any other details?"

"Are ye sure ye want to do this right now, Hads?" Fitz asked.

I was desperate for the answer. I nodded.

"There aren't many details, no," she said. "It only said "fate unknown.""

"'Tis consistent with the warning from the Bean Nighe," Hamish said.

"Ye've encountered a *Bean Nighe*?" Ann asked, her eyes wide.

"She said I would die if I didn't change course. It's one thing to have a creature in the woods tell you of a possible fate. It's another thing entirely when there's a record of it in the future."

"We must heed her warning," Fitz said.

"How can this be?" I asked. "I mean... how can there be a book already written in the future about events that haven't even occurred yet in the past?"

"When we alter the past, though it be our present right now, Fate has already charted the new course. Or at least, I believe it to be so," Ann said.

Fitz dropped his elbows onto his knees. "I didnae believe it would change so quickly. I've long heard of the consequences of Fate, but this... Ye must return to the future," Fitz said, turning to me. "Immediately."

"And what?" I asked. "Just leave you here?"

"Aye, I'll remain for a bit longer." Fitz eyed me meaningfully. He said into my mind, "*I'll see things through.*"

"No," I said, shaking my head. "I won't leave you here."

"The risk is less for me. Ye are in danger."

"I'm afraid the Cardinal Court has sent orders," Izzy said. "They've ordered both of yous to return to our time."

"*What?*" I asked incredulously.

"Aye," Ann said. "They are frightened of losing you, and so are we. Izzy and I support their decision to bring you home."

"But...." I paused, cognizant of how much I should say before Esther, Hamish, Annabel, and Katherine. They knew our goals, but it felt crude to have this discussion in front of Esther. "It's not time."

"That is why I should remain," Fitz said. "Ye are at risk, so ye should return, and I'll follow ye as quickly as I can."

"I can't believe you'd even suggest that," I said.

"That ye follow court orders and remain safe? Aye, I'll readily support that decision."

"I won't leave without you," I said.

"I willnae leave without you both," Ann said firmly.

"Mum," Fitz began.

"No, Fitz," she said in a tone that didn't welcome discussion. Her eyes narrowed in determination. "I lost my husband only weeks ago, and I willnae do the same with my son because of his stubborn nature. We'll all return—I willnae leave without ye."

Fitz fixed his gaze on his fidgeting hands. He wouldn't cross his mother—not publicly, anyway. "Perhaps we'll resume our discussion this evening—give ourselves a bit of time to consider this news."

Ann's expression was unreadable. "A diplomatic answer. Just like your father." Her tone wasn't harsh—a bit of tenderness mixed with her fear, I thought.

The others remained quiet, allowing us to work through our issues as a family unit, but Esther, Annabel, and Hamish were family too, and they had questions that were best suited for Ann. Izzy used the opportunity to move to the sofa where we were seated and settled next to me.

"Is anything amiss? I mean, besides what I already know." Her eyes narrowed in concern.

"No more than we can handle."

Izzy wasn't convinced. "Perhaps I'll work up a bit of my calming herbal tea, and we can have ourselves a wee chat later," she said. "I'll wager Esther has just the right ingredients. For my calming soak too, if we're lucky."

Izzy's eyes were fixed distantly through the window, the sun highlighting the freckles scattered across her angelic face, but her mind was already far away. She twirled a piece of her auburn hair absent-mindedly between her fingers.

"Technically, you're our guest here. I think I should be the one fussing over you," I said.

Her emerald eyes focused. "I like to be useful."

"I worry about you. I know you like to stay busy, but I want to make sure you're taking the time for yourself to heal."

A sly grin rose to her lips as she found her response. "I'm a healer. Healing you will heal a bit of myself. So you just mind yourself, aye?"

"There's no arguing with you, Iz."

"Aye, and you'd do well to remember that."

I smiled. That sounded just like something her brother would say, and in that very tone. My eyes flickered to Fitz. He was listening to our conversation, but the distance in his energy told me he might as well have been miles away.

"This is loads to process," Izzy said, also studying Fitz, I realized. "I know that. But I do ask both of yous to come home with us. I know very well that you're both stubborn as anyone in this world or the next, but know your limits here, aye? The moment Hadley is condemned is the moment all is lost."

"Don't say that, Iz," I said.

"Why not? It is the truth. The councils of this time will not intervene to save you, Hadley. If we lose you, not only will it be devastating to our family, but we also lose a great hope—one half of the prophecy. Do not forget the role you are meant to play in our time just for the sake of this ring in the past. If you are captured, what good will that do?"

"Izzy is right. Ye must leave, Hadley," Fitz said.

"You'll no more tell me what to do than anyone else in this room."

"Oh aye? Because I wish ye ill?" he said dismissively.

"Of course I don't think that," I said, my blood beginning to boil.

"I've only asked ye to share a life with me. I've only gone through hell and back to ensure ye could make yer own decisions and have the life ye would choose for yerself." Fitz's voice was low, but anger burned through it.

"Fitz," I whispered urgently.

"Nae, Hadley. Ye dinnae like being told what to do, and I ken that plain enough. But I am serious when I say that ye *cannae* die here. Do ye understand me? I cannae bear even the thought of it. Do *not* put me through that for the sake of yer own stubborn pride."

"I'm not asking to die here, Fitz," I said, a bit harsher than I meant it. "I am asking to stay long enough to see this mission through. We have a clear warning—we'll know when I become a true suspect, and I'll leave before anything happens. I promise."

"By the time ye're a suspect, it'll bloody well be too late."

"That's not true."

"Hadley…" Fitz said.

"No, I'm serious, Fitz."

"I ken ye are. That's what troubles me."

"We can be smart about this," I said.

"I dinnae wish to make matters worse," Izzy said, her accent already thickening. "But Fate's kindness has its limits, and the court… well, they've given their orders. But that doesnae mean we have to follow the court's instruction *today*."

"And Fate?" I asked.

"We could make the wrong decision at any point. Time is of the essence, but I hardly think a day or two will matter much after everything that's been set in motion."

"I dinnae ken…" Fitz said, his broad Scottish speech as bold as ever.

"Emotions are high right now. Let's all sit on this a moment and reconvene. A couple of hours won't make or break our decision." Izzy eyed Fitz and me warily. "Further discussion after everyone has time to decompress would be ideal."

"Fine," Fitz said reluctantly.

Izzy rose from the sofa and returned to her mother. I turned to Fitz.

"*You and I need to talk,*" I said. "*Away from the others.*"

His gaze remained fixed on the fire.

"Fitz."

Everything had just turned on its head with this news, *and* we'd just agreed to walk down the aisle. My mind was spinning, but nothing would make sense until Fitz and I finally worked out what was going on between us.

Finally, he nodded. "I'm gonnae take a turn in the garden, and I'll meet ye in our room after?" he proposed, looking to me.

"Okay," I agreed. "I'll meet you in our room in half an hour."

CHAPTER TWENTY-SIX

"I can't handle this, Fitz," I said, holding my left hand in front of me. "I can't go through with this… not this way."

He had just returned from his walk, his sights set on the warm fire.

"I dinnae understand. The wedding, ye mean?" Fitz asked, his face flooded with concern. He stood by an old wooden table near the fireside, the light dancing across his face. "I need ye to explain. Please."

I hadn't intended to make him nervous, but when I understood his fear, my heart sank.

"I love you. I want to spend my entire life loving you," I said. "I just can't go through a wedding ceremony until we fix this."

"Fix what?" he asked, though I thought I saw a spark of realization in his eyes.

"Nothing seems wrong from the outside looking in, does it? We're intimate. We talk about our mission and your relatives, Lucio and

Lorenzo, Fate and the future. But we aren't sharing what's troubling our hearts."

Fitz looked down at the floor. "I'd say we're doing a braw job, considering the circumstances."

"We could be doing better. Down the line, we're going to wish we hadn't just stuffed our feelings down and moved on."

"Just moving on? That isnae what I'm doing. Are ye?"

I shot him a sour look.

"I'd say the events of the last year are pretty well on my mind all the time," he said roughly.

"I didn't know," I said.

"I dinnae talk about these things all the time."

"All the time isn't what I'm asking for. But there's an emotional distance here that I don't want to walk down the aisle with."

Fitz sighed.

"Seriously?" I said. "Why can't we just talk about this?"

"Because I dinnae wish to discuss it, Hadley!" he bellowed, his brows furrowed.

The words I had intended to say next escaped me. The hurt must have shown on my face, and I hated that more than anything. Fitz's face fell. He squeezed his eyes shut and leaned onto the old wooden table, his fists clenched.

I crossed my arms. He was hurting, and I knew it. Perhaps I should be the bigger person and apologize for pushing, but I couldn't find it in myself to do that. Every day, his energy grew stranger to me. He was coiled so tightly inside, I was afraid he would never unravel. I was afraid of losing the man I loved so dearly.

When Fitz opened his eyes again, he met my gaze, his features relaxed ever so slightly.

"I didnae intend to yell. I'm sorry."

I nodded, my lips pulled tightly.

Fitz sighed. "'Tis difficult to see ye upset. I hate myself for being the one to have caused it."

The words still stuck in my throat.

"Hadley, please… say something." He ran his fingertips nervously through his hair. "Shout at me if ye'd like. Anything would be better than silence."

His eyes were troubled. Pleading. The war raging inside of him was palpable, from his eyes to the hard line on his lips to his energy buzzing around him.

Finally—"I'm afraid, Fitz."

"No… no of me," he said, almost unsure.

"Of course not," I said, wringing my hands.

"Of what, then?"

"Of losing you."

His quizzical brow betrayed his confusion.

"You aren't yourself. You haven't been since we lost Ian, and I understand. You know I do…" My eyes misted thinking of Ian, thinking of my own father. "You're upset and angry, but you won't discuss it. His death is eating you alive."

"Hadley," he said, his eyes filled with pain. "I am wearing his loss like a blanket. 'Tis all over me, smothering me."

The crackle of the fire was all that disturbed the room. I didn't dare move even an inch, scared I would break the spell between us.

"Aye, I've been quiet. Perhaps I distract myself more than ye're accustomed to, but with all that's at stake here, I cannae lose myself completely to grief. I cannae think about it anymore, aye? I need ye to just let me breathe."

I nodded softly, swallowing hard. "I've been through this. I know what it is to lose a father."

"I know, Hadley," he said softly.

"Maybe talking to me right now is too much, but maybe you could talk to Hamish. Your sister. Anyone. Because if you don't, I'll lose you. Even worse, you'll lose yourself."

Fitz's energy faltered. He turned and began to pace the room. Finally, he paused, turning to face me, his features calmer than before.

"I'm afraid too. But no of losing myself."

"What, then?" It was more demand than question, and I cleared my throat, my impatience surprising even myself.

A smirk pulled across Fitz's lips at my response, before a stoic expression replaced it. "I'm angry with Lorenzo. So truly enraged that I'm afraid to even express it. I'm afraid of what I'm capable of with this hatred. If 'tis locked safely inside, that's one thing, but once I open the floodgates..." he trailed off.

"Some would say you'd feel better once you let the steam out of the pot."

Fitz shook his head. "It'll be... I think... once I allow myself to truly think through this, once I stop deflecting, I'll fill with such a rage that I willnae be able to control it."

I moved closer and reached for his hands. He flinched but didn't pull away.

"We won't let that happen to you."

"How do ye ken?"

"Because I know what you're capable of. I know what *we* are capable of. I know we can channel this pain into power instead of letting it consume us."

He shook his head again, unsure.

"I won't tell you to not be angry, because you have every right. I'm angry too. But if we don't find our way through this, we're playing right into Lorenzo's hands."

"Broken souls make the easiest targets."

"And he's trying to break us. I won't allow it. Will you?"

Fitz's eyes darkened. "Nae, I willnae allow him to have power over me."

"Then you know what we have to do."

He hesitated briefly before nodding. I dropped onto a chair by the fireside. Fitz's eyes studied me.

"What?" I asked.

"What are ye no saying?"

"What do you mean?"

"Yer energy… there's something to it that I cannae sort."

What a loaded question, I thought.

"I just… feel so heavy."

Fitz cocked his head, as though he was making sense of me. He moved closer and knelt to the floor, so he was eye level with me. He slipped his hand under my chin, raising my gaze to his.

"I cannae read yer mind, Hads."

We sat suspended in silence, our eyes locked and energies wavering. I knew what I wanted to say, but I hardly knew where to begin. Finally, Fitz's energy shifted, growing softer, and he broke the quiet.

"Come on. Let's end our torment."

I thought of how to lighten the mood.

"Esther has fresh bread and honey in the kitchen. I couldn't really eat breakfast, so I could go grab that? Perhaps we can talk while we have a snack?"

Fitz chuckled ever so slightly, and I gave him a questioning glance.

"'Tis amusing to hear such a modern phrase in this place. Aye, a braw plan."

I smiled.

We held each other's gazes for a bit too long. My heart thumped heavily in my chest, and my breathing came short. My eyes dipped to Fitz's lips, and involuntarily, I bit at my own. I pulled my eyes quickly from him, quelling my urges.

I had so desperately wanted to talk with Fitz, and not wanting him to change his mind, I stood. He followed suit, and I turned, grabbing his hand to pull him toward the door.

I didn't get far before his arm was around my waist, and he pulled me against him.

"So hasty," he whispered against my ear. "My mind is clouded, Hadley. I can think of nothing but the taste of ye."

That was all it took for my resolve to crumble.

I shuddered longingly under his touch and leaned into him. His free hand traveled to my arms, across my chest, and rested at my collarbone, his fingertips sinking against my neck. His grip on my waist tightened, and his fingers slid up my neck to tilt my head to the side, kissing the tender skin below my ear. My lips parted, and after a moment's work, his fingertips pushed my chin gently back toward him.

His lips brushed against mine before sinking into a kiss. A weight lifted from my chest, and I leaned deeper into his embrace, my lips working against his.

Fitz removed my stays before pulling me around to face him. He tugged at the chemise, and it fell from my shoulders. His lips traveled across my newly exposed skin and gentle euphoria took hold of my mind, pulling me toward pleasure.

He returned to my lips, where we worked against each other, restoring what had been damaged. When Fitz pulled back, panting, he rested his forehead against mine.

"I'd be lost without ye, firecracker," he whispered, pulling me tightly against him. "Two hundred years isnae long enough, but I'll gladly give ye the years I have left."

Fitz volunteered to tell the family we'd be preoccupied and request some food from the kitchen. He was in a disheveled state with his hair wild and his shift askew. I tried to smooth over his appearance, but he resisted my attempts.

"I dinnae much care about that just now," he said before padding down the hallway.

I pulled my chemise back into place and sank into the covers, seeking warmth. My blood still hummed through my veins, and though I needed strength for our upcoming conversation, I decided I could revel in my beautifully lethargic state a bit longer. I recalled Fitz's words back in London—this love of ours might not be easy, but it was real, and I would fight for it. I wondered what that love might look like if we hadn't been placed in these circumstances. It was impossible to guess.

The door opened, and I clutched the covers, hoping it wasn't Millie. Fitz strode in with a tray filled with bread, honey, cold cuts, and two large mugs.

"A bit of mead from Isla," he said. "She gave me a sly smile when she set them down."

I looked him over, and he smirked. "I told you that you looked suspicious."

He chuckled before sliding into bed and setting the tray between us. Fitz drizzled a bit of honey across the bread and took a big bite.

I couldn't help but smile. I loved this man so much.

"All right then," he mumbled through his mouthful. "Tell me what's troubling ye."

"What *isn't* troubling me? Besides all of…" I raised my hands, looking around. "*This.* There's also us. There's been this weight on me ever since we left our team. And the deaths…." I looked down. "Fitz, these deaths haunt me."

Fitz's chewing slowed, and he set his glass of mead back onto the tray. His eyes softened as they met mine, and he nodded.

"Keoni's death has bothered me from the moment it happened, but not only because he's gone. There's so much more to what happened than we know. I know that, but I can't figure it out. His death is tied to information that is needed to keep the living safe."

Keoni had been a trusted advisor in Opimae, but once he'd been killed while double crossing us, countless questions had arisen. We had been kicked off the mission before we could search for an answer to them all.

"Aye, I understand. It doesnae make sense, but we willnae sort that in the past. That is for the team to handle."

"And I'm sure they will," I said flatly. I took a deep breath, steeling myself for my next statement. "And then there's Ian."

Fitz nodded, his mouth tight. He lifted the bread from the tray, busying his hands.

"I don't know… if *I* should talk about it."

"Why no?"

"Because I'm not sure if it'll make things better or worse for you. You don't want to discuss your feelings, but I'm different." I rubbed my aching neck, reflecting. "And then there's what's coming with Esther."

"Ye may speak of what ye'd like, Hads. I think that's clear. I can handle it."

"I don't know what to do with that. I don't know what you're really saying."

"Dinnae harbor yer feelings. Out with it."

I started to bring up our most recent fight before realizing there was something else I needed to say first. Fitz was pulling the bread apart nonchalantly, and looking at him, I almost choked back the words. I spoke before I could change my mind.

"I feel responsible for Ian's death."

Fitz froze, and it was a couple heartbeats before he looked at me. "*Why?*"

"I pushed for us to go to the fortress after the battle."

"Nae, Hadley."

"I did. And if I hadn't… he would still be alive."

Fitz squeezed his eyes shut. "Ye cannae think that way."

"I can't help it."

For a moment, there was only silence. Then he looked at me once more.

"Lorenzo killed my father—it was only him. No yer advocacy for the fortress, no my support of that plan, no my father's decision to join the crusade."

I nodded, knowing he was right, but it still haunted me.

"I cannae convince ye that ye're no to blame," he said. "But I hope ye can come to that conclusion on yer own because ye dinnae wear any of the responsibility for this."

"I want to believe that."

"Then do. Believe *me*. I wouldnae lie to ye, Hadley. We made the best decision we could. The fault lies with Lorenzo."

I nodded again. Knowing Fitz didn't blame me helped minutely. Perhaps… perhaps I could find my way out after all.

We ate for a few moments in silence.

"Now, what else?" Fitz asked.

"We're still not striking the right balance with how protective you are."

"Have ye no considered that perhaps I'd back down if ye'd stop being so reckless?"

I scoffed. "That's ridiculous."

"Ridiculous, is it? Why do ye think so?"

"I'm not saying I never need help—I'm not out of touch—but I can handle myself pretty well these days."

"It isnae always whether ye can handle yerself or no. 'Tis that ye get yerself into situations that ye shouldnae."

"That's not fair."

"Aye, and is that why a man died two nights ago?"

I winced, setting the piece of bread I was holding back onto the tray.

"It's not that simple."

"Of course it isnae. It was self-defense, and ye were justified in protecting yerself and Esther from someone who meant to kill ye," he said before pausing, clearly collecting his thoughts. "However, what ye did was reckless. Ye broke into the bloke's house, almost got yerself caught by the physician and then almost got killed by Duncan."

I sighed. "The thing with the physician was an oversight. But Esther wanted to know for sure if Duncan might talk."

"Weel, I dinnae think there's much chance of that now."

I cut my eyes at him, not amused by his sarcasm.

"That isnae even what troubles me most," he said.

"What is it then?"

"That ye didnae tell me."

"You would have told me not to do it."

"Aye, and I think all things considered, that would've been sound advice."

I raised my hands in surrender. "No one else will die by his hands—human or witch."

"And while I'm glad of that wee fact, I cannae say I'm pleased that ye snuck around to do it."

"I know."

"Do ye?" he asked, his eyes troubled. "Because ye argue with me about being overprotective, but ye'll run straight into the eye of the storm and do just as ye damn well please—every single time. 'Tis hardly fair for ye to be vexed with me when ye willingly put yerself into danger like that."

I wanted to argue, but I couldn't. I popped a bit of bread into my mouth, stalling as I organized my thoughts.

"I'm trying, Fitz. I'm trying so hard to do the right thing."

"I ken," he said, resting his hand briefly on mine. "So am I."

I nodded in acknowledgment. "You can't just order me around and tell me I can't do things. That won't work with me."

"And ye cannae run off into danger when it isnae necessary without speaking to me about it. I ken yer nature, and I love ye all the better for it. I'll be frustrated every time ye put yerself in danger. I'll never be fine with it because I cannae stomach the thought of losing ye. But... I cannae clip yer wings, firecracker. That would be taking the spirit that I love so well. We need to be patient with each other."

"And what about you?" I asked.

"What about me? Who would I be without ye, Hadley? Who would I be if no yer protector?"

"You're far more than that."

"Aye. I have my own life—or I did before this crusade, anyway."

I mulled over my response, certain he would hate it. "I need to know that your life will have meaning if I don't survive this."

His eyes fixed on the fire, darkening, and his body went rigid.

"I know you'd mourn." Of course I did. Henry's and Molly's pains would haunt me forever. "But I just… I need to know you'd be okay in the end."

Finally, Fitz turned to me. "Dinnae say such things."

"You worry too much about me. I need you to focus some of that energy on yourself."

"I'll always prioritize yer well-being. *Always*. It cannae be otherwise."

Even if I worried about his concern for me, it was ultimately the reason I was sitting in this bed in the seventeenth century. He could have walked away from me, from us, when I'd left for Boston, and I'd still be living a life only half fulfilled.

"The life that I have and the beings that fill it… I have these things because of you." My eyes misted. "I know how you've fought and sacrificed so I could truly live, and I'm so grateful to you for that."

Fitz's fingertips brushed my temples before sliding down my jaw, and he left them there, cupping my face. I leaned forward and kissed him. The intimacy of the moment was overwhelming. To be loved in your purest form, to be fully known and fully loved, was a miracle in itself.

When I leaned back, I met Fitz's eyes, and our connection intensified.

"I worry about your protectiveness because I worry you aren't keeping yourself safe. You know that. So, truthfully, our worry is the same. It's founded in love and concern. Fitz, I love every bit of you—even the infuriating parts."

He laughed lightly.

"Maybe we'll always be bickering over my recklessness and your overprotectiveness, but my god, am I glad to be doing that with you. If the time has come to declare our vows, let mine be this: I promise to never stop bickering with you because the moment our concern for each other ceases is the moment our love dies. And I vow to never let that happen."

He kissed me deeply, his hands running through my hair, across my neck, beneath my chemise. The desire that channeled between us was neither hasty nor angry. It was purposeful. It was love.

CHAPTER TWENTY-SEVEN

The following day, Esther wrote to Neilina seeking council from the coven, and Neilina answered within the hour with instructions. She advised us to meet on the far side of the same copse where Esther, Marjorie, and I had encountered The Witchkiller.

A large group traveling toward the edge of town would raise suspicion, so we ventured out in groups of two. Fitz and I left the house just after dusk and met the rest of our family. Esther and Ann were waiting in the shadows. Izzy and Hamish arrived roughly five minutes behind us, and even with her cloak pulled over her head, Izzy's eyes seemed to glow in the soft moonlight spilling across us.

Fitz worried about me drawing attention from the villagers, but I thought perhaps Izzy was in even more danger of that.

Hamish and Fitz trudged ahead of us, leading the way and scouting for danger. Izzy fell in beside me as we traveled down the muddy path, and I turned to the woman who was as dear to me now as a sister. In truth, she was already my sister-in-law, but soon enough, humans would recognize our ties as well.

"Are you married?" Izzy asked quietly as we labored up the hillside, our breaths shortened by our stays.

I tilted my head and then realized. In the excitement of the afternoon, it hadn't occurred to me that how my last name was listed in the mysterious book would raise questions. "Oh, no, we're not married yet."

Izzy raised her eyebrows.

"Hamish suggested we… speed our marriage along so the humans don't discover we aren't legally wed—well, according to human law."

Izzy nodded. "I'm sure he meant well."

"He meant to protect Esther, but that's reason enough."

Izzy glanced at me from the corners of her eyes.

I laughed lightly. "What is it, Iz?"

"Are you ready, then?"

"Of course I am. We've been distracted by this mission even before Fitz's proposal. Even if forming our streams was more powerful than the human ceremony, I grew up in human culture. Witch or not, I want to wed your brother."

"Then you have my blessing. I only want happiness for the two of yous."

I smiled. "Thank you, Izzy. Your blessing means more than you know."

We were silent for a few moments before Izzy changed the subject.

"You know, Esther's name wasnae in the book."

"I'm not too surprised. Fitz said he knew of her death only because of the family archives. Annabel wrote of it in her journal years after it happened."

"I wonder why it wasnae recorded, then?"

"Maybe the witches had it scrubbed, for some reason."

"If that were the case, then why didn't they…."

"Remove my name as well? I don't know, Iz."

Izzy's face grew pensive, and my thoughts turned to another possibility.

"But if mine is there and hers is gone… what if Esther doesn't die this time?" I asked.

"Oh," she whispered. "Because you and Fitz might have altered her course."

Maybe it was foolish for me to hope that it was true. If we'd altered the course of history in such a way, we were bound to reap Fate's consequences. And there was also the haunting detail of my unknown fate. Would I escape? Or would we exchange Esther's death for my own?

Hamish and Fitz paused ahead, signaling us to halt, and the energy of my witch's eye crackled as it searched the elements. Izzy took my hand. Hamish motioned to Fitz, and they moved slowly in opposite directions. Fitz sprinted toward the tree line and disappeared into the darkness. My heart rate increased—and so did Fitz's. His pulse thrummed through me, and I breathed slowly, willing my protective instincts to calm. Fitz was more than ready for a fight.

"*Watch yer six, Hadley,*" Fitz said telepathically.

"*What's going on?*" I asked.

"*Others are here… no allies. Hamish and I are investigating, but they might no be alone—watch for those who might be joining them.*"

Soon enough, Fitz and Hamish doubled back. Fitz wrapped his arm around me, and I moved in closer, seeking both his calming presence and his warmth.

"What's our plan?" Ann asked.

"Well, there's a wee group of men to the north," Fitz said. "We believe they're wandering the woods making trouble. They're sloshed."

"*Sloshed?*" Esther asked. "I dinnae ken that one."

"They've had too much drink," Ann clarified.

"We dinnae think they ken we're here," Hamish said.

"We'll stay to the south and go from there, then?" Esther asked. "Through that wee path?"

"Aye. Dinnae make careless noise as we meander along the forest. Tell me ye understand," Hamish said to the rest of us.

Ann and Izzy looked warily to each other.

"What's in the forest?" Izzy asked.

"Fair folk," he said.

"I thought they all migrated to Opimae hundreds of years ago."

"Many did, but no all."

Izzy turned to Esther, who nodded. "This path is safe from human eyes, but the fair folk are equally dangerous when provoked. They have favored the witches with safe passage through their forest, but ye must remain respectful. They are temperamental beings."

With the group in agreement, we walked carefully to the south, searching for the obscure opening Fitz and I had walked once before. A familiar, ominous energy coated my bones with dread, alerting me that we neared the dominion of the fair folk.

"The faeries will grant us safe passage through their woods," I whispered to Izzy. "You don't need to worry."

"You've been here before?"

"Fitz and I met with their rulers."

Izzy bit at her lip, then nodded.

We came to the opening, and even though I believed I'd be fine, my entire body tensed. The air was filled with the same musky scent, and rain-soaked branches glimmered in the light of the full moon. From Izzy's stiff posture to Ann's grim expression, skepticism was written clearly across their faces.

As we stepped into the forest, the air grew still. Nothing stirred. No animals, no wind, no rustle of grass or leaves. All was quiet, and the stillness brought a certain uneasiness with it. Izzy stared listlessly around her.

"Are you okay?" I asked.

She nodded feebly. "Aye, it's only that the world feels dormant here, and I…." she trailed off, her eyes darting about.

"That's especially troubling for you," I said, understanding. Izzy was a green witch to her very core. The absence of life must have been disturbing.

Esther came to her side, placing her hand just under Izzy's elbow. "Come now," Esther said. "In a minute's time, all will be well. Ye'll see—if ye'll trust me?"

I nodded to Izzy, who returned the gesture.

Ann looped her arm through Izzy's, and Esther did the same at her other side. Hamish fell in line behind them, and Fitz squeezed my hand.

"Another adventure, firecracker," Fitz whispered, his breath warm in my ear. I ran my free hand down the side of his face and smiled.

"Let's do this, MacGregor."

Fitz's chuckle faded as we stepped further into darkness, and in the absence of moonlight, my chest tightened with dread. With each step, the world grew dimmer, and the energy of the faeries grew stronger. Even though we had done this once before, Aladia had lit our path last time. The total absence of light sent an uneasy sensation slithering through the pit of my stomach. I refused to look back, and with that determination, we moved forward.

Slowly, the world grew lighter, revealing tree trunks and long, slender branches with patches of green. Evergreens… the very sight was a comfort to me, a reminder of home. As our eyes adjusted to the illumination, I realized the soft glow wasn't spilling from lanterns nor torchlight, but rather, it was pouring from the beings surrounding us.

A gasp escaped Ann's lips, but there was no fear in our collective energy. There was only wonder and awe, leaving me a bit lightheaded. I recalled the glowing faerie we'd seen dancing in the Opimaean courtyard, and a wave of nostalgic longing rippled through me. Even though we'd seen the glow of Aladia, Queen Tarron, Prince Faolán, and the guards, this was different. The glow radiating from this group was another thing entirely. Fitz and I turned, back to back, as we took in the sight before us.

Roughly thirty faeries encircled us, all glowing with the softest, warmest illumination. Their expressions were neutral, but their gazes nudged curiously at my skin. Their light was steady, but it wasn't singular: it sparked and danced around us as if it were as alive as they were. The faeries were as diverse as any group might be—from dark skin to light, blond hair to brunette, blue eyes to brown—but they all shared two characteristics. Each one of them emitted a soft glow, and their eyes, no matter the shade, glowed with a light similar to what I had seen from Jordan, Saoirse, and Gustavo.

I looked toward the sky, and the evergreens seemed to glow with their light. I thought perhaps I should have been a little more wary of the situation, but a strong sense of calm settled deep within me.

"I feel a bit funny," I said as my mind grew foggier.

"Aye, so do I," Fitz said.

"It is the energy emitted when the fair folk gather." A deep voice sounded behind me. "It is always so with us."

I met the steely gaze of a man who towered over me. He must have been nearly seven feet tall. His long blond hair had been half pulled back, but the rest spilled down his navy plaid overcoat. Beside him stood Aladia, her face even and her arms crossed.

"It has long been our duty to guard weary travelers and grant them rest," he continued. "Much of humanity fears us, but it is our charge nonetheless."

"And will ye grant us safe passage through yer woods this evening?" Fitz asked.

"Aye. That we are pleased to offer ye," he said. "The Queen sends her regards—she is attending to urgent business, but she wishes ye well."

"We are grateful," Fitz returned, bowing slightly.

The man was diplomatic, and I had no reason to suspect he was displeased. But something odd simmered beneath the surface of his energy.

The crowd parted, and a familiar face emerged, a bright grin on their face.

"I hope Lochlan has been sufficiently kind in his welcome to our witch friends," they said pointedly, eyeing the tall faerie who had greeted us.

"Prince Faolán," Fitz said. "'Tis a pleasure to see ye again."

Our group bowed.

"Please, friends. Rise."

They shook Fitz's hand and then my own before greeting the others quickly. "You are all most welcome here."

"Thank you, Your Grace. We hope you and the queen are well."

"Very well, indeed. Thank you for asking. Tarron is dealing with a nasty bit of business in the west, but I am pleased to inform you that I had my own urgent business to attend to, and therefore, I have escaped her fate."

I laughed. "It sounds as though your business is more pleasant then."

"Oh, it is far better. Pierre and I had our first crop of *flùr beag* bloom."

"Little flower," Hamish said.

"It was cultivated from your land, and I wanted to pay homage."

Esther and Hamish seemed pleased.

"As you can see, it was out of the question for me to leave at such a time. It was too risky for me to be away."

"I'm sure the healing benefits of yer new crop are of great interest to ye all," Esther said.

"Absolutely!" Prince Faolán said. "I'm glad Tarron recognized its importance to our folk—and to our work here in Scotland."

"I'm sorry, I dinnae mean to be impertinent, but I would love to hear more about this new discovery of yours," Izzy said, a bit timidly. She stepped forward and removed the hood of her cloak. "I'm a healer, you see, so I've great interest in the medicinal use of natural plants and herbs."

The prince's dark eyes fluttered to Izzy and widened in wonder as they took in the sight of her.

"Yes," they said slowly, their voice soft and distant. "Yes, I'd love to share more with you."

Izzy blushed, her gaze dropping momentarily to the ground. The prince stepped forward, and she looked to them expectantly.

"Perhaps I could show you—I know you have little time now—but maybe soon I could show the flower to you, and we could talk more of it."

"That would be lovely," she said.

The glow emitted by the prince's dark skin grew more brilliant as the two stood seemingly transfixed.

Lochlan's energy darkened as he studied Izzy with Prince Faolán. His eyes were fiery, and his heart raced. Surely, he wouldn't believe Izzy to be a danger to the prince—no, it must have been something else entirely.

As Fitz remarked about Izzy's immense skill as a healer, her attention turned, walking closer to one of the faeries—or so it seemed. But once she was a couple of feet away, she knelt to the ground. It was then that I realized her attention had been captured by something else. A small fox emerged from between the full skirts of two women. It appeared young, with a thick red coat and patches of white around its mouth and trimming its ears.

Izzy extended her hand, and the fox's whisky-hued eyes swept over Izzy before coming nearer.

"Such a well-mannered girl," Izzy said, giggling. "I am honored to meet ye."

"She is always near," a woman said to Izzy. "She protects my daughter."

As if on cue, another red fox stepped around her skirt and sat near the other.

"This is my Catriona," she said.

Surprise registered all around.

"Is shapeshifter your preferred term?" Izzy asked.

"Yes, that'll do well, child," the woman said.

"Is that common with fair folk?" I asked. "I've had the honor before, but I don't recall them holding that particular gift."

"It runs through a few of our familial lines," Prince Faolán answered. "Some of us also have the ability to change our size. Humans fear our abilities, but we know no other way. This is what we are."

"And it's beautiful," Izzy said. "Never believe differently."

The prince smiled and bowed their head to Izzy. The rest of the faerie group followed suit. Izzy looked around, her eyes widening in disbelief. A small burst of energy coursed through me, and I turned to Fitz. He nodded; he had felt it too. The shift in the dynamic around us couldn't be ignored.

"Your healing powers are not the only extraordinary thing about you, I see," the prince said. "You are wise and kind. The animals place their trust in you, and that is most telling."

Lochlan exhaled deeply, the look in his eyes bordering on annoyance. The prince still wore their brightest smile. Even in the dim light, it was clear that Izzy was blushing. I turned to Fitz, and he met my gaze with a smile.

"What is your name, if I might ask?"

"Izzy. Izzy MacGregor."

They skipped a couple of steps forward, pulling a smile from Izzy. They then took her hand and kissed the top of it. "It is a pleasure to meet you, Izzy MacGregor."

"The pleasure is all mine," she said, bowing.

"We are happy to meet you and your companion. We have been anticipating your arrival," Prince Faolán said.

Of course, they'd seen Izzy and Ann coming.

"Thank you," Izzy said earnestly. "I dinnae know how we can repay you for your kindness."

"We ask nothing in return," Prince Faolán said. "It is our duty and our honor to aid this journey."

"We would stay longer if we could spare the time, but the hour grows late. The coven expects us," Esther said.

"We granted them safe passage, and they told us to expect ye," Lochlan said, his words polite but his energy unsettling.

"And, likewise, we shall see you through," said the prince, their eyes narrowing as they looked toward the imposing faerie.

"We are most obliged to ye, yer grace," Hamish said.

The two shook hands, and so began our passage through the western woods.

Izzy fell into step with Prince Faolán, whose crown of dark vines seemed to be lightening. Streaks of soft brown webbed through them, expanding slowly. I couldn't help but smile. Fitz leaned toward me, a conspiratorial look in his eye.

"What's going on over there, ye reckon?" he asked, nodding his head toward Izzy.

"You know as much as I do," I said before laughing lightly. "But it's not nothing."

"This will surely lead to all sorts of problems, and yet… I cannae be angry at it," Fitz said.

I squeezed his hand. "You romantic."

"Aye, that I am, and with my whole heart, I blame *ye*."

I pulled him to me, and we paused, pressing our lips together. In the midst of a forbidden forest, in the warm glow of faerie light, we lingered for a few seconds simply to stay in the magic.

A large fire roared, sending smoke swirling through the night sky, sprinkled with glowing embers that floated toward the stars. The coven had gathered. Sixteen women and eight men were scattered around the fireside. Even though the scene sent a shiver down my spine, my heart warmed at the sight of so many of our magical kin.

Prince Faolán turned to Izzy. "This is where we part ways. I have no business here. I'll be waiting just inside the trees to guide you home."

Izzy nodded before turning to us. I took her hand in mine, and we stepped through the dormant grass, closing the distance between us and the Forfar coven.

Esther's eyes were proud and resolute. Hamish flanked her left side, his stance poised to defend as always. Fitz lent his arm to his mother, trailing just behind Izzy and me, and though he appeared nonchalant, his eyes swept the surrounding area diligently.

As we reached the fireside, a hush fell across the coven, and my skin prickled with the intensity of so many witches' eyes upon us. A woman stepped from the shadows, and the sight of her put me more at ease.

"Katherine," I said warmly. "Was the trek difficult for you?"

"Ne'er ye mind that," she said, extending her hands. I took them in mine, and she smiled softly. "I transported this evening, and before ye ask, I did verra well."

She then turned to the rest of our group. "And to all of ye—welcome to our wee gathering."

I swept my eyes across the coven, and in doing so, I found three familiar faces. Annabel stood not far behind Katherine, and to her right were Thomas and Elspeth. Another woman stepped forward, and her dark eyes glimmered almost amber in the flickering firelight, though her hood cast a shadow across much of her face. When she pulled the hood back, chestnut hair was spilling defiantly from her pins, and her expression was somber.

"Neilina," I said.

"I have feared the repercussions of yer presence in Forfar," she said to Fitz and me. "That fear increased when Esther wrote of yer companions' arrival." Neilina nodded toward Ann and Izzy. "The coven has been at odds. Nothing, it seems, has been right. But tonight, the coven has convened. We believe ye have come to set things right. We are honored to have ye warm yerselves by our fireside, and we stand ready to assist ye in yer quest for information."

"We thank ye for yer kindness," Fitz said. "And we are honored by yer invitation."

Neilina nodded once, and I smiled. I knew this must have been difficult for her, and yet, she had decided to honor her coven's choice. I had to commend her for that.

"We shall first greet the full moon, now that the coven is complete." She stumbled on the last word, surely thinking of Marjorie. "Once we have concluded the full moon communion and received her blessing, we shall channel our power to assist Esther with her visions."

"Will we all join?" I asked.

"All the women, aye. We want only the purest alliance of sisterhood as we connect with the moon, and as such, the men will channel their powers to us so that our energetic levels will maintain the strongest connection to our sister."

"Aye, then let us begin."

I cast a glance over my shoulder to Fitz, and he gave a tight smile before I found my place around the fire with my magical sisters. Katherine was to my right, and she took me by the hand, squeezing it gently. Izzy was opposite the fire from me, and even as the heat distorted the air and sparks danced across my vision, it was clear how Izzy's entire being was alight with magic, her eyes teeming with wonder. She gave a simple nod in my direction, a smile gracing her lips, before closing her eyes and tilting her face toward the sky.

Neilina started the communion by looking to the moon, and after a few seconds of silence, her melodic voice echoed upward toward our lunar sister.

with spirits all in consort
we are unison in mind
we call upon our sister
her glow within us shine

The rest of the coven then joined in, first singing slowly so I could make out the chant, and as I picked it up, the words rolled across our tongues quicker.

into the night do we call
into the flames let it burn
down from above let it fall
the moon betwixt the embers

up from the ground let it rise
let the wind lead us once more
down from above let it fall
the moon betwixt the embers

Once we fell into a steady rhythm with the lyrics, the group began a simple dance. Katherine moved a bit slower so I might mimic her motions, and as I watched the movement of her feet, I worked my way toward proficiency. Annabel played teacher to Ann, and Izzy glowed as Elspeth helped her along. Through steps and sways, our bodies moved in sync. Energy channeled through me, soft but sure, and my entire body buzzed with it.

I turned my eyes to the moon, marveling at her beauty and wonder. She was the same moon that had watched me grow into my power, that fueled Annabel's magic, that smiled down upon us now as I danced alongside Fitz's ancestors. The same moon that shined somewhere on my own. A sense of euphoria crept through me as we completed our chanting. The blessing Neilina had anticipated, I supposed.

It was as though a spell had been cast over us, and I ached with longing, not quite ready to release the moment. I closed my eyes, committing the ethereal scene to memory: the crackling fire as it cast its mysterious light across the coven, the gentle laughter of sisterhood, the moon's bright glow as it peeked over the tops of the evergreens. If magic were a setting, it would be this.

I opened my eyes and swept the scene once more before turning to Fitz. He moved to my side in anticipation of what came next. I swept my fingertips across the side of his face, and he caught my hand, kissing the inside of my wrist. Butterflies rippled through me, the sensation heightened by the lingering joy from the moon's blessing.

"Sisters and brothers of the Forfar coven," Neilina said, breaking the spell. "Hadley and Fitz MacGregor have traveled through the in-between to set matters right in their own time."

Whispers of acknowledgment rippled through the air.

"MacGregor family, step forward," Neilina said.

We followed her instruction and stood united before the rest of the coven.

"This wee group," Neilina said, pointing to us, Izzy, Ann, Esther, and Hamish, "seeks our help. Tonight, we shall aid them by attempting to make sense of Esther and Hadley's connection and Esther's trouble with her visions."

Neilina moved closer to us.

"Come now. Let us combine our powers to request clarity from Fate. Esther, take yer place betwixt Hadley and Fitz." She turned to us. "As we begin our practice, envision Opimae and think of yer companions. Channel yer thoughts and energy toward Esther, and we shall do the same. If her visions are meant to surface, they shall."

Esther followed instruction, and Neilina arranged everyone where their power would be best suited. Izzy moved to take my free hand, and Ann took her son's. Neilina placed Hamish and Annabel in our circle, and as Annabel took Izzy's hand, she studied her carefully. She then looked to me, nodded curtly, and closed her eyes.

The rest of the coven encircled us and clasped their hands together. Neilina called the coven to order, and they chanted, swaying from side to side. At the end of their first verse, they moved around us, still swaying as they stepped. Our inner circle remained still.

Energy popped and crackled, shooting streaks of light across the night sky. My own energy buzzed, unsettled by the influx, and I closed my eyes to center myself. I breathed deeply, in and out, until my heart rate slowed and my energy calmed. As I focused intently on Opimae, my energy fell into place and my witch's eye opened.

The faces of my companions flashed across my mind: Jordan and Henry laughing across the breakfast table from each other, Molly curled up by Isaac's side as she answered his questions about Opimaean customs, James reading a book by the fireside, whisky glass in hand—I saw them all, each one of our crusaders.

I thought of who might try to send a warning beyond our own team—Queen Marina, Charles, perhaps even Gabriella. I pulled the world closer to me as I recalled the lush landscape—the cliffs that hosted the autumnal celebration, the winding canals of Opimae City, the abundant forests of the fire witch nation of Arregaithel, the craggy, snow-covered mountainsides near Lorenzo's fortress.

And then something clicked. An intense burst of energy blew through me, and my witch's eye prickled with knowing.

My breath came short, and my body trembled at the intensity. Fitz's head snapped in my direction.

I shook my head. *"Stay focused."*

Fitz narrowed his eyes, but he nodded and tilted his face upward to the sky. I centered in on the mountains near Lorenzo's lair and traced my path—the trees to the lower ridge where I'd once sneaked across with Fitz, Molly, and Solomon. From there, I wandered through the weak spot in the fortress wall and down the hallways to Lorenzo's office. My energy grew more focused, and I knew I was on the right track.

"Think of Lorenzo," I said to Fitz's mind. *"This vision will relate to him."*

I reached for the door to Lorenzo's office, and I brought my memories of him in that very space to the surface. A flash of bright white light obscured my vision, and when my sight was restored, everything was blurry, like the world wasn't quite real. Esther's energy shifted around me, and I knew.

I was watching Esther's vision.

A fair-haired woman sat at a grand piano in an expensively furnished room. An ornate iron stairwell wound downward behind her, and large windows displayed the night sky beyond her. Fire and candlelight lit her pale face.

Anya, I realized.

The woman I had seen when I picked up the golden band in Lorenzo's office.

Anya's eyes misted. "I… I dinnae understand."

Her accent… she was *Scottish*. The realization blazed through me. Her name had suggested otherwise.

"I know."

Lorenzo. The realization left me stunned.

Anya twisted the gold band on her hand. "Was I married once?"

Lorenzo nodded.

"I cannae recall…" she said, her voice barely a whisper.

Lorenzo remained silent. After a moment, he said, "May I take your ring? I'll keep it safe for you."

Anya met his gaze, hesitating for only a few seconds, before nodding and pulling the band from her finger. She dropped the ring into Lorenzo's open palm, and he closed his hand slowly before shutting his eyes. When he opened them, they were shrouded in mist.

I couldn't make sense of it. Why was he leaving her?

"I know it isn't much consolation, but you were well-loved, Anya," he said.

"Then why did it end?" she asked.

"I cannot tell you that."

Anya pursed her lips, deep in thought. "Then I'm ne'er to ken the truth?"

"No, I'm afraid not."

At that, tears spilled out of Anya's eyes, falling the length of her cheeks.

"Goodbye, Anya. I wish you well," he said before turning away and walking through the door.

The vision blurred, and what had once been an ornate sitting room turned to simple beige stone. Lucio passed by a fire, which cast a soft glimmer to his inky black curls.

"I do not understand the correlation, Father."

"And you won't—not for a long time."

Lorenzo sighed. "What is this about? Why will you not just tell me all I need to know?"

"All will be revealed in time, my son. You must allow things to run their natural course, or we *will* fail."

Lorenzo stood. "I cannot understand it—not this. It feels… unnatural."

"She is the key to everything, Lorenzo. It does not matter how you feel. You keep that in mind. You have not come all this way to fail me now."

The vision wavered, and another scene unfolded. Lorenzo was addressing his followers in the depths of night. I couldn't make out his words over the roar of the crowd. They cheered and shouted, threw their hands toward the heavens and beat them against their chests.

I was startled by a quick change in light as night sprang into day. No, this wasn't the vision shifting into another. I glanced around the fireside to check on our sisters, where the entire coven had been pulled from their meditation and shielded their eyes as they adjusted to the change.

A force blew through my body, leaving behind the traces of its wrath: frazzled nerves, tingling fingertips, and a heavy heart. It was an onslaught of a strong, ancient magic.

The light shifted again. Pale robes billowed in a wind I could not feel, dancing softly through the space. I perceived, rather than saw, the figure of a woman draped in white.

The illumination wasn't the sun. The light poured from her skin and her fair hair.

"Who are you?" I asked, already knowing the answer.

"I am Fate."

"We are honored by yer presence," Neilina said, coming closer and resting her hand on my shoulder. "Ye are most welcome here."

"Am I? There is one here whom I know well, but she does not claim to know me the same. Hadley, my child. Am I also welcome to you?"

I nodded wordlessly. "Yes," I finally said, my voice hoarse.

"I have come to speak with the crusaders."

"We are honored," Fitz said cordially as he slipped an arm around my waist. My energy was wild, and I took a few intentional breaths, steadying myself.

"If you and your companions remain on your current course, Earth and Opimae will both be irrevocably altered by Lorenzo's forces."

"How can we set this right?" I asked, trying to keep a quiver out of my voice. "What can we do to help?"

"You may not set right what others have broken. You have deviated from your course."

"Fitz and I were removed from Opimae by its leaders."

"We wouldnae have left on our own accord," Fitz added.

"The chamber will answer for their indiscretion. Already, they find themselves in the midst of a difficult lesson."

"What does that mean?" I asked, desperate for information. "Our team is not at fault."

"Many suffer who are not at fault."

I looked around, gauging everyone's expressions. Fitz's jaw was set tight, and the coven looked troubled. I couldn't argue with Fate's statement, but I longed to understand *why*.

"Should we not try to stop Lucio?" I asked. "We'll do whatever you ask to keep our team safe."

"That is for you to determine."

"We want to help set things right."

"You have decided… and so your course is altered. If it is so, then blood is the answer to setting things right."

What on Earth was she talking about?

"Blood…?" Fitz echoed, almost to himself.

"Blood will solve all."

"What does blood have to do with any of this?" I asked, growing impatient.

Fate's light flickered softly. "Everything."

"What does that mean?"

"That is for you to discover. Time will bring your answers."

My mind was muddled. Fate was speaking in riddles, and I wanted to scream.

"When the time comes, you will know." Fate nodded, eyeing us meaningfully. "There is one amongst you who is not true. Be wary of them."

And with that, she was gone.

CHAPTER TWENTY-EIGHT

As Fate disappeared, I expected to gaze once again upon the fireside, but the scene before me was much different. The chill of the night air sank deeply into my bones, and the pale moon's glow was all that lit the space around us. Even through my wool stockings, my feet ached against the frigid earth, and the soggy ground dampened my boots. All the coven members were still with us. And not only that, but the group of faeries who had accompanied us to the fireside were standing together at a distance.

We all looked around, confused about what had happened. Fate's words echoed in my mind.

There is one amongst you who is not true.

The fair folk crossed the distance warily.

"Is this a trick of yers?" Thomas asked them.

"No," Prince Faolán answered. "This is the work of Fate, I'm afraid."

"Why should we believe ye?"

"Thomas," Neilina said sternly.

He met her eyes defiantly. "Ye might be willing to risk our fates over propriety, but ye willnae find me doing the same."

Elspeth placed a hand on Thomas's arm, but he shrugged her off and strode closer to Prince Faolán. The other faeries stepped forward, ready to strike. The prince moved their arm to the side, bidding the faeries to stand down. They obeyed reluctantly.

"Is there something more you wish to say?"

"Ye may be royalty, but that doesnae make ye above reproach."

"This was not my doing, Thomas."

Thomas sneered and pulled his arms back. Magical energy poured from his fingertips.

"Well, that's my cue," I said, stepping forward. My hands blazed with fire, and for a few seconds, Thomas froze, seemingly mesmerized. "Don't make any rash decisions."

"I willnae take orders from ye."

"It's not an order, but it *is* advice, which it seems you could use right now."

"Now is no the time to make enemies," Fitz said. "The fair folk have been kind to us. Let us no forget that."

"Aye," Hamish said, moving quickly to Fitz's side. "Mind yerself now."

Esther, Neilina, Katherine, and several members of the coven stepped forward, reminding Thomas of the many reasons he shouldn't act out of line. His eyes narrowed, clearly calculating his next move, but just when I thought he meant to attack, he placed his hands upward in surrender and stepped back.

"Fine," he said. He stepped nearer, his face mere inches from my own. "But when this all turns sour, remember, 'tis this troublemaker ye sided with."

Thomas strode off, and I lost sight of him in the darkness. My pulse quickened. I didn't much like the thought of him lurking in the shadows while his anger burned, but there was another pressing matter to attend to.

"Where do we find ourselves?" Katherine asked.

Though the moon offered enough light for us to see one another, I squinted as I searched the distance, attempting to make out a shape on the horizon.

"I… I think we might be near the old Bruce settlement," I said.

Fitz's eyes were wild as they met mine. Neither of us had forgotten the dark energy that lingered within the walls of those structures.

Esther slipped a hand in mine and squeezed tightly.

"Aye, I feel the troublesome energy," she said as she pointed to our right. "It lies that way."

"Should we return home?" Ann asked.

"Fate brought us here for a reason," I said.

"Aye, and I would be fibbing if I said that doesnae trouble me," Annabel said.

"Something we agree on," Katherine said.

"If she's brought us here, there must be reason, aye?" Hamish asked.

I hadn't expected him to be up for adventure while Esther was among us.

"I've surprised ye, I see. But it isnae the first time we've scoured these grounds, and the first time yielded a bit of intelligence."

"Ye brought Esther out here without me?" Annabel scolded. "I thought ye meant to leave her behind."

"Aye, and she was with *me*," Hamish said. "She was in nae danger."

Annabel huffed. "Sometimes I think ye dinnae have good sense."

I had to smile despite the circumstances, and there was a hint of amusement on Esther's features as well.

"I say we continue on," Esther said. "Discover whatever Fate means for us to find."

"Tell us of yer intelligence, and the coven will put it to a vote," Neilina said.

None of us raced to share of our adventure.

"'Tis only fair," Elspeth said. "How can we decide when we dinnae ken all the information?"

The four of us looked at one another. Finally, Esther nodded, and I began the tale. When I'd finished, the coven sat quietly.

"I'm not sure if your invitation extends to us fair folk, but if it does, we're in," Prince Faolán said.

"Your Grace, are you certain?" It was Lochlan who spoke.

"Fate does not make mistakes," they said softly. "We are not here by accident."

"I'm following the prince's logic," I said. "If Fate has brought us this close to the settlement, I think we're meant to go."

Annabel nodded curtly. "Perhaps this will aid Marjorie in some way or assist us in preventing further arrests. I am willing to take the risk."

"If ye join us, be vigilant," Fitz said. "No only is there great darkness in this place, but the man we sought here—Lucio Belmonte—is dangerous."

"All in favor," Neilina said.

A wave of hands raised.

"All opposed."

Only five hands.

"The ayes have it," she said. "However, if ye are one of the opposition, ye may leave now. It isnae our business to force support."

We waited, but none left.

"Then ye proceed by choice, and yer choice alone."

She nodded to us, and the four of us—Fitz, Esther, Hamish, and I—led the way.

We stepped lightly through the damp grass, closing our distance as efficiently and as quietly as possible. Hushed voices broke through the silence.

"What is the matter?" Fitz asked.

"'Tis Elspeth."

"I cannae find Thomas," she said, panic clear in her tone. "We must find him."

"He was angry. He likely walked back to the village."

"Without me?"

Annabel sighed.

"What is it?" Elspeth said. "Out with it, Annabel."

"Thomas hasnae been himself lately."

"Aye, he's been acting strangely, Elspeth. I ken he wouldnae leave ye behind in his usual state, but—he is troubled now," Esther said.

"I think they're right," I said. "He's been hot and cold, aye?"

"Aye," she said, exasperated. "And that is what troubles me."

"Ye cannae turn back," Katherine said. "'Tis no safe for ye to do so."

"But—"

"I willnae hear of it," Neilina said. "We proceed as a group now. 'Tis too late to turn back. We shall find Thomas when we return to the burgh."

Tears streamed down Elspeth's face, but she nodded, her expression dull, admitting defeat. Katherine wrapped an arm around her, and we pushed on.

Finally, we approached the walls of the first building. I moved closer and rested my hand against it, seeking support. Walking long distances in stays with heightened emotions was not an easy task. But no sooner had my fingertips made contact with the wall than a vision overtook me. Hamish exclaimed, and Esther's energy rippled against me—it had taken hold of her too.

A man crouched in the corner of a stone structure. A dark presence lingered around him, and he crawled toward the doorway until he seized with hysterics. He fell to his side and rolled onto his back. His face was contorted in pain, but it was one I knew instantly. I pushed back against the vision, screaming in protest, and Fitz's voice broke through.

"'Tis all right, Hadley. I've got ye. Just come back to me now."

I focused on his voice and pulled myself to the surface. His face was near mine, his brows furrowed and his eyes closed in concentration as he navigated our connection in his effort to pull me back. I wrapped my arms around his neck.

"I'm okay. I'm back."

He pulled away, searching my face for a hint of anything amiss. Once he was satisfied, he nodded, and his features relaxed.

I found Esther nearby, and we linked fingers.

"Did you see?" I asked.

She nodded.

"What? What is the matter?" Neilina prodded.

"It's Thomas," I said. "He's in some kind of trouble, but I think I know just where he is."

"Hurry!" Elspeth yelled. "We must go now!"

"Quietly," I said pointedly. "I don't know what we'll find, and we have to be smart if we want to help him, okay?"

Elspeth nodded. She whispered, "Please, Hadley."

"The room where I told you I saw that family," I said to Fitz.

He nodded and led us toward the old structure. The same strange energy assaulted my skin with a prickling sensation, far more active this evening.

"I dinnae like the feel of that," Fitz said, his eyes darting to mine.

"Let's try to be quick," I said.

Fitz nodded. "This way, I think?"

I focused on the energies teeming through the air and found a new witch's magic buzzing around me. It grew stronger in the direction Fitz had nodded toward.

We continued forward, mindful of our steps. We'd reached the second building—the one where I'd seen the happy, young family—when movement on the other side of the wall caught my witch's eye. I turned to Fitz, and we signaled the coven forward.

We rounded the corner through the crumbling doorway and came face to face with Thomas. He had been kneeling but rose at the sight of us, grasping a stick in his right hand. A small box sat discarded to the left of a small fire that had nearly burned out. To the right was a symbol drawn with stick and ash. I didn't recognize it, but Fitz swore.

It was a crude circle with a smaller circle resting within it, and between the two circles were words I didn't recognize—Latin, I thought. Two snaking lines intersected at the center of the inner circle, forming a wavy "X" within it, and a single star rested in each of the four quadrants.

"What have ye done?" Fitz asked, disbelief hanging in his tone.

"Thomas!" Elspeth yelled. She ran forward, but Hamish caught her before she reached him. "Let go of me!"

"Nae. Be still, Elspeth."

Thomas cocked his head to the side. "Keeping my wife from me now, Hamish?" he asked, clicking his tongue in disapproval. "Now why would ye do such a thing?"

"Because you aren't her husband," I realized. I couldn't believe how long it had escaped me.

Thomas raised an eyebrow. "I believe the minister would disagree with yer assessment of our marital union."

Thomas's hot and cold attitude.

"That's because he's a simpleton," I shot back.

"Just what do ye mean by that?" Thomas asked.

The feel of something in the shadows.

"Father Evans can't perceive what I can."

"Which is?"

Fate's warning to be wary of the one amongst us who was not true.

"I hear you haven't been yourself lately," I said.

Thomas smirked.

I had even seen a spell for it in Annabel's grimoire.

"You don't seem like yourself because you aren't yourself. You're not Thomas at all, are you?"

"Ye're talking nonsense!" Elspeth said. "Of course that's Thomas. Look with yer eyes, feel his energy!"

Our suspicions that Lucio was already here in the past.

"Of course you feel Thomas's energy," I said softly. "You're connected to him through your streams. But there's the energy of another there too."

It hit me with full force. The room went silent.

"And that's because there's another spirit inside Thomas's body right now. Isn't that right, Lucio?"

Elspeth cried in protest. "Nae, it cannae be. Nae!"

Thomas took a step forward and clapped. "Very good, Hadley. You are just as clever as I'd expected."

"Expected?" I said, my body recoiling at the implication of his words. "You already know about me?"

"Oh, I've known about you for a long time. Fitz too," he said, nodding in his direction.

Fitz moved closer, placing his arm around my waist.

"This cannae be," Elspeth said weakly.

"I fought against you before you were born and again when you were mere children."

My blood ran cold, and Fitz's energy stirred within me.

"What is that supposed to mean?" I asked, subtly finding a firmer stance in the ground.

Gabriella's words echoed through my mind.

Because unlike Lorenzo, Lucio will kill you immediately.

His dark eyes twinkled mischievously, and something dangerous lingered within them, just as I had noticed with his son. His energy permeated the air. He was powerful.

"I *did* know you'd be quite the detective, but unfortunately, you've figured this out a little late." His smirk was insufferable as he motioned toward the far wall. "This sigil was used once before on these lands."

"How do ye ken that?" Fitz asked.

I recalled the markings I had seen last time. They had been too weathered to make out, but could they be what Lucio spoke of?

"The families that lived here were witch hunters. Did you know that?" Lucio asked.

Silence.

"The Bruces in this region were notorious for it. They were ruthless in their killings of our kind, and they offered no more kindness to *your* folk either," he said to the prince. "Not like these simpletons in this village," he added with a sneering laugh. "These people were the real thing, and they learned how to kill us even without power of their own."

I shifted uncomfortably, and Fitz tightened his hold around my waist. He angled himself protectively, leaving me turned to where I could drop into a battle position at a second's notice.

"They amassed quite a few families who sought protection from the *evil witches*, and so their homestead grew. However, the few witches who were left after their killing sprees eventually banded together and cursed the families. One evening, they broke through the Bruce protections and cast a spell on the families so they would sleep soundly."

"What did they do?" I asked, barely a whisper.

"They called forth the type of creature that would kill them swiftly. They summoned a fuath."

"It killed the adults but had the discretion to leave the children alive?" Fitz asked. "I've ne'er heard of such a thing."

"If you work your spell properly, conditions may be inserted. The witches did not want the children to die—they gave them a chance."

"So, the coven took them in?" I asked.

"Precisely. The children were raised with tolerance for all kinds. If they had been raised properly, they would have had a disdain for other humans, but the witches weren't perfect. They did as they saw fit."

Fitz and I looked warily to each other. This was how Marjorie Bruce had come to be a witch.

"And after all this, Marjorie Bruce was arrested for simply being what she is," I said.

"Humans do not change," he said. "They continue in their prejudice. I have told the council elders as much, but Forfar does not seem content to learn from their past mistakes."

"What this town has done is horrible, but they dinnae all deserve death," Esther said.

"And not all of them are meant to die," he said. "Perhaps a bit lenient on my part, but there must always be survivors to tell the story. That was the mistake the local coven made last time by only leaving children."

"How do we stop this?" I asked Fitz.

"I've ne'er dabbled in dark spells like this," Fitz said. *"We need the coven to take the lead on breaking this type of magic."*

"On it."

Fitz continued speaking with Lucio, distracting him as I set to work. I called to the elements, pulling the air to me, and whispered warnings into the night. The air responded, and I breathed life into my message before pushing it toward the others.

"What is it you're doing?" Lucio asked.

"Listening to a whole load of bullshit," I said.

Fitz stifled a laugh, which did not escape Lucio's attention. His anger deepened, souring the air around us. He dropped into an aggressive stance, and his power burst forward in a wave.

But before Lucio could strike, strange noises sounded through the space. We looked around in confusion. I strained, trying to make sense of the ruckus.

"It looks like my messenger made quick work of alerting the council and Father Evans we are here," Lucio said, though almost to himself. "Alas, Malcolm is the only one who has any idea what they've just walked into."

His smile sent nerves crawling down my spine.

"I'll just go welcome them," he said.

"No, you won't," I countered, throwing a fireball in his direction.

Lucio dodged my attempt, but his eyes were wild when he faced us again.

"Take everyone outside. Assess the situation while we deal with Lucio," I said to Esther's mind.

Lucio hurled a blue energy orb at me as Esther led the others from the building, but I was prepared. I ducked below the orb and channeled my own energy toward it. A thud sounded through me as I connected to it and sent it back, tossing it toward Lucio. He wasn't prepared for my counterattack, and his own energy almost connected with his chest, but he batted it away at the last second. His eyebrows rose as he turned back to face me.

Fitz launched energy at him, but he countered the attack, the collision of the two exploding between us. We ducked, and as soon as I found my footing, I sent fireballs spinning in Lucio's direction, one after the other. As he jumped out of the way, I studied his battle strategy. His movements reminded me of Lorenzo, which was no surprise, but his motions were less refined than his son's. Battling against Lorenzo was like playing chess match with a seasoned opponent. I had assumed that had been taught by Lucio, but now I was unsure.

Lucio did possess a considerable amount of power, and he was not without strategy. Which version of Lucio were we battling? Was this the man who had written the plans to Lorenzo that I'd found in his office desk? Or was this a younger Lucio who was only now formulating his plans? With as much research as we had done, our team was still unsure what time Lucio had left when he traveled back for the ring. But then it sunk in: Lucio *knew* he'd find us in the past before he'd traveled back. That sent a live wire down my body.

I was readying my next fireball when the air became too thin. I gasped, my body faltering with the lack of oxygen. Fitz's breathing grew short and irregular, and I reached for him, gripping his elbow.

Don't panic, I thought, the very words I had said to myself when acquiring my powers.

Henry's voice echoed through my mind. *You have the power for it.*

Lucio was strong, but Fitz and I were stronger, especially together—I knew it.

I assessed the air around me, my magic pushing against it, diagnosing the issue. Through my witch's eye, I perceived a shield entrapping Fitz and me. Lucio had created a barrier that was bound to us.

I concentrated on the shield, focusing on finding a loophole. I willed my energy to permeate the barrier, and with a firm push, it shattered around us. My chest heaved as I drew in the unbridled air my lungs desperately needed.

When I turned to Lucio, he was on his knees, gripping his head. I had been so focused on breaking his spell, I hadn't noticed Fitz's counterattack. His memory control power had Lucio in a vulnerable state.

But no sooner had we regained our strength than Lucio disappeared.

I looked to Fitz. "He'll be free of your mind tricks now, and there's no way that guy is missing the show happening outside."

"Let's go see what we're up against."

We met with our group just outside the building.

"How bad?" I asked.

"We cannae count numbers from here," Hamish said. "I think nae more than fifteen."

"We need to split up," I said. "One group needs to look for Lucio's body—or Thomas's, if Lucio has already returned to his true form."

"We'll work on tracing him," Annabel said. "I have a spell for separating spirits from bodies."

"Perfect," I said. "Prince Faolán, you and your folk can't be seen here, and neither can Izzy and Ann. You'll need to leave."

"We'll move to the forest where it is safe, but we won't be far," they said. "If you call for us, look for the lights; we will be there."

"Izzy and I will channel our energy toward you and help as best we can," Ann said.

"The best casters should return inside and work on undoing this summoning chaos," Fitz said. "And the rest of us—we're heading straight into the fight."

"Aye," Neilina said. "We are ready."

"Expect *anything*."

We ran around to the opposite side of the structure. Orange dots scattered across the horizon, marking the torches carried by the villagers.

I sighed. "I think I see an actual pitchfork."

"Hadley," Fitz said, though he chuckled.

"I'm serious—check out that guy all the way to the right."

"I'll be damned," he said. "Ye ken, there's no many of the villagers."

"No, it's definitely not a town event. It looks like a few of them and… the witch hunting committee?"

"Aye, 'tis only Father Evans, the magistrate, a few guards, the rest of the hunting committee, and…" he paused.

"The Forfar Council," I finished.

"Bastards," Fitz said.

"Is there a time period or a universe where at least one council likes us?"

Fitz leaned over and kissed me. "I love ye, firecracker," he whispered against my lips.

"I love you too," I said simply, running my fingers along his jaw.

"At a time like this?" a woman's voice asked.

I turned, already knowing I'd find Annabel. "Where's Thomas?"

"He and Elspeth arnae far behind me," she said. "He was already awake when we found him. It seems Lucio wanted to be back in his own body for this madness."

"Weel, at least that bit is sorted," Fitz said.

"Do we ken yet if the council are friends or foes?" Annabel asked.

"Not yet," I said.

"Perhaps the council has been assisting Lucio," Neilina said. "We have thought it so once ye told us of Lucio and his plans. And Esther—" Neilina paused, clearing her throat. "Esther told us of Lorenzo and yer crusade in the future."

"Why would they help him?" I asked.

I ducked as something whirled by us.

"What the hell was that?" Fitz asked.

Neilina held an arrow. "*Think*, lass—they both wish for chaos. They're sowing those seeds together."

"Lucio said Malcolm is the only one who knows what they've walked into… so maybe he hasn't been working with the whole council. Is this a trap of some kind for the rest of them?"

"Perhaps the council has grown tired of Lucio's schemes, and they mean to remedy the problem?" Neilina speculated.

"This is the last straw," Thomas said, approaching us. "Let this day be one that is well remembered."

"Thomas!" I said. "Are you well?"

"Aye, there's nothing much the matter with me save for a mighty ache in my head—but Izzy and the prince assisted in relieving the pain."

"Now, we *have* to find Lucio—we need to know his next move."

"Aye," Neilina said. "I should turn back now that Thomas is well and assist in disrupting the sigil."

"We need to push our opponents back so we can deal with the spell and Lucio," Fitz said.

"I've got it," I said. "I can at least slow them down."

I pulled my fire to the surface until I was covered in flames, and the result was so intense that even the other witches stumbled back.

"I'll need Fitz—or someone—to stay with me, but the rest of you can work on the spell and find Lucio."

"Dinnae deplete yerself," Fitz said in warning.

Glowing orbs sparkled around me, and energy channeled through me, restoring the power I had lost. The magic was certainly different, an ancient hum coursing through me, but it was life just the same.

The faeries.

I smiled and turned toward Malcolm, Father Evans, and their motley group. A few of them saw me, though they likely didn't know exactly what they were looking at, and we yelled for the villagers to halt.

"Go," I shouted to the coven.

They all ran into the building where Lucio had drawn the sigil, leaving Fitz and me to stall the oncoming mob.

Arrows came flying toward us, but Fitz shielded us, and I used my fire to launch flaming magical arrows back at them. Our plan wasn't to hit them—not yet—but rather to push them back. Once we had them far enough, I laid a line of fire about ten feet wide between us.

"Use my flames and create a ring around the perimeter," I said to Fitz.

He moved his hands in front of him and closed his eyes, whispering under his breath. When he opened them, he extended his arms and the fire spread quickly, forming a ring of flames around the entirety of the homestead.

"That should hold for about ten minutes before we'll need a recharge of flames," he said.

I pulled back on my fire so it only channeled through my palms, conserving my energy as much as possible.

"Should you go check on the coven?" I asked.

"I willnae leave ye here."

"I'm good—they aren't going to break through this, and they'll have a hell of a time extinguishing these flames."

"Nae."

"They might need a push of power from one of us. They're powerful, but…"

"No like us." He grinned.

Fitz moved just behind me, mindful of the flames pouring from my outstretched hands, and slid one hand across my waist, the other underneath my chin. He tilted my head back to him and kissed me. Warm adrenaline pulsed through me, and the torrent of emotion made it difficult to keep my flames lowered. When he pulled back, it was impossible to break eye contact, and our connection surged along with my flames. I would become reckless if he wasn't strong enough to break the moment.

A shriek pierced the night air, and we both jerked away, looking for the source.

"Is that…?"

"The fuath? Aye, I think so."

"Shit. They're running out of time. Go, Fitz," I whispered.

"No," he said firmly. He turned and placed his back to mine. "Yer sword and shield, remember? We stand together, always."

Movement to my right pulled our focus, and sure enough, a wispy figure floated through the flames, followed by a shaggy black dog. The woman's eyes were solid black, and her skin deathly white. Though her small frame was covered by a chemise, stays, and skirts, she wore no garments meant to shield the cold, and the edges of her clothes were tattered. The dog walking beside her had large red eyes, and something dripped from its snarled teeth.

"Shite," Fitz said.

"Blood?" I asked, my stomach rolling.

"Aye."

With each step, the dog left bloody footprints in its wake.

How could this be happening now? After everything we'd over-come, I *really* didn't want to die here in the past, and I decided right then and there, I wouldn't. I gathered my fear like my many sisters before me. It was mine to channel into something greater. My mantra was clear: I would finish this, and I would return home safely.

Fitz was poised, ready to attack, but the fuath raised its hand signaling for the dog to stand down. As it drew nearer, the figure slowly transformed from foot to head, revealing itself slowly as a solid figure. The beautiful woman had dark hair and wore a burgundy dress of fine velvet but was barefoot.

"Stop," I demanded. "You're here to murder these beings?"

"Aye. I am sorrow and death, fear and destruction. I am justice."

"How is this justice?"

"Havenae they come here to claim yer life?"

"I don't know why they're here."

"And yet ye defend yerself with flames? Ye ken why they have come."

I was silent.

"Why are ye doing this?" Fitz asked.

"I was murdered by a man who wanted more than I would give to him," she said. "But in death, I was granted the chance to offer him the same mercy he extended to me. 'Tis now my fate. I am doomed to walk the earth and do the bidding of the one who granted me the chance to settle my score."

"The devil, then?" Fitz asked.

The woman smiled. "Dinnae believe everything the villagers tell ye."

"Well, it surely isn't God. Fate?" I asked.

The woman looked at me but offered no reply. The beast snarled beside her.

"Some believe the black dog to be the devil in disguise," Fitz said.

"Those who believe so are fools," the spirit answered. "What does the devil care for the taste of human flesh? His desires are those of the mind."

I shivered. I wanted to be rid of these spirits. "Have you come to kill us?"

She looked at me long enough to make it uncomfortable. I would've thought she didn't hear me, except that she seemed to be considering us.

"I dinnae think so," she said. The dog barked at her answer. "I dinnae think it yer time, though… dinnae hinder me from my task, or I cannae make ye that promise."

"We can't stand by and just let you kill them all," I said. "Some of them might deserve it, but still."

"Then face my wrath," she said.

She rose from the ground, and her limbs pulled in each direction as her human facade withered away like dust scattering in the wind. The wispy form we'd first encountered was all that remained, and she took off at full speed, her hound fast on her heels.

"I'm genuinely torn between going out there and returning to the coven," I said.

Screams sounded from beyond my flames, and I knew the conflict in Fitz's eyes matched mine. I looked to my palms, which were still alight with flames.

"Perhaps the council will finally be useful," Fitz said. "Perhaps they will save lives instead of taking them."

"Truthfully," I said, swallowing hard as I came to terms with my true feelings, "any human out there has persecuted innocent humans and witches, and they will implicate more."

Fitz reached for my hand, and I extinguished my flames, taking his hand in mine. With one step, we were inside the building with the coven.

"The fuath has arrived," I said.

Every head jerked up.

"Aye," Fitz said. "Now what is going on in here?"

"The spell Lucio cast, we found a way to reverse it, but we cannae break his to begin our own."

"I can help with that," I said.

Neilina looked to me, her eyes narrowed. "'Tis a strange energy. 'Tis—"

"Tied together with strange magic," I said, cutting Neilina off. "Yeah, I feel it. Just a minute."

Lucio had pulled some of the dark energy of the space and used it to bind the spell.

"Shit," I said. The energy at my fingertips was sickening.

"What is it?" Fitz asked.

"He used dark magic to bind it. I can break it, but it'll take a lot of energy. I'll need a boost."

"We will assist ye," Elspeth said.

I found the wisp of Lucio's energy that would unravel the spell, just as I had done with his son's spells on several occasions, and tugged. The energy that coursed through my fingers set my body ablaze, and I yelped with the pain.

"Hadley!" Fitz said.

"It's okay," I choked out. "It just hurts… like… hell."

He was soon behind me, his hands on mine sending calming energy through my system.

I bit back the pain and pushed forward. "*Now.* I need energy now."

I had anticipated the surge of my magical brothers and sisters, but I was not prepared for the vitality that swam through my system. I ground my jaw at the onslaught of magic before channeling the energy at the dark magic.

The resulting spark exploded, lighting the dark room and propelling me backward against Fitz's chest. We fell and rolled over onto our knees. The floor that once bore the sigil was now covered in black soot.

Neilina, Annabel, Esther, and Elspeth were ready with the replacement spell, and another bright light flashed across the room. Annabel ripped her skirt and scrubbed the soot across where the sigil had been, ensuring it was erased.

"'Tis done," Elspeth said.

We raced from the building, and through the waning ring of fire. The fuath was in combat with the witch council. The council and their companions hadn't escaped without casualties. Several bodies littered the ground.

"Shouldnae she be gone?" Elspeth asked.

"Perhaps our spell didn't hold," Thomas said.

"Nae," Annabel said. "It was correct, and it held. I'm certain."

"Can we banish her?" Fitz asked.

The coven members looked to one another.

"I dinnae ken with certainty. Ye havnae done this before?" Neilina asked.

"Fitz and I haven't had much use for spell work in our time," I said.

"I have a thought," Elspeth said. "Annabel once taught me a spell that might be useful."

She and Annabel exchanged a look, their thoughts surely rolling across each other's minds.

"If we work the spell together—all of us," Annabel said pointing to Fitz and me, "asking for favor from the elements, it may work."

"Let's give it a try," Fitz instructed.

Annabel turned to Elspeth, who nodded. They gathered us all in a circle, and we clasped hands. The fuath screamed in the background, and the council members were yelling instructions to one another. I cleared my mind and pushed the noise away, focusing intently on Elspeth and Annabel.

Their chanting was in Scots Gaelic, and I focused on the rhythm as the others joined in. The wind picked up and blew violently across the clearing.

Our hair whipped and leaves scattered in the breeze.

And still we chanted.

The spirit screamed, and the council elders channeled their highest magic.

And still we chanted.

The remnants of my fire blazed back to life.

And still we chanted.

The sprits of the land ebbed and flowed, granting us unmatched vitality.

And still we chanted.

Finally, Annabel looked to me and yelled, "Now!"

Fitz and I pulled at the elements. They answered, feeling the imbalance of the scene, and air, earth, fire, water, and moon came together. The surge of energy was oppressive in its brilliance, and it took every bit of my strength to remain standing. Thunder rumbled across the sky, and the fuath released an ear-shattering cry.

The black dog burst from the tree line, where I could only assume it had chased those who had fled, and jumped into the arms of the fuath. Lightning flashed across the sky, and with the next rumble of thunder, they disappeared.

I scanned the area and met eyes with several members of the council across the clearing.

"Did ye summon that creature?" one of them asked.

"Lucio did," I yelled back. "But he had some help from Malcolm, didn't he?"

The anger that registered on Malcolm's face was his condemnation.

"Is this true?" a red-headed man asked. "Have ye been working with him?"

"How dare ye make such an accusation!"

"Well, it is the truth, is it not?" Lucio yelled from behind me. "You see, what we have done here is a beautiful thing."

I took a step back.

"When our brothers and sisters across Scotland learn of the corruption and persecution, they will be appalled. But when they learn of this uprising and how evil can be mended..." His eyes gleamed. "We'll have ourselves an uprising then. And do you know the best part?"

Silence.

"Uprisings lead to revolutions."

"Unbelievable," I whispered.

It didn't escape Lucio's attention. He smiled at me.

"It seems my work here is done. I thank you all for the role you have played in this first act. A small reckoning, but the seed we planted here tonight will grow."

With that, he disappeared.

PART THREE

CHAPTER TWENTY-NINE

The following morning, Fitz and I joined his family, along with Thomas and Elspeth, by the fireside to discuss the events of the previous evening, to make sense of what had happened and take our next steps accordingly.

"Are ye well, Thomas?" Hamish asked as they embraced warmly. Thomas was moving a bit slowly.

"Aye, my head is much improved, and I feel… weel, much more myself."

We had to chuckle at his description.

"The type of magic used for such a spell is unusual," Annabel said. "It alters the mind, but the body is mostly unharmed."

"I cannae recall much," Thomas said. "Will I e'er recover these memories, or are they lost?"

"Lost, I'm afraid," Ann said softly. "Though your mind was present for those actions, it was unconscious. Lucio's spirit, and his mind, were in control. The memories remain with him."

Thomas's shoulders slumped slightly. "I thought it would be so."

"I'm sorry I dinnae have better news," she said.

"It isnae yer doing. I suppose 'tis better to ken the truth than to have hope that will ne'er come to pass."

The door swung open, and we hesitated until Katherine and Izzy strode through the doorway.

"Perfect timing," Fitz said. "But where did ye get off to this morning?"

"Did ye no receive our note from Millie?" Katherine asked. "I took Izzy to the woods."

"To the woods or to the fair folk?" I asked.

Izzy blushed, her gaze fixed on the floor. The answer was clear.

"And how was Prince Faolán today?" I asked, eyeing Fitz.

"Oh, they were lovely. They showed me a number of plants they're cultivating in their wee bit of forest. And the flower they spoke of… it's fascinating, really."

Fitz smiled broadly.

"This is quite the council Katherine and I have wandered into," Izzy said, pivoting. "Discussing our visit from Fate?"

"Nae," Esther answered. "But we must sort through yesternight… all of it, in truth."

"For my part, I cannae understand why Fate wouldnae speak plainly," Hamish said. "All riddles and mysteries, that one."

"'Tis her way, I reckon," Thomas said. "She willnae give instruction, but if ye decide on the wrong course, God be with ye." He smiled sympathetically.

"She did make one thing clear—she wishes ye both to return to Opimae," Ann said.

"Aye, and we will give it our best efforts, but only so much is within our control," Fitz said.

"The Opimaean chamber will fight us," I said.

"And if that is true even after we share Fate's instruction, we have a greater problem than we realized."

"When will ye depart for yer time?" Esther asked.

I turned to Fitz, and we held each other's gaze for a moment.

"When our work here is done," he said.

"Fitz," Ann said. "Might I remind you that Izzy and I are here to bring you and Hadley home?"

"I mean to see this mission through."

Mother and son sat wordlessly, their defiance matching.

Finally, Izzy broke the tension. "You're stubborn—both of yous," she said, turning to me. "But perhaps it is time, aye?"

"I understand your concerns," I said, "but now that we know Lucio has been working with Malcolm, we can't just leave."

Now that the council knew that Malcolm was in league with Lucio, would this alter the council's fight against the witch trials? Could this alter Esther's fate?

"Dinnae you see the tangled mess you'll leave behind?" Ann challenged. "Only look at last night."

"Perhaps those lives were already marked by Fate," Fitz said.

Ann sighed.

"Fate didn't outright forbid it," I said pointedly.

Fitz nodded. "We willnae dally, but we traveled here to prevent Lucio from stealing this ring. We'll do our best to see that through." He turned to his mother. "We will leave the moment it is done. Ye have my word."

Ann's features hardened as she considered her son's words. Finally, she nodded.

"For my part, yesternight only strengthens my opinion that Malcolm works dark magic," Esther said.

I agreed. "Lucio clearly does, and if they're connected...."

"We'll look into it further," Hamish said. "Perhaps this shall aid us in discovering Malcolm's true purpose."

"I have long heard rumors of Malcolm's practice of the dark arts," Elspeth said. "I cannae say it surprises me."

"Nor I," Thomas said. "If I happen to recover memories that will assist ye, I'll be sure to inform ye."

Annabel stood and walked closer to the fireside. When she turned back, her eyes were troubled. "What do ye make of Esther's vision? Did it grant us any useful knowledge?"

"If anything," I said, "it's only reinforced what we already supposed to be true—Lucio is the mastermind of all this."

"His trail has gone cold," Fitz said. "We could repeat the locator spell and keep after him."

"I regret not following him now," I said.

"You made the right decision," Ann said. "Your mission is to prevent him from taking the ring, not chasing him to who knows where."

"Aye, ye could have landed in grave danger," Hamish said. "The locator spell is a braw plan. 'Tis wise to track his movements."

Hamish was right. If we were able to keep our eyes on Lucio, maybe it would help us stay ahead of him.

"Ye warned us that he was dangerous, but it isnae only that," Hamish said. "He's reckless."

"Ye're certain about this ring, Annabel?" Elspeth said. "Ye're certain about this risk—even though the ring could fall into the hands of such a madman?"

The room froze, and all eyes locked on Annabel.

Her jaw was set tight and her eyes defiant. "I have spoken at length with the family—all of them—and we believe the answer for Esther is the ring. We will focus our efforts on preventing the ring from falling into the wrong hands." Annabel's voice faltered, and she cleared her throat. "Whatever has happened in Fitz and Hadley's past, Esther willnae die at the hands of the witch hunting committee."

Annabel met Esther's gaze, daring her to contradict her words, but Esther remained silent. She wouldn't argue with Annabel in front of the others, but in her energy, I didn't find the slightest indication that she'd changed her mind about the ring.

Would Esther's fate play out just as it had before?

"I have this feeling Lucio wants something from me," I said. "Fitz, too. If we knew exactly what he wanted, we could perhaps use that to distract him while the rest of you take care of the ring whenever the time comes."

"Esther may no be able to give up the ring," Annabel countered.

"At some point she will, no matter what the future holds. Lucio will attempt to steal it one way or another. Esther grows more at risk the longer she has the ring."

"Aye, so keeping it forever isnae an option," Fitz said. "We must come to an agreement on when the ring is destroyed."

"It should remain with Esther as she draws breath," Annabel said. "Ye willnae remain in the past that long. She will live a long life."

Annabel was living in the delusion she'd built for herself, existing in absolute denial.

"And if I live another seventy years, should I be looking over my shoulder for all that time, wondering when Lucio might come for it?" Esther asked. "Anyone in the future might ken when I die, whether it be in these trials or no. Lucio could formulate a plan at any moment, and we're at the mercy of whatever plan he devises. He will have far more time to plan than us."

"Fitz and Hadley could warn ye before that happens once they are back where they belong."

"Once we're in our present, our own fates aren't certain. If we can return to Opimae to continue our mission, there are no guarantees we'll come back."

"Aye, yer plan requires a guarantee we cannae give ye," Fitz said.

"Esther, are ye certain ye willnae leave Forfar?" Elspeth asked.

"It isnae right," she said. "My bairns… weel, I willnae risk their safety."

Hamish and Thomas exchanged a meaningful glance. I had little time to consider it before a knock sounded through the house. We shouldn't have heard a knock at such a distance—whoever was at the door was making a scene.

A ruckus sounded from down the hallway. Voices shouted over one another, creating a muddled roar, but one voice rang loudly above the others.

"You will take us to the witch. Now!"

I braced myself and met Fitz's gaze as everyone rose to their feet.

"Transport Izzy out of here!" I whispered to Ann. If the minister saw Izzy, our troubles would only increase.

Ann nodded, and then they were gone.

Fitz pulled me protectively to him. Hamish positioned himself in front of Esther, as did Annabel and Katherine, and Thomas pulled Elspeth into an embrace.

The MacGregor staff burst into the room, attempting to stay ahead of the witch hunters at their heels. Ten guards flanked the minister as they rushed into the room. Draped in dark wool and armed with muskets and daggers, the guards stopped just inside the doorway, meeting our gazes defiantly, and Father Evans took a step forward. Malcolm was right behind him. I looked at Esther as I ticked through whatever options we might have to defend her.

"What right have ye to storm into my hame?" Hamish boomed.

"Pardon me for the intrusion," Father Evans returned. "But your staff was uncooperative."

Father Evans straightened his posture and leveled his dark eyes at Hamish, clearly attempting to make himself more domineering in the presence of such a man. Though the minister was tall and square, he lacked the presence Hamish brought to a room.

"Aye? Weel, they *are* accustomed to visitors with manners," Hamish shot back.

The minister's eyebrow rose. "I have business with a woman who seeks refuge here."

Hamish narrowed his gaze.

"Hadley MacGregor, you are under arrest for violation of the Act Against Witchcraft of 1604 under the law of King James the First, God rest his soul."

The minister bowed his head at the mention of King James I, and the guards followed suit.

The breath left my body as Fitz's grip on me tightened.

My vision swam.

This couldn't be happening.

"Guards," Father Evans said, nodding to me.

They took a step forward, almost in perfect unison, though everything moved in slow motion.

"Wait!" Fitz yelled, placing himself in front of me. "On what grounds?"

I gripped Fitz's arm, recalling the promise he had made me. *If anyone tries to harm you, I'll kill them.*

"Perhaps you should listen—for violation of the Witchcraft Act, as I have said."

"Willfully misunderstand me if ye must, but I am asking: what are the charges? What has she *allegedly* done wrong?"

"She was seen just yestereve working magic of the devil, crafting fire from her very hands."

There would be no reasoning my way out of this one. Everything would fall apart. Lucio would obtain the ring, and Esther... she would still die. No. Even if it angered Fate, I couldn't let this happen.

"That's outrageous," Fitz said, his voice rising. "How dare ye make such a baseless claim!"

With each passing minute, I felt less frightened, less shocked... and I grew angry.

"It is not baseless. I'm afraid several of our flock saw her in action, including Malcolm Campbell."

My eyes darted to Malcolm, whose icy stare prickled across my skin.

"Outright lies!" Hamish cried out.

"Ye cannae fight the truth, Hamish," Malcolm's deep voice boomed.

"If there's a witch standing in this verra room, it isnae Hadley," Hamish said, his eyes traveling in an accusatory manner across Malcolm.

"Ye dinnae want to challenge me," he threatened.

"And why not?" Hamish asked, seething. "Ye practice dark magic, and everyone kens it."

"Enough!" Katherine cried out. "'Tis time for the truth, and the truth ye all shall hear."

She strode to the center of the room. Her energy was troubled, but strong.

"The villagers did see Hadley yesternight, or so their eyes told them. But she was an apparition."

I was dumbfounded. What was she doing?

Katherine continued. "I have hated Malcolm Campbell for many years, and in truth, I've wished ill on him. I have cursed him."

Mumbles sounded through the crowd. "Yesternight, I casted a spell to increase the potency of my curse. My anger toward this burgh burned hot, and I decided Malcolm wasnae enough."

Fitz pulled me closer.

"*Dinnae say a word*," he said.

The minister's face grew stern.

"In order to hide my dark deeds, I used Hadley's likeness so that if anyone were to see, they would blame her."

"No!" I said, my voice hoarse. She couldn't do this.

Katherine's gaze was defiant. "*Dinnae protest.*"

"I am sorry, Hadley," she said aloud. "I shouldnae have done it, but I was in the middle of the spell before I realized I hadnae hidden my trail. The devil called to me, and I was in a right hurry to answer."

Gasps sounded. She was receiving just the reaction she sought, and my heart shredded with the realization that she would leave here a prisoner before she would allow them to take me to the tolbooth.

"Katherine," I said.

"Nae, dinnae say it," she said, closing her eyes in pain. "I ken ye trusted me, and I am sorry for it. I hope ye can forgive me now that I willnae let ye suffer the consequences of my actions. I pray ye can forgive me, just as I pray our merciful God will forgive me."

"How dare ye say the name of our Lord, witch!" Father Evans yelled, his cheeks flushed.

Malcolm stood in the corner, his arms crossed and his face blank. Before I could break into his mind to see what he was thinking, Father Evans and his words sucked the soul right out of my body.

"Guards, arrest her immediately!"

But his pointed finger led to Katherine.

"Nae!" Elspeth screamed.

"You wish to defend such a depraved woman?" he asked. "Perhaps I should take you all to the tolbooth and find out just how much you have all been keeping from me!"

"That willnae be necessary," Thomas said, tightening his hold on Elspeth, who was doing her best to break free.

"How do I know you weren't involved?" Father Evans asked, looking to me.

"Hadley is a fine, godly woman. She would ne'er participate in such evil!" Fitz said. His energy wavered at his final word, but he didn't flinch, his stare held firmly on Father Evans.

"He speaks the truth," Katherine said. "Hadley is nae witch. She is innocent, Father."

The minister's eyes lingered on me long enough to make me uncomfortable. My nerves were a live wire screaming through my entire body.

Fitz tightened his grip on me.

"*If he steps forward, move to the side,*" he said to my mind. "*I'll strike him down before he takes a second step.*"

My breath hitched. He couldn't do that… it would create a mess. Bigger than it already was.

But I couldn't die here.

Father Evans turned his gaze to Fitz, and in his eyes, I saw fear. He recognized Fitz for the threat he was. We waited in suspense. Finally, Father Evans nodded and turned back to Katherine.

"Let us be done with this," he said.

The guards moved forward, but Hamish, Fitz, and Thomas were across the room in the blink of an eye, wrestling with the guards. Every fiber of my being called me to utilize my Opimaean training to fight, but to do so would make everything so much worse. Instead, Esther, Annabel, Elspeth, and I linked arms, shielding Katherine. The other guards were quick to overpower us. Before I knew it, a guard had pressed a dirk against Elspeth's neck. I screamed, as much in agony over stifling my powers as in fear of them slitting her throat.

Thomas froze, the blood draining from his face. Fitz and Hamish followed suit.

"A wise choice," the minister said.

The guard took hold of Katherine and moved to the doorway, standing next to the minister.

"Katherine shall be transported to the tolbooth for questioning, and a fair and reasonable trial shall follow."

Hamish sneered.

Father Evans called the guards to his side. They were in varying states, some unharmed, others bruised and bleeding. Katherine's hands were already tied, and she stood motionless beside the minister, a guard holding onto her bound hands.

"Mind your ways and alter your hearts, lest you be next," the minister warned. His eyes swept over us, and I was surprised to find neither anger nor contempt. Instead, I found curiosity… and a bit of sadness. I wanted to know more, but Esther's sob pulled my focus. She was tucked under Hamish's arm and clung tightly to him as tears streamed down her face.

Esther had stood beside Katherine even when everyone in her life told her she shouldn't… even when they had pushed her to think of her own safety. Esther had been friend and confidant, Katherine's full support system. This was an unhappy ending we'd all feared, but none would take this so hard as Esther.

The guards exited the room, surrounding Katherine on all sides. The minister followed, but at the last minute, he paused in the doorway. He turned his head, looking back over his shoulder, his eyes downcast.

"I *am* sorry it has come to this," he said before clearing his throat and passing through the doorway. I turned to Fitz, whose face held the same questioning expression on my own features. Something about the minister's apology nipped at my witch's eye. We needed to find out what was happening.

Ann and Izzy entered back into the sitting room as soon as our unwelcome visitors left. The room was suspended in silence, all of us seemingly in shock.

Esther dropped her head in her hands. "I cannae believe this."

Elspeth moved closer to Esther and pulled her close.

"It's my fault," I said, pain flooding through me.

"Nae," Esther said. "We freed Thomas and saved the village from a fuath."

"They dinnae ken they just arrested one of the beings who saved their miserable lives last night," Fitz said, his eyes distant.

"Esther is right," Annabel said. "They might have seen ye pushing them back with flames, but we all were in danger of being discovered."

"Simpletons, the lot of them," Thomas said. "I feel responsible myself."

"Ye can hardly blame yerself for being overtaken by Lucio," Annabel said.

"Perhaps no, but still, I feel it."

"Perhaps something can be done," Esther said.

"We are the few who would speak for her, but we are all in danger of falling next," Thomas said. "None are safe."

Hamish finally broke his stillness, and his eyes held a quiet determination that I had not yet seen from him.

"We're leaving, Esther."

"Hamish—"

"Nae," he said. "We've discussed this till we hardly had life left in us, but nae more. I willnae sit idly and allow this same fate to come to ye."

Esther stared at him, her eyes hollow.

Hamish continued. "We will collect the bairns and leave for Opimae."

"We dinnae ken that it will work."

"Aye, but we ken what this path holds, and I cannae abide it. We will fight, damn it!"

Esther didn't answer.

"Ye should leave, just as Hamish says." The despair in Annabel's tone was palpable, and my eyes filled with tears. "Save yerself, lass. Take yer future into yer own hands."

Esther raised her gaze to mine, then to Fitz. "What would ye have me do?"

"Ye ken we cannae answer that, Esther."

I nodded, though my eyes must have been pleading with her, desperate as I was for Esther to either run from her future captors or to fight against them.

She moved her head ever so slightly to nod. "What is the date of my death?"

Hamish winced as the words left Esther's lips.

"We dinnae ken," Fitz answered. "Several women's fates are un-known, and a few more still whose exact dates of death are uncertain. The records are missing."

"Was her death certain?" Elspeth asked, a glimmer of hope in her eyes.

"Aye, I'm afraid so. There are accounts of it—only the date was uncertain."

"Do ye reckon 'tis close at hand?" Esther asked.

Fitz hesitated before nodding, and when he again spoke, his voice was low and his energy hollowed out. "Yer date of capture was recorded as the thirtieth of November. If we havenae disturbed the natural order of things, ye have only a few days."

"Why have ye no told us this before!" Hamish demanded.

"Because I asked him no to share it," Esther shot back. "I didnae wish to ken the date, and I didnae wish to risk Fitz being punished by Fate for sharing details he shouldnae."

Hamish exhaled angrily.

"Only four days," Annabel said. "We have much to prepare."

"Aye, just enough time to settle matters before we depart," Hamish said.

All eyes were on Esther, and the room was suspended in silence until finally… she nodded. "Aye, I'll go."

Relief flooded the room, but my own body was in a flurry. My energy was muddled as I considered how Fate would respond to this plan. Would they have reached this decision without me? Had they decided on this plan in the original version of the past?

I breathed deeply and scanned the room.

"This must remain in the confidence of only those in this room," Esther said. "My bairns are at risk otherwise."

"Should Fitz and Hadley accompany us?" Hamish asked. "For additional protection?"

"And the ring," Elspeth said. "Should they join ye to assist in destroying it once ye're safe?"

"What is safety?" Annabel challenged. "When do we consider Esther safe?"

The room quieted as we considered this question once more.

"There is nae guarantee," Fitz said. "Of that, I believe us all certain."

"If we return to the future and discover when Esther was truly safe, we'd have to send someone back to tell you all," I said.

"The thought of the ring going to Opimae makes me uneasy," Ann said. "Does that make it all the easier for it to follow its current path… I mean, where it is in *our* present?"

"Aye, we might be playing right into Lucio's hands," Izzy said. "But if we do agree to this plan, I'm the only other living MacGregor in our time who can return to ensure we destroy the ring."

Fitz and Izzy exchanged a meaningful look. Without Ian, they were the two legacies on whom we'd rely.

"What if we destroy the ring once those in power die? Hamish and I could return to Scotland once the witch hunts have quieted." Esther said.

"Aye, there's a thought," Thomas said, looking to Fitz. "When do these witch hunts end?"

"A good question," Fitz said. "Things will ease here in Forfar in a few years. The last time a person will be tried and executed for witchcraft in Britain is 1727, so a while yet before the last of this comes to pass."

A tear rolled down Elspeth's cheek. "So many years yet for our sisters to be persecuted."

"We'd have a fair stretch of life before us, Esther," Hamish said. "We could come back, and our bairns would still have the chance to truly ken Scotland."

"Ye keep the ring until 1727, and then ye destroy it," Elspeth said. "No a bad plan."

"Ye must guard it carefully for many years yet. Dinnae forget that," Thomas said.

"I'll increase the strength of my protection spells. We'll ensure its safety," Annabel said.

My pulse quickened. We were really doing this. Esther was going to escape.

"The braw thing about this plan is that by coming back to Scotland, ye willnae alter more of the future than necessary," Fitz said. "Ye're returning where ye're meant to be. Bringing yer bairns back where they're meant to be."

"Aye," Hamish said. "We'll die on Scottish soil yet, but on a natural course."

"If ye learn of anything going amiss, will ye promise to come back and destroy this ring?" Esther asked.

"Aye," Fitz said, looking to Izzy and Ann. "Should I fall in Opimae, Izzy can take care of it."

"If anything were to happen to Esther, any witch in this room has my blessing to destroy the ring after that time," Annabel said.

"It should die alongside me should that death occur prior to 1727." Esther nodded curtly. "Do we have an accord?"

Each of us gave our agreement.

"There is one bit of business left to attend to, then," Esther said. "Should it be nae bother to anyone, I would verra much like to see Hadley and Fitz married."

CHAPTER THIRTY

We spent the following day planning our wedding in earnest. Though Fitz and I had told Esther we could wait until our time to be wed now that she had chosen to leave for Opimae, she wouldn't hear of it. While Esther whisked me around the house making plans and seeking my approval on this and that, she dispatched Millie on errands around the burgh as Isla planned a menu with Ann and Izzy. I insisted Esther not make too big of a fuss since she was in the middle of preparations for her journey, but as it turned out, our marital felicity was a very welcome distraction amidst the darkness of the trials.

But even our upcoming nuptials couldn't soften our fear for Katherine's well-being. Esther insisted on seeing Katherine that evening, and though everyone advised against it, she won. I was to accompany Esther while Hamish and Annabel continued preparations for their departure, and Ann and Izzy continued with Esther's wedding plans.

Fitz was waiting in a horse stall just next door in case we ran into trouble and needed backup.

Midnight found us meeting with Ivan, a guard Esther paid off to allow us entry.

"Are you sure we can trust him?" I asked.

"Aye, for a bit of coin, he grants access—for humans and witches alike. He willnae manage an escape—they'd have his head for that—but he doesnae much care for the witch hunts and he's keen to line his pockets."

The prison beneath the tolbooth was dark, musty, and damp, and my skin crawled at the very thought of Katherine existing in such a place. The air was bitterly cold, and the old stonework only enhanced the uncomfortable chill. Our footsteps echoed through the barren hallways, and water—or at least, I hoped it was water—trickled. The lower we traveled, the riper the air grew with human stench and… something rotten. I tried not to think about the source. As we turned a corner, we startled a large rat, which ran across my shoe, causing my heart to leap through my chest. Perhaps I'd found the other source of smell within the old, dirty structure.

When Esther took my hand, I wasn't sure which of us was shaking harder. I pulled my shawl tighter with my free hand and gave her an encouraging nod.

"Are ye coming or no?" Ivan barked ahead of us.

"Aye," Esther called. "Just startled by a rat is all."

"Rats will be the least of yer concern if ye dinnae move quickly. I dinnae much care for the prospect of being seen by another guard."

Finally, we reached the cells.

A long row of iron gates ran to our right, disappearing into the darkness. We held our torches further out in front of us, seeking a better view of what lay ahead.

At the first gate, my breath caught in the back of my throat. My torch caught the glow of two eyes staring back at me. A woman lay huddled in a tattered blanket, her head resting against the iron bars of her prison. Her expression was blank, even as she stared straight at me. Esther tugged at me, urging me to move on.

At the next cell, an arm reached through the bar and grabbed hold of Esther's skirts.

"Please," a raspy voice called out softly. "Please help."

The shirt covering the woman's arm was filthy, covered in dirt and blood. I raised my torch, revealing a face that was cut and bruised from only God knew what. Her brown hair was cropped short, and patches were missing along her skull. I swallowed hard at the sight, suppressing tears.

Ivan pointed a finger toward the woman, his brow furrowing.

"Let go of 'er, or 'tis the branks for ye, Janet!"

The woman recoiled, and recalling photos from Fitz's research of the horrific device, I took a step away from Ivan myself. Death wasn't the only thing Katherine had saved me from. The branks—or the witch's bridle—were secured over a woman's head with a bit that suppressed the tongue, sometimes even puncturing it. My stomach lurched as I thought about the pain and humiliation it had caused my sisters—witch and human alike.

The next cell held a hunched figure, her brunette strands falling through the bars. A rat was chewing on her hand, and Esther and I shooed the creature away.

"Get on with ye, wee beastie!" Esther scolded in a strong whisper.

"Are you okay?" I asked the woman.

There was no response. I looked to Esther, whose eyes held a sad knowledge. I bent down to check for signs of life, but Ivan beat me to it. He pushed against the woman's shoulder, and she fell over onto the ground. Ivan sighed before removing the keys from his belt and opening the cell. He entered, bent down, and swore.

"She's dead all right. Been gone long enough to be cold." He emerged from the cell and carried on, leaving the gate open.

"Do… do you need to do anything about that?" I asked.

"What would ye have me do?" he sneered. "She's dead. The officials would have my head for waking them over such a thing. Nae. 'Tis cold enough. She'll keep til morn."

Esther stiffened next to me. My eyes must have been the size of saucers.

"The rats…" I said, trailing off.

"Aye, and what of them? They'll leave the living alone for tonight."

Nausea overtook me, and I bent over, breathing deeply.

"Dinnae make more work for us," Ivan said, tossing a bucket my way. The bucket held remnants of something rank, and that was the last of my willpower. I retched as Esther rubbed my back. Once I was done, I wiped my mouth and stood.

"Done?" Ivan asked, a hint of annoyance in his tone.

I nodded.

At the next gate, I was surprised to find the conditions much different.

"Esther MacGregor," a woman's voice said. "I didnae expect to see ye here. At least, no on the other side of the bars."

Esther froze. "Helen," she said, before turning.

"I suppose I shouldnae be surprised now that I've learned of Katherine's arrest."

"Learned of Katherine's arrest?" Esther said coldly. "As if ye werenae the reason for it."

Helen rolled her eyes. "Dinnae be so self-righteous, Esther."

I surveyed Helen's cell and found a clean cot, several wool blankets, a tray that held the remnants of dinner, several books, and a stick.

"The rats have learned to leave me be," Helen said with an unsettling smile.

"You seem to be living quite comfortably," I said, recalling Helen's "usefulness" to her captors.

"She's rewarded for betraying other women and compromising the innocent around these parts," a voice called from a nearby cell. "It's afforded a few comforts. Aye, Helen?"

Helen turned her head lazily in the direction of the voice.

"Dinnae fash. She'll die like the rest of us in the end, and the fires of Hell will warm her bones for all of eternity."

I moved my torch closer to the source of the voice and found a middle-aged woman with long caramel hair. Her face was cut and bruised, much like the others, but her health hadn't yet declined as far. Newer to the fold, I assumed.

Esther rushed to the gate. "Agnes!" she said urgently, her eyes welling with tears. "Agnes, I... I came to help ye, to warn ye, but it was too late."

"Esther, please," Agnes said, taking her by the hand. "What good would it have done?"

"I am sorry," she returned.

"If ye wish to set anything right, leave this place. Leave Forfar before this disloyal *levereter* claims yer life," Agnes said, her narrowed eyes cast in Helen's direction.

"They have my bairn, Agnes. I'll drag ye all to Hell before I'll allow her this treatment."

"Ye're destroying families," Esther began. "Ye may say whatever ye wish, but it doesnae change that."

"Ye might have Father Evans hanging on yer every word, but it doesnae appear to be helping, does it?" Agnes asked.

"Malcolm makes my work more difficult." Helen looked as though she tasted something sour.

"Isnae their bickering yer doing?" Agnes asked.

"They're fighting?" I asked.

"Och aye," Agnes said. "Heard them clear down the hallway only yesterday."

"About what?"

"It seems Father Evans was true to their cause in the beginning, but as of late, he's questioned their actions," Agnes said.

Perhaps this explained the minister's conflicting energy.

"Their cause?"

"Chaos suits their interests," Agnes answered. "The witch hunts arenae meant to protect the villagers from witches. They are meant to ripple until they create havoc across all of Britain."

"That'll be enough from ye," Helen said sternly.

"Don't like when others share secrets, Helen?" I asked, sarcasm dripping from my tongue.

"Mind yer tongue, ootlin," Helen shot back. "Ye almost found yerself amongst us, aye? One tale from me, and ye'll be the next in that wee cell." She pointed in the direction of the deceased woman.

I held her gaze, unyielding. Intimidation wouldn't work on me, and I *would* get to the bottom of Malcolm and Father Evans's web.

"How can ye do this?" Esther said in disgust.

"Ye wouldnae do the same for yer bairns? Are ye no risking everything for them, even now?"

"Dinnae play into her games, Esther," Agnes said.

"Esther?"

The voice was one we knew well. Esther's eyes were pained when they met mine.

"Where are you, Katherine?" I asked.

"Two cells past Helen's."

Esther and I moved quickly, though my stomach lurched. I hadn't realized how difficult it would be to face Katherine until this very moment, how much I would blame myself for her current treatment.

Katherine was lying near the door, and we crouched nearer to her. She extended her hands to us. They were like ice.

"Och, Katherine," Esther said. "Ye'll freeze through."

Katherine nodded. "I willnae long survive this."

Esther nodded, her eyes filling with tears.

"'Tis a blessing, Esther." Katherine raised her head, looking around before dropping her voice. "Look at these women. I dinnae wish to share in their fate. I pray God takes me quickly."

Esther closed her eyes, tears spilling down her cheeks.

"You shouldn't have taken the fall for me," I said weakly.

"It was an easy sacrifice."

"But—"

Katherine cut me off. "Nae. Ye have many years ahead of ye, lass. A mate who loves ye dearly and an entire world to save."

"Perhaps we can prove yer innocence and have ye released," Esther said. "Perhaps we can both escape."

"Nae. My innocence is Hadley's guilt. Besides, I did make quite the spectacle of myself." Katherine smiled fiendishly. "When asked, Helen agreed that I was a witch, and the magistrate has a taste for blood that the minister wishes to whet. I have no the slightest hope."

"How can Helen live with herself?" I wondered, not bothering to keep my voice low.

"Verra weel, thank ye," she said, her voice echoing down the corridor.

Katherine's eyes flickered weakly. Already, her energy was waning. She was unwell before she ever entered this tolbooth, and a couple of days in these conditions would do her in. I wanted it to be different. I wanted to tell Katherine she was wrong and there was hope, but that would be a lie. Her only hope was to defy the council and use her power to free herself. But even so, the chill of death had already crept into her body—a body already weakened by illness and grief. I knew she longed for release, regardless of how horrible her last few days might be. When she entered the tolbooth, she had not meant to return.

"Where is Marjorie?" Esther asked.

"They removed her earlier—we dinnae ken."

Esther and I exchanged a fearful glance.

"Make me a promise," Katherine said, looking to Esther.

"Anything."

"Run, Esther," she whispered. "Run to Opimae and fight for a life with Hamish and yer bairns. And Hadley," she said, turning to me, "see yerself married immediately. Make a life for yerself with Fitz, and dinnae succumb to this ending like the rest of us. Ye dinnae belong here, dear one. Return to yer time and set things right."

Katherine fell into a coughing fit, and Esther and I exchanged a pointed look.

"I will," I whispered. "I'll be wed tomorrow."

Katherine smiled weakly. She reached for my hand and patted it. "Good. Verra good, Hadley."

"Hamish and I leave in two days' time." Esther said it so softly, I wasn't sure Katherine could hear her. But then, a slow smile returned to Katherine's lips.

"My life has unfolded in three acts," she began. "The first was a charmed existence. The second was filled with love and happiness. The final act—weel, it has held loss, grief, and the promise of death. I have lived a full life, and I dinnae begrudge those who have happiness ahead of them in this life, for I have happiness ahead of me in the next. I shall see my husband soon, and I cannae think of anything I've longed for more than that."

She coughed again, though this fit lasted only a few seconds.

"I am grateful that death isnae the end of me. The love I have given and the magic I have worked will live on after my earthly body draws its final breath," Katherine said. "We are only as good as the love we have given. Go far away from this place, the both of ye, and love well. Set yerselves free from the evil that plagues this burgh."

She gripped our hands tighter.

"*Live*," she whispered.

CHAPTER THIRTY-ONE

The early afternoon sun was a pleasant surprise for late November, and it soaked the edges of the dining table with a gentle warmth. Millie positioned three large cups of steaming tea in front of Fitz, Esther, and me, along with a plate of shortbread cookies. Hamish had gone into the burgh to settle matters with his business before his and Esther's departure. Annabel and her husband, John, were to see to things in their absence. Likewise, Esther had been sorting through trunks all morning as she and their household staff prepared for life without their employers.

I was glad to see Esther taking a break for tea. Her quiet determination and steadfast spirit shone brightly, and I hoped they were enough to see her through her next chapter. Leaving their known lives behind for the possibilities of Opimae would not be easy, but if their family remained intact, it was a change worthy of the effort.

Izzy had been dispatched to the forest to make an inquiry of the fair folk after I had awoken in the early morning from a night terror, fearful that the witch hunters would barge into the MacGregor home during our wedding ceremony. Though I was trying to wait patiently for her return, my nerves had me on edge.

"This really is a lot to ask of the faeries. Maybe I shouldn't have suggested we stray from our plans."

Esther waved off my concerns. "Yer time with the fair folk has been marked with quite serious matters, but that isnae always so with them. And in fact, they are usually quite pleased with any reason to enjoy a mighty feast."

"Aye, Esther is right, Hads. Fair folk lore has always depicted their love for feasts and gatherings."

"All will be well with yer wee wedding," Esther said. "Ye'll see."

Fitz turned a bit abruptly toward me, his eyes clearly lost in thought. "Ye ken, I really shouldnae be in this room right now," Fitz said.

"For what possible reason?" Esther asked.

"'Tis bad luck for the groom to see the bride before the wedding." He gave his best serious face.

"I think it's too late for that," I said. "We're already in a world of trouble. I don't think seeing me before our wedding is going to make much difference."

"Oh aye?" he said playfully. "Weel, I dinnae ken about yer feelings on the matter, but I consider myself to be quite fortunate in love, even if everything else is quite the mess."

I couldn't help but chuckle. "You've got a point, MacGregor. We *are* lucky in love, at least."

He reached for my chin and held it softly before planting a kiss on my lips.

"Aye! Now, that is just what a day like today calls for." Izzy's smile was bright as she skipped across the room to me.

"Don't make me ask," I said to Izzy, my face scrunched as I braced myself for the verdict.

"They've agreed to host us!"

"Wait, really?" I asked.

"Aye. Quite enthusiastically, actually. Faolán is quite chuffed over the whole affair. They said they are honored to host the wedding."

I didn't miss the familiarity Izzy showed in calling the prince by their given name. She beamed, and my heart tore a bit at the sight. What would they do when it was time for Izzy to return to the present?

"That's grand, Iz. Thank ye," Fitz said.

Izzy hugged her brother. "Dinnae mention it," she said. "It was quite the easy task. Apparently, the fair folk adore parties, and it took nae convincing on my part."

When Esther turned to me, her expression said, *I told ye.*

"Now, it's time to get to work. We have a wedding to prepare for!"

"What should we take to the forest?" Esther asked.

"Whatever we need for the ceremony," Izzy said.

"There's nothing else needed of us?" Fitz asked.

"I think a bit of the scran we had planned would be well-received, but Faolán said that a proper wedding banquet was under the jurisdiction of the fair folk." She eyed the plate of shortbread.

"Oh, faerie scran. Now, that will be a fine experience to be sure," Fitz said.

"It isnae often the fair folk offer such an honor to those from outside their species," Esther said. "Quite a gesture, this is."

"Now I'm even more excited," I said. "What time do they expect us?"

"Faolán said about an hour before sunset would be grand," she said, grabbing a cookie.

"We'd better set to work," Ann said, entering the room. "Sorry, Fitz—we'll be taking yer fiancée now."

The rest of the afternoon passed as I imagined most wedding days did. There were conversations to be had and running around to be done, but as Izzy beckoned me to the sitting room to begin my bridal preparations, a flurry of nerves hit the pit of my stomach.

"Pre-wedding jitters?" she asked.

"Isn't it silly? I've already made my true commitments to Fitz. This is just another way of saying something I've already said a hundred times."

"Though this ceremony isnae as common for witches, it does have meaning," Ann said. "It isnae silly at all."

"Aye, and ye were immersed in human culture for much of your life. I'd imagine it would have an additional impact for ye," Izzy said.

I was grateful for Ann and Izzy and their unwavering support, but the thought of human culture pulled feelings to the surface that I had attempted to stuff down. I missed Momma and Gram greatly, and I longed for their presence in this moment.

I hadn't thought all that much about my wedding when I was younger—I wasn't that kind of daydreamer—but I had always assumed my parents would be there with me. Now, with the loss of my father and my mother centuries away, a sadness crept into my soul that I couldn't uproot. I was forever fighting Fate when it came to my family.

"Is everything all right?" Izzy asked, eyeing me.

"Oh aye. I'm just thinking."

"Care to share?"

"Well… I wonder if customs will be different, considering we're doing the ceremony on faerie land," I said, skirting away from the true issue at hand.

Izzy paused, considering. "Perhaps. The faerie woods hold a different type of magic, and it is… well, it is ethereal. At the very least, I dinnae see how it couldn't add something more."

"Aye, double the magic," Ann said, smiling.

Esther entered the room to the sounds of our greetings.

"Have ye come to join us, Esther?" Ann asked.

"I'd be mighty pleased to stay, if ye'll have me."

"Of course!" I said. "I'd love for you to be here if you don't need to be anywhere else."

"That's braw, because I've brought a wee something borrowed," Esther said.

My look of surprise was enough to garner an explanation.

"We shared the custom with Esther, and she's assisted us in our search for all the proper items," Izzy said.

"Something old, something new, something borrowed, something blue," she quoted dutifully as she set a few items on the table.

I gasped in delight, which brought smiles and laughter to the faces of the three MacGregor women.

"Something borrowed," Esther said, handing me a hair pin. It was formed of hammered gold and held a sizable piece of agate.

"Oh, Esther," I said softly. "This is beautiful."

"Scottish agate," she said proudly.

The stone was a deep bluish-gray at its edges, but its next band was lighter and flecked with silver. The center was soft white, almost the color of pearls.

"This is perfect. Thank you."

Izzy picked up another item from the table and crossed the room to me. Sitting in the palm of her hand was a set of earrings. Two sapphires sat in gold circle settings, and I imagined they must be quite precious in this time.

"Hamish procured the sapphires and had them sent to Edinburgh to be set." Esther smiled, blushing. "It was extravagant, but he said he wished to make our first anniversary one to remember."

"They're gorgeous," I said. "Hamish did well."

"Aye, and I thought perhaps this could be yer something old and something blue. They arnae quite so old, but I thought they were just old enough to work for both."

"Of course. Thank you, Esther."

"And this," she said, holding a sixpence in the light, "is for yer shoe."

"My shoe?"

"Aye, ye'll place it in yer shoe for good luck."

I took the coin from her and followed direction.

"And lastly, something new," Ann said.

She moved closer to me, removing her pearl necklace and securing it around my neck. "Though these arenae new in our time, they did travel from over three-hundred years in the future. Ian gave these to me when Fitz was born. They seemed a proper fit."

I laughed, tears gathering at the corner of my eyes. "I'd say that qualifies. I'm surprised these made the journey with you."

"Modern trinkets do ensure a more difficult journey into the past, but when the time came, I found I couldnae bear…" Ann paused, her emotion clear. "I couldnae bear to part with them."

I nodded, and a tear rolled down Ann's cheek. Izzy moved closer and placed an arm supportively around her mother.

"I wish more than anything that he could be here today." Her voice was barely a whisper.

It reminded me that I wasn't alone in missing my loved ones. I enveloped Ann in a gentle embrace. When we released each other, it was with the exchange of sad smiles.

"Anyway, let's get on, shall we? Have a seat, Hadley, and Izzy will set to work on yer hair."

The rest of our time passed in smiles and laughter, anecdotes and banter, and I found my heart swelling with happiness by the time we'd pulled my wedding look together. We opted for simple and timeless. Izzy pulled the sides of my hair into French braids, which gathered at the back of my head in a loose bun. The lower half of my hair hung loosely down my back with a few strands framing my face. It was a whimsical look, fitting for a wedding hosted by fair folk.

Esther excused herself, and when she returned, Millie assisted her in bringing a beautiful gown through the doorway. The dress was crafted of fine silver silk that shimmered like snow in the afternoon sunlight. Knotted hearts were embroidered on the bodice and the elaborately full skirts, a timeless symbol of eternal love. Even the cream-colored laces gleamed as they caught the light, adding drama to the garment.

"Wait... seriously? This is for me?" I asked.

"I had a vision a few years back of a wealthy family whose daughter was to wed a Scottish nobleman. But she was ne'er to wear her wedding gown, for the ship carrying her family's belongings sank, and the dress was lost." Esther sighed heavily. "Perhaps it was foolish to replicate the wee thing, but I couldnae help myself."

"Esther," I whispered.

She smiled. "It was meant for ye, sure as I am standing here. It *looks* like magic, aye?"

My eyes filled with tears, and Izzy handed me a handkerchief.

"It does. It's absolutely perfect."

"Are ye certain? I want ye to be pleased with what ye wear today."

"More than pleased." I laughed. "I thought we were going to rummage through my closet for something."

Esther rolled her eyes playfully. "Hadley, ye do say the most shocking things at times."

We all fell to laughter. And yet, the tears still came.

I embraced Esther, all the while expressing my enthusiasm for the gown.

"We shall see ye safely to the forest and reach back for this, aye?"

"A good call," I said. "Best to not raise suspicions."

"Speaking of which… are we ready, then?" Izzy asked.

"Aye, I'll just gather my things," Esther said.

"Where's Fitz?" I asked.

"He should be nearing the faerie path by now," Izzy said.

"Oh. I thought he would walk with us."

"And see ye in this state?" Izzy said, horror in her wide eyes.

"We said we'd do a first look," I said defensively.

"Aye! In the forest, once ye look…" Izzy paused, gesturing to me. "*Proper.*"

I laughed lightly.

"He and Hamish will have walked together," Esther said. "Ann will transport Izzy to the forest's edge to prevent her from being seen. Annabel will accompany us. We are to meet her just near the edge of town."

My anxiety roared to life, and Izzy closed the gap between us. She placed her hand on my cheek and whispered. A soft breeze of peaceful energy channeled through me, and I relaxed with the changes occurring inside of me.

"I know ye dinnae wish to grow reliant on it, but it's your wedding day. There's loads happening and Fitz isn't here to calm ye, but your anxiety should be quieted enough to enjoy every bit of today."

I nodded. "Thanks, Iz."

She smiled broadly and took her place next to her mother. Ann wrapped her arms around Izzy and looked to me.

"We'll see ye soon, sweetheart."

"I'll be the one in silver."

The walk to the faerie forest was a quiet one. Annabel had begun to speak of Esther's departure, but Esther wouldn't hear of it.

"This is Hadley's evening, and we willnae sully it with the talk of taking leave or the witch hunters to come."

Annabel simply nodded, and we pressed on.

Our food offerings had been sent ahead of us, along with any items needed for our ceremony, and even with it being my special day, I felt a bit guilty for not helping. When I expressed the sentiment, Annabel looked at me like I was a puzzle to her, but Esther only chuckled before assuring me they were happy to have made the arrangements.

We reached the edge of the forest just as the sun neared the horizon. Sunset wouldn't be far behind, but we paused briefly before proceeding into the tree line. I recalled the strange energy that would accompany my re-entry into the realm of the fair folk and steeled myself for the shift in the atmosphere. But before I approached the entrance, a familiar figure with cascading blonde hair stepped through the opening.

Lochlan bowed. "It is a pleasure to see you again, Hadley—and on such a joyous occasion." His expression was pleasant, but he seemed irritated, his energy like sandpaper on my skin.

"The pleasure is all mine," I said, bowing in return. "Fitz and I are both so grateful to your folk for your willingness to host our wedding."

"These times are troubled. It is a welcome distraction."

Everyone had been adamant in their belief that faeries loved to host a party, but Lochlan's energy sure suggested otherwise.

He invited us into the forest, and we stepped inside. As the sunlight waned in the thick of the trees, the soft glow of his skin grew more brilliant. We followed him across the narrow path until we came upon Izzy and the prince. A magically lit lantern floated above them, though it was unnecessary with the prince glowing brightly beside Izzy.

At the sight of them, Lochlan's expression soured, and he took his leave. Though the prince clearly noticed the change, Izzy was too preoccupied with our entrance.

"You're here!" She beamed.

"What a joy it is to see you!" the prince greeted.

"Prince Faolán," I said, "I really don't know how to thank you for this. You are very kind."

"We are pleased with this diversion. The village really doesn't afford the most joyful energy at present."

"That's putting it mildly."

The prince chuckled. "But here? We shall revel in true celebration. I've heard you'll be wearing a dress fit for a queen."

"It's exquisite," I said.

"Then let us not tarry. Izzy?"

"Yes! This way."

Izzy pulled the floating lantern to her and led us off the path and further into the trees. The air shifted, and the way it rippled across my skin indicated that the elements were intertwined in magic. A privacy spell.

We stepped into the protected space, and Esther wasted no time in calling forth the gown. Izzy helped me shed the outer layers of my dress until I was standing in my chemise. Then, the three of them helped me into the new gown. Once I was laced into place, they each took a step back. Annabel gave a satisfied nod, Esther's eyes welled with tears, and Izzy squealed in delight.

Izzy pointed to a corner, where a floor length mirror was propped against a tree. I took a deep breath and moved slowly toward the mirror. Studying my reflection, I couldn't help but smile. From the gown to the hairstyle to the borrowed jewelry, I was dressed in love. It was perfect.

"Shall we send for Fitz?" Izzy asked.

"Sure. Send him in," I said, turning back to where the group stood.

"What? Nae," Izzy said, exasperated. "Ye must make a grand entrance! Step just outside the shield over there, so I can send Fitz in."

"What if I bump into him?" I asked.

"Ye'll be fine. Fitz is under strict instructions to stay where he is until I tell him otherwise. I'll lead him to the proper spot."

I couldn't help but laugh, but I followed Izzy's instructions dutifully and waited until she was ready for me. When she signaled me forward, my nerves quieted at the thought of Fitz being so near, and I made my way to the edge of the shield. Izzy nodded, and I stepped across the magical barrier. In my brief absence, magical lanterns had been placed strategically on the forest floor and in the trees. Another hung lazily above us.

"Wow," I whispered.

Fitz turned, and his eyes sparkled as they swept over me, the softest smile gracing his lips.

Fitz had never seemed more himself than he was in this moment, standing blissfully in the forest, draped in the clothing of his ancestors. Magic rippled through the air all around him, joyful and untamed. My breath hitched… My god, was he a sight to behold.

He wore a white shift of fine linen underneath a dark coat and a big wrap, or a belted plaid, as he called it. As Fitz had once shared with me, the belted plaid was the precursor to the modern kilt. Comprised of the ancient MacGregor red-and-black tartan, the plaid was draped over his shoulder and ran across his torso, where it was secured by a leather belt. A MacGregor crest bearing the coat of arms was pinned to the top of the plaid near his collarbone.

We stood silently for only a moment before I walked deeper into the shield. Fitz was frozen, it seemed, and as I drew near, his gaze dropped to the forest floor. He shook his head softly and chuckled. When his eyes met mine, tears escaped them.

We were both overcome, suspended in our cocoon inside the realm of the faeries. It was Fitz who closed the final gap between us.

"We've formed our streams and made our commitments to each other, so tell me why I'm emotional seeing ye in that dress."

"It's just a human ceremony, remember?" I grinned.

"Nae," he whispered. "'Tis much more than that."

Fitz kissed me gently, and for the first time since we'd crossed into the past, our energies flowed openly and freely, uninhibited by grief and fear. Our troubles wouldn't disappear, but we could forget them for a few precious hours.

Fitz traced his fingertips along my cheek. "Perhaps 'tis trite to say this, but ye are bonnie—bonnie as ye've e'er been."

"No makeup, no hairspray, no painted nails or designer shoes." I smiled. "And yet… I've never felt more magical than I do right now."

"Aye. Ye dinnae need a bit of that, my wee witch. Tonight, ye are brimming with magic. Ye glow like the faeries."

I traced my fingertips across the MacGregor crest.

"You're wearing your… what was the Gaelic name of this?" I asked, pointing to the plaid.

"*Feileadh mor.*" He grinned.

"Very dapper," I said.

"Hamish was well chuffed to take this out of his closet. The king didnae overturn the ban on the MacGregors until last year. Unfortunately, another will be placed on our people. But for now, we Mac-Gregors are safe from being murdered for using our name, at least."

"That'll officially include me in about fifteen minutes."

Fitz's gaze turned tender.

"It'll be quicker than that if I have anything to say about it. Come on, firecracker. Let's get ourselves wed before ye go changing yer mind on me."

CHAPTER THIRTY-TWO

Our ceremony site lay on the west side of the forest, far away from the main path used by humans. The sun peeked above the horizon, and the light had taken on a soft, golden quality. Fitz and Prince Faolán stood near the trunk of a Scots pine, and our family stood to either side of them, all turned expectantly in my direction. I pulled the fresh air deeply into my lungs and made my way closer. Fallen branches had been arranged to form an aisle, which perfectly complemented the natural bouquet Izzy had harvested for me. As I neared the scene, floating bits of light caught my eye. The buzz of magical energy was palpable, and I soon realized the glowing orbs were the faeries. They'd shifted to their smaller forms to create the illusion of fireflies dancing on the evening air.

As I took my place across from Fitz, my eyes were intensely on his, and I knew with more certainty than ever that I wanted to tie myself to Fitz.

"How can I be this lucky?" Fitz whispered.

I smiled and wiped the single tear trailing down his cheek.

The prince called the wedding to order, and in my previous life, I couldn't have imagined being wed by a faerie prince. After welcoming us all into such a magical evening, they led us through promises and vows. There was something timeless about traditional wedding vows, in the reciting of words that had joined together countless humans and beings before us, and that countless lovers would offer long after we'd returned to dust.

Our ceremony truly reflected the complexities of our love and our journey, intertwining both modern and ancient wedding practices. It was surreal to finally utter these vows—to make these enduring promises before our family and friends. I wanted to take it all in, every single bit of the night, but in these fleeting moments, I couldn't bear to remove my eyes from Fitz. Our energy traveled warmly across our streams, channeling an ancient and ethereal magic.

Hamish handed a braided cord to Prince Faolán. The prince bound our right hands together, wrapping the cord around them. With the vows complete, Hamish extended his hand to Esther. She followed his lead, and they joined us where we stood.

He nodded to Fitz, who then looked tenderly to me.

"Just as this ring has no beginning nor end, my love for ye is so. Our souls are intertwined, understanding each other by a steadfast and boundless love. Time is said to be infinite, but my love for ye is longer still."

Tears spilled down my cheeks, and my grasp on Fitz's hands tightened. My blood hummed so loudly within me I thought the whole woods must be filled with the song of my magic… with the vibrancy of my love for this man.

"With these vows, our wee family acknowledges Hadley Weston-MacGregor as one of our own."

A breathy laugh escaped my lips. I hadn't realized just how much it would mean to me to hear those very words.

Hamish continued in Gaelic, and Fitz whispered the words in English.

Mìle fàilte dhuit le d'bhréid,
A thousand welcomes to you with your marriage,

Fad do ré gun robh thu slàn.
May you be healthy all your days.

Móran làithean dhuit is sìth,
May you be blessed with long life and peace,

Le d'mhaitheas is le d'nì bhi fàs.
May you grow old with goodness, and with riches.

Esther stepped forward and draped a tartan shawl around my shoulders before securing it into place with a silver pin, which bore the Clan Gregor coat of arms, their motto surrounding the roaring lion.

"Welcome to the family," Esther said, beaming. "I ken ye'll do us proud."

I couldn't wipe the ecstatic smile from my face, and Fitz's expression was equal to mine.

When we sealed our promises with a kiss, our family erupted in applause, and Fitz and I fell to laughter as we clung to each other. Izzy and Ann wrapped us in embraces, and Esther was quick to follow.

But the night was just beginning. The fair folk had planned a reception fit for royalty.

It was a woodland dream set in the soft light of twilight, weaving the simplest magic of the forest into every detail. Wreaths made from fir and spruce trimmings and decorated with berries and ribbon adorned the wooden chairs set around the tables, which were topped with glowing candelabras and magical lanterns nestled in a bed of vines and additional tree trimmings. One long table held the feast for the evening, and I led Fitz, hand in hand, to survey our meal. There were roasted vegetables and smoked fish, nuts and berries, steaming soups and soft breads. My nerves were gone, and the pang of hunger was fierce.

After a hearty dinner, we moved deeper into the forest until we came to a clearing. Fire pits roared to life, and the faeries clapped and whistled at our approach, all quick to offer their congratulations. We smiled and waved and exchanged pleasantries with the fair folk, until the prince arrived at our side with mugs of whisky.

"We could ne'er repay yer kindness," Fitz began. "But please accept our most hearty thanks for all ye've done."

"You've given us a night we'll never forget," I said. "Thank you, Your Grace—truly."

"Please, don't trouble yourself with the formalities. I believe we are past that. Call me Faolán."

"I don't imagine your sister will be pleased with that," Fitz said.

"Probably not, but as I'll share with her, it isn't her business. I gave the crown to Tarron, and with that act, I am now able to be less… *regal.*"

"You were meant to rule?" I asked.

"My father left the crown to me, but I did not care for it. So, I named Tarron queen and stepped away."

"Are you the eldest, then?" I asked. Faolán didn't give me "oldest sibling" energy.

"No, but my father wanted me to become a strong male leader. He told me I'd grow into the responsibility and who I was meant to become—or rather, who he thought I was meant to become. It was an irresponsible decision on his part, really. Tarron was clearly the best suited to rule, but my father cared little about that. Bit of a misogynist, that one."

The thought of misogyny in their culture surprised me, and I realized I still idealized other beings too much. At times, I still thought like a human, naively believing these magical cultures lacked prejudice, but I had learned that wasn't true firsthand in Opimae. From my encounters with the druids to our troubles with our own councils, it was far too prevalent. This was yet another reminder that every species had its problems, and in many of them, we all shared.

"Do ye often provide council to the queen?" Fitz asked.

"Of course," Faolán said. "We're a team. Being a ruler is difficult, and I'm happy to be of service to her. It is often difficult to know who you can trust."

"That, we can understand," I said. "Deciding whose advice is self-interested, and who is simply trying to advise you to do the right thing."

"Exactly," they said. "I might not always be right, but my heart is always in the right place. That, at least, I can claim."

"Speaking of which," I began, "is everything all right with the member of your guard who greeted us today?"

"Oh, Lochlan." The prince cleared their throat.

"I don't mean to pry… I just realized something has been off with him, and I wasn't sure if we'd offended him."

"Do not trouble yourselves. Lochlan and I had a bit of a fling for a brief time. We were far too different to be compatible in the long run, so I called it off."

"Oh," I said softly. Izzy.

The prince nodded. "Lochlan wasn't pleased with me, but he's remained a loyal member of the guard—he refused to be reassigned."

"Has that been awkward?" I asked, my face scrunching.

The prince laughed. "Perhaps at first. Things settled for a while, but then he saw me with your sister." He turned to Fitz.

"A bit of jealousy, then," Fitz said.

"Fair folk are a bit different than witches in the romance department. Perhaps we are not as singularly minded on our path through life, but when we do find love, it is just as indestructible as what the two of you have." They paused, taking a deep breath. "Fitz, what I've felt for anyone in my past doesn't hold a candle to the way I feel for your sister."

The prince searched Fitz's expression, seemingly unsure if they should continue. Fitz nodded.

"Our circumstances aren't simple, but I hope you won't oppose our wishes to become better acquainted."

"I havenae seen anything thus far that troubles me when it comes to yer intentions," Fitz said. "But I do fear ye're playing at a game ye cannae win."

The prince nodded, their eyes distant.

"My entire world shifted when I first laid eyes on Izzy." They chuckled lightly. "Her beauty is beyond words, but it was much more than that. I felt as if our energies were meant to know each other's, that our minds would find the most reassuring intimacy together, that I'd found a piece of my heart that had always been lost. All in a mere moment. It was something I had thought to be impossible."

"That sounds incredibly powerful," I said, eyeing Fitz.

"Am I making sense at all?" Faolán asked.

"Aye," Fitz said. "Much more than ye ken."

It had been the same for me and Fitz. When I met Fitz, I hadn't known who I was—I had no idea I was a witch or what any of this meant. Even so, my world had changed forever with one glance.

"Is that your blessing, then?"

We couldn't help but laugh.

"Aye, 'tis our blessing."

"You'll have a fight ahead of you—we all do," I said. "But Izzy would hardly be the first MacGregor to fight against all odds for love."

Fitz kissed me then, and it was with difficulty that we broke away.

"Well, if I have your blessing… come and dance. Let's make merry."

A festive group of fair folk were gathered at the far side of the clearing with a variety of instruments at the ready: a harpsichord, fiddles, a Celtic harp, a flute, mandolins, and more. The fair folk were quick to teach us their dances and traditions, and we joined them for several dances before needing a bit of rest. Something eased in my chest at the sight of the merriment. Though this began as a celebration of Fitz's and my union, this night belonged to us all.

Fitz and I found nearby seats, and we sat quietly, observing our companions. Izzy danced to every song with the prince. The two of them were absolute magic together. Faolán was as ethereal as God ever made anyone, but when they stood next to Izzy, the glow from their skin grew even brighter and their eyes only looked upon her as they twirled her about the earthen dance floor. Izzy's hair was unbound, wild and free, and her feet were bare. Her laughter was unguarded, and it occurred to me that the prince wasn't only helping heal her loss but also unburdening her from the chains she had so carefully placed around herself. She was too magical, too ethereal for our world not to take notice—but in this forest, she was exactly as she was meant to be.

Seeing her like this reminded me of a summer's night long ago, when I'd observed her working magic with her skin alight.

"I see that smile of yers," Fitz said. "And I see who holds yer attention."

"It worries you."

"I fear it can only end in heartache. Of course it worries me."

I squeezed his hand. "You've given your blessing—this is their fight now. We'll support their decision however we can."

It was then that I noticed the prince's crown of vines. They had faded to a softer brown than before, and orange buds sprouted from them, seemingly ready to burst forth with new life. Their smile was vibrant, and their energy was utterly alight.

"They'll work it out. I have to believe that for them. Surely, after such devoted service on the prince's part, Fate wouldn't be so cruel."

"There's such goodness in them," Esther said, taking a seat next to Fitz. "I didnae mean to interrupt. I only saw who's captured yer eye."

"You're never an interruption," I said, smiling. "And aye, you're right. We're hoping that Fate will offer her blessing."

Esther nodded. "Stranger things have come to pass, but only time will tell. Faolán's case is unusual to be sure."

"I trust ye're enjoying yer last night in these bonnie woods," Fitz said, changing the subject.

"Verra much. I cannae think of a better way to spend my last evening in Forfar."

"Ye and Hamish seemed to be getting on quite well on the dance floor."

Esther laughed. "There was a time we loved nothing more than to dance. That was many years past… before the trials drew near and Fate sent trouble to our doorstep."

"Now you'll have that chance again," I said, taking Esther's hand.

She squeezed it gently. "Aye, perhaps ye are right."

"Thank ye, Esther," Fitz said. "For all of this. For taking us in when ye didnae have to. For believing in our mission—in us. For being a part of this special night."

"Och aye," she said, waving her hand dismissively. "It has been my great honor. There are few who can boast that they've taken in their descendants."

"I've spent years wondering about my many times great-grandmother," Fitz said, a sad smile rising to his lips. "Our time together will always be near to my heart."

Esther's eyelids fluttered, and she took her hands in her lap, twisting them absentmindedly.

"Is everything okay?" I asked. "Have we upset you?"

"Nae," Esther said, shaking her head, though her lashes were damp when she looked to us again. "'Tis only… Och, how I long to live to earn that title—*grandmother*. I long to meet the young bairns who would call me grandmother and chase them about the park. I long for my hair to fade to gray, and for the lines on my face to reflect a long and well-lived life."

"Oh, Esther," I whispered.

Esther shook her head again. "Nae. Dinnae fash. This evening is a celebration. 'Tis only… I wish I had more time with ye both."

"Aye," Fitz said softly. "Aye, we ken."

Hamish came wandering up and seated himself next to his wife. "What is the matter?"

"I'm only feeling sentimental this evening."

Hamish smiled. "Aye, I cannae begrudge ye for that. No on a night such as this."

We sat in silence for only a moment before Hamish broke the quiet. "I wish to say something to ye, Fitz. I ken what ails ye, the grief ye hold close to yer heart, but I ask ye to release it. This marriage—it willnae heal ye, but Hadley will walk by yer side as ye heal yerself. She'll hold yer hand and keep it warm. Dinnae forget the purpose of yer life. Aye, ye are meant to save beings in yer time, but ye are also meant for love—and yer love is what will save the world at the end of it all."

Fitz nodded, his eyes distant. "Aye, I hear ye, Hamish. Thank ye."

"Our time wears thin," Hamish said to Esther. "Shall we have another dance before returning hame?"

Esther smiled. "Aye, Hamish. Dance with me."

Hamish led Esther to the dance floor, and she laughed as he spun her around before pulling her against his chest. Esther's laughter faded to a dreamy smile, and she closed her eyes as Hamish guided her in time with the music. Despite the years of worry and the arguments over what was best for their family, it was clear that nothing stood between the two of them tonight.

I swallowed against the ache in my throat, uncertain if the emotion was sadness over their plight or happiness over their choice to leave for Opimae. Hamish looked tenderly at his wife and kissed the top of her head.

"A dance seems a fine idea," Fitz said. "If ye'll have me for yer partner, I'd like to dance with my wife."

The butterflies that hit my stomach at the word "wife" surprised me. "I would very much like to dance with my *husband*."

Fitz grinned. He stood and bowed before me, his hand outstretched in silent request.

I tilted my head upward as we made our way across the beautiful clearing. The night sky was sprinkled with stars. The clear weather meant an extra chill to the air, but thankfully, the thick forest protected us from the wind, and the fires kept the space comfortable. It was purely lit by firelight, magical flames, and the glow of the fair folk. We were tucked safely in a cocoon, and I wished life could always be so. I breathed deeply, pulling in the clean air marked by the fresh scent of evergreens and the warm tones of the smoke.

Fitz pulled me closer to him, and we moved in time with the music. Fitz tightened his grip on me until it felt as though we were dancing as one. With every turn, each subtle movement, we were speaking one of the most timeless languages lovers had ever known. My eyes traced each part of his face carefully, as though it wasn't already committed to memory: his bright emerald eyes and chiseled jawline, his strong brow and chestnut hair. I'd always found Fitz attractive, but there was something more than that. He was *beautiful.* In the rush of recent months, I hadn't taken the time to appreciate him for the man he was. I would do better, I vowed.

"Keep looking at me like that, Hadley, and we willnae finish this dance."

"Don't say something like that if you don't intend to follow through," I countered.

"The fair folk don't expect us to stay until the end. Iz already asked Faolán about their customs."

I raised my eyebrows.

"And as bonnie as ye are in that dress—and my god, ye *are* bonnie—I'll be damned if I'm no desperate to get ye out of it."

My breath shifted, my throat growing thick with desire, and Fitz slipped his arm further around me, finding a firm grasp at my waist. With his other hand, he flipped my arm over and slowly kissed the soft skin of my inner wrist. My pulse quickened with the brush of his lips, and when our eyes locked, it was decided.

It was time to return to our quarters.

Our room was aglow with warm flickering light from the fire Millie had built in our hearth. A sizable stack of wood had been placed nearby, and our water storage had been replenished—Millie wouldn't be disturbing us this evening. I removed my jewelry and placed them on the nearby table.

"Mum adores that string of pearls," Fitz said absentmindedly.

"I'm sorry Ian couldn't be here tonight. I know he would've loved every minute of this."

Fitz's smile was bittersweet. "And I am sorry Matt wasn't here to walk ye down the aisle. I can almost see his face, how proud he would have been."

I laughed lightly. "Dad would have been ecstatic."

"Have ye e'er thought much about yer wedding day?" Fitz asked. "What it would be like and that sort of thing?"

I thought hard. "Not really. I mean, when I was younger, it was a game some of my friends liked to play—dreaming of princess gowns and large cakes."

Fitz laughed.

"But seriously? I can't say that I have. I was rather career-focused, and there wasn't anything to really dream about. Not until you showed up... you and all your complications." I grinned mischievously.

"How can ye say such a thing?" he said, feigning offense. "Here ye sit in this seventeenth-century home in an absolutely stable time period with nae danger after being wed by a faerie prince. What's complicated about that?"

"Aye, well, when you put it like that..."

Fitz leaned against the wooden post at the far side of the room, studying me.

"What is it?"

"Oh, 'tis nothing," he said. "I was only wondering if there was anything missing tonight from yer early years of playful wedding planning."

His concern was endearing. "Truthfully, I think the only thing I knew I wanted was to dance at the reception to 'Something'—the Frank Sinatra version. Otherwise, my desires were left open to be charted with my future husband."

"Yer husband would love to chart yer desires with ye."

"I'm sure he would," I said. "Then he'd better read my mind and get me out of this gown. Beautiful as they are, stays have never been comfortable."

Fitz meandered toward me as he sang the first few lines of "Something."

"Better sing along, *mo chridhe*. My voice is lonely."

Soon enough, we were singing and laughing as he loosened my laces. He twirled me around to face him, and the laughter halted for a slow, deep kiss. When he pulled back, the promise of him sharing his thoughts was evident in his features.

"Hadley... tomorrow begins a new chapter, and I dinnae ken what to expect from Fate. But of one thing I am certain: we have faced countless trials, and every challenge only brought us closer together. Nothing can part us now."

"Uncertainty from outside factors is nothing new to us," I said. "We will navigate this new course together, and Fitz, I *will* fight for us until the bitter end."

"My brave witch," he whispered, his fingertips running through my hair. "Ye have my love, my loyalty, and now… ye have my name. I am yers, Hadley. To the end of this world—or any other we may cross into—I'll go there for ye."

I kissed him then. Our lips moved in perfect unison, imparting our vows through touch. The feel of his body against mine was euphoric. Fitz's hands slid across my back to the top of my shoulders, where he gently massaged tension away. I dropped my head back and sighed, and he ran his lips lightly along my neck, sending goosebumps rippling across my skin. He found my lips once more, and I was lost in his taste as my fingers twisted through his hair. I pulled back and gazed into his eyes, my thumb running gently across his lips.

A sort of feral desire guided my movements as I took stock of my husband. I removed the MacGregor pin from his plaid, freeing his upper body from the cloth, before moving on to the leather belt at his waist. I tossed the items onto the bed, and the plaid fell to his feet with a thud, leaving him only in his shift. I placed my palm against his chest and closed my eyes at the feel of his heart thumping against my skin. My witch's eye roared to life, and our connection blossomed. His heartbeat was everything, thrumming through me as though it were my own. My lips parted, and Fitz leaned forward and kissed me until our hearts beat in time with each other's.

I pulled back and pushed the linen garment up and over his head, and he tugged it free and threw it toward a chair. His emerald eyes gleamed with desire, and the thud of my pulse was palpable in my neck. Fitz kissed that very spot before stepping back.

"Was this yer plan, then?" he asked, a wry smile forming at his lips. "To study me?"

He raised his arms in question, and my eyes answered as they swept the masculine shape of his body. From his broad shoulders and long torso to his muscular thighs and strong arms, the sight of him deepened my desire. His toned physique now held the remnants of battle, and I couldn't help but to study his scattered scars. I had stood by his side for much of the carnage, and my own body bore markings to match. I stepped closer and traced the outline of his body with my fingertips. Fitz held still, his eyes cast downward to watch me at work, only closing them as I reached the areas that pulled breathy noises from him or caused him to nibble at his lip.

When I slid my arms around his waist, he lost no time in flipping the scene.

"My turn," he whispered, his breath warm on my ear.

Fitz finished the work he had begun and removed my skirts. My wedding day chemise tied in between my collarbones, and Fitz held my gaze as he tugged at the strings. Much to his satisfaction, the top fell open, and he ran his hands down my chest, followed by his lips. My mind was already falling into a haze, and I closed my eyes to better focus on the feel of him studying the curves of my body.

"Fitz," I whispered, desire clear in my tone.

"Nae," he returned, his voice gruff. "I'll command ye tonight, firecracker."

I opened my mouth to protest, but he met me in a deep kiss.

"'Tis my turn to study ye," he whispered against my lips. "And I plan to be… thorough."

I gripped the chair behind me to steady myself, and taking notice, Fitz lifted me from the ground and onto the bed. He planted his knees on either side of me, and I arched my back sharply, my mind growing thicker with want, as a surreal urge pumped through my body. I slid my hands across his chest, his back, his taut arms supporting the weight of his body.

Then, dipping his head, he kissed the sensitive skin at the base of my neck near my collarbone before sliding his hand along my throat, his thumb running back and forth just under my jawline. He made good on his word to study me, until I was desperate for his lips on mine. I reached for him, resting my hands on either side of his face.

"Ye've ne'er been bonnier than ye are right now, lying beneath me cast in firelight." I moved my thumb against his lip, tugging his mouth open ever so slightly. "Promise me it'll always be like this, that you'll always want me as you do now."

Fitz lowered himself gently, and I gasped at the feel of him.

"How could it e'er be otherwise, my love?" he asked, his eyes searching mine. "I love ye too fiercely for these desires to fade."

I tugged him closer to me and gripped him tightly as he moved against me, our marital union complete.

CHAPTER THIRTY-THREE

Esther

The wedding did me good, and it seemed to be so with Hamish as well. We passed much of the evening recalling our own vows, considering our future in Opimae, and making promises—both in words and actions. The next day, we rose before first light to prepare for our journey. My body was tired, but my mind was clearer than it had been in months. Though I was riddled with worry over the fate of our bairns, our most trusted family and friends were resolute in their belief that Opimae was best for us. I decided to trust in Hamish and myself, trust that all would be well with our wee family.

When I stepped into the sitting room, Hadley was awaiting my arrival.

"Where's Fitz?" I asked.

"Readying the carriage with Hamish," she said. We had debated our transportation, but we had decided to journey by carriage. It was costly, but the coachmen were from Edinburgh. They wouldnae be recognized, and it allowed us to pack more provisions than we might on horseback—luggage, weapons, food. The carriage awaited us just outside the woods of the fair folk.

Fitz and Ann had offered to transport us to the portal, but I believed that to be too far from our natural course. I couldnae say whether I would have decided on Opimae without Hadley and Fitz crossing our paths, but I could say that Fitz and Ann should have ne'er been in our time. They couldnae interfere that far.

"What's that you have there?" Hadley asked.

I smiled, holding the doll out for her to inspect. "A favorite in this household."

Hadley observed it carefully.

"I see she's been well-loved," she said, combing the hair down with her fingers.

I chuckled. "Elsie loved her dearly, but when she grew too old for such things, she passed her along to Ainsley. We forgot to place the wee thing in Ainsley's trunk before she went away."

Hadley handed the doll back to me.

"Have you said your goodbyes?" she asked, her eyes soft and her tone tender.

"Aye. I've taken my leave." I paused. "Millie has wept enough for us all."

A soft smile graced her lips. "Poor Millie," she said. "But you'll see her again one day."

"Aye, I am certain ye are right."

"Well, if you're ready, Elspeth will be waiting on us at the edge of town."

I took one last look at the sitting room, thinking of the many evenings we passed by the fireside, Hamish reading aloud while

Callum and Archie performed scenes from the story, Elsie grow-ing—thankfully—proficient with the pianoforte, Ainsley taking her first steps near the chaise by the window. Hamish and I had truly made this a home.

Tears welled in my eyes. I longed to steady my nerves, but even my deep breaths did nothing to dispel the fluttering in my chest. I couldnae afford to be sentimental, and I cleared my throat as I faced the doorway. Though I turned away from the place that held many dear memories of our wee family, I took solace in the fact that we would soon be together once more.

Hadley took my arm and looped it through hers, supporting me as we made our way to the foyer. The staff had gathered near the doorway, tears falling down their faces like the rain upon the win-dowsill.

"I thank ye." I swallowed hard, holding back the emotion that threatened to spill out of me. "I thank ye for all ye have done for us. Hamish and I will see ye again."

Millie's attempt to stifle her soft sobs was unsuccessful, and her emotion threatened to break me. I offered a brave smile and looked away, hardly able to meet her eyes. Hadley pushed us along, and we had neared the door when a loud knock sounded from the other side. We each looked to the other, and my heart thumped hard in my chest.

The knock came again, this one more violent than the last.

"Around the corner," Hadley instructed. She pushed me gently in the proper direction before moving closer to the door with Millie. She nodded, and Millie unlatched the door.

"Hadley!" Annabel's voice croaked. "Where is Esther?"

"Come in," Hadley said before closing the door. "We were just leaving."

I moved into sight. "What's amiss, Aunt? I thought ye were to meet us at the woods."

"Aye, I was nearing the center of town when the crowds grew restless. Father Evans had only just finished speaking to them."

"What has happened?" I asked impatiently.

"He means to try Marjorie today."

My spirit broke. Hadley closed her eyes as her face fell.

"I thought it best to accompany ye and Hadley to the edge of the burgh rather than meeting ye… in case of trouble."

"Do you think we need to give it a minute?" Hadley asked.

"They'll only grow more restless as the trial draws near," Annabel said. "We should take the outside path to the west and cut through the park. We'll meet Elspeth just as planned, though perhaps a bit late. Whatever we do, we must avoid the areas around the tolbooth."

"Aye," I said. "Let us go now."

We moved swiftly from the house and shortened our trek by walking through my garden. The wee patch was sodden, all mud and mess from the heavy rains of the last few weeks. But come time, Millie would tend it for me, keeping it well until my return.

As we reached the park, my breathing grew more even. Danger could still befall us, but with the excitement in the burgh, it wasnae likely we'd meet villagers on the path. We continued wordlessly, in a hurry to be done with this part of the journey. Elspeth was waiting on the far side of the park, and we continued on, our arms looped as we enjoyed the last few moments we had together.

Who would be here when I returned from Opimae? Would Elspeth survive the trials? Would Murdina still be baking bread in Annabel's kitchen? Would Annabel—I stopped myself. This was futile. Instead, I would reflect only on the land that had been my refuge since my earliest days in the burgh, when the villagers had first thought me strange.

The pure scent of evergreen filled me, along with the clean air of the forest, and I exhaled the impurities of the burgh. As we neared the western wood, we dared to slow our pace.

"Esther, are ye well, lass?" Annabel asked.

I nodded. "Much better now that we've left the burgh."

"Aye," Annabel said, smiling. "I thought this day would ne'er come."

"When will ye return to yer time, lass?" Annabel asked Hadley.

"We plan to wait a day or two and keep up appearances so Esther and Hamish aren't immediately missed."

We'd taken a few steps more when the edge of my sight blurred.

"A vision," I whispered. "Help me move into the tree line."

My companions guided me into the safety of the forest. We tucked just into the tree line, and they propped me against a tree trunk.

The vision wavered, but the ripples of energy bursting through me promised it would yet surface. I dug my fingers into the damp earth, connecting with my element, hoping it would assist me. Steadily, the scene grew stronger, and a room stretched before me. Several witches and a few elves were seated at a long table, their faces marked with trouble.

"I don't know what can be done about it," a man said, his voice anguished.

"Well, something must be done, Charles. We are wasting precious time." It was Henry who spoke, his voice filled with anger. I had seen him enough to be certain of it.

"Yes, it does… but we can't just storm in there."

"Hadley would have the answer to this," an elven woman with blonde hair said.

"Hadley *is* the answer," Molly said, staring blankly at the wall.

"Aye, it is well past time. The councils must convene. If they willnae allow it, then we'll find a way to smuggle them in."

Charles dropped his head into his hands.

"We are out of options." The woman who spoke was regal. I had seen enough of the water witches in Opimae to think she might call Thalassa her home. As the vision crisped, I made out her dark skin and hazel eyes, her lavender robes and gold crown, and I knew it then—this was Queen Marina, whom Hadley had spoken of.

My vision went dark, but someone whispered in the shadows. I strained to hear and understand.

"Bring it in, musketeers," someone said faintly.

"Love you guys."

"Always."

"Forever."

Everything went black before my eyesight restored itself. Annabel, Elspeth, and Hadley were on the ground beside me, their concern clear.

"Hadley, did ye see?" I asked.

"No," she said. "I don't know why, but I saw nothing."

"'Tis strange," I said. My mind was a bit muddled, and it took me a moment more to continue on. "Once before, ye said the word 'musketeers?'"

Confusion marked her face for a brief second before recognition sparked. "I made a comment about the three musketeers the other day."

"Aye... does the word mean anything to ye?"

"Jordan, Tanner, and I call ourselves the three musketeers."

I shared the contents of my vision. "I think yer friends are in trouble. They need ye."

She chewed at her lip before nodding. "We almost have you on your way to Opimae. We'll be returning to our time *very* soon."

"Aye, let us be done with this," I said.

"Can ye stand, or do ye need a bit of rest?" Annabel asked.

"I can walk."

Hamish's voice broke through the damp air. "Esther!" he called, though quietly. "Are ye here?"

Hadley stepped into the clearing and returned with Hamish and Fitz.

"Are ye well?" Hamish asked, immediately dropping to his knees beside me.

"Aye, a vision is all."

His hand cupped my face. "Let us get ye into the carriage and be on our way. Ye can rest inside."

The carriage was already worth the spend, considering my vision would have required us to stop while traveling on horseback.

Hamish cradled me in his arms and carried me from the woods, our wee family just behind us. Just as we reached the carriage, a noise startled us. Hamish's hand traveled to the firearm just inside the carriage, while Fitz and Hadley positioned themselves before me. The leaves shook with a disturbance, and finally, a branch moved to reveal Prince Faolán, followed by Izzy and Ann.

"Yer Grace!" Hamish called. "We feared the worst."

"I apologize. I only came to wish you a safe and pleasant journey."

"And we thank ye for yer kindness," Hamish returned.

"You will be sorely missed, but for my part, I am glad to see you take your leave. Go to Opimae with our blessing, and live a long and harmonious life."

Hamish shook their hand. A gentle breeze blew from the forest, carrying warmth and peace. Magic nudged my skin, and I closed my eyes for a moment, taking my leave of the forest that I had loved so well.

It was a proper goodbye from the fair folk.

Hamish took my hand to help me into the carriage when another disturbance pulled our attention. I feared we wouldnae be so fortunate twice.

"Take Esther and Izzy back into the woods," Hadley commanded the prince and Ann.

We followed Hadley's instruction, unsure of my next move, but kenning this would grant me a few moments to consider. Our position afforded a view of the proceedings from the shelter of the trees. Father Evans topped the hill, and with him were twelve guards and five villagers. My vision swam.

There was nae reason for him to be here. He had found us out.

"What do we have here?"

"I am traveling with my kin to Edinburgh," Hamish replied.

Father Evans looked around. "And Elspeth?"

"She was out walking, and we stopped momentarily for Hadley to speak with her."

"Walking here all alone?" Father Evans asked.

"Nae. Annabel accompanied me to collect a wee bit of thistle for the shop."

Annabel's face was resolute, her eyes fixed on the minister. Her gaze threatened to burn a hole through the man's head.

Father Evans looked less than convinced. "And you saw her from the carriage?"

"I'm not feeling well and wanted to walk beside the carriage for a bit," Hadley said. "I saw Elspeth and Annabel in the distance."

"How convenient. What business do you have in Edinburgh?"

"Why do ye ask? Our business is our own," Fitz answered.

The small group of villagers looked to one another, shocked.

"It looks as though you are attempting to escape."

"Escape from what? Hadley and I are returning home. I dinnae ken why that is anyone's business besides our wee family's."

"Why are ye harassing my kin?" Hamish asked.

"Where is Esther?" Father Evans asked, ignoring Hamish and Fitz's questions.

"She is hame."

"Odd," he said. "See, I just stopped by, and they told me she was out."

"Then she must have stepped out," Hamish said, exasperated.

The minister nodded.

"We'd better be going," Hadley said. "Daylight is burning, and we don't want to be on the road past dark. Thieves, you know."

"Of course. We'll let you be on your way."

"We will?" a villager asked.

"Yes, there's nothing amiss here. Let us return to the village and make our next visit."

The villager looked confused, but he didn't dare contradict the minister. He nodded, and the group turned around.

"*I don't trust them,*" Hadley said to my mind. "*Cut through the woods with Prince Faolán, and we'll pick you up on the other side.*"

Hadley

The minister and his band of misfits moved on, but I didn't trust they wouldn't be lurking along our path, waiting to catch Esther. I communicated my thoughts quietly to our group.

"Annabel, ye and Elspeth must walk home as though nothing is amiss," Fitz instructed.

Annabel protested. "I cannae leave Esther under these circumstances!"

"Ye must," Fitz said. "If the minister is watching, and sees ye walk on with us, our plan is as good as dead."

Annabel's eyes flicked to mine.

"You need to go back, and be careful what you speak of on the way home. The minister or his little helpers could be planted anywhere," I said.

Annabel wrung her hands, her eyes troubled.

"I ken ye want to be useful to Esther and ye havnae had a proper goodbye, but Annabel, one wrong step and we will be the reason Esther is sent to the gallows."

With that, Annabel pulled an envelope from her pocket. "Please see that Esther receives this immediately."

I extended my hand, and she pulled back.

"If I'm going to alter history, it won't be in this moment," I said. "I swear to you, I will put this in Esther's hands."

Annabel hesitated, but Hamish nodded, and she handed off the package to me.

"We must sort what to do with ye now," Hamish said, looking to me and Fitz.

"Let us travel on with ye until we're certain ye're safe. Then, I'll transport Hadley and myself back to yer house to send word to Annabel and Elspeth. We'll depart immediately after."

"Let's set things into motion," I said. "We really are burning daylight now."

Annabel made Hamish give her a number of promises regarding Esther's safety before hugging him fiercely. Elspeth bid Hamish a heartfelt farewell, and with that, we were on our way. The three of us walked beside the carriage, as I was determined to keep up appearances, and it was better for dispelling our nerves. We'd all feel better once they were on the road.

"How do ye suppose he found us out?" Hamish asked.

The disappointing answer surfaced.

"When Esther and I spoke to Katherine, we kept our voices low, but… it's possible Helen overheard us."

"Ye told her of Esther's plan!" Hamish's volume wasn't above a whisper, but his tone somehow gutted me more than if he had simply shouted. I held my tongue.

"It was a bad idea, and I said so myself. But the two of ye are stubborn as mules."

"Hamish, we dinnae ken that Helen overheard. This is speculation at best, and this isnae helpful," Fitz said, looking pointedly to us both.

Hamish grumbled under his breath.

Fitz was right. We didn't know for sure. After the arrests of Marjorie and Katherine, and with Esther's original capture date growing near, I suspected Father Evans had been monitoring our comings and goings for some time now.

"I wonder…" I said, halting. "Should I spy on Father Evans for a moment, just to find out if they're really returning to the village?"

"Yer spirit-travel, ye mean?" Fitz asked. He and Hamish stopped only a couple paces ahead of me. I nodded.

"A fine idea, I'd say," Hamish said. At least he was cordial, despite the edge in his voice.

I sat below a large evergreen and slipped away, navigating toward the edge of the woods nearest the path from town. Sure enough, the group was stopped near the road. Huge clouds rolled beyond them in the distance, painting the sky an ominous dark blue. I hoped Esther and Hamish were well on their way before the rain set in.

"These times are troubled, dear ones, but all will be well again soon," Father Evans said.

"Ye're certain we can trust Malcolm?" one of the villagers asked.

"I fought alongside Malcolm in the war. He swore a vendetta against Charles and his lineage. He will see this through."

The villager nodded, though it was plain to see in his eyes that he wasn't convinced.

I moved closer, hoping to learn more, when Father Evans looked directly at me. Though it was unnerving, it wasn't possible that he saw me.

Still, Father Evans held my gaze for several seconds longer, before finally giving the order.

"Let us move on. We shouldn't linger," he said, pointing in the direction of the storm clouds.

I returned to Fitz and Hamish, and we pressed on.

The forest was larger than I expected, and I realized much of it had been cut back in our time compared with the sprawling length of it in this era. Once we finally made it around, we paused, awaiting Esther's signal. A light glimmered about twenty yards down, and we rushed over.

Hamish took Esther in his arms and kissed her gently.

"We mustn't tarry, *mo ghaol*," he said.

"Aye."

Esther turned to me, and I passed the envelope to her from Annabel. She tore it open and held the ring in the light. The moonstone glimmered.

"There's no time like the present," I said.

Esther hesitated only briefly before sliding the ring onto her finger.

"How does it feel?" I asked.

"Strange." She moved her finger. "Though comforting… My parents' energy is strong. 'Tis as though they're with me."

After everything this ring had put us through, I was at least pleased to know it brought Esther some comfort as she fled her home.

I looked up as the mist set in and then turned to Fitz. "Children of the mist," I said, echoing the words Sir Walter Scott would one day attribute to the MacGregors.

He grinned and extended his hand to assist me into the carriage. "Hadley and I are to accompany ye for a wee bit. Have ye said yer goodbyes to Mum and Izzy?"

"Aye, and Prince Faolán as well. Let us be on our way."

We climbed into the carriage. Though it was a bit cramped for four witches, we'd appreciate the roof over our heads, especially when the downpour started. I could only imagine what it must have cost Hamish. The ride was bumpy on the muddy path, but Esther seemed to pay it no mind. She instead smiled as she studied Fitz.

"I cannae find the words to properly express how I've treasured our time together," she said. "It has done my heart good to ken ye, Fitz. Ye do us proud, and Hamish and I are pleased to see how the MacGregor line lives on in ye and yer sister."

"I'll ne'er forget ye, Esther," he said as they clasped hands. "I ken now that ye'll always be with me—with us both," he said, nodding to me.

Esther touched his face, her gesture timelessly maternal. She then turned to me.

"I hope ye dinnae find it presumptuous that I call ye my dear companion, for that is what ye've become to me."

"And you to me," I said.

She took me by the hands. "I thank ye, Hadley—for all of it. Ye brought back a courage in me that I thought was lost forever."

"Thank *you*," I said. "I've learned so much from you—and not just how to mend a shirt or warm milk by the fireside."

She chuckled before leaning forward. We hugged tightly.

The mist turned to rainfall, pattering against the small window in the carriage. My nerves wouldn't ease until we'd put several miles between us and Forfar, but I couldn't say that our final moments together weren't pleasant. Though the old path wasn't smooth, the jostling grew less severe as we neared the main road that would lead us toward Edinburgh. Once there, Esther and Hamish would change carriages and disappear.

The carriage slowed as we met the main road, but the horses neighed loudly, and the coachmen brought us to a complete stop.

"Stay here—please," Fitz said as he and Hamish exited the carriage.

Esther and I clasped hands and sat silently, my blood thumping uncomfortably in my ears. When Fitz threw open the door, we both jumped.

"Get to the trees!" Hamish exclaimed to Esther over Fitz's shoulder.

"Run, Hads," Fitz said, helping us from the carriage.

The minister and his angry mob had sneaked along the eastern forest, and they were jogging down the main road, their weapons drawn. I reached out for Esther, and we sprinted for the trees.

Hamish pulled out a dirk and turned to buy us time, quickly followed by Fitz, and we made it safely into the woods. Izzy, Ann, and Faolán awaited us just inside.

"You're still here," I panted. My stays were far too tight for this.

"We followed you along the tree line," Ann said. "We couldnae bear to part with you just yet."

The commotion near the carriage grew louder, and I strained my eyes to make out what was happening.

In his rush to protect Esther, Hamish had left himself vulnerable. The guards had overpowered him and were tying his hands behind his back. Fitz raised his hands in surrender, and a guard stood nearby with his musket pointed in his direction. My blood boiled at the sight.

A hand slipped onto my arm, and I turned, finding Faolán.

"They won't harm Fitz as long as he remains calm. Do not cause a scene that will compromise you all."

Ann's eyes were troubled, and Izzy took her by the hand. "Faolán is right, Mum. Fitz knows what he's doing."

Amid our conversation, we hadn't realized Esther was about to clear the tree line.

"Wait!" Izzy shouted as she ran to Esther. "Think about this. Ye cannae go!"

Esther opened her mouth to speak, but she was cut off by Faolán groaning as they gripped their head.

Izzy was quickly at their side. "What is it? What's the matter?"

The prince rubbed at their temples before leveling their gaze at Esther.

"Esther has decided." Faolán's voice was strained, and their glow dimmed as their eyes darkened. "And so has Fate."

Esther looked sadly at me. "I am sorry, Hadley."

The world tilted off its axis. "Fate is charting your course based on your decision. You still have time to change this. The ring is still yours to use."

Esther's eyes misted, but she turned and continued wordlessly through the trees.

"No!" I yelled, my blood humming hotly through my veins, but she didn't pay me any mind.

"Flee, Esther!" Hamish yelled. "Ye have time. Fitz!"

Fitz looked around, clearly calculating how he could even reach Esther.

"Nae," Esther said as she walked closer to the guards. "And ken that I exchanged my life for my husband's?"

The guards held still, seemingly understanding that Esther wasn't going to run.

"I couldnae live with myself." She turned to the guards and held her hands up. "Release him. 'Tis me ye want."

"We will hold him until he is no longer a danger, but we shall set him free as long as you follow instructions."

She nodded as they pulled her hands behind her back.

"Esther MacGregor," Father Evans said, "you are under arrest for doing the devil's bidding by reading the future to alter it for his purposes and for your own gain. You shall stand trial, and if convicted, you will be put to death in accordance with the Act Against Witchcraft of 1604."

I fell to my knees, my heart shattered, as they hauled Esther and Hamish from our sight.

CHAPTER THIRTY-FOUR

We were all denied access to visit Esther, so I took a page from her playbook. As soon as we arrived home, I dispatched Millie to deliver a note to Ivan, the wayward guard at the tolbooth, seeking admittance to see Esther.

Hamish was being held at the tolbooth overnight due to his behavior. Apparently, when they'd released him after taking Esther to her holding cell, he'd started fighting the guards. Annabel and John decided to stay at Esther and Hamish's with us so we'd all learn of any news as quickly as possible.

Though she didn't outright accuse us of being the problem, Annabel alluded several times to how things would've gone differently had she remained with Esther instead of allowing us to carry on without her.

I was glad for John's presence—he was calm, and he did a fair job of keeping Annabel from doing anything too out of line—but even so, Annabel's presence was anything but helpful. Ultimately, I didn't care. No amount of conversation was going to pull her from her delusions. If she blamed us and it gave her a place to channel some of her fear, then that was fine by me. I'd never anticipated Annabel's friendship as a result of this mission, and it was clear she was never going to bestow it.

Finally, as night drew near, Millie found me in my quarters and delivered a note from Ivan. I thanked her and closed the door, drawing near the fireside to read the contents.

10 p.m. at the side door. Dinnae knock.

Fitz insisted on accompanying me, but I put my foot down about him coming inside.

"Stay out here and keep hidden," I whispered as we slinked near the edge of the tolbooth.

"I dinnae like the thought of ye going in there without me."

"You'll know if something is wrong. Come for me then." My eyes pierced his. "I told you what I was doing instead of sneaking off, but I need you to support me, not fight me."

Fitz's energy was tight, but he nodded. "Fine. But at the first sign of trouble, I'll be there, and I'll do whatever necessary to ensure yer safety."

I knew that very well. I placed my hand along his jaw and pulled his forehead to mine.

"Thank you," I said. "This will be over soon."

The side door swung open, and Ivan's bulky frame filled the doorway.

"Quickly," he said. He eyed Fitz as I slipped inside. "Only one of ye tonight."

"He's just waiting outside for me."

"Tuck around that corner," he said, pointing toward an alleyway. "A new guard patrols this evening, and he is… easily excitable. Ye dinnae wish to be caught lurking here."

I crossed the threshold, and when he slammed the door shut, my chest tightened with the sound. I focused on breathing evenly, rather than the draft of the building or the stench that I had prayed I'd forget.

We wound our way to the stairwell, and to my surprise, we climbed the stairs rather than descending underground. I wanted to ask questions but couldn't risk being heard. The thought of being taken somewhere and locked up crossed my mind, but if Esther had trusted Ivan, I guessed I would too.

After one flight of stairs, we came to a wooden door, which led us down a narrow hallway. At the other end, we passed through another door, where we found two holding cells. Esther's auburn hair gleamed in the moonlight, and I ran to her.

She clasped at the bars, clearly surprised at my entrance. I slid my hands through the barricade, cupping her face and turning it side to side, checking for damage. My eyes darted over her. She was a bit dirty, but otherwise, she seemed in decent condition. Her sorrow and nerves filled the space, prickling at my witch's eye and coursing through my veins. She was chained to the wall, and the very sight of it made my blood boil.

"They havnae harmed me," she said. "I've cooperated."

My muscles tensed. "What does that mean exactly?"

"They interrogated me, but I've answered all of their questions… thus far. I think tomorrow they mean to ask me about members of the coven, and that… those are questions I willnae answer. I willnae implicate another woman," she said, not daring to meet my eyes.

I took her hands in mine. My chest swelled with emotion, making it more difficult to breathe.

"Don't let them torture you, Esther. Use the damn ring if you have to."

"Hadley," she whispered.

"No," I said, grasping her hands more firmly. "This isn't fair. I can't sit by and watch this happen. They're barbaric, and the council isn't doing their damn job. I agree with Annabel—take your fate into your own hands."

"Ye cannae influence the past," Esther said. "Do ye nae longer fear Fate?"

"The past be damned," I said. "Surely Fate doesn't condone the murder of innocent women."

Esther's breath was uneven, and her hands trembled in mine.

"Fight, Esther."

My blood sang with my words, my magic buzzing all around me. I wanted her to fight. I couldn't stomach the thought of her succumbing to this cruel fate.

"My bairns," she began.

"Will be just fine," I said. "We'll see to that."

Her eyes flitted to mine, and her torment was plain.

"Do it tomorrow. Take down the minister first, and Fitz and I will be here to aid you. Annabel, Hamish—hell, I'm sure half the coven will support your actions if you'll just make the first move."

"We dinnae ken that," she said.

"Esther, if you take a stand, others will follow. I promise you that. You have the power to save yourself, but more than that, you have the power to save your sisters. Don't let these murderers win."

Esther grew quiet, her eyes distant.

"Oh, I almost forgot," I said, dropping her hands so I could rummage through the pocket sewn into my skirts.

I pulled out the doll Esther had held just this morning. She took the toy in her hands, squeezing her eyes shut. I reached through the cold iron bars and pulled her hand back into mine.

"You have such courage, Esther. I know you wish it were different—that you didn't have to be brave—but you *are* one of the bravest souls I've ever known. And I've known many brave beings in my short season." I cleared my throat, pushing back against the ache of grief. "Your fear fills every fiber of my being, and yet, you've never strayed from the path you've believed would save your family. You inspire me endlessly, Esther, and I—" I stifled a sob and choked out, "I am better for knowing you."

Tears spilled down Esther's cheeks, and she crumbled. Her anguish filled the air. She pressed herself against the bars to pull me closer. I wanted to rip the heartless iron from between us, but instead, I gripped her tightly and stroked her hair until her shaking grew less intense. Finally, she rocked back on her knees and cradled the toy to her chest. There was something so childlike in the act. It brought out an instinct that was so protective, I was taken aback.

She wiped her eyes and took a few shuddered breaths. "Thank ye for bringing a bit of hame to me. I regret that my bairns ne'er had the pleasure of meeting ye," she said, sniffling. "I've written letters to them."

I gasped softly. "You knew the escape wouldn't work?"

"Nae… or rather, I wasnae certain, and as such, I wrote letters so I might say the many things to them that I wished. I told them of ye and Fitz. I told them how bravely ye stood by my side and risked yer lives for the sake of all that is good in our world. I want them to ken that even if such evil exists amongst us, that good exists also. That powerful warriors walk amongst us, and brilliant faeries, and strong, deep magic—legacies that will live on long after our time."

I wiped my own tears and nodded, unable to find my voice just then.

Esther pulled the ring from her finger and held it out to me. "I need ye to take this."

"I won't take this from you—not yet. You need it."

"Dinnae succumb to yer emotions, Hadley. Remain resolute in what is right."

"And in our version of the past, no one took this ring from you before you walked to the gallows." I stumbled on the last word, but I regained my composure. "It didn't happen before, and it won't happen now. We'll wait until it's time."

Perhaps that wasn't my only reasoning, but I hoped it was enough to quiet Esther's arguments. The door swung open behind me, and I turned, my heart falling. Ivan was trailing another guard—one I had seen hauling Hamish off into the tolbooth.

"Ye have nae business here, witch!" he said. "Be gone."

I rose to my feet.

"Do it again, and I'll report ye, Ivan."

"I was only speaking to my family."

"She isnae allowed visitors." The guard gripped my arm, and I winced, pain shooting from elbow to shoulder.

"Release her!" Esther shouted.

The guard paid her no mind.

"Hadley!" she shouted to me.

The guard shoved me through the door.

"Forfar, May 2, 1998. When the time comes, ye'll ken!"

The date rang a bell—the paper clipping we'd retrieved from Lucio's hideout, I realized. It had been only one day later.

I glanced over my shoulder one last time, and Esther's anguish was written on her face.

"I'll remember," I said to her mind.

The guard pulled me down the stairs, and I stumbled, missing steps and trying to stabilize myself. All the while, he held his death grip on my arm, and my wounded shoulder continued to sear with pain. It took every bit of self-restraint I had to not blast him with my fire magic.

"Ye ought to be chained next to her, witch," the guard spat. "Soon enough it will be so. Dinnae waste yer freedom while 'tis yers."

We'd finally reached the exit. He threw open the door, which banged against the stone wall. He shoved me so hard, I stumbled on the steps and fell to my knees in the thick mud.

"Dinnae return until ye're ready for yer own cell."

With that, he slammed the door closed.

CHAPTER THIRTY-FIVE

Fitz and I sat uncomfortably across the breakfast table from Annabel and John. Izzy and Ann had left early to speak with Faolán about our prospects of saving Esther while Fitz and I remained home to await news of Hamish. Nothing much had been uttered since we sat, and there was some relief in that simple fact. I thought perhaps conversation would make things even worse.

The scraping of plates and clinging of utensils reminded me of another tense meal we'd had at this very table. Emotion gripped my chest, and my hands shook. I tried to think of something, anything other than our meals with Esther and Hamish, until my eyes stopped burning. Fitz laid his hand on my back, and I nodded at him. I just needed a moment.

I caught Annabel looking at me from the corner of my eye, but I ignored it. The last thing I needed was for her to find a way to make me feel bad for being upset. She scraped the last bit of porridge from her bowl before setting it down with a thud.

"I attempted to see Esther yesternight, but the guards turned me away," Annabel said curtly. "I need to ensure she still has the ring."

I debated for a few seconds before responding. "She does."

"How can ye be certain?"

"I saw her last night," I said, laying my napkin on the table.

"Ye saw her? At what time?"

"Around ten."

Annabel looked affronted. "Why would they let ye in and no her own aunt?"

I held my tongue.

"What did ye speak of?"

"A number of things. I asked if she would use the ring. I asked her to fight."

"What did she say about the ring? She'll use it?"

I didn't hesitate. "No, I don't think she will."

A ruckus in the hallway pulled our focus. Fitz and John stood from their chairs, ready to defend us from whoever might walk through the door, and we fell silent. A voice we recognized floated through the doorway a heartbeat before its owner.

"Hamish," Fitz said warmly. "We're glad to see ye a free man again."

Hamish and Fitz clasped each other by the shoulder.

"'Tis good to be hame—now we may strategize."

"Does Millie know you're back?" I asked as he clasped John's hand and found his seat.

"Did ye hear the clatter in the hallway?" he asked. I nodded. "She dropped a whole load of things when she saw me."

I smiled. Good. Breakfast would already be on its way then.

"What news do ye have for us, Hamish?" Annabel asked.

"I was allowed to see Esther briefly when they released me. She's in good spirits, considering."

"Does she have a plan for escaping?" she pushed.

"Nae. She's refusing to use yer wee ring."

Annabel swore, and Hamish raised his eyebrows.

"I ken. 'Tis only… must she be stubborn right now?"

"That's hardly fair, coming from ye," Hamish said.

If looks could kill crossed my mind.

"I should have been there—in the forest. We could have prevented her from being taken."

"Aye?" Hamish asked. "What would ye have done that we didnae?"

Annabel huffed.

"I understand the sentiment, but we were outnumbered," I said.

"Magic would have helped."

"There was no point if Esther wasn't going to use the ring."

"I could've convinced her."

"It all happened so fast," I said. "And if you haven't convinced her by now, you aren't going to."

"How do ye ken?" Annabel bellowed. "Ye think ye ken everything because ye come from the future, but ye shouldnae be so sure of yerself. Do ye no even understand how much ye've changed?"

"Of course we recognize that, but Esther's will is still her own."

Annabel slid her chair back just as Millie entered with Hamish's breakfast.

"Ye cannae see it. None of ye can. I will find my way into that building. I willnae allow her to walk to the gallows."

"Dinnae storm about my house like ye are the only one here concerned for Esther's safety!" Hamish boomed. "This willnae do, Annabel. Esther tempered me around ye, but ye willnae rattle on so. Ye upset Esther with all this ring madness!"

Annabel's face fell.

"I have demanded that she fight for herself," he said. "Demanded that she allow me to fight for her, begged and pleaded with her—if it could be done, I have done it. But to keep pushing this ring on her when ye ken she doesnae want to use it…'tis wrong. Ye must see that."

"She is worried about ye! About the bairns, about everyone but herself. I cannae fault myself for caring more for her fate than she does. Someone must keep her best interests."

The words had barely left Annabel's mouth before Hamish's chair slid harshly against the floor. He rose from his seat and brought his fist down on the table. "Dinnae make the mistake of believing that any-one in this world cares for Esther more than I do. That anyone holds her interests more than I do. That anyone loves her more than I do!"

"Ye dinnae push her like ye ought. Ye—"

"Okay, enough!" I said, my voice rising above every other. "Enough of this. This is not a competition. Everyone in this room loves Esther. We all want what's best for her. We're all on the same team here, in case you need a reminder. I know emotions are high and everyone is upset, but bickering isn't going to save Esther."

All eyes were turned to me.

"That *is* what we're meant to be doing right now, aye?"

"Aye," Hamish said, returning to his seat.

"Take the damn ring off the table for a minute," I said. "What is our plan?"

"Aye," Fitz said. "She willnae use it. So, what's the alternative? We break into the tolbooth and remove her?"

"'Tis a possibility," Hamish said. "In the dead of night, there are usually only two guards on duty at a time, and the whole of the burgh is asleep."

"Aye, I think that's the way to do this," Fitz agreed.

I looked across the table. "Thoughts?"

Annabel was pacing behind John. "Aye, it might work."

"I agree," John said.

"So, we formulate our plan to break in quietly and remove Esther," I said, turning to Hamish. "Then we reunite you with your children and get you all across the portal expediently."

Hamish nodded.

"At this point, Fitz and I are tempting Fate anyway." I looked to Fitz. "It's up to you how much you want to tempt her, but…"

"Aye, I could transport ye to Gregor land so ye're ahead of the witch hunting committee. I dinnae wish to speak for Mum, but perhaps we can transport ye to yer bairns. Are there others who time-walk so we might move ye and yer family quickly?"

"Marjorie is the only time-walker in our coven," Annabel said.

Hamish's eyes narrowed. "I have an uncle who is a time-walker. He might be prevailed upon to assist us."

"That would be grand," Fitz said. "The faster we get ye to Opimae, the better."

"Okay, so once that is sorted out, then it's just the fate of the ring," I said.

"We'll keep with the original plan on that one, aye?" Annabel said firmly.

"Why is your tone so accusatory?" I asked.

"Pardon me?" Annabel asked.

"You act like I've done something wrong."

"Ye're always trying to get yer hands on that ring."

I looked to John, who very much looked like he wanted to be anywhere else. I didn't blame him for not wanting to interfere in witch business, but why wouldn't he try to reason with Annabel?

"I am trying to make sure the ring is disposed of properly," I said.

"Ye need to leave it be."

"I will not. You've committed a crime that puts the entire world in danger! This world and the next!" I shouted. "I am trying to prevent that from happening, but you seem content to destroy the entire world for a plan that won't even work!"

"Ye think if ye speak long enough, ye'll change my mind? That I'll become the hero? Is that it? Weel, lass, ye're sorely mistaken about that. I'll sacrifice yer world to save my niece, and I willnae think twice of it. I'll save mine, and ye save yers, ye understand?"

She stormed to the door.

"Where are you going?" John asked.

"Home!" she yelled. "I need a moment's peace!"

Hamish sighed. "Just as I expected."

For the first time since his release, I truly looked at him. His eyes were hollow, and his coloring was sickly. His energy was a mix of despair and anger.

He wasn't fully here without Esther.

I stood.

"And where are ye going?" Fitz asked.

"I'm following her. We need to be in agreement if we're going to save Esther."

The last thing I saw before walking out the door was Hamish dropping his head into his hands.

The streets were busy and stares were plentiful, but rage pushed me forward. I might have drawn attention to myself, but as I knocked on Annabel's front door, I couldn't count my action as a mistake. There had to be a way to find middle ground with her.

I knocked again, and still, no one came. I knew Annabel was home—I felt her energy. I knocked a third time.

Murdina finally opened the door. Why was the kitchen maid answering the door?

"I've come to speak with Annabel," I said.

"Aye? Weel, she's just arrived hame and is in a rare mood."

"I'm afraid I'm one of the reasons she's angry."

Murdina opened the door the rest of the way, allowing me inside. "Follow me. She's in the sitting room, but dinnae say I didnae warn ye."

Murdina pushed open the sitting room door. Annabel was crouched in a fighting position, her hands ready to expel energy. Near her, Alannah lay across the floor. Murdina started.

Lucio Belmonte stood across the room from Annabel.

"Hadley, what an unexpected surprise."

"What are you doing here?" I asked.

"I've come to collect my ring."

"You're not leaving with it," I said.

My power roared to life, and as it coursed through me, I felt more brazen than perhaps I should have.

Lucio sent a stream of blue-tinged power surging toward Annabel. She jumped out of the way in time, but she didn't have the training or the energy to last in a battle with Lucio.

"Your little energy blasts aren't going to get you what you want," I said, trying to keep his focus on me.

Sure enough, he fired at me, and I dodged his attempt, batting the energy back toward him. He moved just in time. I hurled fire at him, but he deflected. Still, it was a distraction.

Murdina was sneaking over to Alannah, and if she could only remove her from the room, she could also call for backup. Annabel attempted an energy ball, but it wasn't strong enough to affect Lucio. He sent the energy back and rushed toward her. Annabel fell from the impact. I intercepted Lucio, wrapping my arms around his torso and using my foot to trip him. We went tumbling to the ground, fighting for control.

I rolled my way on top with my palms still burning, and Lucio growled in protest at the heat. He flipped me over, slamming my shoulders onto the ground. An unbearable pain shot through my arm, but I breathed through it. We were struggling against each other when Murdina neared Alannah. Lucio fired in her direction, but I bumped his arm at the last second, and he missed his target. I used the distraction to free myself of his grip.

This seemed to anger him.

Lucio fought against me with renewed strength. He catapulted back toward me faster than I'd anticipated, and as he slammed against me, my head hit the floor with a violent thud, causing my vision to swim.

Annabel had pulled herself from the ground using a nearby armchair for support and blasted Lucio with a burst of energy. It made impact, and he leaned away from me, clutching his arm. He rolled to his feet and threw an energy orb at Annabel. I yelled in disbelief as it left his hands, knowing I would be too late to stop the deadly energy.

Murdina launched herself in front of Annabel, taking the brunt of the damage. She fell instantly and lay unmoving. Small fragments of the orb escaped during impact and bounced at Annabel. She screamed and fell to the floor, limp.

My anger burned as I turned back toward him, and I called deeply inside of me, pulling at the extra wisps of magic, before launching a packed fireball at Lucio. He hadn't yet recovered his footing from his attack, and the fireball hit him, suppressing his magic momentarily. I used the time to fire again before working up my own energy ball and hurling it at him. He was able to avoid it but fumbled over a stack of wood, tumbling toward the fireplace. He had almost corrected his fall when his head hit the corner of the mantle. My fireball made impact on the wall just behind him, and as it broke, flecks of fire and energy assaulted him. He bellowed angrily, batting at his face. Blood poured down the side of his head, flowing from the new wound, and when he met my eyes, his expression made it clear this round was over.

Fitz ran through the door, followed by Hamish and John. Of course, Fitz had felt my distress through our connection.

Lucio was outmanned and outmaneuvered, and he knew it. His eyes were seething with anger when they met mine.

"This isn't over," he said before disappearing.

We immediately ran to those lying on the ground. A small amount of Lucio's energy attacked Annabel's system, but Fitz and I pulled the power from her and disposed of it properly, just as we had learned to do in Opimae. Annabel needed rest to heal, but she'd be okay. Alannah too.

But Murdina did not share in the same fate.

I placed my fingers against her throat for a pulse, already knowing what I'd find.

"I'm sorry," I said to John. "I know she's been with you and Annabel a long time. I know she is more than your staff."

John nodded, tears in his eyes. "Annabel will take this poorly," he said, barely audible. "Help me get yer aunt and Alannah to bed."

He was looking to Fitz when he spoke. A strange warmth filled my heart at John's words. Annabel might not consider us family, but it was obvious John saw things differently.

"Aye," Fitz said. "Hadley and I will assist ye. Hamish—perhaps call on the coven to see how we best handle Murdina's death. She deserves a dignified burial, but we cannae risk the wrath of the witch hunters."

Hamish nodded. "I'll handle it."

By the time we returned home that night, I was sore, bruised, and exhausted. My shoulder was loud with pain, aching all the way down to my elbow, and rubbing it only made it worse.

Fitz stepped next to me. "Let me examine ye."

I winced as I raised my arm. "This shoulder *just* healed from Opimae."

"Come here," he said softly, leading me to the bed. He found his grip on my thighs and lifted me, and I wrapped my good arm around him. He set me down gently, and I tugged at his neck, pulling his lips to mine, memorizing the taste of him like I'd done countless times before. But this time was different. Esther and Hamish had been ripped apart. John had nearly lost Annabel. I didn't take it for granted that I could kiss my husband, that I could run my fingers through his hair and slide my hand underneath his shirt to feel the thump of his heart's song.

When I pulled back, his eyes were closed and his lips still parted, and when his eyelids fluttered open, my breath hitched. His hands slid to cradle my head, his thumbs rubbing gently across my cheeks.

"I am grateful to still hold ye in my arms, Hads," he said, his voice breathy.

I smiled. Of course he knew.

"Now, about that shoulder."

I nodded. He unbuttoned my overcoat and helped me shed my outer layers before pushing my chemise over my shoulder. A pensive look rested on his features.

"Do ye plan on leaving our quarters again tonight?" he asked. "It would be best to remove yer stays."

I ran my hand through his hair just above his ear. "If my husband will bring me room service, I'm happy to rest by the fireside tonight."

"Aye, he can do that."

He untied my laces and pulled them apart without ever breaking eye contact.

"You've become quite proficient at that."

"I've untied them more than ye have," he said, a sly smile rising to his lips.

He pulled the stays from my body and tossed it onto the bed before untying the top of my chemise and sliding it down my arms. He kept his face even, but he bit at his lip.

"Bad?" I asked.

"Och, ye've had worse, firecracker."

I laughed. I didn't doubt that assessment.

He moved his fingers deftly over the damaged area and maneuvered my arm this way and that.

"No sprain, I think. Certainly bruised—a nasty one, at that. We'll give it a bit of rest, aye?"

I nodded with a sigh.

"Yer energy is sad, *mo chridhe*."

"Everything just feels like a mess right now," I said.

"Aye, cause it is."

"There's Esther, but I also can't stop thinking about our team," I said, resting my head in my hand. "I'm terrified something bad has happened."

"I understand. I've done a fair bit of worrying myself, but we are here, and they are there. We cannae ken anything for certain until we're back in our time."

"I don't know which I'm more worried about. I mean, I feel like Esther isn't going to change her fate. That just… *sucks*. There's no other way to put it."

"Aye," Fitz said, his eyes distant.

"I'd feel guilty for leaving now with Esther locked away. We can't just up and leave as everything gets tough for her and Hamish. But I feel guilty staying when we know things are bad in Opimae."

"I willnae say we should choose Esther over our other wee family, but our team is filled with trained warriors. Nor am I saying we should choose our family in the present and abandon… my grandmother. There's nae winning on this one, Hadley. Even if we returned to the present, there's nae guarantee we'll make back into Opimae with their chamber against it."

I sighed. "Our team is the more prepared of the two, but that doesn't mean they don't need us."

"I think about it like this: we have opened a can of worms in the past. We have to at least try to sort things before we leave. If we leave right now, what are the odds we could return to Opimae? And what we are doing here right now affects the future."

"So what if we leave something undone that becomes the reason for the future's troubles?"

"Exactly. Everything we do in the past is an alteration—we know that. Do we further intervene? Do we act to save Esther? Do we keep plotting with Hamish and take an active role in her release? Esther was arrested a day early. Is that because we altered the past and changed the timeline, or is that because Fate wouldnae allow a change to her charted course?"

"Crap," I said.

"Ye encouraged her to consider Opimae, and to fight her way from the tolbooth, aye?"

I nodded sheepishly.

"'Tis all right, Hads," he said. "We've already played into these events. Does it even matter now? Is it too late for the rest to matter?"

I sighed as I unlaced my shoes.

"For my part," Fitz said, "I think we try."

I paused my task and looked at him. "That isn't what I expected you to say."

He raised his eyebrows. "Perhaps my reckless wife is having some sort of adverse effect on me."

I laughed lightly.

"We've meddled enough for ye to receive visions and for us to warrant an appearance from Fate. I dinnae wish to make matters worse, but maybe this truly is our chance to tidy up our mess. Do what we can."

"And if we make an even bigger mess?"

"Then at least we can go home saying we tried."

"Okay, MacGregor," I said, smiling. "These witch hunters think we're all bound for Hell anyway. So, let's take them with us."

"Aye, now that's the spirit."

CHAPTER THIRTY-SIX

The next day, Fitz and I consulted with Hamish over what our best approach might be to break Esther out. After the events at the Bruce homestead, I wondered if the council anticipated this from us—and what the council knew in general.

"How much do we think the council knows about Fitz and me?"

"I'd reckon they ken most everything about ye," Hamish said.

"I'm not so sure," I said. "Malcolm probably knows everything Lucio does, but if Malcolm told the council we were from the future…"

"Then surely, they would have sought an audience with us already," Fitz said.

"Exactly. It doesn't make sense."

Hamish rapped his fingertips on the table, his eyes distant. "Perhaps he has kept that information from the council, then. He does seem to be one for secrets."

"Perhaps Malcolm doesnae want us gone yet," Fitz said. "But if he's kenned this entire time, and he was complicit in Father Evans's attempt to arrest Hadley, what does he want from us?"

I hoped we'd all escape before we found out the answer to that question.

"We must go!" Millie shouted, bursting into the room. "The officials are moving Mistress MacGregor outside the tolbooth! They've called for Marjorie and Agnes to be executed."

The horror on Hamish's face would haunt me forever. We jumped from our seats and scrambled for the door.

"Wait!" Millie called, catching us as we reached for our overcoats. "Isla said several guards were being sent here. I dinnae ken if they mean to bring ye to the tolbooth or keep ye from it."

"So, we don't risk it," I said. "We exit through the back windows and run along the park."

"Perhaps ye should remain here," Fitz said to me.

"No chance," I shot back.

"'Tis more dangerous for ye than e'er." Fitz's eyes were cloaked with fear.

I rested my hand against his cheek. "We will persevere, no matter what happens today. I will not stay here and fold to these murderers."

After a beat, Fitz nodded. "Ye have to be careful this time, Hadley. Ye must be smart about this. Promise me."

"I promise," I said, my voice barely a whisper.

Millie dispatched a messenger to Annabel's house as we crawled through a window in the sitting room. My boot met the damp ground with a squish. Fitz had me by the hand to hold me steady, and I cursed my garments for the thousandth time since I'd landed in the past.

We made good time and were relatively unobserved, except for a few stares through the neighbors' windows. Though the weather had let up, dark clouds spread across the horizon. The cold air burned my lungs as we weaved around trees and gardens.

We finally reached the rain-soaked streets of Forfar. Villagers, carts, and horses littered our path, slowing us as we neared the heart of the burgh. Fitz's heartbeat pounded through my chest from both nerves and exertion, and I wondered how we'd have any breath left in us when we reached the tolbooth.

Hamish shoved through the chaos like the hounds of Hell were on our heels. I prayed we would make it before they had Esther up on the gallows for the whole burgh to see.

Two guards stepped around a cart, and for a heartbeat, we all froze.

"Stop right there!" a guard yelled.

"We dinnae have time for this," Fitz said.

"Find your way to the tolbooth!" I yelled to Hamish. "We'll meet you there."

Fitz and I cut down the nearest street, weaving around some villagers and bumping into others. Despite startled yelps and angered screams, we continued our furious run. Finally, we found a deserted alleyway and tried the first door. The old hinges groaned in protest as Fitz flung it open. I ran inside and he shut the door behind us, panting hard. When we turned around, we were surprised to recognize the startled woman.

"Naw," she said sternly. "Out with ye both."

"Fiona," I said.

"I willnae hear it."

"Esther is at the tolbooth," I continued.

"Aye, being tried for witchcraft, and we all ken she's guilty of it."

My face fell, and Fiona huffed.

"I dinnae much care whether the lot of ye are witches or no, but I willnae have ye arrested in my shop."

"We only need a moment," Fitz said.

"It hasnae even been a fortnight since I opened shop. Do ye ken how I have worked for this? I willnae waste my progress for the likes of ye."

Fiona opened the door, though slowly, and poked her head out. She turned back to us.

"There are nae guards about," she said. "So out with ye."

I nodded, and we stepped across the threshold.

"For what 'tis worth, I *am* sorry for these foolish men and their wicked ways," she said. "I dinnae agree with it, but I cannae change it either."

She shut the door, and we rushed toward the gallows.

We snaked up the alleyway and stepped into the market, where the sheer volume of people slowed our pace to an unbearable crawl. Every second seemed to mock us as we meandered through the thickening crowds.

"Did ye see it?" one villager asked to another. "Marjorie ne'er took her eyes from Father Evans."

My heart dropped. Marjorie was gone. I gathered my thoughts quickly and wished Marjorie well on her journey across the veil.

"Aye, and Agnes either. She cursed the minister and the magistrate with her last breath."

The villagers gave the sign of the cross, as if God would protect their rotten souls. I knew it was wrong, but I hated them with every fiber of my being. A rank crowd of lowlife idiots, the whole lot of them.

I was as angry as I was devastated by the events of the day, and even more than that, I was afraid. I was truly afraid we were too late to save Esther. We scanned the area around the cross, and though we were in clear sight of the tolbooth, Esther was nowhere to be seen.

"Let's check the side door."

Fitz nodded.

We rounded the corner and nearly slammed into the procession of guards guiding Esther from the building.

"Stop!" Hamish cried, finding us just in time. "Please stop!"

The guards paused, but despite recognizing Hamish, they ignored his pleas and carried on.

"Stop them!" I called. "Can a husband not even speak to his wife before she is hauled away to the gallows?"

The guard who seemed to be in charge was far enough away that I couldn't decide for sure if he had rolled his eyes at me, but he seemed resigned.

"Fine," he said, his English accent thick. He raised his hands for the guards to pause. "Make it quick. The crowds are not easily managed at this time."

The guards parted, and we were allowed to draw nearer.

Esther had mentioned the night before that she would be further questioned in the morning light, and my stomach grew queasy as I anticipated the shape we might find her in—how Hamish would remember her in this moment. Fresh bruises and scrapes littered her exposed skin. Though she wasn't as bad as I had feared, those final answers they wanted from her this morning must not have come easily. I swallowed hard as we stepped closer.

"Go," Esther said gravely, looking to me and Fitz. "Ye cannae save me, but ye may save yer wee family in Opimae."

"Esther," I said.

"Nae." Her determination was clear. "I have decided my course, and none will sway me from it. I will protect my own—and that includes the two of ye—so, be gone. Return to yer time."

Tears spilled down my face, and her eyes softened.

"I will be with ye always."

She turned to Hamish. He had tried to move closer to her, but the guards held him. She looked to the head guard, who nodded.

"She willnae flee. Allow her closer."

The guards pointed their weapons at Hamish as they released him. He hugged her fiercely, cupping her face, running his hands over her hair, sliding his hands along her arms, desperately taking stock of her.

"What have they done to ye?" His eyes burned with rage, but his words to her were tender.

"'Tis time, Hamish. I am sorry for it, but 'tis so."

"Nae," he said, barely above a whisper.

"We walked together for many years, *mo ghaol*. They cannae take that away from us."

"Esther, use the ring," Hamish begged, tears falling down his face.

Esther's lips pursed sympathetically.

"I will cut down every human here."

"Hamish."

"Naw, I will do it. I will tear this burgh apart," he growled.

"Ye cannae do so without hurting me. Our bairns will suffer for yer actions."

"No, none will still stand who might harm them."

Hamish's hands were balled into fists.

Esther closed her eyes, and calming energy sprinkled across Hamish. He batted at the air around him, attempting to outmaneuver her spell.

"I will be with ye always in dreams. In the whisper of the wind as it touches yer face."

Hamish's features were scrunched in grief, and he shook his head violently, as though it would change his wife's fate.

"In the soil as ye tend our garden," she continued. "In the eyes of our bairns as they meet yers."

"Esther," he whispered.

Esther leaned forward and kissed him. Hamish laid his hands on either side of her face, tears streaming down both their cheeks.

"Keep me well in memories, *mo ghaol*, and honor me in life. I shall be waiting for ye." Esther's voice broke. "But dinnae rush. Raise our bairns, live a life that is full, and when 'tis yer time, I shall welcome ye hame."

At this, the guards pulled her away, and she faced her captors bravely. Doubt flashed through one of their eyes—I was sure of it—and his energy stirred. He wasn't sure about his duty, I realized.

"This is the last of the prisoners today," one guard said to another. "Agnes Cameron, Marjorie Bruce, and Esther MacGregor."

"And Helen?" I asked.

"Helen is still useful," he said.

"Katherine?"

"Katherine is dead."

My energy quivered through me. "What? When was she was executed?"

"Found dead in her cell this morning," Father Evans said as he approached us. "She did not live to see justice served."

I tensed at the sight of him. My fingers sparked, and I had to remind myself why I couldn't incinerate the evil man on the spot.

"I'd put that away if I were you," the minister spat. "Malcolm has officially requested your arrest. I had not intended to do so today, but mark my words, if the villagers see your eyes and fingertips ablaze, this burgh will come apart."

"Father!" a loud voice called above the chaos. "Arrest this woman now!"

I didn't need to turn to know I'd find Malcolm's overzealous eyes.

"Looks like your luck has run out after all," the minister said, smirking.

"Ye willnae touch her," Fitz spat.

"We need to do something," I said, turning to Hamish while Fitz argued with the minister.

Hamish didn't respond, his eyes distant.

"Hamish!" I shouted. I shook him by the shoulders.

He looked at me, shock registering on his face. Esther's spell had left him confused.

Shit. This was the last thing we needed today.

I didn't wish to dishonor Esther's attempt at keeping Hamish safe, but we needed him. I closed my eyes briefly until I found the edge of Esther's energy. One little tug at her spell, and it was done.

Hamish's eyes focused.

"Ready?" Fitz asked.

Hamish pushed through the crowd with a force no one contested. He was every bit a bloodthirsty Viking in that moment, and he had never seemed more imposing. Fitz had his arm protectively around me, pushing with his other as we moved beside Hamish. I'd seen Fitz cut down his enemies on the battlefield, and yet, he had never looked more dangerous than he did at that very moment. The villagers recoiled from us, and their fear permeated the air. I would have been more pleased by that little fact had I not been consumed with anger, fear, and the grief that filled my chest.

We paused momentarily, taking stock of the scene.

"This is it," I said. "There's no reasoning our way out of this one. We're out of time."

"We fight, then."

Fitz laid his hand on Hamish's shoulder. "Aye, we fight."

Guards lined the steps of the gallows. The witch hunters weren't just ruthless—they wanted to make a spectacle of the whole thing as a warning to any of those that might have thoughts about saving a victim.

A few more steps, and large barrels came into view. My stomach recoiled at the thought of the contents. Fitz had told me, in the safety of our flat in Edinburgh, about the barrels of hot tar that were used for the bodies immediately following their strangulation or hanging. I bit back my fear and leaned forward, seeking a better view. Auburn hair whipped around in the wind.

Esther.

Her hands were bound to prevent her from escaping, and she stood with her eyes resolutely on the crowd.

"Stop!" Annabel yelled, finally approaching. Her gait was slower than normal, and John was at her side, holding her steady.

"Quiet, witch!" a nearby guard bellowed. "Or we'll toss ye up there after yer niece."

"I demand ye stop these proceedings at once!" Annabel yelled. As she grew closer, I noticed a sizable bruise on the right side of her face.

"Oh aye? I bet ye do." He chuckled, looking at the guard to his right.

"Let us pass," Hamish said. "We must speak with the magistrate immediately."

"Nae," the guard said.

"Ye will be punished for this." Fitz said.

"And will that punishment be coming from ye?" The guard laughed again. "Can ye believe this?"

Hamish's patience ran out, and he punched the guard square in the face. The man clutched his nose, which was gushing red. Two others rushed forward and grabbed at Hamish. John ran over to help, but two more guards jumped in, squashing the scuffle.

"Remain calm," Fitz whispered, surely worried about my temper.

"Let us pass or you'll regret it," I said, raising my voice above the chatter. The words tumbled out, and I hardly knew what I was saying.

"Quiet!" one of the guards shouted. "Or we'll feed ye to the barrels next."

My eyes squeezed shut as a rush of anger blew through me—Fitz's anger—and I realized he was about to ignore his own advice.

"Threaten my wife again, and I'll stain the soil with yer blood," Fitz growled through gritted teeth.

"Threaten me again, and I'll send yer wee bitch up to the platform where she belongs," the guard spat back.

Fitz launched himself at the guard, and they fell into utter chaos. Annabel hadn't recovered from the events with Lucio, but she fought as best she could, kicking the guard who was fighting against Fitz. Meanwhile, Hamish pulled against his captors, trying the strength of their bonds. I pushed to the side, using the distraction to get eyes on Esther. She was watching the whole scene unfold with wide eyes. She met my gaze.

"*We've come to free you*," I said.

"*Ye should go*," she replied. "*Ye cannae win this. Get Hamish away from this place. I ken what ye're thinking. Put that out of yer mind or else they'll throw ye in the tolbooth.*"

A guard pulled me back, preventing my reply, and tied my hands behind my back.

I realized the guard holding me was Ivan, and I exhaled at the sight of him. Perhaps all wasn't lost. Ivan wasn't exactly a standup guy, but he wasn't an exemplary government employee either.

"This is our last chance to free Esther."

Ivan scoffed.

"What?"

"Even if the magistrate will hear ye—and he willnae do that—mark my words, this crowd is too far gone for ye to turn the tides. It'll be all out rebellion if they move to save Esther's neck now."

"No," I whispered. "Ivan…"

"Dinnae say more."

His eyes pierced mine. I understood in an instant: plausible deniability.

I nodded and turned back toward the platform. Esther was being led forward as the magistrate spoke her case.

"… And we cannae allow such evil to take root in our burgh! Think of our children! 'Tis with such thoughts in mind that I arrive at my final decision…."

"Hang her!" a woman shouted near me.

A chorus of "ayes" and further insults followed. The villagers drowned out the magistrate, but when he was ready to give the verdict, a hush fell over the crowd.

"Guilty," his voice cried out.

Hamish's screams would always be with me. He pulled so hard at his ties that he broke one of the ropes.

I pulled against Ivan, who held me back firmly. I couldn't breathe with Hamish's crippling despair surrounding us. As hard as he tried, he couldn't break free of the guards. His eyes lightened just as Tanner's did when his electrokinesis activated, and my breath hitched.

"Ye cannae do this!" the guard said through gritted teeth. "Ye cannae reveal yer magic to the humans."

This was one of Malcolm's agents, then.

But it was too late. A human man standing close to the action clocked Hamish's eyes, and he stumbled backward. Terror flooded his face, and his fear rippled through the air. My blood hummed with pleasure at the feel of it.

One of the guards looked around before gripping Hamish tighter, his hands glowing with the effort. Hamish yelled angrily, though his scrunched features already told me he was in pain.

I couldn't stand there any longer and watch the horrific scene unfold. The guards were stronger than me without the aid of my power. To use my magic in this moment would be treason, but Hamish had already crossed that line. As a second guard's magic roared to life, I realized it might be time to commit my crimes against the Forfar Council. I might as well give this burgh a real reason to hate me.

But a thousand thoughts flashed through my mind: the threat of Fate's wrath, Esther's children, Hamish's grief, an altered future, my spouse's safety, the well-being of my team… every risk was made plain to me in a matter of seconds.

Then I met Esther's eyes.

As filled with emotion as they were, as clear as it was that Hamish's pain and grief were ripping through her, as firmly as her jaw was set… when I concentrated enough to isolate her energy, it wasn't simply grief or fear I found there.

Esther was up to something.

"Help Hamish… please," she said to my mind.

"I will, but if I do… we'll all have to fight. Are you prepared for that?"

"I have a plan," she said. *"I only need the minister to step forward to make his official statement with the magistrate before the crowd."*

Her energy overwhelmed me, filling me with a heartache I had never known. I stifled a sob.

"They're frightened of me," Esther said.

"As they should be," I said. *"Give them hell, Esther. Don't hold back."*

She smiled bitterly. It was during the most impossible moments that we discovered exactly how much fight coursed through our veins.

"Aye. I think I will."

"To sisterhood," I said softly.

The minister stepped forward, and I waited with bated breath.

"Prepare yourself," I said to Fitz. *"Esther is up to something, and I don't know what kind of chaos will follow."*

Fitz still struggled with the guard, but his eyes widened and met mine. The determination I found in them was clear—he was ready for a fight. He channeled his energy until the feeling of it was almost unbearable and then gripped the guard by the neck. The guard's eyes widened in shock before his eyes rolled back and he slumped to the ground.

The guards pushed Esther to her knees, and Annabel's cry rose above the crowd. She pushed toward the gallows' steps, her features resolute.

"Stop her!" the minister called, pointing to Annabel. Guards raced in her direction, but she eluded the first few attempts. John broke away from his skirmish and raced toward Annabel, but he was caught by a guard.

She had reached the steps of the gallows when a guard slipped his arms around her and pulled her back. She thrashed against his grasp, but he held firm. A glimmering light wavered from her fingertips, and I knew: they'd never allow her the chance to reveal her magic.

"What's the matter?" Fitz asked.

His face fell as he registered the scene.

The guard pulled a dagger from his hip. He met the minister's eyes, who nodded his approval, and then the guard deftly slit Annabel's throat.

Blood gushed freely down her neck, and her eyes widened before growing vacant. The guard dropped her body to the ground, and the scream that erupted from my body surprised me, matching the volume of the grief-filled shriek that escaped Esther. John struggled against his captor, his shouts incoherent. The chaos of the crowd increased with their realization of what had just happened.

A roar filled my head as my vision twitched. I would have dropped to my knees if not for Ivan holding me upright.

Annabel. This couldn't be happening.

My mind reeled. It seemed impossible that Esther's fiery aunt lay lifeless on the ground. This wasn't right—Annabel wasn't meant to die like this. I could hardly make sense of anything around me.

But even as the hysteria threatened to overtake me, I couldn't allow it to consume me. Esther wasn't safe. We wouldn't allow her to meet the same fate. I reclaimed my mind, steadying my nerves as much as possible, and reminded myself that remaining calm was the only way we'd make it out alive.

Esther looked to the sky and spoke words that were lost on the crowd, and dark clouds gathered above us, swirling ominously. Gasps echoed, and every head turned to the sky. The wind tore through the throngs of people as thunder boomed, bringing the villagers to silence and then to scattered cries and exclamations.

"Did you know this was one of her powers?" I asked Fitz.

He studied the chaos. "She's full of surprises."

I crafted a message to Izzy and entrusted it to the elements. I wasn't sure I cast it properly, but we were about to find out if my spell work was paying off.

"Let the name MacGregor be said henceforth with reverence in their voices and fear in their hearts," Fitz said. His energy was dancing ominously through the air, dripping with rage. The guards nearest to us exchanged a wary glance, but neither seemed ready to make the first move against Fitz.

"Remove yer hands from my wife, or I'll kill ye right here and now," Fitz said.

Ivan hesitated, and Fitz moved closer to us. His eyes were wild, and danger rolled off him in waves. Ivan quickly decided he wasn't willing to give his life for the cause, and he released me, stumbling backward.

My breath hitched. Fitz's energy didn't just feel dangerous. He was.

Esther raised her arms above her, and with a strike of lightning, the ropes broke, sending waves of disbelief through the crowd. Tears streamed down her face, but as she leveled her gaze at the crowd with her hair whipping in the wind, she was absolutely terrifying.

"Get her back in her bindings!" Father Evans yelled. "She is far too dangerous to be released!"

The minister didn't know how true his words were, but with the crowd's pandemonium, it was growing more likely that I could make my way near the gallows.

Fitz and I rushed at the guards subduing Hamish. One of them reached for me, and Fitz knocked the man unconscious. The other looked at the fallen guard before slipping quickly through the crowd.

"Let's go!" I screamed above the noise.

Fitz and Hamish were right behind me as I knocked bodies out of my way. At one point, a man turned to me, ready to fight, but one look at my blazing eyes silenced him. He backed away before falling into the hysteria and disappearing from my sight. We reached the minister and the magistrate at the same time as Esther. She used her magic to tilt the magistrate over the edge of the gallows as the minister turned and found himself uncomfortably close to a witch. He flinched when he registered the flames in my eyes.

"Merciful God," he said.

"You may call to God if you wish," I said. "But he does not answer the pleas of evil men like you."

"How can you say such a thing? It is blasphemy."

"Blasphemy? No, that doesn't quite add up."

The minister took a step back.

"I've been dealing with different versions of you my whole life—people who claim they are good, but actually hold their own self-interests above all, regardless of who else suffers." I clicked my tongue. "Just like the Pharisees who crucified Jesus, striking fear into the hearts of the vulnerable and persecuting the good and true. You are a disgrace to the one you claim to follow, and He will deny you at the gates of heaven."

There was little I detested more than a heretic and a false prophet, and he was both.

I couldn't stop myself—I blazed with fire. Flames licked the air all around me, and I shot fire near his feet. His eyes grew large, and he jumped away from me.

"Dinna fash," I said in broad Scots, moving us closer to Esther and the magistrate. "Just a foretaste of what's to come."

"I cannot save you now," he said, scooting farther away from me.

"Who said I needed saving?"

He gave no answer.

"Now, why don't you tell me what you and Malcolm have been up to?"

Father Evans held out a crucifix but remained silent.

"Seriously? I'm not an evil spirit, you idiot." I held out my palm tauntingly. "Answer me or it'll be you who burns today."

Father Evans looked around, but no one was close enough to hear us.

"I know you met Malcolm fighting in the war."

Surprise flashed through his eyes. "It was your spirit the other day."

"How did you…" I trailed off. "Malcolm."

"Malcolm has taught me much." Father Evans looked down at my hand, contemplating for only a moment. "After his father's death, he swore a vendetta against Charles the First. Chaos and uncertainty breed fear and anger among the people. If the monarchy can't provide stability for its subjects…."

I thought about what we'd heard from Annabel and Hamish—about Fitz's research on King James I, which he'd shared with me before all this madness began. Witch trials had happened across the world, and they had never been about eliminating the threat of witches. The realization raced through me. "You want another ruler on the throne. You want to overthrow Charles the Second."

Father Evans remained quiet, his eyes fixed on mine. My rage simmered.

"All of this!" I yelled pointing around us. "All this blood on your hands for a vendetta against one man—a man who is already dead!"

I pulled the air from his lungs, and he panted in his feeble attempt to breathe.

The minister's eyes filled with fear. "You'll pay for this."

"Tell me, which do you fear most: death or a lifetime of looking over your shoulder?"

"Get away from me, witch!" he choked out.

"If people don't stop calling me witch as an insult, I swear I will *burn* this entire village to the ground." My fingers tingled hotly, and they dripped with flames as though to illustrate my point. I tossed fire at the minister's feet. "Get used to hellfire, you bastard."

A crow swooped down and cawed. It stopped a foot in front of my face and held my gaze for a few seconds before flying off.

"Izzy," I whispered.

A murder of crows dotted the horizon in a black swarm, and I smiled at the reinforcements. I allowed hope back into my heart.

The crows swooped strategically, pecking at the minister, the magistrate, and the remaining guards who fought against Fitz and Hamish. The humans seemed a bit shell-shocked. They dashed about in chaos and either ran away or hid behind the market stalls. I would have celebrated had it not been for the council members walking toward us.

"Esther MacGregor! Hadley MacGregor!" they called. "Cease this now or face the consequences."

Father Evans made the most of the distraction and disappeared.

Esther and I both pulled back, though not before delivering a few more assaults on the remaining villagers as we moved toward the stairs. I jumped down from the gallows, intending to run wild through the remaining crowd, but two council members moved toward me.

"Hadley MacGregor! Ye'll stand trial and answer for yer actions!"

Fitz intercepted one of them, and though they met him in combat, they were rank with fear. Little wonder. Fitz was splattered with blood, and little of it was his own.

"Aye," Fitz said. "This is what comes of those who threaten my wife."

I turned on my heel, meeting the other in battle. We struggled against each other, and I channeled my magic hotly through my veins. Once I had overpowered her, she fell unconscious to the ground. My relief was short lived as I turned and found Malcolm advancing toward me.

"Ye *will* stand trial as a witch and answer for yer crimes."

"I'll do no such thing."

"Ye willnae escape as ye did once before," he said. "Ye'll pay this time."

I called my fire to the surface, but it fizzled out before I could launch a fireball at Malcolm. The air grew sour and prickled with the dangerous energy of dark magic… Malcolm's magic. Fitz still battled the other council member. Hamish was locked into a skirmish with a guard while Esther fended off another. Without combining power with another witch, I might not be able to overcome Malcolm.

I ran through every magical trick I'd learned, but my power seemed to strike against a wall. He'd stunted it, I realized. My heart raced, and for the first time, I truly believed Ann and Izzy's warning might come to fruition.

This can't be how I die.

Malcolm stood just in front of me. He gripped my shoulders, sending pain shooting through my bad one, and reached behind my back to bind my hands with rope. I struggled against him, but Malcolm was far too strong for me to overtake him without my power. He was so close his breath was warm against my ear, and the scent of his lye soap mixed with his sweat was pungent. The rope burned my wrists as he finally secured it into place.

"Let's go," he commanded, pulling me behind him.

"I'm not going anywhere with you, murderer!" I yelled as I squirmed, trying to break free.

"That's enough from ye," Malcolm said, his energy growing wild and dangerous.

I dug my heels into the mud and pushed my weight against him, attempting to slow us down. This only enraged him further, and he shoved me forward. I fell to the ground, and though I broke my fall with my forearms, the impact seared all the way up to my shoulders, and my injury from the day prior burned hotly. I winced at the pain and rolled over. My thick skirts were coated in mud, but my knees were unscathed.

Malcolm grabbed my bound wrists and pulled me up to stand just in front of him. The rope cut my skin, and with the ache of the cold, they burned intensely.

"Unhand her, *now*," Fitz's icy voice called out.

Malcolm turned us around and spat in Fitz's direction. "Ye dinnae command *me*," he ground out through gritted teeth.

"When it comes to Hadley, I certainly do," Fitz countered. "Let her go, and I'll spare yer life."

Malcolm chuckled at Fitz's response, and though I wasn't sure what he was doing, the disturbance in the air suggested he was launching some sort of attack on Fitz, whose anger swirled so thickly that the air grew thin. A rush of energy blew through me.

Fitz scoffed. "Ye think ye'll stifle my magic so easily?"

Fitz's connection to the elements was steadfast. I'd never known a moment when he hadn't been so thoroughly enmeshed with the elements that I truly knew where his energy stopped and the elements began. Malcolm's trick wouldn't work on him.

"Hadley will answer for her sins," Malcolm said. "Ye willnae prevent me from seeing her punished on those verra gallows."

"*Fall to yer knees*," Fitz said to my mind.

The very second I cleared Fitz's line of sight, he hurled an energy orb so violent that it sent Malcolm flying backward. He hadn't let go of his grip on me immediately, so I was pulled back with him. But before I could hit the ground, Fitz caught me in his arms.

"Good thing you're powerful, MacGregor," I managed.

After a kiss that set my veins aflutter, he untied the rope from my wrists. They were bright red and smarting, but it was a small wound in comparison to what Malcolm had intended.

"Get out of here," Fitz said.

"And leave you here with him?" I asked. "No way."

"Yer magic is stunted. There's nothing ye can do."

"I can't leave you."

"Hadley, my anger burns so deeply, I could match Fate herself."

I hesitated still.

"I am perfectly serious," he said. "*Go.*"

Malcolm rose to his feet, and Fitz kissed me once more before twirling me away from him. Fitz was buzzing with magic and alive with rage… it lingered in his kiss; it peppered my skin and pierced through our connection. It was dizzying.

As he turned to face Malcolm, I pulled myself together and ran for Esther.

At the bottom of the stairs, I was met by a few villagers who had not yet fled. Though their eyes held terror, they were poised to fight. I ran toward the opposite set of stairs, but one of the men overtook me, and I crashed to the ground. I braced myself for the fall, but there was little I could do. The cobblestones scraped my bare hands, and they stung from the impact and the cold. Pain was loud through my shoulder, the ache immediate, and though my face didn't hit the cobblestones with much force, it was enough. It would leave a nasty bruise.

Two sets of strong hands yanked me from the ground. I yelped in pain, but that only seemed to please the men further.

"Will ye cry out as we slip the noose about yer neck?" one man said rather enthusiastically. His breath was horrid, and I swallowed the bile that threatened to rise from my stomach.

"She doesnae seem so powerful," another said. "Perhaps we should take a better look at yer shop, aye?"

It was then I realized I had seen the first man before. He was the blacksmith who had eyed us on our first day in Forfar. The very first human villager I had seen.

"Perhaps we should leave this to the minister," the third man said. His energy zipped around, nervous.

"The minister has his hands full," the blacksmith said. "This is for us to decide."

Deep within me, my power tingled as it roared back to life. Only a moment longer, and I was certain I could again expel fire. Perhaps I could fight my way free, but with my magic so close, I decided to give it a few seconds more.

"Aye, we can handle this wee bitch ourselves."

I struggled angrily against the blacksmith, which seemed to humor him and his more aggressive companion. The latter reached his dirty finger toward my face, and I bit at the air.

The men laughed.

"Fiery, are we?"

"You have no idea," I said.

The man slapped me across my face, and my anger burned brightly as my head rolled to the side. It was the final push I needed to reignite my magic.

Fire burned from my palms, and the blacksmith released me as he jumped back.

"I hope you can run fast, boys."

To their credit, they could. Still, they were no match for my fire. I shot three quick arrows, which met their mark on each man. I didn't think I'd kill them, but it was enough to knock them down. Without examining the damage, I ran back toward Fitz.

He was still locked in battle with Malcolm. I pushed energy across our connection, and Fitz's power ignited so brilliantly against mine, it seemed to explode, ringing across the courtyard. I fired an arrow at Malcolm, which connected with his core at the same time Fitz released an energy orb.

Unable to deflect both, he fell.

"Hadley!" Fitz yelled, pointing behind me.

Three council members rushed toward me. I shot fire at their feet, and they halted.

"If ye dinnae cease this at once, we'll be forced to take action," the woman said—the same woman I'd left unconscious.

"I'd like to see you try," I spat. "You have the blood of innocent women on your hands, and you will answer for it. I do not fear Forfar and its fire, but you damn sure better be scared of me."

"Ye must cease this madness. Ye have exposed us in a most infamous manner to the humans."

"Why are you doing this?" I asked. "How can you allow our sisters to suffer for the sake of a new monarch on the throne?"

"What is this ye speak of?" one of the men said, as the council members looked to one another.

It hit me then. "You didn't know? Malcolm has aligned himself with these human leaders and with a dangerous witch. He's placing our entire world in danger—for the hope of a different monarch on the British throne."

Their gazes flickered to Malcolm, who still fought against Fitz.

"Nae. Wait. This cannae be true," the first man said.

"And why no?" the woman asked. "He lied to us about Lucio."

"Aye," the second man said. "We kenned something was amiss with the trouble at the Bruce homestead. I believe her."

Their eyes flickered to mine.

I turned toward Malcolm, pointing. "Then fix this."

He was rising to his feet, clutching his chest, as Fitz bent his knees, ready to pounce.

"I have tired of Malcolm's games," the woman said. "He gives orders incessantly, but we ken he only shares half-truths."

The second man nodded, and the first sighed, resigned. Finally, he nodded, and they rushed toward Malcolm and Fitz.

I scanned the area again and found Hamish entangled with another council member. Maybe I could reason with this man, too. I sprinted toward them, my breath coming short against the pressure of my stays. I yelled for him to stop. I begged for him to listen, but he would not. I paused for only a heartbeat, assessing if I could help take him down without killing him, but in those few seconds, Esther was already at work. I caught sight of her through the corner of my eye as she stood on the gallows, reaching toward the sky. Lightning struck near the councilman, sending him flying backward.

Esther had aided us, but the cost was dear. I hadn't seen Father Evans and the executioner climbing the steps of the gallows, and they were already grasping at her arms. Several guards rushed at Hamish, and he charged at them, yelling just as two men pushed Esther to her knees. The birds pecked at them, but the magistrate yelled for them to persist.

Fitz stooped to the ground. When his fingertips touched the cobblestones, the earth rumbled and cracked at his touch. A fracture raced around Malcolm, and dirt crumbled through the crack. Malcolm stumbled again, and Thomas seemingly appeared from nowhere, tackling him to the ground.

Esther raised her face to the sky, and a flurry of snow fell thickly toward the earth. As the snowflakes neared the ground, they burst into flames.

I pulled my arm back, ready to launch fire as soon as I had a clean hit, and Fitz raced up the steps. I took a shot at the executioner and connected to his left shoulder. I drew back again, but he was too quick. The executioner set his hands on either side of Esther's head and twisted.

She fell limp, and I fell to the ground, my hands blazing hot. I screamed so loudly the entire burgh must have heard me. Hamish's screams rivaled mine, but I could hardly make sense of it all.

I envisioned the burgh of Forfar in flames. I saw myself silhouetted against the rising flames as the tolbooth, shops, homes, everything was ablaze.

And I didn't care.

More than that—I wanted it so badly, I already tasted the smoke on my tongue.

I threw my first fireball toward the minister, then the magistrate. I was just about to release fire toward the first council member when Fitz wrapped his arms around me and pulled me against him.

"Nae, Hadley. Ye cannae do this."

I trembled violently, sobbing as he held me. "I will raze this burgh to the ground. They'll pay. They must."

"Look at me."

I couldn't focus.

"Hadley, look at me," he repeated, and this time, I did.

"'Tis over, *mo chidhe*," he said, tears falling down his face. "We did what we could, but 'tis over now."

Sobs burst from my aching chest, and tears blurred my vision. Fitz held me in the midst of the falling snow, and I stood motionless, shell-shocked.

"We need to get out of here," I said.

"Hadley, look!" Fitz said.

Lucio Belmonte had materialized in the crowd.

"Distract him," I said, before running toward Esther.

I blinked hard against the tears blurring my vision as I raced up the steps. My mind didn't want to focus, but I pushed through the haze, my will to survive slowly eating away at my shock.

As I reached Esther's body, I froze. Hamish had dropped to his knees and was draped over her, sobbing. I looked over my shoulder. Fitz and Thomas were attempting to stop Lucio, and Malcolm was nowhere to be seen. Still, I needed to work fast.

"Hamish," I said softly.

He didn't move.

I squatted next to him and placed my hand on his shoulder. He flinched and turned quickly. His tear-soaked face gutted me, but it was the anger burning in his eyes that took my breath away. He turned toward the skirmish happening below us. Malcolm had returned, and it was impossible to guess who might win.

"I'll make them pay," he said.

I nodded once, and he rose. He jumped from the platform, running straight into the fight.

I turned to Esther. The executioner had let her fall to the side, and she was turned toward me. My throat ached, my entire body feeling like it had been hit with a live wire. I fought back against the emotion that threatened to collapse me and dropped to my knees. Loose strands had fallen across her face, and I ran my fingers through her hair, twisting it back into place. I gently pulled her eyelids closed.

I would never look into her emerald eyes again, and the realization blew any last composure right out of me. A sob escaped me as I pulled Esther's hand into mine, and sure enough, my fingers met cold metal. The ring rested on her delicate finger. Emotion burst wildly through me, and my body shook violently. But even so, I pulled the ring from her finger and slid it onto my own.

I'd dreamed of pulling the ring from the Belmontes' grasp, but in this moment, I was horrified as I realized that it also meant removing it from Esther's.

Nausea rolled through me, and my mouth watered as my stomach lurched. I tilted my head back for a few seconds, manifesting a bit of relief, before pushing forward. My trembling hand pulled my own moonstone ring from my finger and slid it onto Esther's.

"I am so sorry I failed you, Esther," I said through my sobs. "I'll carry you with me always."

For a moment, I could almost imagine her sleeping, and I whispered a desperate prayer that she had found peace. I gently wiped the snowflakes from her pale face and kissed her forehead. Cold air rushed against me as I removed my overcoat and laid it across her broken body.

I stood, taking a few deep breaths as I steadied my legs. They quivered as the cold filled my bones and heartache almost consumed me, but I forced myself to move toward the stairs. I paused only once, looking over my shoulder one last time. My mind attacked me, calling me a traitor for leaving her behind, but I had to focus now on helping Fitz.

I wouldn't lose him today too.

I found him wrestling against Lucio Belmonte, but at the sight of me, Fitz disappeared, leaving Lucio to his own devices. Lucio smirked, clearly thinking he had scared Fitz away, before running onto the gallows and dropping near Esther—just as Fitz had intended. Fitz appeared at my side at the same moment Lucio took Esther's hand in his and removed the ring.

Another wave of nausea rolled through me at the sight of him touching Esther's skin. The council and the guards all rushed toward the platform. Lucio found Fitz and me in the crowd and gave us a wicked smile before disappearing.

I met Fitz's sad gaze.

I loved that ring. It held Fitz's energy and had comforted me through such difficult seasons. Knowing it was gone brought the tears back to my eyes.

"A noble sacrifice," Fitz said, barely above a whisper.

"Its final task."

Fitz kissed my forehead softly.

A cloaked figure materialized beside us. Even in the low light of the stormy scene, ethereal green eyes shone and auburn hair spilled from the hood.

"Get her out of here," Fitz said to Ann. "I'll find Hamish."

"Come, child," Ann said softly.

Her arms wrapped around me, and then, I was in Esther's sitting room.

CHAPTER THIRTY-SEVEN

I didn't think it was possible to cry anymore. My eyes were swollen, and my face was puffy. Izzy stroked my hair gently as I grieved, my head in her lap. Ann had wrapped a blanket around me, but I couldn't stop shaking. Finally, Fitz burst into the room, followed by a few men of the coven who supported Hamish as he walked listlessly through the door. I sat up, my eyes following Hamish's progress.

"*Leave him be,*" Fitz said.

I wanted to do just about anything but that, and yet I nodded—completely defeated.

Neilina followed, and behind her were several more coven members.

"Bring him to this room," I heard Fitz say. "Millie, I ken this is difficult, but we need ye, aye? Hamish needs ye more than e'er right now. Think of Esther—she's entrusted ye with her household."

Millie nodded, sniffling. "Aye," she said, hiccupping from crying.

"Ye ken just what to do," Fitz continued. "Help us get everything sorted."

Isla came bounding from the direction of the kitchen. "What might I do to be most useful?"

"Fetch what Esther had in the kitchen for relief," Fitz ordered. "Hamish will need a bit of aid to make it through the night."

I rose from my seat and made my way to Fitz. His relief was palpable as he pulled me into his embrace.

"My brave witch," he whispered. "Ye fought valiantly."

"It wasn't enough," I choked out.

"Fate hasnae allowed us to change Esther's course, but she didnae go quietly in the end… that is worth something."

"And I am glad for it," I said. "She was so brave."

"Aye," Fitz said, squeezing his eyes shut for a moment.

"Annabel wasn't meant to die," I said. "I keep thinking it's our fault. What if it was Fate punishing us?"

"Hadley," Fitz said.

"No, seriously. Anything that was different this time was our fault."

Fitz sighed. "Can we talk about this later?"

Millie and Isla dashed up and down the hallway, and several coven members stepped out of Hamish's room and gathered near the door, chatting a little too loudly.

I nodded. "I need to busy myself," I said. "Otherwise, I'll fall apart."

I left and bounded toward the kitchen. Millie and Isla moved quickly, lighting fires, pulling the milk from its storage space, mincing herbs. Even through their grief, they were ready to help the rest of us with whatever we needed. It was clear they did their jobs out of loyalty and love. Alongside them, Esther had built a beautiful household.

I pulled a bottle of whisky from the counter, and warm pain shot through my shoulder. I rubbed it until the edge subsided and took a healthy swig before grabbing a couple glasses and heading for Hamish's room. Millie and Isla joined me.

We were halfway down the hallway when I heard his screams. We picked up our paces, running the rest of the way before bursting through the door.

Millie ran to Hamish's bedside and attempted to calm him.

"Nothing is working," Neilina said. "He willnae accept assistance."

I nodded, setting the bottle and glasses down, and moved closer. "Hamish."

He continued screaming and thrashing about.

"Send for Izzy," I ordered Isla. "She can work a calming spell on him."

I neared the bedside. "Hamish!"

His eyes focused on me, but tears continued to pour from them as he thrashed.

"Hamish, I need you to take a deep breath for me."

He coughed, choking on his own grief. "Esther!" he screamed. "It cannae be. I cannae lose her."

"Shhh," I coaxed. "I know."

"Ye dinnae ken," he yelled. "Ye dinnae ken anything."

"I know you need to breathe, so we can get you calmed down."

Hamish turned to his side, gripping the woolen blanket furiously. "She isnae gone."

We talked in circles until Izzy was brought into the room.

"I'm sorry it took so long," she said.

"It's okay," I said, holding onto Hamish's wrists. "He just needs to be calmed down. I think he's hallucinating, and I'm worried he's a danger to himself right now."

Izzy nodded and bent near Hamish's head.

"Hamish," she said lowly.

"She is all I have."

"I ken," Izzy said. "She is a lovely woman."

"Esther?" Hamish said, his eyes wide with hope.

Hamish's grief and confusion were gut-wrenching. Seeing such a strong, powerful, and commanding witch fall apart was traumatic in itself.

Izzy looked to me, her eyes troubled.

I nodded.

Her brow furrowed as she turned back to Hamish. She moved her hand slowly toward his head but froze when her fingertips were mere inches away. She took one deep breath, and as her features relaxed, I knew her decision was made. She smoothed back Hamish's hair, which had come loose from his tie, and smiled.

"Aye, Hamish. I am here to help ye," she said, her voice even and tranquil.

Hamish was transfixed, holding perfectly still as he studied Izzy.

Izzy moved her hand to Hamish's forehead and whispered lowly. Slowly, his eyes grew more distant, and his energy calmed. After a couple of minutes, Izzy stepped away.

"I'll go to the kitchen and prepare broth," Isla said. "He willnae want it, but we'll need to force something down him later."

I set the bottle of whisky on the nightstand.

"He might need a nip of this later," I said to Millie.

Izzy rubbed my arm gently, her eyes troubled. "Come on, love. Let's get ye to the fireside and let Hamish rest."

I followed her lead, but at the doorway, I paused, taking one more look at a man who had lost the woman who had been his very will to live—a woman who had been an irreplaceable light in the darkness of this fear-mongering town.

Malcolm had fallen unconscious in the square due to his injuries. Overnight, he succumbed to those injuries.

Though we were all stricken by grief, the witch hunters had not ceased their efforts with Esther's death, and so we were forced to keep moving. Our sources informed us that Father Evans planned to arrest me this morning and try me as a witch. My fate had changed with my arrival—Ann and Izzy had the proof—but in fighting Malcolm, I had altered my course yet again. We needed to leave, but we hadn't expected Annabel's death, and that made the last bit of our mission much more difficult than we had anticipated. Fitz and I were convening with Ann, Izzy, and the Forfar coven in the cover of the faerie realm. Only Hamish remained in the burgh under the careful watch of his staff.

"The time has come for ye to destroy the wee ring and return to yer time," Neilina said. "The witch hunters will certainly come for ye today."

"They'll all wake up in Hell too," Fitz said.

"Ye cannae kill more humans," Neilina countered.

"Aye, I can and I will. If they threaten Hadley in any way, I'll put every last one of them in the ground."

"Fitz," Thomas began.

"Nae," Fitz said. "I ken ye mean to help, but I willnae allow Hadley to meet the same fate as Esther. Consequences be damned."

The fire in his eyes matched the ice in his tone. He seethed venom, and the room fell quiet.

"They're right. It's time for us to go," I said softly, resting my hand on Fitz's. I turned to the group. "We don't wish to stir up trouble, but we must finish our mission with this ring."

"I ken ye wish to destroy the wee ring here, but I dinnae ken what else to do," Neilina said.

Annabel had forged the ring with blood magic, and even I couldn't find the loophole in her spell. There had to be a way.

"There's nothing of this in Annabel's grimoire?" Thomas asked.

Izzy shrugged. "We don't know. We searched all night for the grimoire. It's still missing."

Faolán placed their hand supportively around her, and Izzy's worried expression eased ever so slightly.

"I've tried to break through her spell every way I can, but I've never seen one so tightly woven. She made this one impenetrable," I said.

"Ye believe it to be a lost cause?" Elspeth asked. Dark circles were visible under her eyes.

"No, I don't. But I'm out of tricks… at least, for right now."

"Ye dinnae recall anything useful in her grimoire from before? From yer studies in yer time?" Elspeth asked.

"Nae. Hadley and I combed through it quite thoroughly. There was nothing else."

"I think Neilina is right," Faolán said. "Return to your time and seek council from others there. Perhaps fresh eyes will help."

"The ring was meant to be destroyed here," Fitz said.

"Perhaps it was meant to be destroyed here, but it wasn't," Faolán said. "In removing the ring to your time, you aren't doing anything that has not been done before."

I turned to Fitz. "Faolán has a point."

"Perhaps our council's records will hold something helpful," Fitz said.

"The grimoire might hold changes in yer time," Neilina said.

"Annabel's journal held entries after Esther's death, as did Hamish's," Fitz said. "What will be lost once we return to our time?"

My heart sank at the thought, but then a spark hit. "We did make really thorough notes and copies of so many entries. I wonder if they'll still exist when we return home."

"Now, that is a very intriguing thought," Faolán said.

"There's but one way to find out," Ann said. "I think it wise to return and seek our instruction from the grimoire and our councils."

Finally, I agreed. "The past holds nothing more when it comes to this ring, but the longer we stay here, the more we change."

Fitz nodded, considering my words. "My only concern is this: if we had destroyed the ring here, then we'd return to a present where the ring doesnae exist. In returning to our time with the ring, no only does it still exist, but we dinnae ken how it might affect… weel, e'erything."

"Because the ring will already be in our present, with Lorenzo in Opimae," I realized.

Fitz nodded, his lips forming a hard line.

"Would it simply… disappear in yer time?" Neilina asked.

We all looked to Faolán.

"Ye have the most experience with Fate," Fitz said. "Any insight?"

Faolán's face was pensive. "I've never seen anything quite like this, so I can't be certain. I do believe the ring would be displaced in your time."

"If ye cannae access the ring, do we think the Belmontes would have better luck?" Ann asked.

"Aye, do we fear the ring more than we should?" Izzy asked.

"Well, he's gaining a boost from the ring at the very least—or at least, we think so," I said.

"How so?"

I lifted my finger, considering the small object. "The ring enhances my magic even now. I can't tap into the full power of it, nor can I destroy it, but… it does increase my power. I feel its magic running through me."

"Enough that it would have given ye an edge over someone like Malcolm?" Izzy asked.

"Without actually tapping into it fully? Maybe not much, but it would have made a difference, for sure."

"Powerful wee thing," Thomas said, his gaze resting on the ring.

Elspeth sighed. "Why did Annabel have to use blood magic?"

"To be fair, if ye're gonnae create something like this, it would be irresponsible *not* to use blood magic."

In the end, the unanimous decision was for us to return to our time.

As we took our leave of the faeries, my energy grew tight. Ann and Izzy were to return with us, and Izzy's visits with Faolán were to cease for some indeterminable amount of time.

"You are most welcome any time in Cadhla," the prince said. "All of you."

"Hopefully, we'll be in Opimae very soon," I said.

"When this is all over… please make your way to Kevardhu. Once there, Cadhla is not far. You will always find refuge in our halls."

Fitz and I bowed, taking our leave.

"Now, what did I say about formalities?" they asked mischievously.

"Sorry, Your Grace," I said through a smirk. "Old habits die hard."

They laughed lightly.

Faolán took leave of Ann, and when she moved to stand by us, Faolán was left staring at Izzy. They smiled timidly at each other before Izzy stepped forward.

We turned to grant them privacy, but when Izzy joined us, tears soaked her face. I wrapped my arms around her, and we each said our goodbyes. Ann disappeared with Izzy, and Fitz and I made our way back to the MacGregor home.

CHAPTER THIRTY-EIGHT

When we arrived home, Millie had tea service waiting. Thomas and Elspeth returned with us to check on Hamish, and we invited them to stay—for the last time. We settled quietly by the fire and poured the tea. It felt odd to gather in the sitting room without Esther, and I thought it might be a while before I felt any semblance of normalcy.

Her favorite teacup still sat on the far table. Millie was thoroughly tidy, and my throat ached at the sight of something she clearly didn't have the heart to remove.

It was as though she knew Esther was on my mind, for Millie handed me a small cloth bag. It was bound by a navy ribbon, and my name was scribbled across a paper tag.

I swallowed.

"What's the matter?" Fitz asked, his hand rubbing gently across my back.

"It's in Esther's handwriting," I whispered. I looked to Millie, who nodded, tears welling in her eyes.

"She asked that I deliver it to ye in—" She broke off.

The room froze.

"I'll open it later," I said. "I don't think—" The words stuck in my throat.

"Aye," Fitz said. "'Tis quite all right if ye need a bit of time."

I caught Elspeth's supportive nod.

Fitz opened his mouth to speak, but he froze, his attention shifting near the fire. Wisps of smoke traveled through the air, and we all rose to inspect it further. I tucked the bag in my skirt pocket and moved closer. It wasn't smoke from the fireplace. It was some sort of magical fog coming from... thin air.

"Lucio," I said.

He had found us out. He was here for the ring.

My realization came only a mere second before Lucio stepped through the fog.

"What in God's name?" Thomas said. He grabbed Elspeth's hand and ran toward us. I took Fitz's hand and Fitz grasped Thomas's. Millie burst through the doorway, and just before the darkness of the in-between overtook me, I yelled.

"Run, Millie! Get out of here now!"

The cold air took my breath as we stepped back onto solid ground. Brief as our journey had been, the in-between was warm, and the shift in temperature was jarring. The moonlight was soft, and I looked around, realizing we were in the forest. We needed to move quickly, but there were far too many fallen leaves for us to remain stealthy.

"How did you...?" I asked.

"Short distance," Fitz answered. "It wasnae easy."

I nodded. "Where are we?"

"Where we entered this time," Fitz said. "Near the loch."

"Look!" Elspeth said.

Lights danced nearby.

"The faeries," Fitz said. "They'll help distract Lucio."

"Make haste before he finds ye. Take care of yerselves," Elspeth said, hugging me quickly. "We will think of ye often, MacGregors. May God bless ye and keep ye."

"Thank ye for all ye have done here," Thomas said. "Ye will be sorely missed."

Thomas placed his arms around Elspeth as tears filled her eyes. Her tight smile was the last thing I saw before the world went dark.

The in-between enveloped us once more, but where the journey had been quick and smooth before, it was now long and rocky. We jostled around the empty space, and Fitz's breathing grew labored. I thought of home and channeled extra boosts of energy his way, but it seemed like it wasn't helping at all.

"What's wrong?" I asked.

"I dinnae ken. 'Tis just… no going well."

"Do you need to rest?"

"I dinnae feel tired. 'Tis almost as if someone is calling to us, beckoning us elsewhere."

"Someone like Lucio?" I asked.

"I cannae tell if they mean well or no. But I—" He paused. "I think we must exit."

When we stepped onto solid ground, the moon was a waxing gibbous, and it was clear we'd walked through time—and not only because of the change in location.

Footsteps sounded near us, and Fitz and I positioned ourselves for a fight. Two figures emerged from the forest, and as the moonlight shone on their faces, we stood down.

"Friends, how lovely it is to see you again," Faolán said.

Fitz and I exchanged a glance, our eyes wide.

"For you, it has been two hundred years," Queen Tarron said to Faolán. "For them, it has been two hours."

They chuckled.

"We've just left 1662 with Lucio chasing us," I said. "Fate still has you stationed in Forfar?"

"Not exactly," they said. "But tonight, we have returned for you. We didn't hold Lucio off for long, but I thought if we called to you in the in-between that we could help you pepper a trail that is difficult to follow—and perhaps grant you a few moments of reprieve."

Fitz embraced Faolán warmly. "Thank ye for this."

"No need for thank yous," they said. "It is possible that Lucio will turn up here, so we should act quickly."

"Where should we go?" I asked. My mind was spinning—where were we safe?

"You could travel through Cadhla," Faolán said.

"No, Faolán. We can't risk our folk," Queen Tarron said.

Faolán meant to argue, but I intercepted. "We wouldn't risk your folk. Perhaps another year."

"Wherever you go, he will find you," Queen Tarron said. "His power is strong, and tracking appears to be one of his greatest strengths."

"So wherever we go, it needs to be where we can really take a stand against him—perhaps pass off the ring immediately and know we have backup."

"Our time. Council headquarters," Fitz said.

A disturbance in the nearby branches caught our attention.

"Go!" Faolán shouted.

They and Queen Tarron drew their swords, and their magic roared to full force in an instant. Fitz reached for me just as the culprit stepped forward. It was Lochlan, the blond-headed faerie who'd been involved with the prince. Fitz and I clocked it at the same time as Faolán and Queen Tarron, and we all paused.

I let out a sigh of relief.

"We are glad it is you," Faolán said, laughing lightly.

Lochlan nodded to Fitz and me. "It has been many years."

"And for us, only a few days." I smiled. "It is good to see you just the same."

"I fear you will feel quite differently in a moment," he replied.

My witch's eye prickled at his words.

A child's scream pierced the cold night air.

Fitz instinctively placed his arm in front of me, and I readied my fire.

Aladia stepped forward, her dagger poised just under the child's jaw. I looked at Fitz in horror, which only amplified as the realization kicked in. This girl looked just like Catriona, the young shapeshifter girl we'd met during our second visit to the faerie realm.

Maybe faeries did live incredibly long lives, but two hundred years into the future... it must have at least been Catriona's daughter. She released another blood curdling scream, and I took a step forward.

"Hadley, no," Fitz whispered.

"*We have to do something*," I said to his mind.

"*I ken, but Aladia has a dagger to her jaw. Stop and think.*"

My eyes darted around the forest, assessing the scene.

"What are you doing?" Queen Tarron asked. "Release the child at once."

"Sorry, my queen," Aladia said. "I'm afraid I can't."

"What do you want?" Faolán asked.

Lochlan smiled. "I want what I was promised."

"And what were you promised?"

"Power," a voice said behind me.

Lucio.

I attempted to turn around, but it was too late. Arms pulled me backward, and I found a dagger's tip just below my own jaw. Fitz's eyes flooded with terror, and his energy roared with anger. I could scarcely breathe between the arm squeezing my torso and the rush of energy channeling through my connection with Fitz. Fear gripped me, but I pushed back, attempting to breathe slowly and evenly.

"Let her go, ye bastard," Fitz said to my captor.

"Of course. All Hadley needs to do is allow us to remove the ring, and we'll be on our way."

My mind reeled. When had he infiltrated the ranks of Cadhla?

"How did you know we'd be here?"

"Witches aren't the only beings with foresight."

The faerie traitors looked pleased.

"Why would you do this?" Queen Tarron asked her subjects.

"We have tired of serving Fate," Lochlan said. "You might be pleased to follow her all your days, but we won't do so any longer."

"We met quite by chance in another time," Lucio said. "I couldn't be more pleased with how the stars have aligned."

A cloaked figure stepped to my right, and they reached for my hand. I waited until they'd gripped my hand in theirs before roaring to life with fire, expelling it through my palm. The faceless figure screamed, and almost simultaneously, a great weight slammed into the side of my head. Stars danced across my vision. Fitz took a step forward but paused at the sound of another scream. Realization flooded his bloodstream, and his nerves trickled through me.

Either I'd die or the child would.

"Fitz, no!" I yelled, though it was more a groan than anything else. "Keep her alive."

"*Hadley,*" he said to my mind. "*Are ye all right?*"

"*Yeah, just a nasty hit to the head. You can't make a move—they'll kill that child.*"

"*No if I kill them first. I willnae lose ye.*"

I noticed Faolán had inched closer to the young girl. The other faeries were talking with Lucio and Queen Tarron, running on about their "oppression" and justifying their betrayal.

"*Faolán,*" I said to Fitz.

"*Aye, I see them.*"

Someone took my hand again, but this time, between my groggy mind and their quick motion, the ring was gone.

"*No!*" I screamed, my entire body blazing with fire.

At my distraction, Faolán grasped Aladia's wrist and pulled the dagger away from her young prisoner. I shot fire like a spray of bullets, causing chaos as my captors attempted to distance themselves. Fitz moved as close as possible without running straight into my assault.

I ran toward Lucio, Fitz hard on my heels, but he disappeared before we reached him. I extinguished my flames, and Fitz had his arms around me in seconds.

"Go," I said.

"Ye're no well enough."

"Yes, I am. Go!"

Fitz didn't hesitate the second time, and the world fell away as Faolán's last words rang in my ears.

"May Fate guide you."

The in-between's warmth was stifling after what we'd just encountered. I was sweating profusely under my oppressive layers, and my throat was thick and dry.

"We're almost there," Fitz said intuitively.

"How strong is his path?" I asked.

"Incredibly. We're no far behind him…" Fitz's words slowed. "Hold on tightly. The exit looks strange, and I dinnae ken what we might come across."

I strengthened my hold on Fitz and prepared for the worst. Light glimmered, and I breathed easier. Almost there.

But as we neared our exit, the atmosphere jostled us around. I gripped Fitz even tighter as we shot through the exit. Even as skilled as he was, the impact was severe, and we fell to our hands and knees.

"Thank god it's grass," I said.

"How is yer head?" he asked.

I might as well have been hit with a baseball bat. I touched the side of my head and found a sizable knot. When I pulled my fingers back, they were coated in blood.

"Shite," he said. "Let me see."

"I'm okay."

"I *will* assess the damage, so the quicker ye allow that to happen, the quicker we'll find Lucio."

His eyes narrowed. I sighed, knowing he was perfectly serious, and turned my head. He inspected it quickly. "I dinnae think it'll need stitches, but *'tis* a nasty gash."

"So, where are we?" I asked, changing the subject as I looked around.

"I think we're near Forfar, but we've changed locations slightly. Look over there."

The Bruce homestead.

"We meet again," I mumbled.

"Aye, we cannae escape it, it seems."

"I feel Lucio's energy," I said.

"His trail willnae keep long."

"What year is this?" I asked.

"Nineteen sixty… one? I think. Let's take a wee look about," he said. "His energy lingers in this direction, which is toward town."

Fitz grabbed my hand, and we ran in pursuit of Lucio's energetic trail. My breath came short—and quickly—with the restrictive garments. By the time we arrived at the edge of town, I was panting hard.

Though many of the stone buildings of Old Forfar had clearly stood the test of time, electric lights illuminated the burgh far differently than I'd grown accustomed to over the past few weeks, and cars were parked along the streets. The dirt paths were no more, and our shoes clicked along the cobblestones.

"It's strange to see the town like this," I said panting.

"Aye, it doesnae seem right."

Once we reached Castle Street, a car barreled toward High Street. Fitz tugged me into a nearby alleyway where we tucked out of sight until the vehicle had passed. My heart raced, warm adrenaline pumping through my system. Not only was this the wrong time to draw notice, my eyes ached at the sight of the bright headlights.

As we approached the city's center, the pounding in my head grew worse, exacerbated by the exercise. I needed to catch my breath.

We stopped in the shadow of a large, two-story building just where the tolbooth should have been.

Though I was relieved to know that innocent women didn't sit on the other side of these stone walls, awaiting their deaths, my mind was reeling, struggling to make sense of the changes.

A figure moved across the street, and even in the dark, I knew instantly that it was Lucio. A glowing light next to him caught my attention, and I froze. What was he doing? As we neared, the illumination grew clearer, revealing an energy orb, though it held a blue hue, same as the power he'd expelled.

"Shit," I said.

"What is it, Hads?"

"Lucio is a water witch—Queen Marina told me that."

"Meaning his power is waning the longer he's away from Opimae," Fitz said. "Why is that a bad thing?"

"It's not a bad thing, but think about it. He relies on energy boosts from other witches while he remains on Earth and has to return to Opimae to truly recharge. So, he has to really make the most of every trip he takes here."

Fitz's eyes grew wide with realization. "He means to make as much chaos as possible with every trip. That's why he's stopped here. He isnae done planting his 'revolution' seeds."

We both took off running, hoping to stop whatever he was planning. We had almost reached him when a menacing smile spread across his lips, and he disappeared, leaving the energy orb behind.

"He's gonnae get away," Fitz said.

I hesitated, torn. But then Esther's words echoed across my mind. *Forfar, May 2, 1998. When the time comes, ye'll ken!*

"I think I know where he's headed. We can catch up with him, but we can't just leave this here."

We assessed the energy orb and quickly realized it was locked with a powerful blood magic spell.

"As soon as a being attempts to dismantle this, it'll explode," Fitz said.

"How far into the sky could you send it if you stabilized with your power?" I asked.

"How far will yer fire arrow go?"

"Far enough," I said confidently.

"It'll wake the burgh, but so would an explosion on the ground."

"And this will save lives."

Fitz's energy crackled wildly, and I formed my fire into a bow. Fitz used his energy to stabilize the orb as he rose high into the air, then tossed the orb into the sky. As soon as it was clear, I pulled back my bow and launched an arrow into the darkness. The orange flames blazed brightly against the night, and as it burst through the edge of the floating blue orb, a deafening explosion rang out.

Then I tucked myself against Fitz, and the world disappeared.

We were sorely out of place. Of that, I was certain. But we did have one thing going for us: it was the middle of the night, and little stirred in the streets of Forfar. We studied the building that had replaced the tolbooth.

Something was amiss.

"Do ye feel him?" Fitz said.

My eyes grew wide as the realization flooded through me. "A little, but his energy is mixed with another."

"What is the matter, Hadley? Who is it?"

"It's… Lorenzo."

Fitz glanced around wildly.

"That way," I said, pointing to the stone building.

We jogged over and checked the perimeter, hoping to follow Lucio's footsteps. A door was ajar at the back of the building, and I wiped the sweat from my brow, bolstering my courage as Fitz opened the door wider. The lock had been severed, and though the hinges whined, it was soft enough that we might just escape the Belmontes' notice. The energy grew stronger toward the stairwell, and we crept silently toward the second floor. At the landing, we paused to assess where the energy led us next.

"They're certainly on this floor," Fitz said.

We walked softly down the hallway until the trail ended at a large wooden door. A plastic sign hung at eye level.

"Private—No Entry."

"Subtle," Fitz said.

Despite the circumstances, I had to laugh.

"Ready, firecracker?" he asked.

I grinned. "Let's go kick some Belmonte ass."

Fitz flung the door open, and sure enough, Lucio and Lorenzo Belmonte stared back at us. We stepped across the threshold and faced our opponents.

"Very good," Lucio said, clapping.

"Don't patronize us," I said.

"Feisty as ever, I see," Lucio said. "That's all right. I like spirit."

Lorenzo stared blankly, as though he didn't recognize us.

"Would you care to greet our guests, son?"

"Your guests? This isn't your office, may I remind you," I said.

"And may I remind you that you know nothing about me."

I crossed my arms.

"Hadley," Lorenzo said softly. "And Fitz."

"*He doesn't know us yet,*" I said.

"*This is the Lorenzo of the past,*" Fitz said.

This is what Lucio had meant when he said he fought us before we were born, and when we were children. Somewhere in this time, we were mere children.

"You knew we'd fight you across time."

"I suspected you would follow me, yes. My seers can't predict everything, but they've provided me with great intelligence."

I shook my head. This was absurd.

"And you killed that man back in Forfar?" I asked. If he was answering questions, I might as well ask.

"You'll have to be a bit more specific," he said.

"The one who saw my eyes ablaze."

"Of course."

"*Of course?* Seriously?" I asked.

"This is the problem with the both of you. You expend far too much energy on the wrong issues. You should have eliminated him as soon as you recognized him as a threat. He might have compromised you—and believe me, he did try."

"Well, you'll have to excuse us. We are compassionate, after all."

"Messy is what you are," Lucio shot back. "You should do better at cleaning up after yourselves."

I scoffed.

"Don't get self-righteous with me, Hadley. I know you murdered The Witchkiller." He laughed. "And I thank you for that. You saved me the trouble."

I couldn't hide my exasperation. Lucio only smiled.

Lorenzo seemed to be taking everything in. He hadn't spoken again, and at times, his father's words seemed to trouble him. Was this how Lorenzo had been before his father pushed his plans on him?

"As enlightening as this has all been, I'll be taking my family's ring now," Fitz said.

"I don't think so," Lucio said. He smiled slyly.

He was enjoying this.

I called my fire magic to the surface, and Fitz's energy echoed through my body. He was fully connected to the elements and prepared for what followed.

"You mean to make a stand?" he asked. "That's fine. Let's see what you're capable of."

I launched fire at Lucio, and he deflected as Fitz lunged at Lorenzo, fully charged. They fell into a skirmish as Lucio readied himself for my next attack. I wasn't sure which of them would have the ring, but I knew we'd have to take them both down if we wanted to ensure it didn't remain in their clutches. I raced toward Lucio and released a fireball in his direction. He jumped away, but the fireball connected with the side of his core. As he fell, he released a bit of energy that hit my injured shoulder.

I groaned at the impact, gripping my shoulder tightly.

Lucio pulled himself from the floor and reached into his right pocket.

"*He has the ring,*" I said to Fitz. He was ensuring it was still in his pocket—I was sure of it.

Lucio's figure wavered. He was trying to leave to keep the ring safe. Fitz clocked it at the same time and raced toward him, soaring through the air. He grabbed ahold of Lucio just as he grew hazy and pulled him back. They tumbled to the floor, throwing punches. Fitz was able to get in a clean hit and used the few seconds he'd gained to rise from the floor.

Lorenzo looked around, and I realized this version of him wasn't yet the well-trained threat I knew in our time. Suddenly, another figure appeared—one I recognized from Opimae.

Alexander. Lorenzo's trusty, time-walking guard.

It appeared he was already Lorenzo's protector in this time as well. He ran to Lorenzo, dodging my flame assaults, and as he reached him, the two of them grew hazy.

In an instant, they were gone.

I turned to help Fitz with Lucio. The water witch's energy was truly beginning to waver. If we could keep him in this time, we could overpower him. Fitz and I tackled Lucio to the ground, and I plucked the ring from his pocket.

Fitz put his arms around me, and we stepped through the in-between into the 2000s.

We tumbled to the ground, and as we stood, I extended my hand, passing the ring to Fitz. I realized as he clutched the ring that Fitz held the object he'd spent countless years researching and searching for… even across planets and centuries.

I smiled broadly.

"We need to form a plan," he said. "Lucio will be looking for us, and I think he'll go straight to our time."

"Should we hide the ring?" I asked.

"Aye. Perhaps in time for a bit?"

I nodded. "Good idea."

Fitz took us in and out of time, weaving a trail that would be difficult to follow. We made our way to the Bruce homestead ruins in the year of 2010. I stooped near a bit of upturned stone and dug into the earth. But as I placed the ring in the dirt, a disturbance pulled my attention away from my task.

Lucio, Lorenzo, and Alexander stood ten feet away from us. I slipped the ring onto my finger and turned.

"You're outnumbered," Lucio said. "Hand over the ring, and we'll leave you both alive."

I ground my jaw, holding firm.

"Have it your way then."

The three men launched themselves at us. I tousled with Lorenzo, while Fitz took on Lucio and Alexander. Even with Lucio's waning powers and Fitz's vast prowess, I was nervous. Being outnumbered was never a good thing. Lorenzo was finding his footing. He put up a good fight—not as impressive as his future self, but still.

Lorenzo blasted me against the stone wall, and I looked over to see Lucio and Alexander pulling Fitz's arms behind his back.

"No!" I screamed. "Leave him alone!"

"We will," Lucio said raising his hands as Alexander held onto Fitz tightly. "As long as you hand over that ring."

I froze.

"Come on, Hadley. Just hand it over, and no harm will come to Fitz."

"Dinnae listen to him, Hads! Keep the ring." Fitz's eyes were pleading, but the reality was that I couldn't take Lorenzo fast enough to deal with Lucio and Alexander before they could harm Fitz.

I raised an eyebrow. "If you'll release him, then this is yours."

"You first," Lucio said.

"Simultaneously." I stepped forward, though my fire magic still blazed brightly. "Final offer."

"Put that out," Lucio said, eyeing my hands.

"No chance. If you double cross me, I'll have no defense."

"I will be good to my word."

"I don't believe you."

"I will kill him," Lucio said, pointing to Fitz.

"Then you're a fool, because he is the only one who can unlock this ring for you," I said, hoping Lucio didn't possess my talent for detecting lies.

Lucio wore a brave face, but his eyes flickered with uncertainty. "Fine."

Lorenzo took Lucio's place beside Fitz, and Lucio stepped closer, keeping his eyes on my hands. I held up my hand, and the ring glimmered in the moonlight. Lucio reached for it, and I closed my hand.

"Have Lorenzo and Alexander step away from him."

Lucio hesitated but finally turned his head over his shoulder and nodded to them. They stepped away, though it was clear in Alexander's energy that he didn't approve of the plan.

I opened my palm. Lucio looked to the ring before his gaze traveled to the side of my head. He reached with his left hand and touched the wound that still dripped blood. I pulled away, but his hand was covered in my blood. His eyes flickered. He reached for the ring, nodded to Lorenzo and Alexander, and they disappeared.

Fitz rushed to my side, and we embraced tightly.

I winced, pulling back as I reached for my aching shoulder.

Fitz slipped my chemise over my shoulder to assess it. I reached for my head with my free hand. It was still pounding, and my spirit was broken. I wasn't sure what hurt worse.

When I pulled my hand away from my head, my fingertips were covered in blood.

Blood.

I recalled the blood in Fate's vision. The thought tugged at me, but I could make no sense of it. Fitz pulled my hand to his, turning it over.

"Let's get going. We should get ye to medical."

"And we have to tell Chloe and Solomon about all this time-jumping. I think we just found out how Lorenzo is passing in and out of Opimae unnoticed."

CHAPTER THIRTY-NINE

Our flat was in pristine condition, though a bit cold, as we crossed the threshold of the space we'd begun to make our home before everything changed. Fitz's research books were just where he'd left them while writing his new course material for the University of Edinburgh. My tote bag hung from the same hook where I'd left it on my last day of work at Edinburgh Castle. The small reminders of the life we'd vacated for the crusade tugged at my heartstrings.

"Come on," Fitz said. "Let's get ye cleaned up."

Though the healers had worked their magic, I'd have to be mindful of my injuries for the next few days. Fitz carefully removed my dirty and tattered clothes before shedding his own layers and helping me shower off. I almost wept in joy at the sight of the steaming shower, and even though I had to avoid water running freely across my injuries, I enjoyed every moment of the luxury of running water.

We reviewed the physician's orders for wound care, and as Fitz set me on the counter, I wrapped my legs around him, pulling him close. We sat in silence for a few moments, simply clinging to each other. When he pulled back, Fitz kissed me before tending to my wounds. Though the process left me a bit lightheaded, the sharp pain was fading to dull throbs, and the promise of healing was at least some consolation.

Fitz helped me into one of my loose, oversized sweaters, which was glorious after weeks in seventeenth-century clothing, but I insisted I could handle slipping into my lounge pants on my own.

I padded off to the sitting room while Fitz finished dressing. I walked to the first east-facing window and tugged at the wooden shutters.

Edinburgh Castle stood boldly beyond the windowpanes, bathed in the soft glow of the city's warm light. I sighed, pushing back at the wistful thoughts that would change nothing about our current circumstances.

I turned as Fitz crossed the living room, opening the old bench that held kindling and pulling a handful from the stash.

He offered a weak smile. "First things first."

"I'll pour us a drink," I offered.

I pulled our favorite tumblers from the cabinet and reached for the unopened bottle of Glenfiddich that lay on top of the bar. A small tag caught my eye, and I swallowed hard as I pulled it closer, anticipating the penmanship scribbled across it.

A favorite in the MacGregor household for the newest MacGregor. I can't wait for the day we see you walking down the aisle.

Welcome to the family, Hadley.

With love,
Ian

My body shook once with the initial burst of emotion, and I gripped the countertop as I hung my head and succumbed to grief. Ian's loss was only deepened by the deaths of Esther and even Annabel. Standing in my cold kitchen with only Ian's words and the hollow pit in my stomach, I allowed myself to feel the full onslaught of it all.

If only I hadn't pushed us to continue to the fortress that day, Ian would still be alive.

If only I hadn't meddled in the past, Annabel wouldn't have died before she was meant to.

If only I'd been smarter, Esther would have made it to Opimae.

My tears splashed against the countertop like the raindrops on the windowsill. Jazz music trickled in from the living room, and a flickering glow told me Fitz's task was complete. I took a shaky breath and wiped the tears from my face. Fitz walked into the kitchen, and with one look at me, his expression softened. He came to me quickly and tugged me into his arms. The tears came back, and he held me patiently as I cried. He laid his head against mine and ran his fingers against my hair, soothing me in the way only he knew how.

Eventually, we pulled back, and his eyes tenderly searched mine. He wasn't going to push just yet, but the question was clear in his gaze. There was no use in keeping the note from him, though I was nervous for his reaction.

I slid the note closer to Fitz. Even as he reached for it, his face fell. He read it quickly before closing his eyes, his brows furrowing, and running his thumb across the surface. I stood perfectly still, afraid even the slightest movement would break the spell. When he opened his eyes, they were shrouded in mist. His mouth twisted before he found his words.

"Dad cared deeply for ye, Hads. No one was happier about our engagement than him." A breathy laugh escaped Fitz's lips. "Old man turned out to be quite the romantic in the end."

I laughed lightly. Fitz was right. I'd found that endearing about Ian.

Fitz pointed to the bottle on the counter. "Let's have a wee dram in honor of the man who bought that for us on a happier occasion."

As the golden liquid trickled into the glasses, I sniffed deeply, willing my mind to fall back into old patterns, to feel the comfort of home, rather than the uncertainty of the future or the grief of the past.

"Live in the present," I whispered to myself.

I finished pouring the healthy servings before pausing.

"What's the matter?" Fitz asked.

I opened the mahogany cabinet and grabbed another tumbler. I poured a third glass of Scotch, and when I turned to Fitz, a sad smile graced his features. He leaned forward and planted a kiss on my forehead. We grabbed our three glasses and the bottle and headed toward the fireplace.

The flames were roaring comfortably by the time we entered the sitting room, and I stretched out before the fire.

"How does this feel to you?" I asked, looking around the flat. "Being here, I mean."

Fitz took his time answering as he settled next to me.

"I'm no sure. 'Tis a bit strange to be back."

"It feels like home, but…" I trailed off.

"It feels a bit empty… like something is missing," he concluded.

"Exactly. I mean, we're home, but… home's half-empty without our whole family."

"Aye."

The clouds broke, and I stared at the raindrops as they streaked down the windowpanes, allowing my mind to fall deeply into itself. My thoughts rolled ceaselessly.

The fireside was warm, and the soft glow of our lamps was comforting. Despite the solace I found in our updated flat, I'd sacrifice it all for another few moments with Esther.

"I miss Esther," I finally said. My throat ached at my confession, and tears clouded my eyes. I took a deep breath, but I trembled with the emotion that threatened to spill out.

"Aye, I do too," Fitz said. "I kenned how it would turn out, but that didnae keep me from hoping her fate might change."

"I've never felt more broken," I admitted. "And I've also never felt such rage before."

"The hatred of that time…" Fitz trailed off.

"It was bad enough to lose Esther, but the villagers' hatred was salt in the wound," I said. "They say history repeats itself, and I fear we will discover just how true that is."

"Aye, if we should fail against Lorenzo, it will ignite old hatreds that should have never existed in the first place."

"We have to stop him," I said, my voice barely above a whisper. "We stand to lose everything."

We grew quiet, but Fitz beckoned me closer to him on the couch. I stared through the window at the cold December rain enveloping the city. I took another sip of whisky as I eyed the bag Millie had given me just before we left. I hadn't been able to face it yet. I wasn't sure I could face it even now.

"There's no time like the present, Hads."

"Did you… just make a time joke?"

Fitz smiled mischievously, and I rolled my eyes. But then, he grew serious. "Ye dinnae have to open the wee thing, but it will torment ye until ye do."

I huffed, finding his accuracy quite annoying, though finally, I nodded. I set my drink on the table as Fitz lifted the bag and handed it off to me.

I froze.

"What's the matter?" Fitz asked.

My eyes were glued to a book that lay just underneath where Esther's bag had been. The antique volume was in pristine condition, all things considered. It was bound in a maroon hardcover, and in gold, it read *Accounts from the Witch Trials of Forfar, Scotland*.

"One thing at a time, Hads," Fitz said. "We dinnae have to face this all at once."

I nodded, but I knew myself too well. I'd obsess over the volume until I flipped through the pages myself. Fitz sighed before passing the book to me.

"Let's get on with it, then."

The book was charged with a magic that was familiar to me. I was certain it didn't belong to anyone I knew, and yet… I knew the feel of this magic somehow.

I bolstered my courage and flipped through the pages until I found the one I sought. I scanned through the list of names, and a small intake of air betrayed my surprise.

Esther MacGregor…. Found guilty & executed.

Hadley MacGregor… Fate unknown.

My nerves buzzed loudly through me, the word "executed" a punch to the gut.

"Annabel isnae listed," Fitz observed.

Of course. She had died trying to save Esther. She hadn't been tried and found guilty.

"Esther's name was never listed anywhere before," I mused.

"No, this is a first." His eyes were filled with concern. "Are ye all right?"

"I think so." I took a moment to parse through my thoughts. "I just didn't expect my name to still be here."

"Malcolm and Father Evans did call for yer arrest," Fitz said. "They must have recorded it after all the madness of that day."

Madness was the perfect descriptor for that tragic day. So many women lost in so little time. I thought of Katherine as I set the book back on the table, and I started at the memory of the book she'd had in her possession.

"Fitz, we never returned *The Hound of the Baskervilles* to the homestead."

Fitz's gaze was tender. "It was lost in the chaos… dinnae fash. I'm sure it will be fine."

I wasn't sure if he actually believed that, but I allowed myself to believe it all the same.

I nodded, and Fitz wrapped his arms around me, holding me until my nerves steadied.

"Okay," I finally said. "It's time."

I took a deep breath and pulled at the navy ribbon. It floated into my lap. I tugged at the bag's opening and pulled two letters from it. "Hadley" was written across one and "Fitz" across the other. I handed Fitz's letter to him and stared at my own.

I picked it up and focused my mind on the paper. Sure enough— Esther's energy lingered, and I closed my eyes for just a moment to savor the feel of it. I opened the letter and ran my fingers across the ink before reading.

If ye find this letter in yer hands, then I am gone—whether that be to Opimae or at the hands of the human leaders. I have always thought Fate would bring me to the gallows. We often dream of changing our fates, but that isnae a destiny meant for us all. I fear this is true for me. Hadley, I thank ye from the verra depths of my heart for what ye have done here in Forfar. Ye've convinced me to fight, and ye and Fitz reminded me of the many happy years Hamish and I were blest to walk together.

I have enclosed a wee something special for ye. From the moment I saw this sitting in yer fiery strands, I kenned it was yers. Think of me at the first snowfall of winter as it blankets the earth in white, for with it, ye shall find me. Ye will be with me always, and my spirit always with ye.

Until we meet again.

Affectionately yers,
Esther

When we'd finished reading the letters, Fitz and I looked at each other as tears scattered in our lashes. He pulled me close to him, and we sat in silence, allowing our emotions to run free, to feel the full weight of Esther's loss.

Finally, I pulled the hair clip from the bag. The Scottish agate nearly glowed in the light, and I ran my fingertips across it.

"My something borrowed."

"Aye. As bonnie as Scotland itself."

I held the hairpin as Fitz held me, and we talked about our loved ones and grief. When we grew quiet, my mind wandered back to the events of the past—to those we had left behind—and a spark ignited deep within me.

"What is it, Hads?" Fitz asked.

"Give me just a moment."

I stood and placed the hairpin carefully on the table before walking into our bedroom near the wall where I'd hidden Annabel's grimoire. I tugged at the elements, and the book flew from the wall and into my waiting grasp. When I reemerged into the living room, Fitz's gaze was curious. I handed the grimoire to him.

"'Tis still here," he marveled.

"This should have been the first thing I did when we walked through the door."

"We've just returned from hell. An hour's delay did little harm."

"You're right, but now that we have it—check for anything new?"

His eyes lit. "Do ye think?"

"I know Annabel was riddled with fear for Esther's fate, but I think she understood the stakes for our time. I just have this feeling, Fitz. The grimoire is actually still here—let's see if she left another page for us."

Fitz nodded and thumbed through the book, his eyes closed in concentration. They popped open, and my breath caught.

"Hadley," he whispered.

My pulse raced.

Fitz whispered a few words in Scots Gaelic and reached toward the spine of the book. When he pulled his hand back, a glowing page came with it, just as it had the night we first looked through the magical book together.

"Oh, Annabel," I said softly.

Fitz's eyes scanned the page. "Aye, 'tis what we need."

My mind was racing. "We should talk to Chloe and Solomon. Maybe this is our ticket back through the portal."

"And if it isnae?" he asked. The creak of the front door halted our conversation. "That ye, Iz?"

"Aye!"

"Join us, will ye?" Fitz asked.

Izzy rounded the corner. "What have ye got there?"

"Annabel hid the spell for us in the grimoire. This might be the leverage we've been looking for."

"Oh!" she exclaimed. "That's grand. Unfortunately for the chamber, Lorenzo has made great strides on Opimae. Fortunately—for your current wishes—members of the chamber are questioning the decision they made to send ye back to Earth. If they knew ye held the answer to releasing the power of the ring...."

There it was—the spark of hope.

"We have to get across that portal," I said. "Whatever it takes."

"We cannae get ye across before Tuesday. They'll vote on Monday evening our time, and we'll have ye ready to cross Tuesday morning, should they vote in your favor."

I nodded, my brain racing through ideas.

"What are ye thinking?" Fitz asked.

"That we should take a page from Lucio's playbook," I said.

Fitz's eyebrows arched.

"You're a time-walker. Let's make use of our advantage."

"Ye cannae be serious," Fitz said, his eyes lighting in realization.

"Dead serious. If they don't vote us back, let's travel back in time, cross over, and travel back to the present."

"And do what? Go rogue? They'll catch us."

"We have compelling information. They'll vote yes to hearing our briefing in person."

"If it isnae compelling enough to vote us back, I dinnae think it'll be enough once we return."

"That's not what I'm saying. I think the chamber would absolutely vote for our return if they heard this information. What I'm worried about is if our information will make it to the right people with the information breakdown that was happening before we left."

"Aye, and I dinnae know if Jordan has had enough time or resources to have sorted it, though she was making strides when we left," Izzy said. "For what it's worth, I think this is a plan worth trying, if it comes to it."

"I think they need us too badly to penalize us right now, and once we're across the portal, they'll see that. All we'll do is cut through their bureaucratic red tape so we can get to our team quicker."

Fitz sighed.

"I swear to the heavens, Fitz. If you tell me to have patience right now…"

His lips twitched.

"We know what's at stake now. Please, Fitz."

Fitz hesitated, but finally, he responded. "I think ye're right about speaking with Solomon and Chloe. They willnae betray us, but they'll have the best perspective."

"Okay, we'll talk to them tomorrow during our debrief."

Izzy stood. "It's settled then," she said, before walking to the kitchen.

When she returned, it was with steaming mugs in hand.

"I made oodles of this tea just before Mum and I left to find ye," she said, handing the mugs to us. "It has loads of healing properties in it. *This* is what ye should be drinking right now, aye?"

Fitz's mug rested on his chest, and steam wound through the air, contrasted by the dark windowpanes beyond. He stretched out on the couch, his free arm tucked underneath his head of chestnut hair. It was strange to see him wearing his cream-colored sweater and dark gray joggers after our attempts to assimilate in Opimae and then in the past, but seeing Fitz in his usual style made my heart flutter. It reminded me of the man I'd fallen in love with several summers ago.

Izzy followed my gaze and laughed lightly.

"What?"

Izzy shook her head. "Oh, just the two of yous."

We'd silently sipped our tea for some time before Izzy spoke again. "Hadley, there's something I need to tell ye. I asked to be transferred to field work shortly after ye left for the past, and my request was approved."

I gasped softly and turned to Fitz.

He nodded, rising to sit with his arms over his bent knees.

"No that we've e'er done a braw job at keeping secrets from Iz, but there will be no helping it now." His attempt at keeping his tone light wasn't enough to fool me. His concern coursed through my blood.

Izzy laughed.

"You already knew about this?"

"I learned of it tonight while ye were in with the healers," Fitz said.

"Did the council pressure you to do this?" I asked.

She crossed her arms, indignation settling across her features. "No, so dinnae go meddling. I volunteered. And before ye say anything, ye should know Fitz already made fuss enough for the both of yous."

I almost laughed, but the gravity of the situation prevented it. "Why would you do this?"

"I couldnae help myself. Ye both are at the heart of this crusade, whether the Opimaean council still believes that or not. I see the way ye're continuing yer fight, especially after journeying into the past. It's inspiring. There's also the fact that this meant a great deal to Dad, and he… well, he was willing to give his life for the cause."

Tears welled in her eyes. I nodded, understanding.

"My skills are useful—even Dad said so. I cannae sit by and watch anymore. I cannae just wait…" she paused, suppressing tears. I grasped her hand, waiting until she was ready. "I cannae just sit there waiting for news of ye anymore. Not after what happened to Dad. No, I need to be useful, more so than sitting in that council office. So, I started training while ye were away in Forfar."

"I do understand. Completely," I said. "But I don't know about this."

"You cannae control Iz," Fitz said.

"I'm not trying to control her. I just… I'm so tired of worrying. And honestly, it's really out of character for you to be okay with this."

"Okay? No. But I cannae control it, and I—"

"What?" I asked.

Fitz shrugged.

"Just say it."

He eyed me unhappily for a few seconds before responding. "I'm just tired, Hadley."

My mouth tugged to the side, a display of my uncertainty. I didn't even know what to say.

"We all are," Izzy finally said. "None more than the two of yous."

"I'm sorry to be difficult," I said. "It's not that I don't think you're capable—of course you are. It's just been a really rough year."

Izzy nodded and then pulled me into her embrace. I found Fitz over her shoulder. His expression had relaxed, and he nodded, resigned.

Izzy sighed as she pulled away. "Sorry about that. It's been a rough year for us all, and the last month or so… not so grand."

"You know I understand," I said. "So, what exactly will you be doing?"

"That depends on what's decided next for ye—I'm meant to join the team, but I'm stationed with ye and Fitz. I suppose this all hinges on the Opimaean chamber and if they grant the court's wish for ye to return."

"Fieldwork is tough," I said simply.

"Aye. My healing powers will be most useful with the team. Since I work with wild animals, ye know—bears, wolves, elk, Fitz—the councils believe I have the presence of mind to handle it."

Fitz tossed one of our decorative pillows at her, laughing, but she caught it with ease, smiling in return.

"The council offered me a job after my internship, ye know… watching ye, but I declined. I didnae care for fieldwork at the time. They're chuffed at my decision."

"Ye'll make a brilliant addition," Fitz declared.

"I'll make ye proud."

"Ye already do, Iz."

CHAPTER FORTY

My hand slid roughly across the castle's stone wall as I walked toward my old office. Someone else would be occupying it, performing the work I'd loved prior to my departure. I wouldn't allow myself to step inside or view James's office. I needed to picture them as they were—to keep them intact in my mind, just as James and I had furnished them during our employment. Just as they were when Ian was alive and walking through these very halls.

Though we'd been told the new employees were qualified temps who would continue our work in our absence, I couldn't help but think of them with jealousy. They were only doing the work that needed to be done, but they were imposters in my mixed-up mind.

I paused briefly outside my office, scanning the hallway for even the subtlest change. It was the same—well, except for the Christmas decorations. I walked on toward the council offices, smiling at the holiday wreaths on the doors and the tiny Christmas trees sitting on the desks that were visible through windowpanes. The castle was closed for a few days—a massive maintenance issue was the official reason given for the closure, but in reality, it was swarming with council members who'd gathered to debate Earth's position on the Opimaean crisis. Fitz and I were waiting for Chloe and Solomon's prior meeting to wrap before we could start our debrief. I had used the delay to walk the halls of this special place alone—perhaps for the last time.

When I finally made my way back to Fitz, dusk had fallen into full darkness, and the city lights of Edinburgh twinkled across the horizon. The Royal Mile was especially festive during the holiday season, and people laughed and chattered happily in the warm glow of holiday lights. Fitz wrapped his arms around me, and we gazed at our city in the chilly evening air.

"I've missed her," Fitz admitted.

"In another life, we're decorating our tree right now," I said, my voice nearly cracking. "I mourn for who we could have been here."

"A month ago, I would have said that if I could give ye anything, it would be the life we would've had without this crusade."

My grip tightened on his arms. "And now?"

"A life without the crusade means we wouldnae have had time with Esther."

Emotion flooded through me.

"I'm grateful for many of the beings that have come into our life, even with the heavy price, but I dinnae ken that I'd say it was all worth it until recently. Our time in the past has changed me forever."

"It was brutal," I said. "And it was worth every wound."

The past had forged us into something new. We had been tested more than ever and heartbroken to our very cores. We were grieving and finding our rhythm once more, but Fitz was right. Our time in the past was worth the pain.

"I can't imagine who I'd be without you, and I am so grateful it is you who walks by my side."

I turned to meet his gaze, my words meaning even more after all that had happened in recent months. He nuzzled his face into the crook of my neck and held me quietly. Despite the cold, I was happy to stay in our peaceful moment, but eventually, I checked my watch.

"We'd better get going. It's almost time for our meeting."

I'd been in this meeting room countless times before, but my biggest concern back then was wondering if Mark, my work nemesis, would ever tolerate me. Now, this room would hear much bigger, and much more important, concerns. Solomon was sitting at the far side of the room looking at his tablet while we waited for Chloe. His jaw rested on his hand, and his features were grave.

"Everything okay?" I asked.

Solomon forced a weak smile to his lips. "Just more bickering between the nations," he said, waving his hand dismissively. "Perhaps one day we'll find ourselves on the same page, but until then...."

Fitz set his worn leather bag on the counter. I'd seen him cart it around countless times to the University of Edinburgh and all around the city, but it had never carried such precious contents as it did today. He unzipped it and pulled out the grimoire, setting it gently on the table.

I steadied my nerves. Debriefing on this mission would not be easy.

Chloe was in deep discussion with another court member as they entered the room. Her companion was a short woman with raven hair, and even before she turned to face me, I knew her porcelain face held glacial blue eyes. What I didn't anticipate was how her face would fall when she saw me.

"Great to see you too, Mia," I said.

Fitz bit his lip to avoid a smile.

"Hadley," Chloe began. We have news from Opimae."

My heart plummeted from my chest.

"What's happened?" I asked, setting my trembling hands in my lap.

"It's about Jordan," Mia said.

My breath caught. "What's happened to her?"

"She's been captured by Lorenzo's forces. Prepare for immediate departure to Opimae City."

EPILOGUE

Jordan struggled to fight her way free, but the guards held a firm grip on her arms, forcing her through an arched doorway. The fortress' stone walls were to blame for the bone-biting chill in the hallways, but the lavishly furnished room before her was quite warm, thanks to a roaring fire and expensive rugs. As they shoved her toward the far side of the room, her foot caught the edge of an uneven stone. She launched forward. Just before she hit the floor, her face mere inches from the stones, strong hands cradled her body and hoisted her to her feet. Jordan turned to face her rescuer, and a loud intake of air betrayed her surprise.

"Lorenzo," she whispered.

His expression was as hard as the stones beneath their feet, and after ensuring she was standing upright of her own accord, he turned his icy gaze on the guards. Their expressions ranged from uncertainty to outright fear, and one guard swallowed hard as he met the eyes of Lorenzo Belmonte.

"Is that any way to treat our guest?" he said, his words barely more than a deep growl.

The guards didn't dare to make a sound.

His voice was venom. "*I said*, is that any way to treat our guest?"

"No, Signore," they responded in unison.

"Do it again, and I'll have your left hand for that."

The guards kept their gaze fixed on the floor.

"You're dismissed."

They didn't tarry, and the last guard closed the door as he exited the room.

"I apologize for the lack of a civilized welcome."

Jordan held Lorenzo's gaze, her breaths coming short and her nostrils flared.

"You're angry. You have every right to be." Lorenzo motioned toward a table near the window. "Why don't you make yourself comfortable?"

Jordan eyed the table warily.

"I insist. You are my guest, after all."

"Guest?" Jordan asked.

"Are you not?" Lorenzo asked.

"I guess I'm just a little confused because your guards captured me and then dragged me here. That doesn't seem like I'm a guest."

"You *are* Hadley's best companion. I shouldn't be surprised that you share in the same logic."

"What does that mean?"

Lorenzo motioned toward the table once more. Jordan sighed, but she didn't protest. She strode to the table and took a seat. Lorenzo followed behind her and sank into the chair across from her.

"Wine?" he asked.

Jordan couldn't keep the exasperated laugh from her lips. "What is happening right now?"

A wicked grin rose to Lorenzo's face.

"Come on," Jordan said. "You're going to have to help me figure all this out because I don't have a clue what's going on right now."

Lorenzo nodded. "You trespassed on my land, and my guards escorted you here so that we could discuss why you would do such a thing."

"That's an easy one. You're murdering innocent people, and I want to stop you."

"It isn't quite so straightforward though, is it?" he asked.

"Yeah, it kind of is."

The disdain was clear. But Jordan's attitude seemed to humor Lorenzo. A soft smile crept into the corners of his mouth, but he cleared his throat, pushing back against it.

"Why don't you just get to the point?" Jordan asked.

"I'm not sure what you mean."

"I mean, I wouldn't be here if you didn't want something from me. So, what is it?"

Lorenzo nodded. "Intelligence."

"That's what I figured," she said. "Unfortunately, you won't get anything from me."

"We'll see about that. You've amassed quite the collection of knowledge," he said. "I can't have you sharing all of my secrets with my opponents."

Jordan rolled her eyes.

"I think you'll find this to be a comfortable place to wait out the storm," he continued, seemingly indifferent to her annoyance.

Why hadn't Jordan used her magic? She shook her head and closed her eyes momentarily. Lorenzo studied her quietly. He was draped lazily in his seat, his elbows resting on the arms of the chair and his chin propped on his balled fists.

Jordan's eyes snapped open at the precise moment Lorenzo's head jerked in the direction of the doorway. Shuffling feet sounded on the other side, and as the door cracked open, a woman's icy voice floated on the chill that penetrated the room.

Lorenzo sighed before rising from his chair. "If you'll excuse me, I must attend to an urgent matter." He bowed ever so slightly before crossing the room, closing the door behind him.

Jordan released a long, deep sigh, her relief palpable. She rose from her chair and walked to the doorway just beyond the table where she had conversed with a murderous villain. She opened the door, and wind blew cold and furious across the room, sending the curtains whipping through the air. Jordan raised her hand to protect her eyes, but she pushed forward into the mad flurry of snowflakes. The suns had almost fully set, only the softest glow visible beyond the horizon through a break in the clouds, but it was enough to illuminate the side of the fortress. The sheer drop was sobering, but Jordan had magic... so why wasn't she using it?

Perhaps a new protection had been set around the fortress, or perhaps it was something else entirely, but Jordan turned back to her room and used her full weight to close the door, until the soft click finally brought the room back to its tranquil state. But no sooner had Jordan stationed herself by the fireside than a knock came from the opposite door, followed by footsteps as the intruder entered her room. Jordan poised herself for a fight, but she lowered her arms at the sight of her guest.

"You might not remember me," the woman began once she'd closed the door.

"Gabriella. I never forget an ally." Her eyes searched Gabriella's. "You *are* an ally, aren't you?"

"I am your most faithful ally," Gabriella returned sincerely. "I do not wish for Signore's plans to succeed. It would be very bad, indeed."

Jordan sighed in relief.

"I have news," Gabriella said. "Hadley and Fitz—they have returned to Opimae. That is what Alexander came to tell Signore."

Jordan gasped.

"We must be strategic in our plans," Gabriella continued.

Jordan's brows furrowed. "Hadley will come straight for this fortress."

"Just what I was afraid of," Gabriella said. "Signore—he is counting on it."

Hadley

Róisín had known just what she was doing. I had barely stepped out of the car in front of HQ when she greeted me, all embers and smoke. When I had reached for her, the power of the vision had been so intense, I cried out in pain as I lost consciousness. Now, I opened my eyes to several familiar faces and one long snout.

"A vision?" Fitz asked. He cradled my head in his hand.

"Yes," I murmured weakly as Róisín nodded enthusiastically.

"She's been having *visions*?" Henry asked.

"Aye. We thought that would disappear with the past, but we were wrong, it seems."

I sat up, though slowly, supported the entire way by Fitz.

"It's Jordan," I said, my voice trembling. "Help me inside? I think I know what to do."

GLOSSARY

Arnae – aren't

Aye – yes

Bairn – kid

Bonnie – handsome, pretty, beautiful.

Braw – good looking, beautiful, really nice.

Cannae – can't

Couldnae – couldn't

Didnae – didn't

Dinnae – don't

Dinnae fash – don't worry

Hadnae – hadn't

E'en – even

Gonnae – going to

Gowk – foolish person

Greet – to cry

Ken – to know

Loch – Lake

Mo chridhe – my heart

Mo ghaol – my love, my beloved

Nae – no

Ne'er – ever

No – (in certain contexts) used in place of not

Och – oh

Ootlin – outsider

Scran – food

Shouldnae – shouldn't

'Tis – it is

Verra – very

Wasnae – wasn't

Wean – child

Wee – little

Weel – well

Willnae – won't

Wouldnae – wouldn't

Ye – you

Yon – that

ACKNOWLEDGEMENTS

This book took more blood, sweat, and tears (literally) than any book of my books to date. I couldn't have made it through the sleepless nights, the grueling research material, or the emotional toll of this story without these wonderful people.

My first thank you, as always, is to my husband, Trent. A forever thank you for your support through the happy milestones and the moments of heartache. Thank you for stepping into so many roles to allow me to tell this story properly and often knowing what I need before I do. Time to book those tickets to celebrate, aye?

Thank you to my incredible editor, Jamie Ryu. Jamie, you continue to inspire me endlessly and you keep me on track with such grace. If I've said it once, I've said it a million times: authors dream of a working relationship like ours. Now, let's celebrate before we start the next one ;)

Thank you to my amazing beta readers: Kathryn Gaddy, Vee Elle, Britt Byrd, Darrian Kirksey, Leah Block, and Charlotte Gilgallon. Your commentary has left immeasurable value on these pages, and your lively commentary kept me smiling even on the hardest days.

Thank you to Jon Stubbington for another beautiful cover! I'm continually amazed by your ability to take our concepts and bring them to life so beautifully. The snowflakes bursting into flames is one of my favorite details yet!

Thank you, Summoned Patreon Team!!! President Rachael Dunn, Musical Artist Cherish Danae, and Assistant Extraordinaire Darrian

Kirksey, you three keep the magic alive. And to our Patrons… as always, YOU ARE THE REAL MAGIC! We couldn't do what we do without you, and this book is all the better for your support. SITM <3

Thank you to my business partner and dear friend, Samantha Rose Baldwin. Your love for Hadley and this world will never be taken for granted, and your relentless belief in me has kept me going so many times. Time to celebrate—save me a seat at the Grill?

Thank you to Cherish Danae for your hard work on the sisterhood chant. I can't wait for readers to hear this come to life for the first time!

Thank you to Taylor Novak for that Fitz line that lies within these pages. A piece of *Forged* history that will undoubtedly turn to myth and lore.

Thank you to my family & friends. You continue to be the most patient and supportive, and I will forever be grateful for my incredible loved ones. You all know who you are, and I can't wait to celebrate in the ways only we know how.

Thank you to my littlest companion Midnight for keeping my feet warm and the chair next to me occupied in equal measure. My long days would be much lonelier without my little boogs.

Thank you to Rod Fleck for lending research materials, sending Scottish language inspiration, and supporting my author journey in ways that make me believe I can reach for more.

Thank you to my Miller Tree Inn team! Marissa, Julia, Jalisa, Maria, Teresa, Bella, & Triana: you have each played such a large role in allowing me to chase my dreams as an author, and even more, you are such a big part of my and Trent's lives. I am so grateful for the light you bring to our days and the hard work and support you've put in over the last few years.

Thank you to the Summoned Team!! You ROCK. It's such a beautiful thing to watch my world be brought to life so authentically and with such love. From the characters lifting off the pages to original music (including a *Forged* song!!), and beyond, it's a dream come true to be doing this with you. ILYOP.

And finally, thank you to the team over at Contrarian Publishing for putting in the hard work and long hours so my story could finally reach readers. You have truly created a safe space for writers to explore and reach our highest potential, and I am grateful to be a Contrarian Publishing author. Y'all are magic.

M.B. Thurman traded her career as an executive assistant to fulfill her lifelong dream of becoming an author. She spends her time writing and operating her bed and breakfast, the notable Miller Tree Inn. Though her Southern roots run deep, Thurman has embraced the lifestyle of the magical Pacific Northwest with her husband and feisty feline, Midnight.

Thurman's book settings echo her love of travel—especially areas of the world that brim with magic and echo ancient marvels. Her company, Firecracker Entertainment, is dedicated to bringing Thurman's novels to life through immersive storytelling in mediums ranging from screen to audio and beyond.

Visit her at mbthurman.com or @mbt_writes.

Learn more at thesummonedseries.com or @thesummonedseries